IT'S YOUR FUNERAL!

R.I.P. MARNIE WINTERS

written by Emily Riesbeck
art by Ellen Kramer
letters by Matt Krotzer

IRON CIRCUS COMICS

strange and amazing

inquiry@ironcircus.com   www.ironcircus.com

writer
Emily Riesbeck

artist
Ellen Kramer

letterer
Matt Krotzer

publisher
C. Spike Trotman

editor
Andrea Purcell

art director/cover design
Matt Sheridan

print technician/book design
Beth Scorzato

proofreader
Abby Lehrke

published by
Iron Circus Comics
329 West 18th Street, Suite 604
Chicago, IL 60616
ironcircus.com

first edition: July 2020

ISBN: 978-1-945820-52-6

10 9 8 7 6 5 4 3 2 1

printed in China

It's Your Funeral!

Publisher's Cataloging-In-Publication Data
(Prepared by The Donohue Group, Inc.)

Names: Riesbeck, Emily, author. | Kramer, Ellen, 1987- illustrator. | Krotzer, Matt, letterer. | Spike, 1978- publisher. | Purcell, Andrea, editor. | Scorzato, Beth, designer.
Title: It's your funeral! / Emily Riesbeck, Ellen Kramer & Matt Krotzer ; [publisher, editor, C. Spike Trotman ; editor, Andrea Purcell ; writer, Emily Riesbeck ; artist, Ellen Kramer ; letterer, Matt Krotzer ; book designer, print technician, Beth Scorzato ; proofreader, Abby Lehrke].
Other Titles: It is your funeral! | R.I.P. Marnie Winters
Description: First edition. | Chicago, IL : Iron Circus Comics, 2020. | Interest age level: 12 and up. | Summary: "A recently deceased girl and her helpful afterlife caseworker embark on a series of hilarious mishaps and misadventures throughout the space-time continuum as they try to close her file so she can move on"–Provided by publisher.
Identifiers: ISBN 9781945820526
Subjects: LCSH: Dead–Comic books, strips, etc. | Social workers–Comic books, strips, etc. | Future life–Comic books, strips, etc. | Space and time–Comic books, strips, etc. | CYAC: Dead–Fiction. | Social workers–Fiction. | Future life–Fiction. | Space and time–Fiction. | LCGFT: Graphic novels. | Humor.
Classification: LCC PZ7.1.R537 It 2020 | DDC 741.5973 [Fic]–dc23

Department
of
Spectral Affairs

Chapter 1

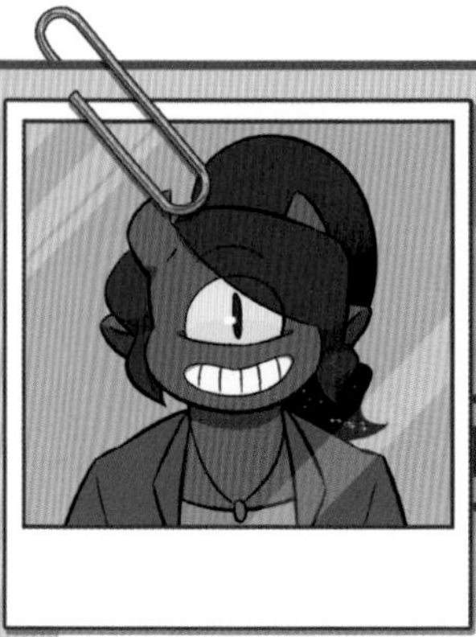

FOR OFFICIAL USE ONLY

Name: X'lakthul

Pronunciation: Zel-Ack-Thul

Pronouns: She/her

Age: ∞

Position: case worker

Likes: Paperwork, the satisfaction of a job well done, helping the spirits of Earth.

Dislikes: Misfiled papers, being mean.

X'lakthul

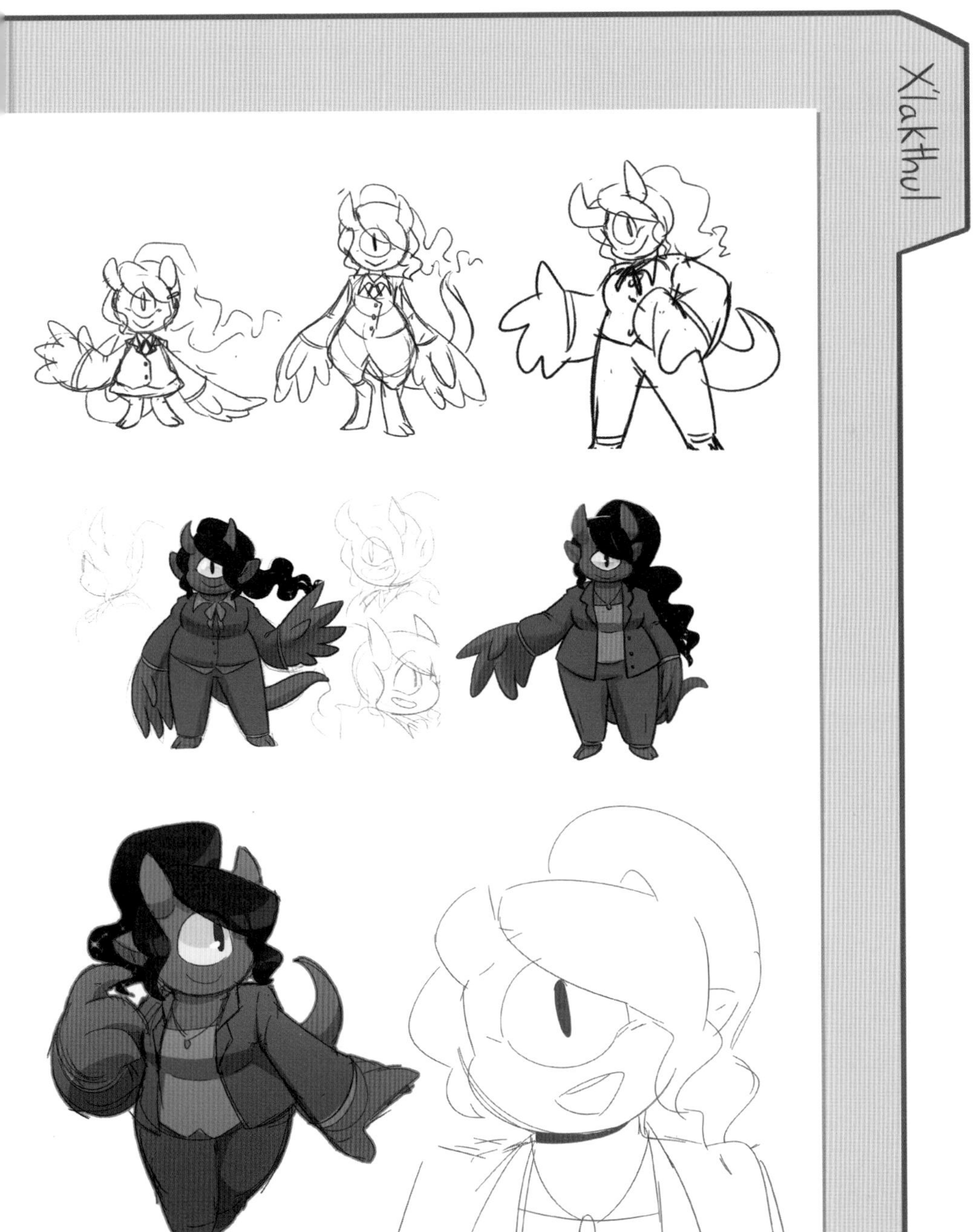

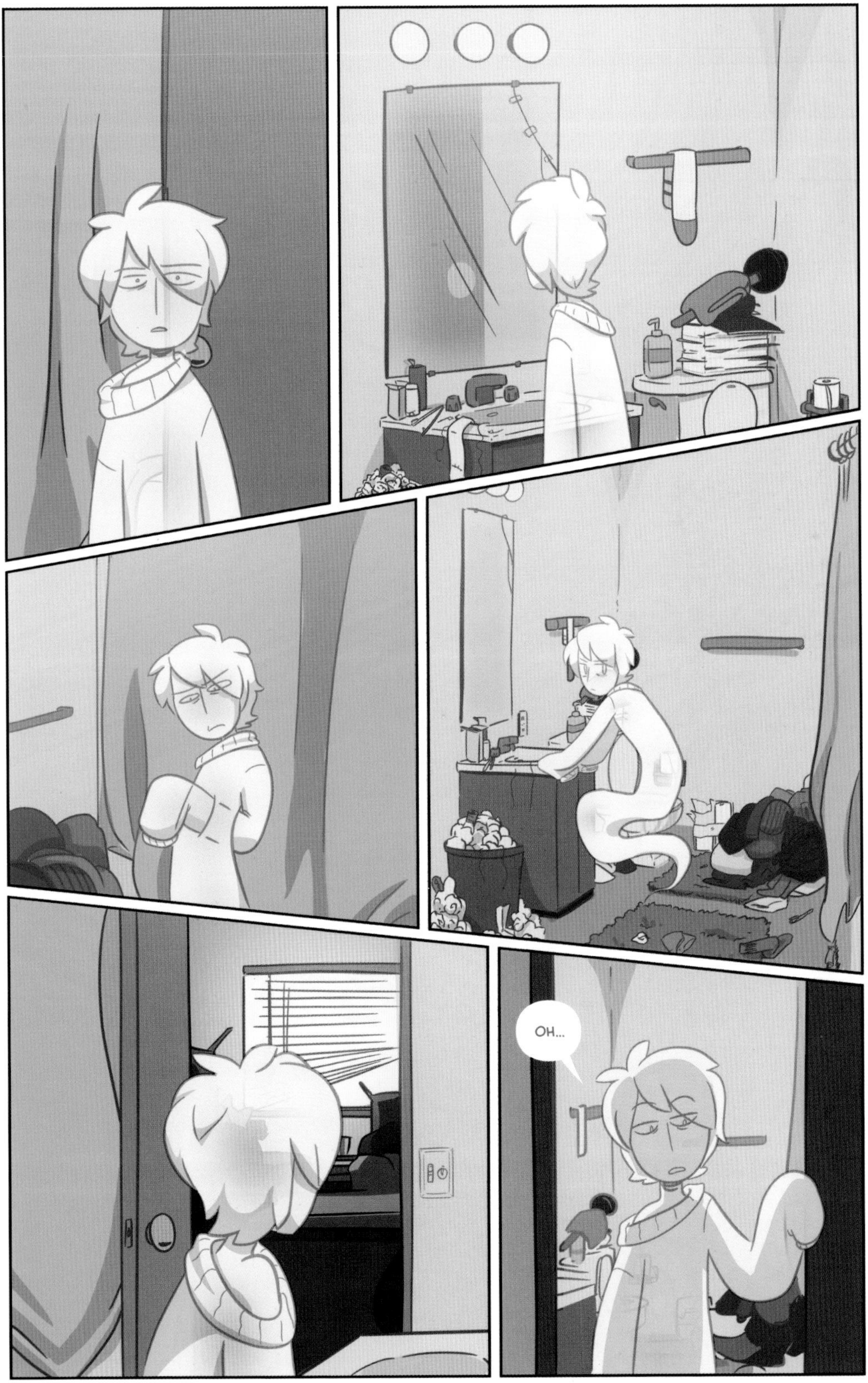
OH...

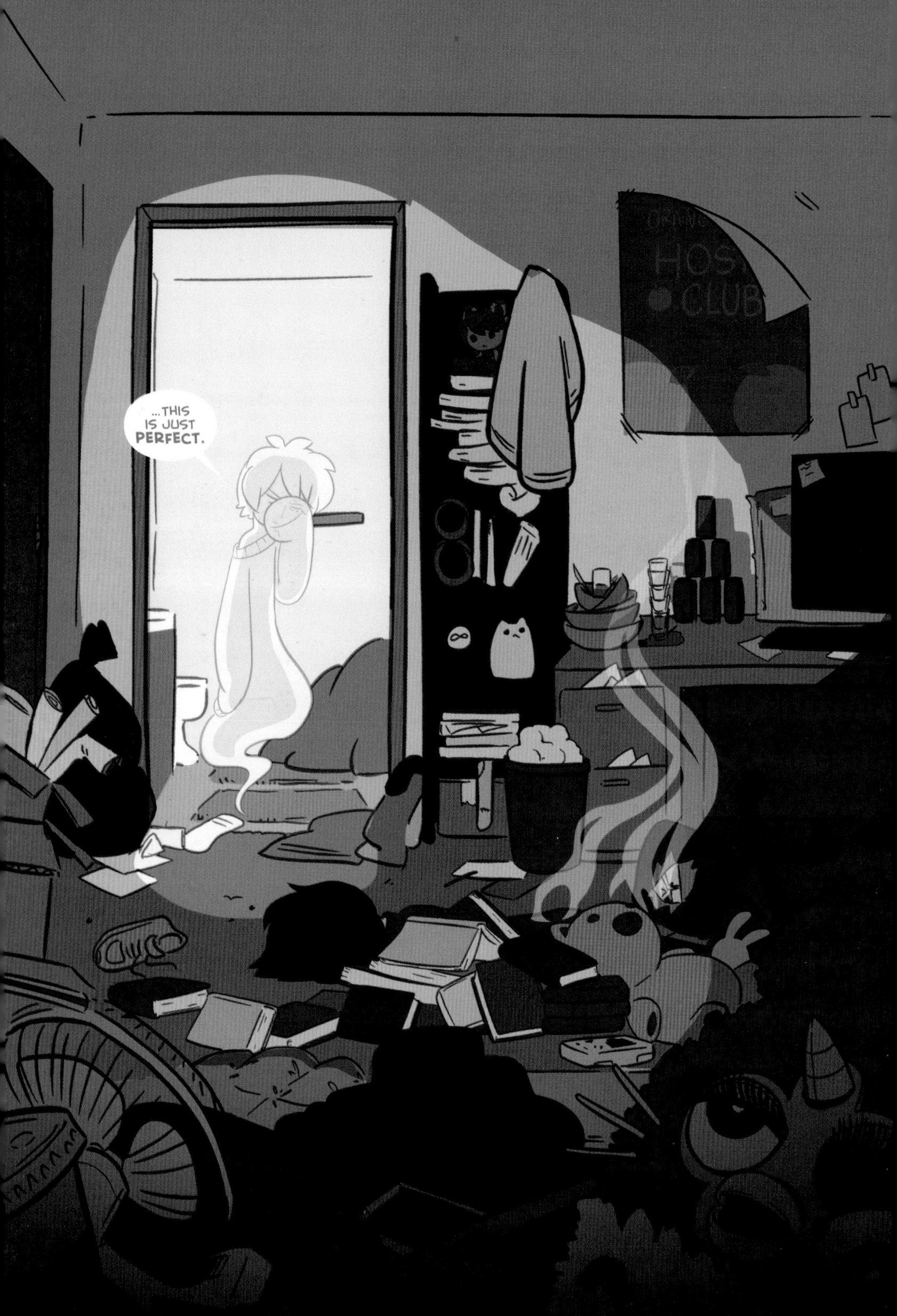
...THIS IS JUST PERFECT.

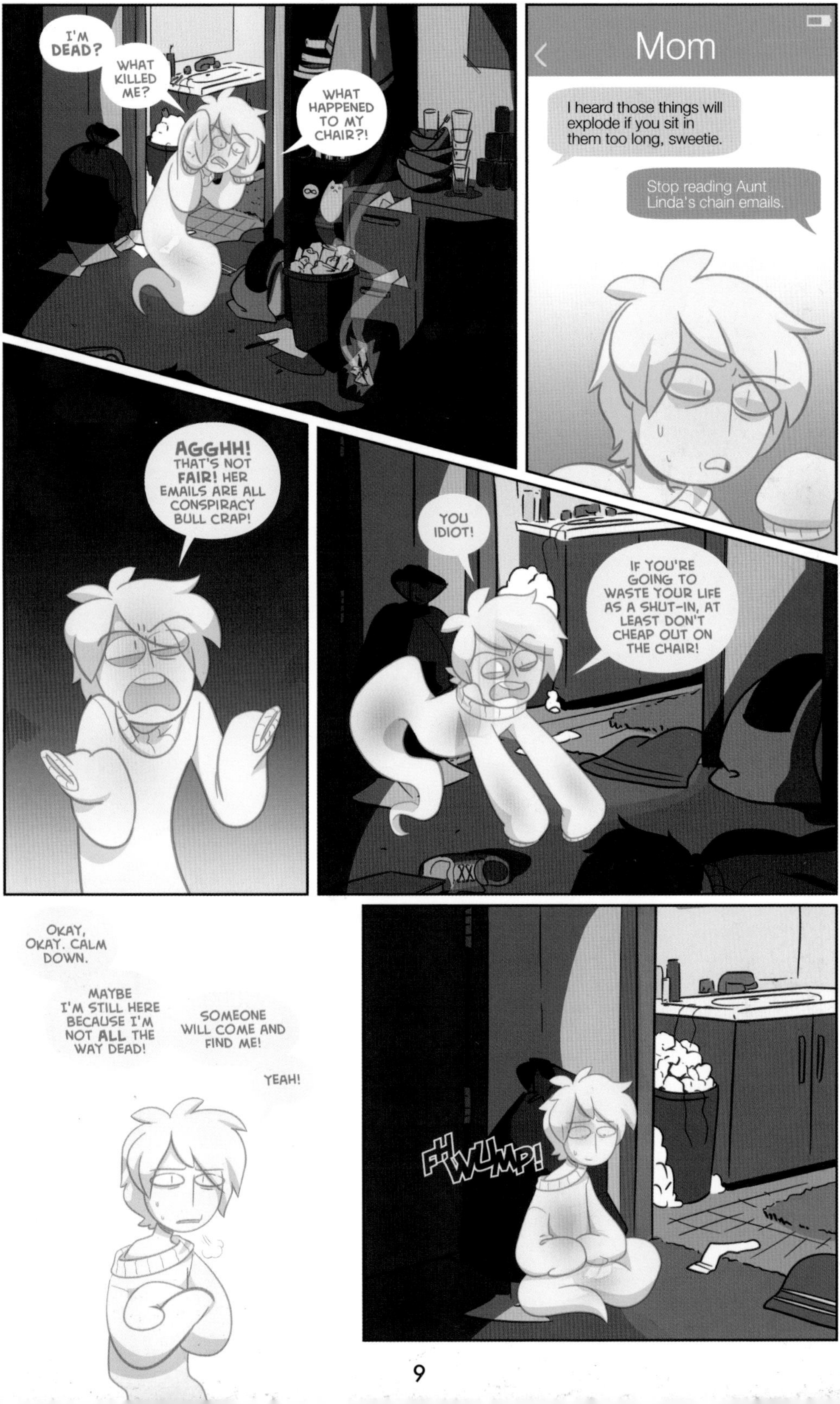
I'M DEAD?
WHAT KILLED ME?
WHAT HAPPENED TO MY CHAIR?!
Mom
I heard those things will explode if you sit in them too long, sweetie.
Stop reading Aunt Linda's chain emails.
AGGHH! THAT'S NOT FAIR! HER EMAILS ARE ALL CONSPIRACY BULL CRAP!
YOU IDIOT!
IF YOU'RE GOING TO WASTE YOUR LIFE AS A SHUT-IN, AT LEAST DON'T CHEAP OUT ON THE CHAIR!
OKAY, OKAY. CALM DOWN.
MAYBE I'M STILL HERE BECAUSE I'M NOT ALL THE WAY DEAD!
SOMEONE WILL COME AND FIND ME!
YEAH!
FHWUMP!

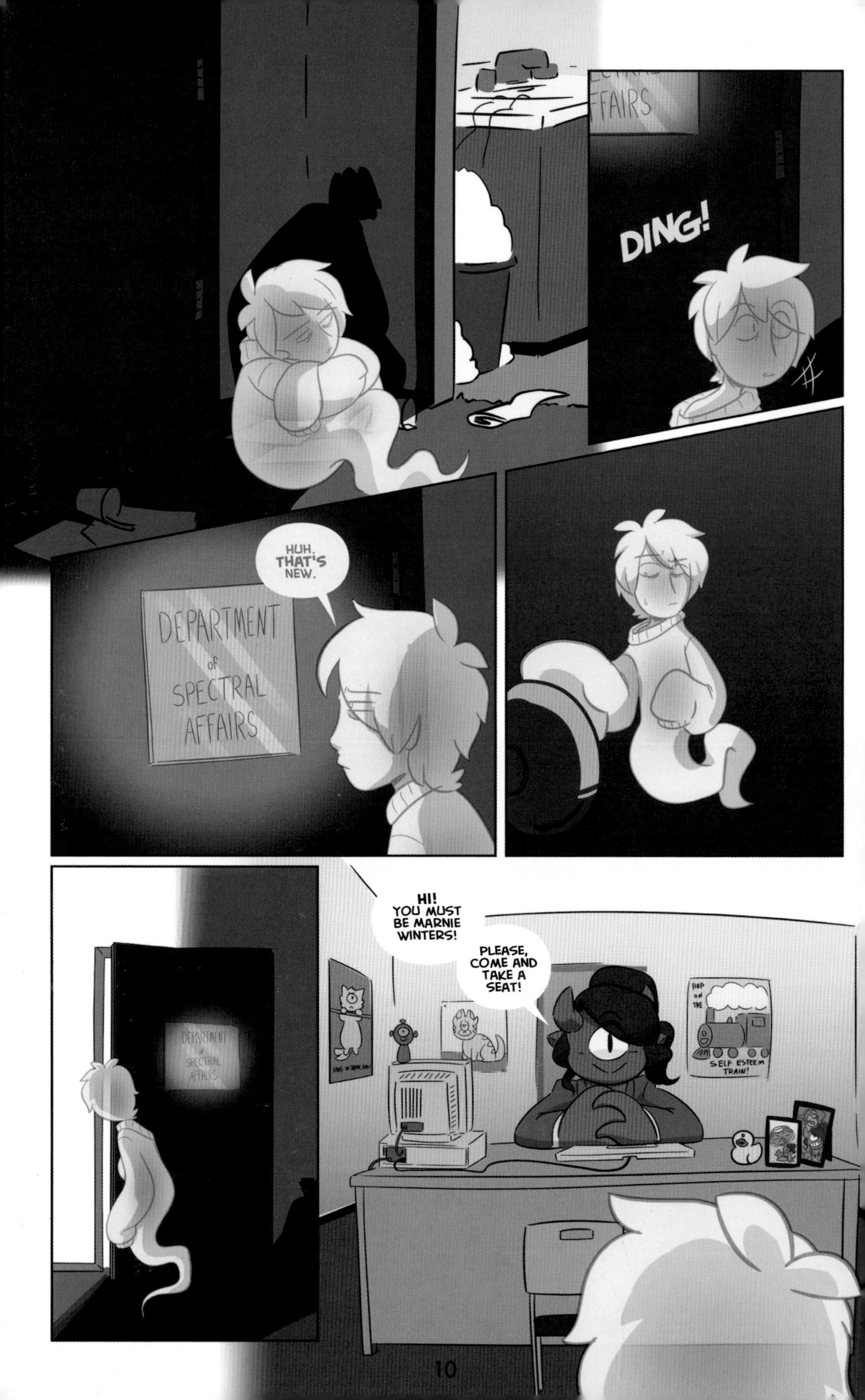
FFAIRS
DING!
HUH. THAT'S NEW.
DEPARTMENT of SPECTRAL AFFAIRS
HI! YOU MUST BE MARNIE WINTERS!
PLEASE, COME AND TAKE A SEAT!
DEPARTMENT of SPECTRAL AFFAIRS
HOP ON THE
SELF ESTEEM TRAIN!

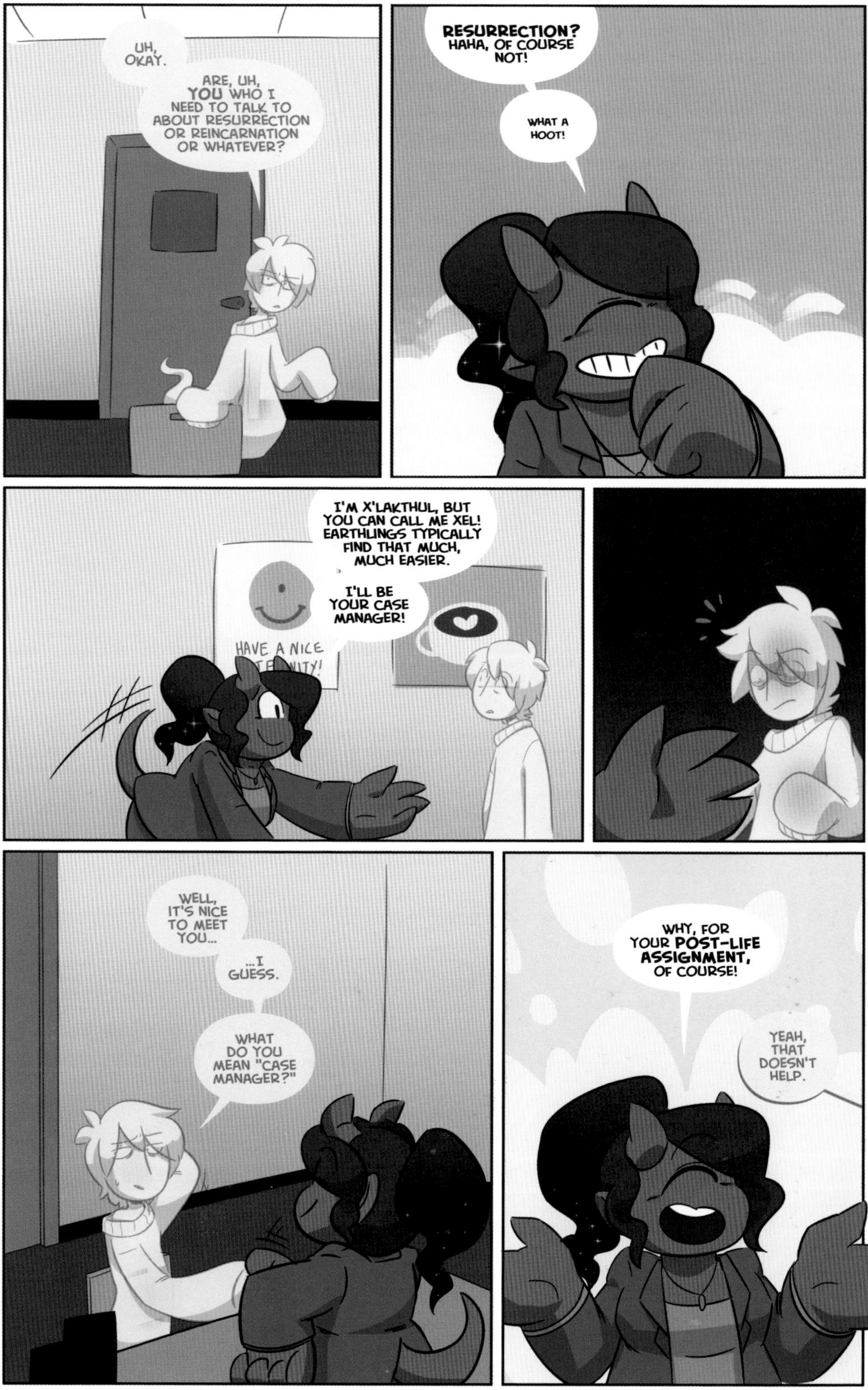
UH, OKAY.
ARE, UH, YOU WHO I NEED TO TALK TO ABOUT RESURRECTION OR REINCARNATION OR WHATEVER?
RESURRECTION? HAHA, OF COURSE NOT!
WHAT A HOOT!
I'M X'LAKTHUL, BUT YOU CAN CALL ME XEL! EARTHLINGS TYPICALLY FIND THAT MUCH, MUCH EASIER.
I'LL BE YOUR CASE MANAGER!
WELL, IT'S NICE TO MEET YOU...
...I GUESS.
WHAT DO YOU MEAN "CASE MANAGER?"
WHY, FOR YOUR POST-LIFE ASSIGNMENT, OF COURSE!
YEAH, THAT DOESN'T HELP.

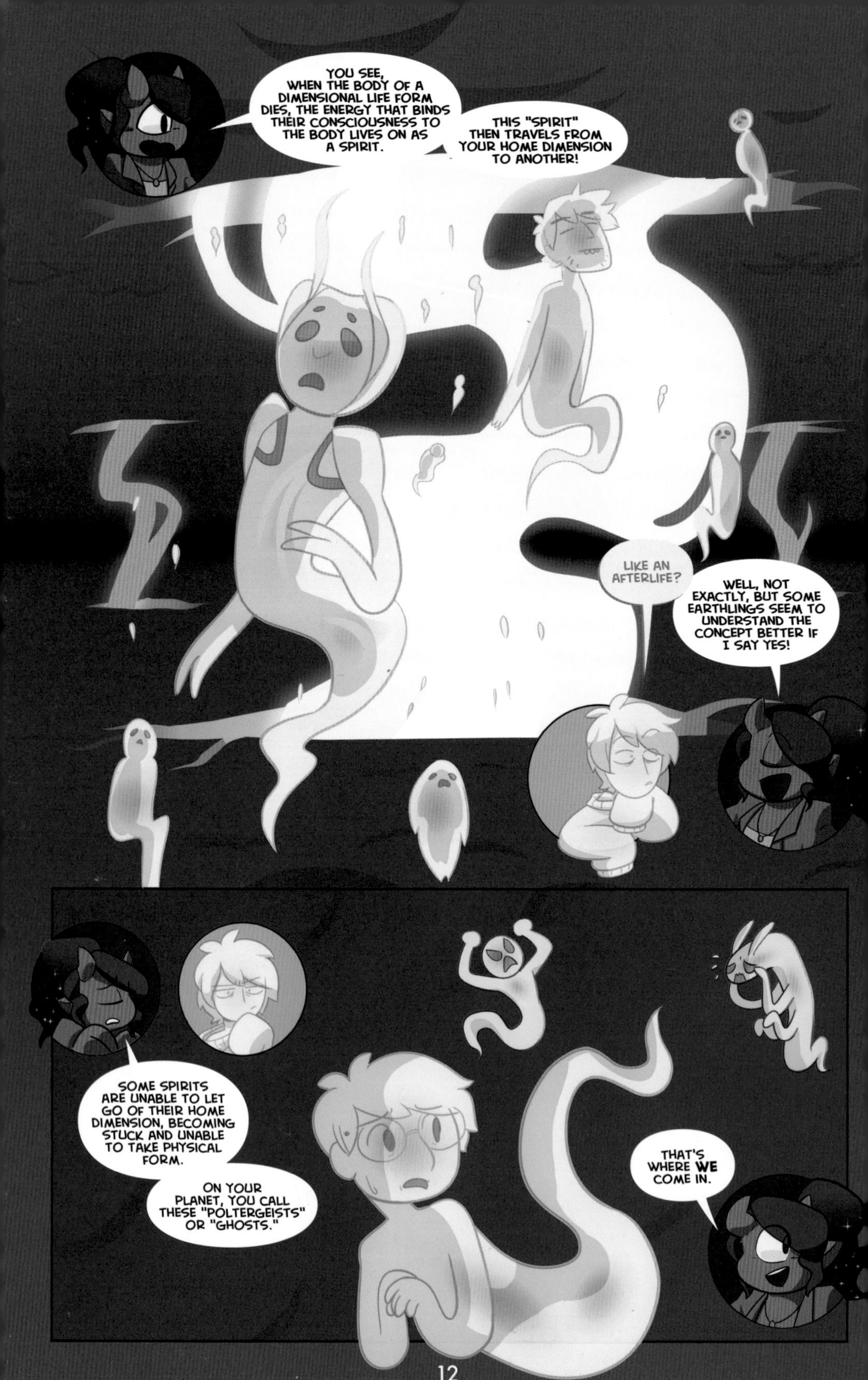
YOU SEE, WHEN THE BODY OF A DIMENSIONAL LIFE FORM DIES, THE ENERGY THAT BINDS THEIR CONSCIOUSNESS TO THE BODY LIVES ON AS A SPIRIT.
THIS "SPIRIT" THEN TRAVELS FROM YOUR HOME DIMENSION TO ANOTHER!
LIKE AN AFTERLIFE?
WELL, NOT EXACTLY, BUT SOME EARTHLINGS SEEM TO UNDERSTAND THE CONCEPT BETTER IF I SAY YES!
SOME SPIRITS ARE UNABLE TO LET GO OF THEIR HOME DIMENSION, BECOMING STUCK AND UNABLE TO TAKE PHYSICAL FORM.
ON YOUR PLANET, YOU CALL THESE "POLTERGEISTS" OR "GHOSTS."
THAT'S WHERE **WE** COME IN.

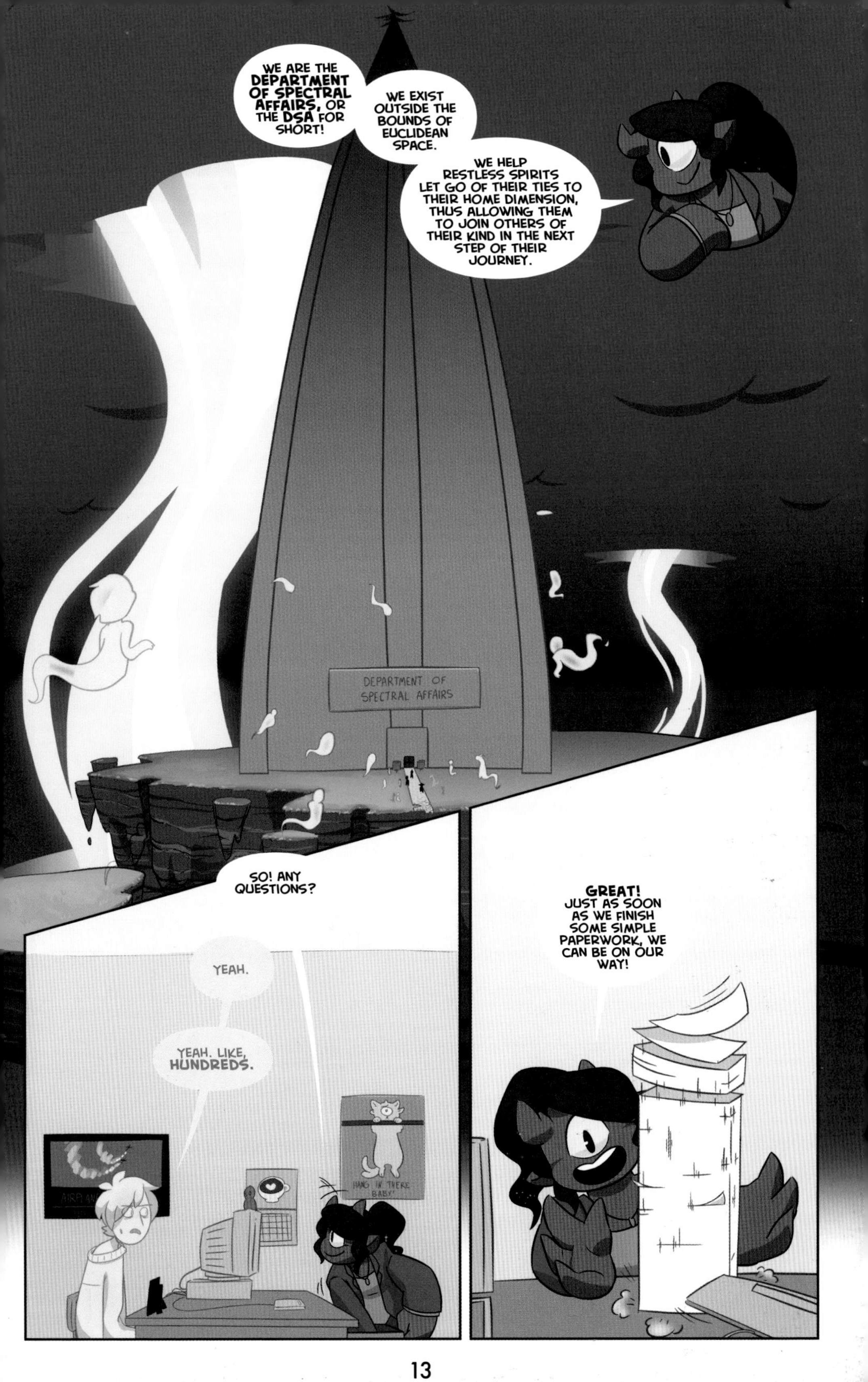
WE ARE THE DEPARTMENT OF SPECTRAL AFFAIRS, OR THE DSA FOR SHORT!
WE EXIST OUTSIDE THE BOUNDS OF EUCLIDEAN SPACE.
WE HELP RESTLESS SPIRITS LET GO OF THEIR TIES TO THEIR HOME DIMENSION, THUS ALLOWING THEM TO JOIN OTHERS OF THEIR KIND IN THE NEXT STEP OF THEIR JOURNEY.
DEPARTMENT OF SPECTRAL AFFAIRS
SO! ANY QUESTIONS?
YEAH.
YEAH. LIKE, **HUNDREDS.**
HANG IN THERE BABY!
GREAT! JUST AS SOON AS WE FINISH SOME SIMPLE PAPERWORK, WE CAN BE ON OUR WAY!

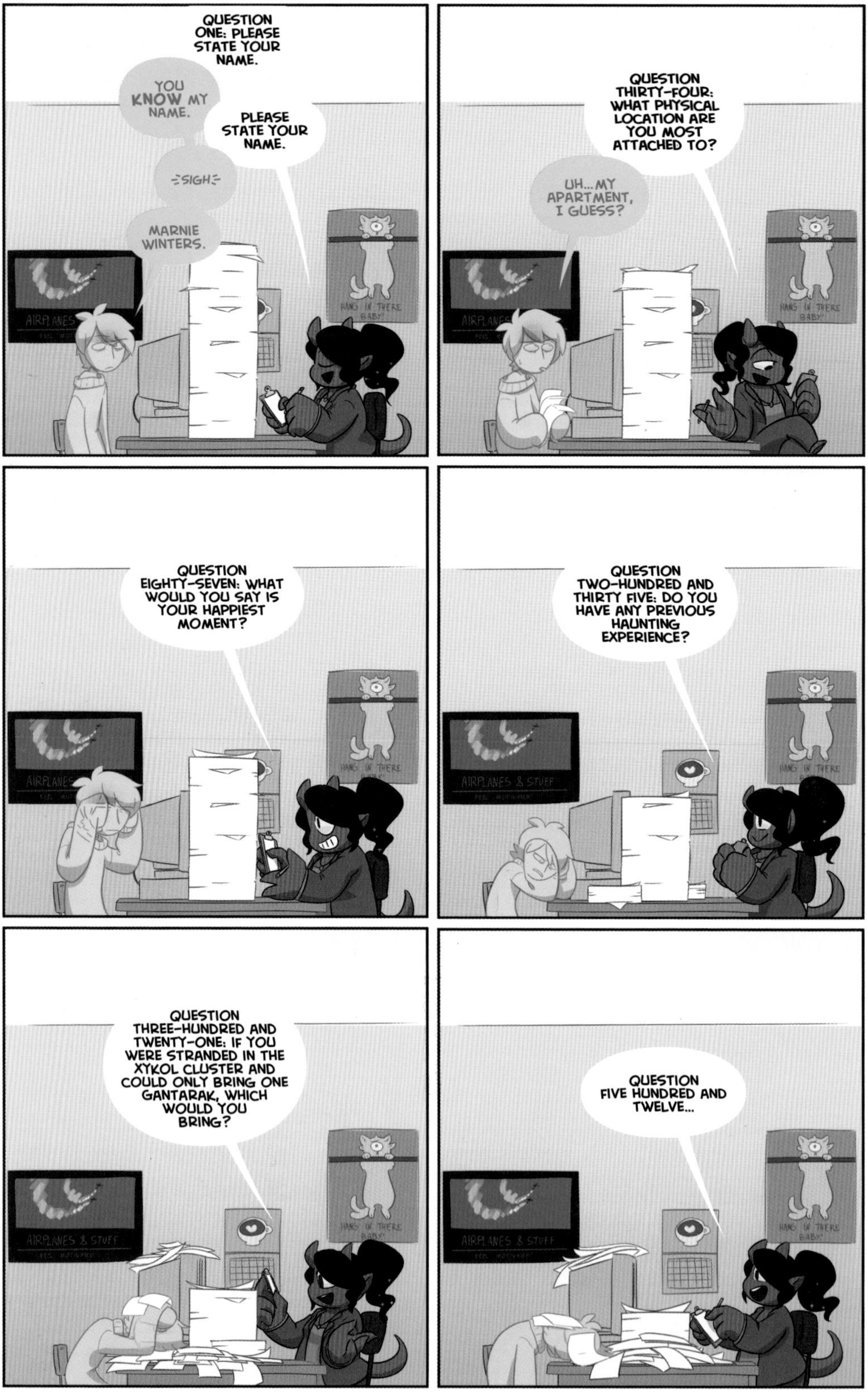
QUESTION ONE: PLEASE STATE YOUR NAME.
YOU KNOW MY NAME.
PLEASE STATE YOUR NAME.
-SIGH-
MARNIE WINTERS.
AIRPLANES
HANG IN THERE BABY!
QUESTION THIRTY-FOUR: WHAT PHYSICAL LOCATION ARE YOU MOST ATTACHED TO?
UH... MY APARTMENT, I GUESS?
QUESTION EIGHTY-SEVEN: WHAT WOULD YOU SAY IS YOUR HAPPIEST MOMENT?
QUESTION TWO-HUNDRED AND THIRTY FIVE: DO YOU HAVE ANY PREVIOUS HAUNTING EXPERIENCE?
AIRPLANES & STUFF
QUESTION THREE-HUNDRED AND TWENTY-ONE: IF YOU WERE STRANDED IN THE XYKOL CLUSTER AND COULD ONLY BRING ONE GANTARAK, WHICH WOULD YOU BRING?
QUESTION FIVE HUNDRED AND TWELVE...

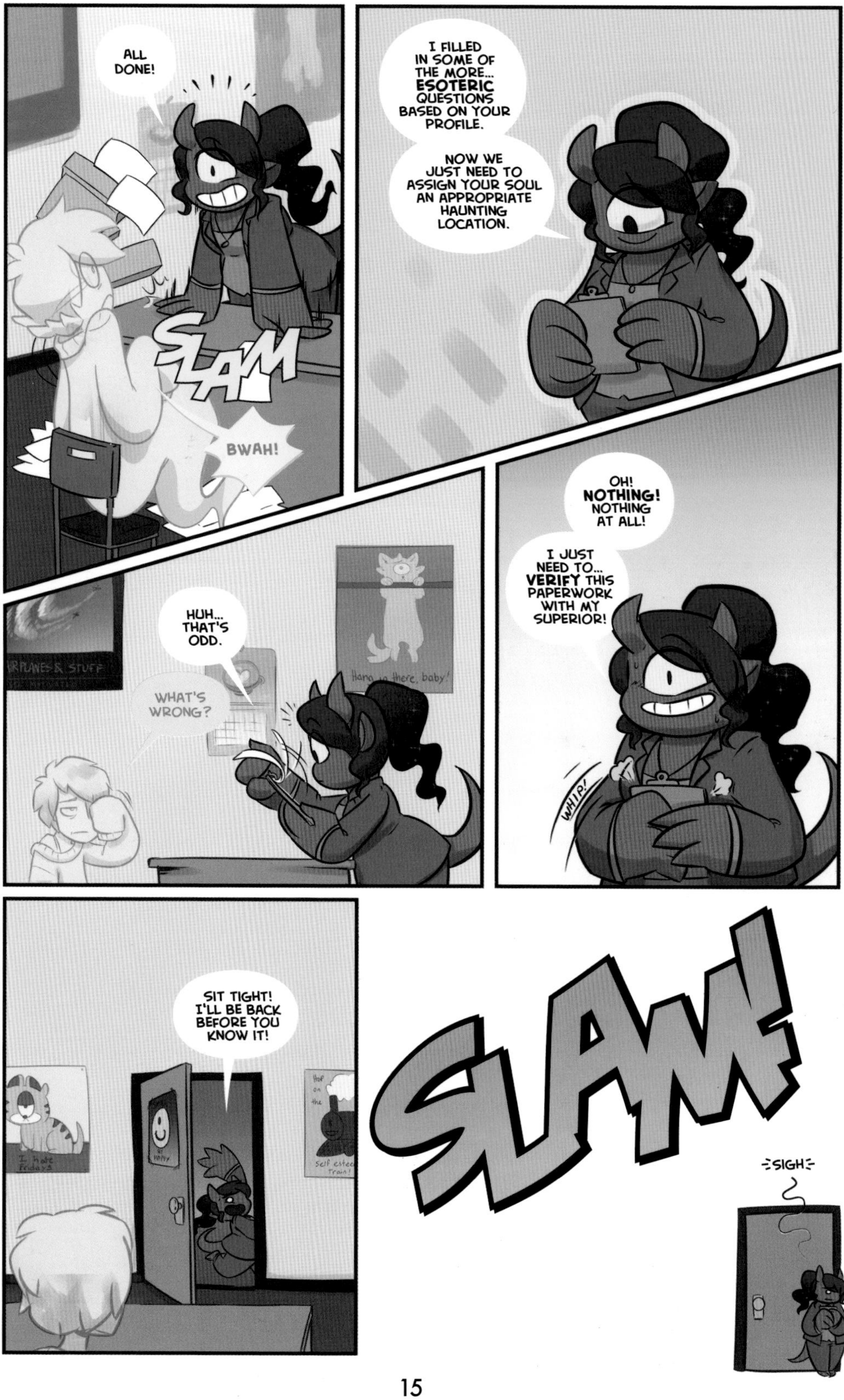
ALL DONE!
SLAM
BWAH!
I FILLED IN SOME OF THE MORE... ESOTERIC QUESTIONS BASED ON YOUR PROFILE.
NOW WE JUST NEED TO ASSIGN YOUR SOUL AN APPROPRIATE HAUNTING LOCATION.
HUH... THAT'S ODD.
WHAT'S WRONG?
Hang in there, baby!
OH! NOTHING! NOTHING AT ALL!
I JUST NEED TO... VERIFY THIS PAPERWORK WITH MY SUPERIOR!
WHIP!
SIT TIGHT! I'LL BE BACK BEFORE YOU KNOW IT!
I hate Fridays
Self esteem Train!
SLAM!
SIGH

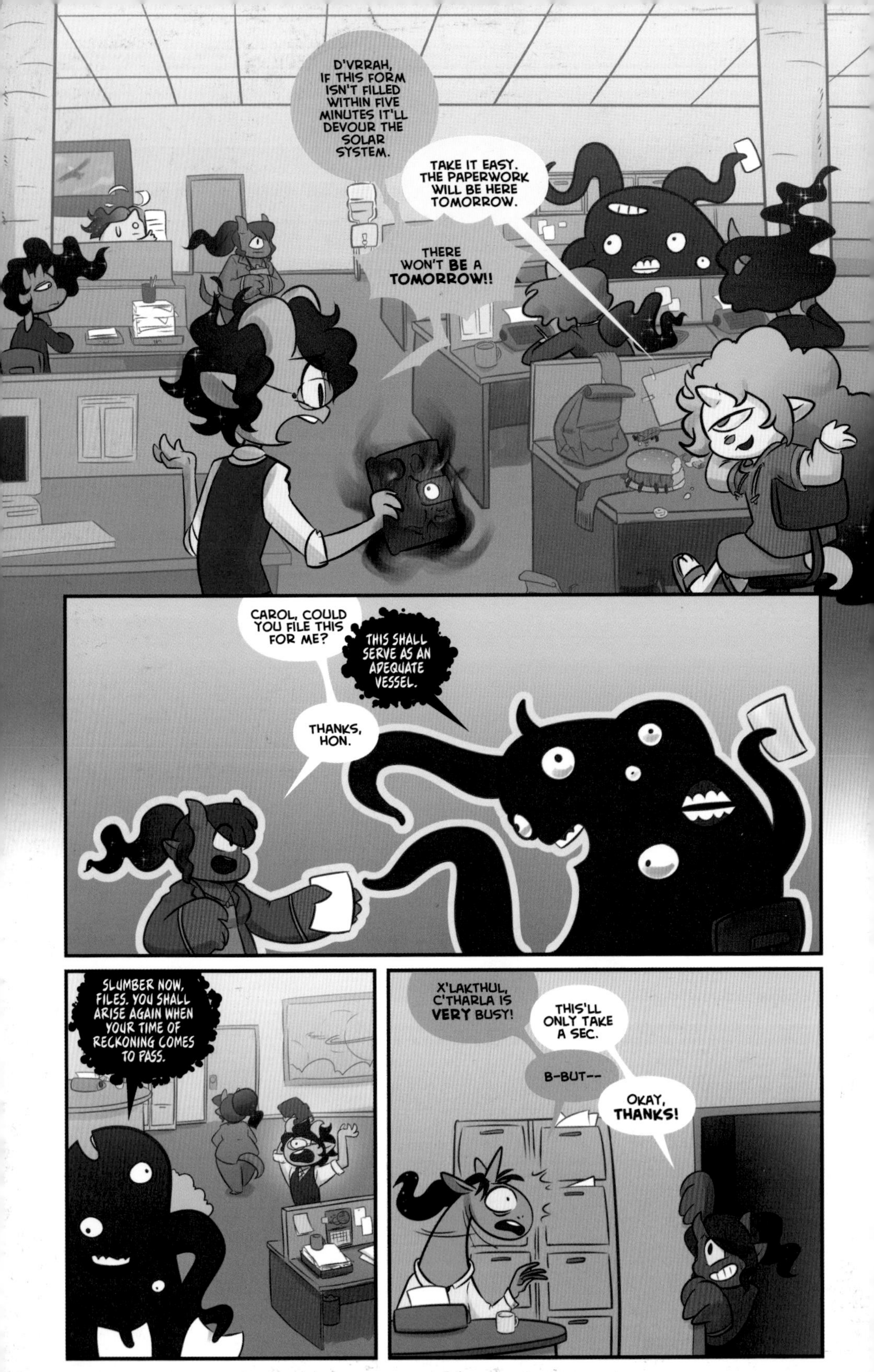
D'VRRAH, IF THIS FORM ISN'T FILLED WITHIN FIVE MINUTES IT'LL DEVOUR THE SOLAR SYSTEM.
TAKE IT EASY. THE PAPERWORK WILL BE HERE TOMORROW.
THERE WON'T **BE** A **TOMORROW!!**
CAROL, COULD YOU FILE THIS FOR ME?
THIS SHALL SERVE AS AN ADEQUATE VESSEL.
THANKS, HON.
SLUMBER NOW, FILES. YOU SHALL ARISE AGAIN WHEN YOUR TIME OF RECKONING COMES TO PASS.
X'LAKTHUL, C'THARLA IS **VERY** BUSY!
THIS'LL ONLY TAKE A SEC.
B-BUT--
OKAY, **THANKS!**

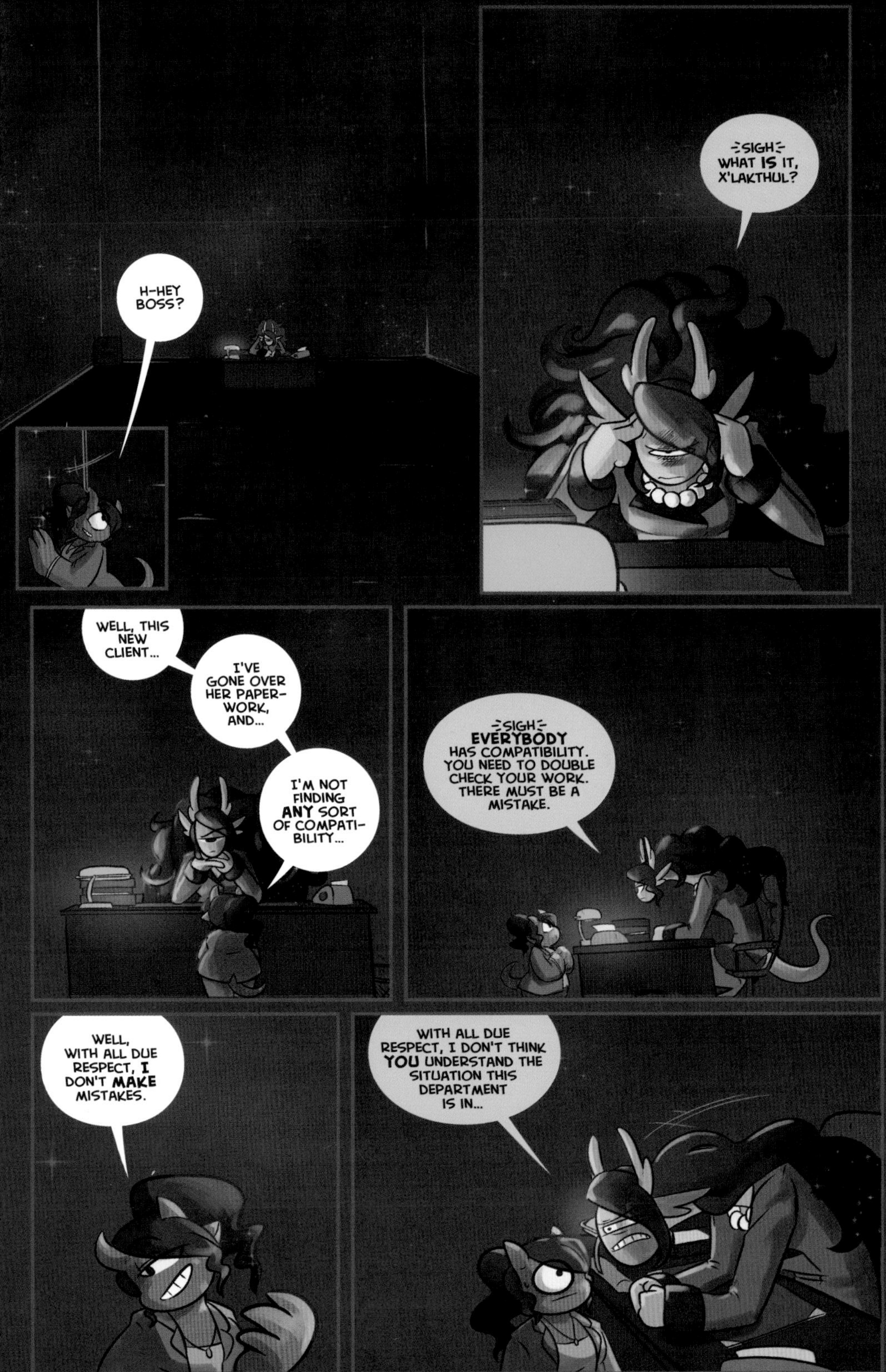
H-HEY BOSS?
-SIGH- WHAT IS IT, X'LAKTHUL?
WELL, THIS NEW CLIENT...
I'VE GONE OVER HER PAPER-WORK, AND...
I'M NOT FINDING ANY SORT OF COMPATI-BILITY...
-SIGH- EVERYBODY HAS COMPATIBILITY. YOU NEED TO DOUBLE CHECK YOUR WORK. THERE MUST BE A MISTAKE.
WELL, WITH ALL DUE RESPECT, I DON'T MAKE MISTAKES.
WITH ALL DUE RESPECT, I DON'T THINK YOU UNDERSTAND THE SITUATION THIS DEPARTMENT IS IN...

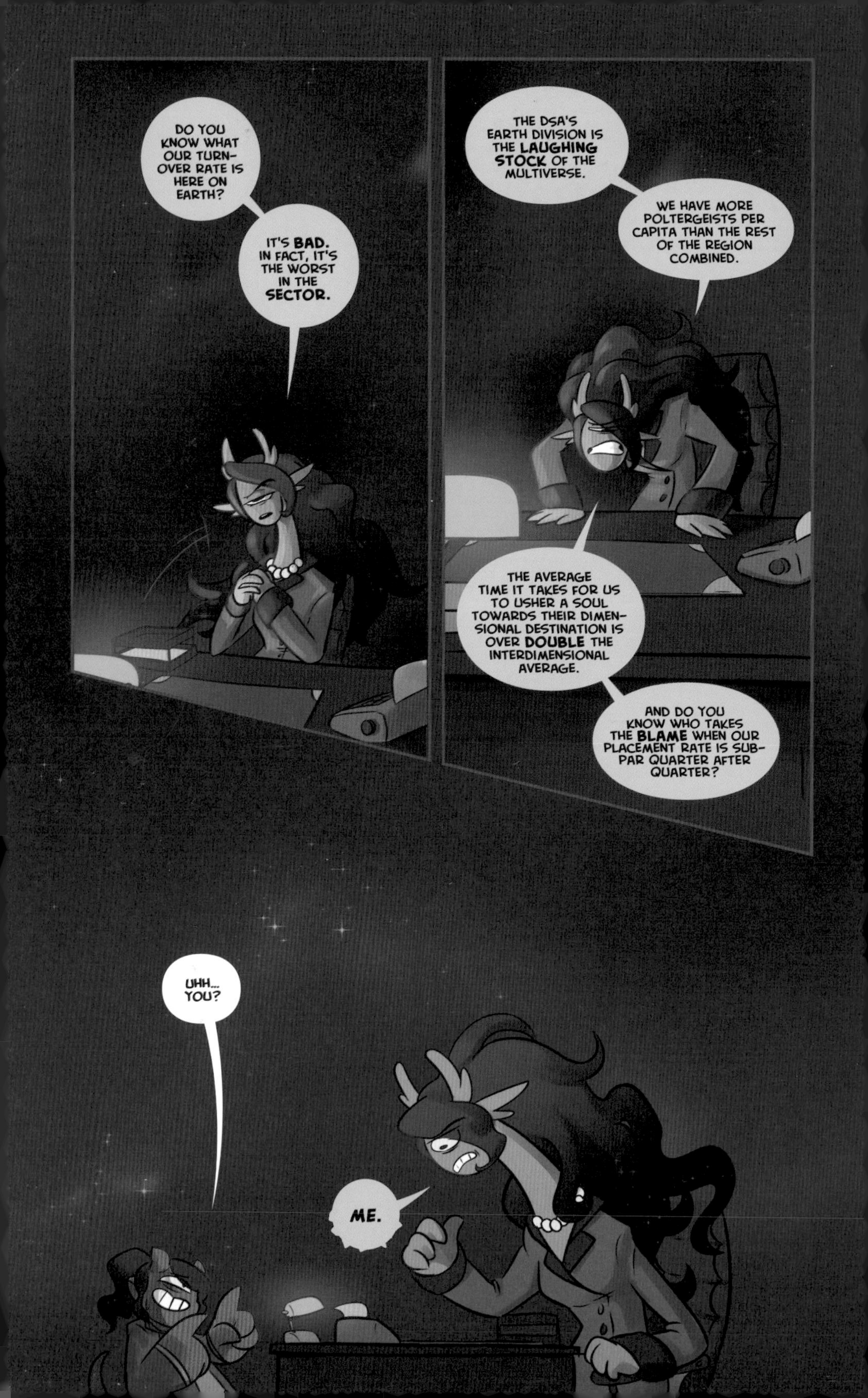
DO YOU KNOW WHAT OUR TURN-OVER RATE IS HERE ON EARTH?
IT'S BAD. IN FACT, IT'S THE WORST IN THE SECTOR.
THE DSA'S EARTH DIVISION IS THE LAUGHING STOCK OF THE MULTIVERSE.
WE HAVE MORE POLTERGEISTS PER CAPITA THAN THE REST OF THE REGION COMBINED.
THE AVERAGE TIME IT TAKES FOR US TO USHER A SOUL TOWARDS THEIR DIMEN-SIONAL DESTINATION IS OVER DOUBLE THE INTERDIMENSIONAL AVERAGE.
AND DO YOU KNOW WHO TAKES THE BLAME WHEN OUR PLACEMENT RATE IS SUB-PAR QUARTER AFTER QUARTER?
UHH... YOU?
ME.

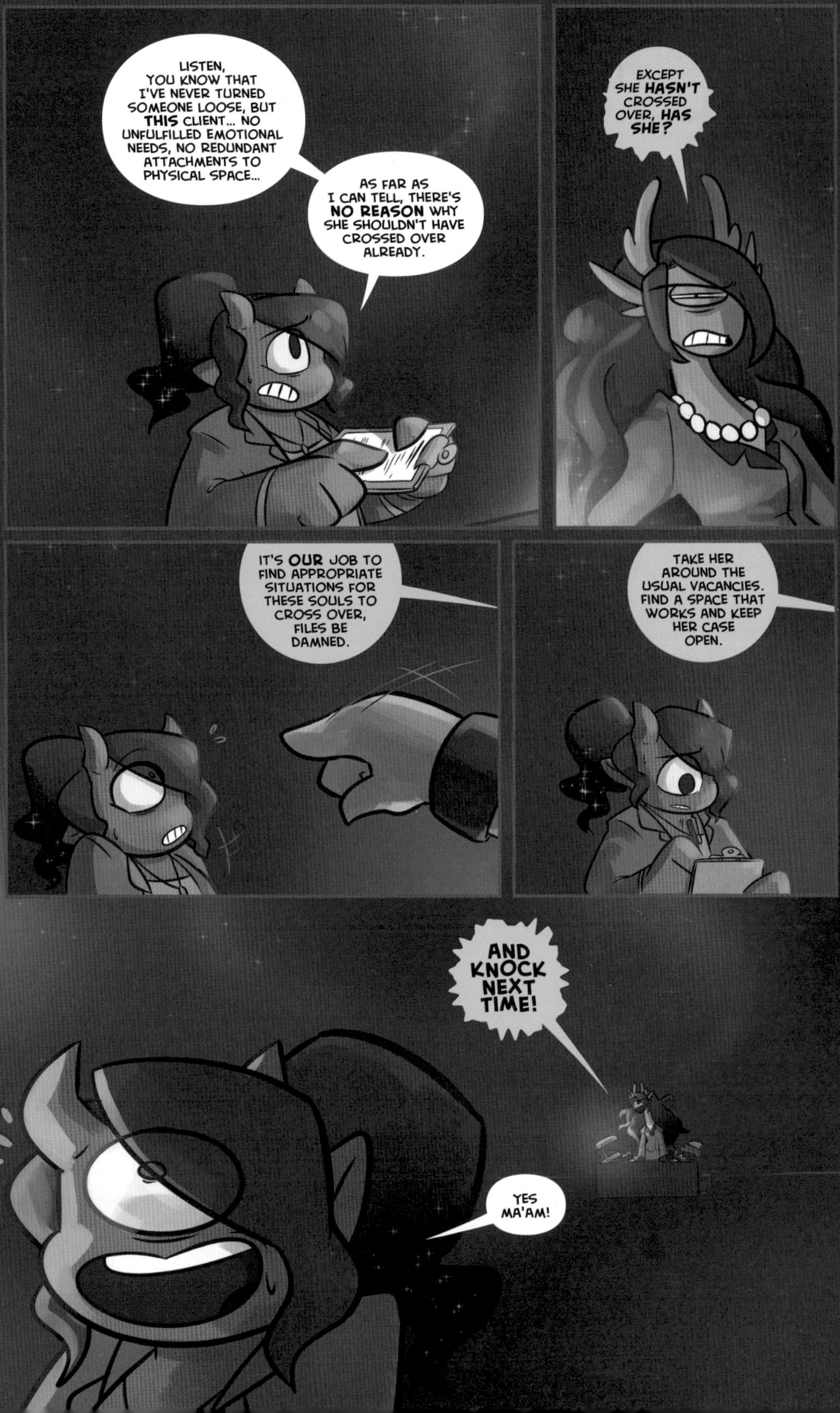
LISTEN, YOU KNOW THAT I'VE NEVER TURNED SOMEONE LOOSE, BUT THIS CLIENT... NO UNFULFILLED EMOTIONAL NEEDS, NO REDUNDANT ATTACHMENTS TO PHYSICAL SPACE...
AS FAR AS I CAN TELL, THERE'S NO REASON WHY SHE SHOULDN'T HAVE CROSSED OVER ALREADY.
EXCEPT SHE HASN'T CROSSED OVER, HAS SHE?
IT'S OUR JOB TO FIND APPROPRIATE SITUATIONS FOR THESE SOULS TO CROSS OVER, FILES BE DAMNED.
TAKE HER AROUND THE USUAL VACANCIES. FIND A SPACE THAT WORKS AND KEEP HER CASE OPEN.
AND KNOCK NEXT TIME!
YES MA'AM!

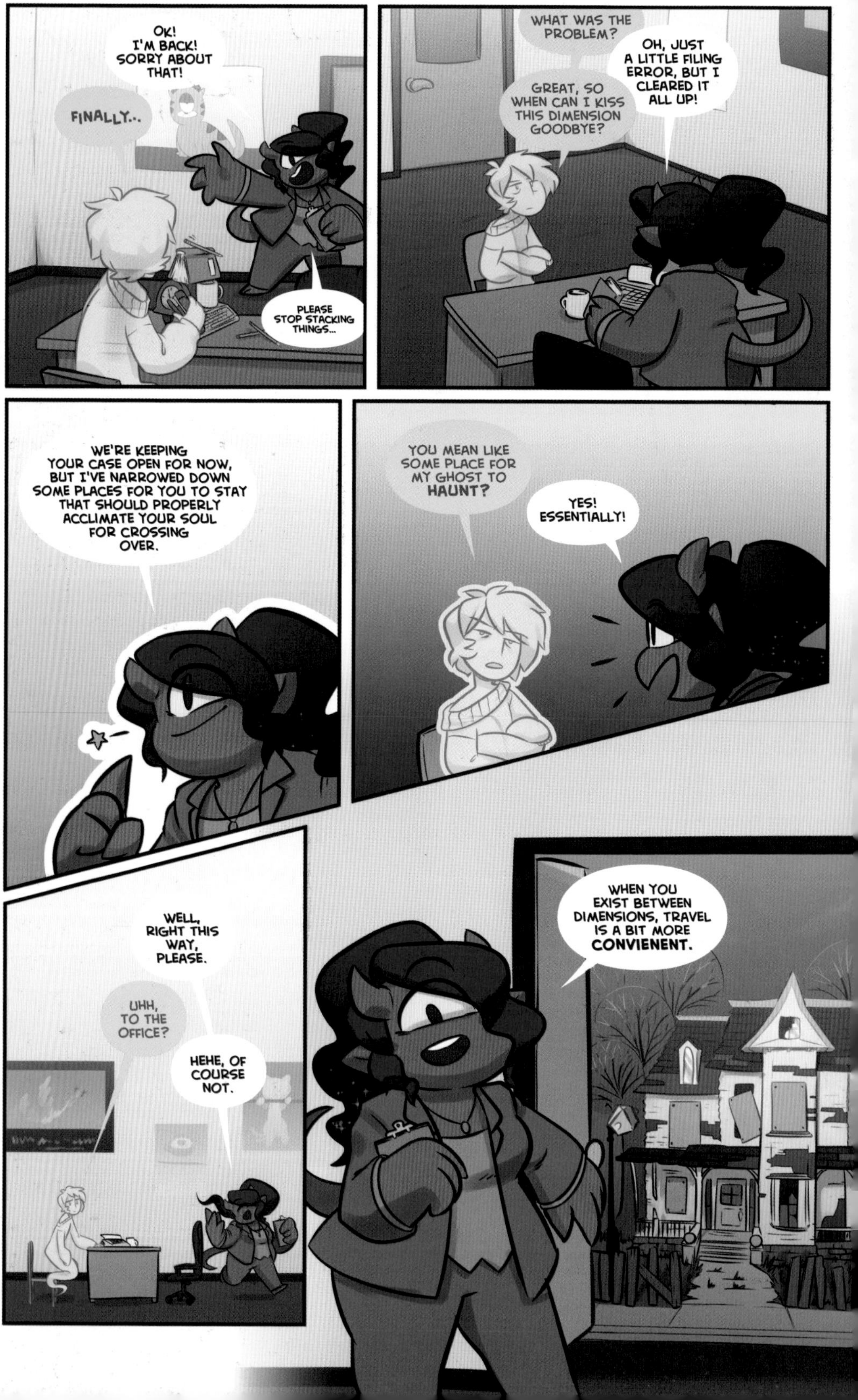
OK! I'M BACK! SORRY ABOUT THAT!
FINALLY...
PLEASE STOP STACKING THINGS...
WHAT WAS THE PROBLEM?
OH, JUST A LITTLE FILING ERROR, BUT I CLEARED IT ALL UP!
GREAT, SO WHEN CAN I KISS THIS DIMENSION GOODBYE?
WE'RE KEEPING YOUR CASE OPEN FOR NOW, BUT I'VE NARROWED DOWN SOME PLACES FOR YOU TO STAY THAT SHOULD PROPERLY ACCLIMATE YOUR SOUL FOR CROSSING OVER.
YOU MEAN LIKE SOME PLACE FOR MY GHOST TO **HAUNT?**
YES! ESSENTIALLY!
WELL, RIGHT THIS WAY, PLEASE.
UHH, TO THE OFFICE?
HEHE, OF COURSE NOT.
WHEN YOU EXIST BETWEEN DIMENSIONS, TRAVEL IS A BIT MORE **CONVIENENT.**

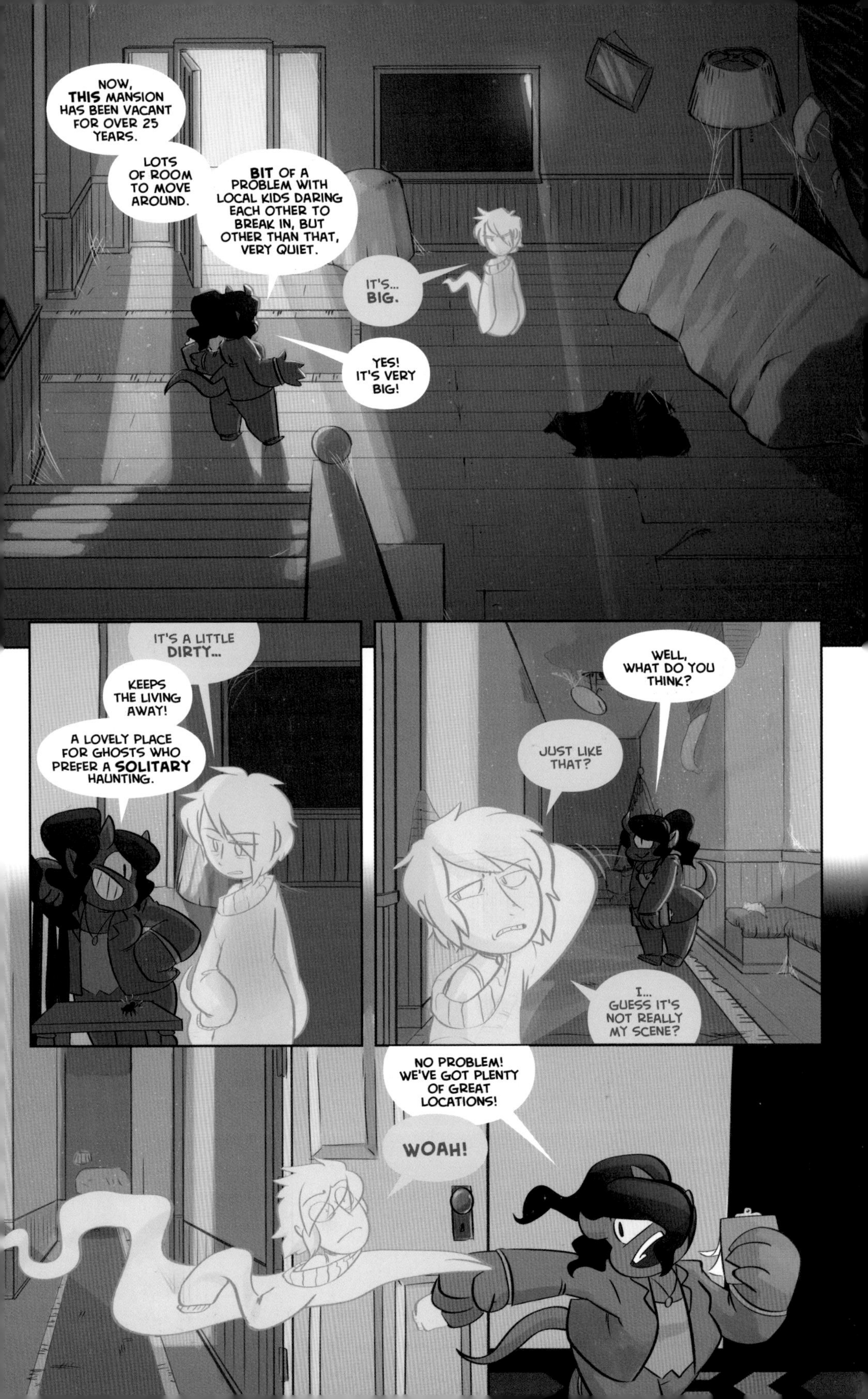
NOW, THIS MANSION HAS BEEN VACANT FOR OVER 25 YEARS.
LOTS OF ROOM TO MOVE AROUND.
BIT OF A PROBLEM WITH LOCAL KIDS DARING EACH OTHER TO BREAK IN, BUT OTHER THAN THAT, VERY QUIET.
IT'S... BIG.
YES! IT'S VERY BIG!
IT'S A LITTLE DIRTY...
KEEPS THE LIVING AWAY!
A LOVELY PLACE FOR GHOSTS WHO PREFER A SOLITARY HAUNTING.
WELL, WHAT DO YOU THINK?
JUST LIKE THAT?
I... GUESS IT'S NOT REALLY MY SCENE?
NO PROBLEM! WE'VE GOT PLENTY OF GREAT LOCATIONS!
WOAH!

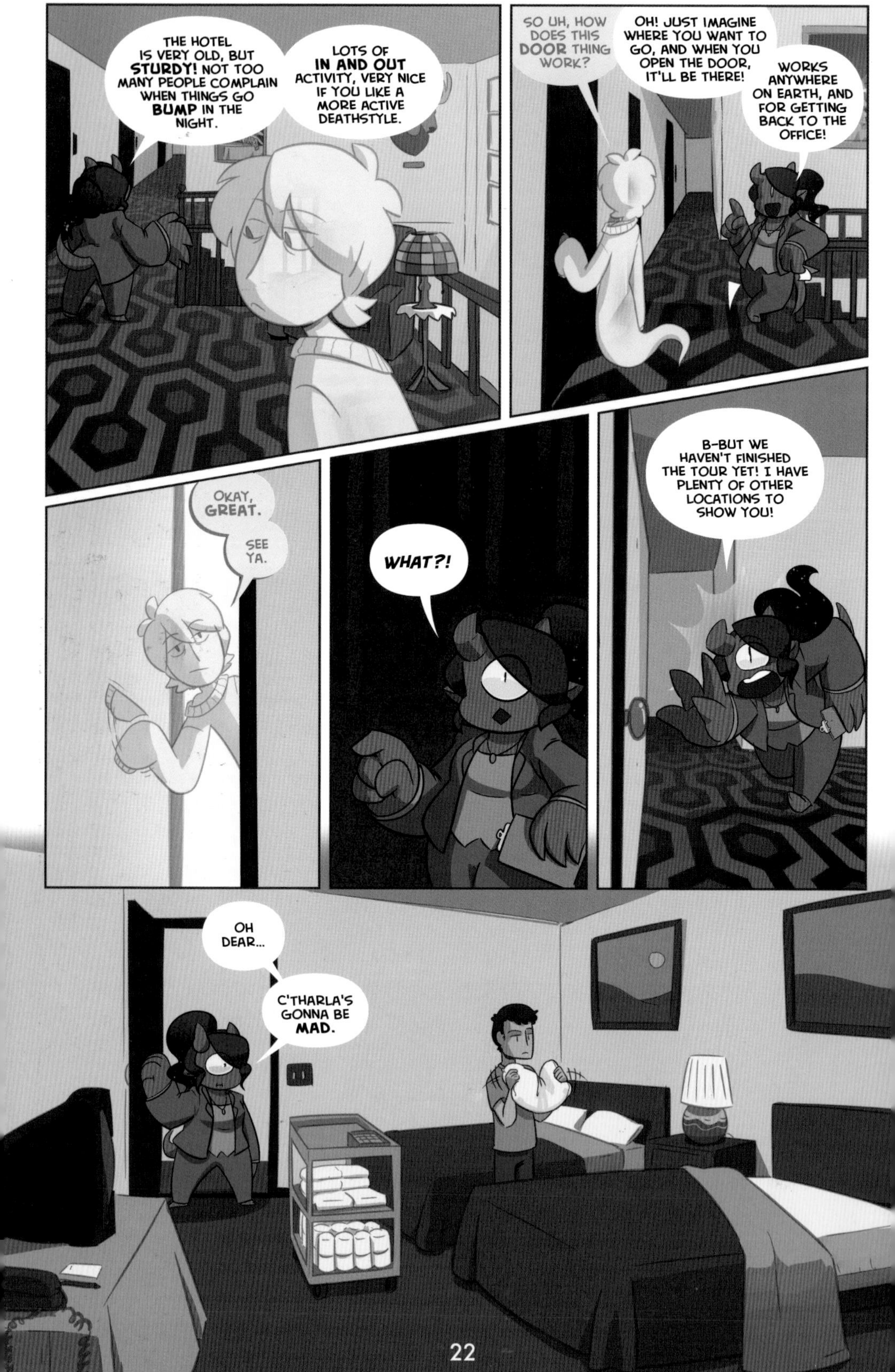
THE HOTEL IS VERY OLD, BUT **STURDY!** NOT TOO MANY PEOPLE COMPLAIN WHEN THINGS GO **BUMP** IN THE NIGHT.
LOTS OF **IN AND OUT** ACTIVITY, VERY NICE IF YOU LIKE A MORE ACTIVE DEATHSTYLE.
SO UH, HOW DOES THIS **DOOR** THING WORK?
OH! JUST IMAGINE WHERE YOU WANT TO GO, AND WHEN YOU OPEN THE DOOR, IT'LL BE THERE!
WORKS ANYWHERE ON EARTH, AND FOR GETTING BACK TO THE OFFICE!
OKAY, **GREAT.**
SEE YA.
WHAT?!
B-BUT WE HAVEN'T FINISHED THE TOUR YET! I HAVE PLENTY OF OTHER LOCATIONS TO SHOW YOU!
OH DEAR...
C'THARLA'S GONNA BE **MAD.**

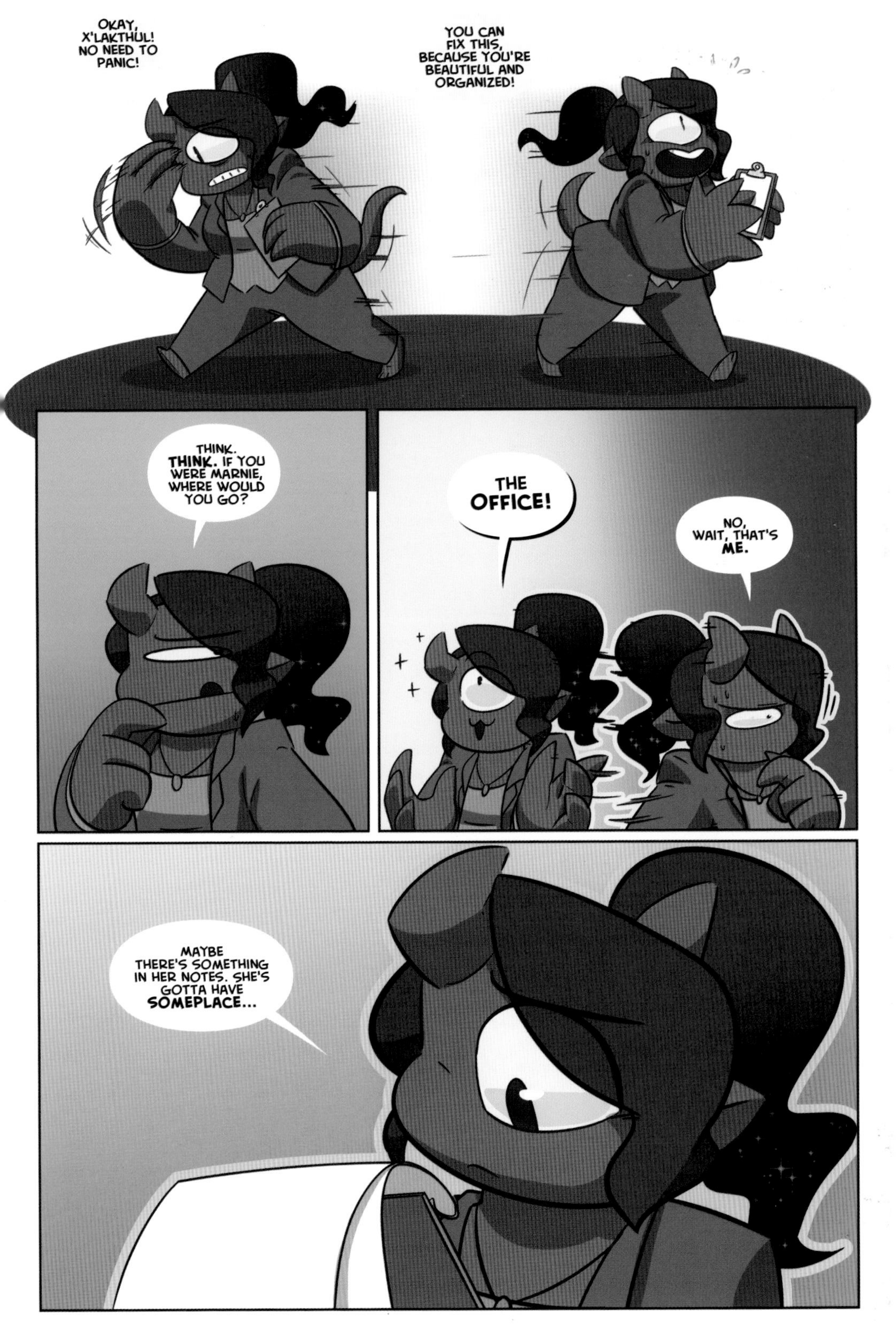
OKAY, X'LAKTHUL! NO NEED TO PANIC!
YOU CAN FIX THIS, BECAUSE YOU'RE BEAUTIFUL AND ORGANIZED!
THINK. THINK. IF YOU WERE MARNIE, WHERE WOULD YOU GO?
THE OFFICE!
NO, WAIT, THAT'S ME.
MAYBE THERE'S SOMETHING IN HER NOTES. SHE'S GOTTA HAVE SOMEPLACE...

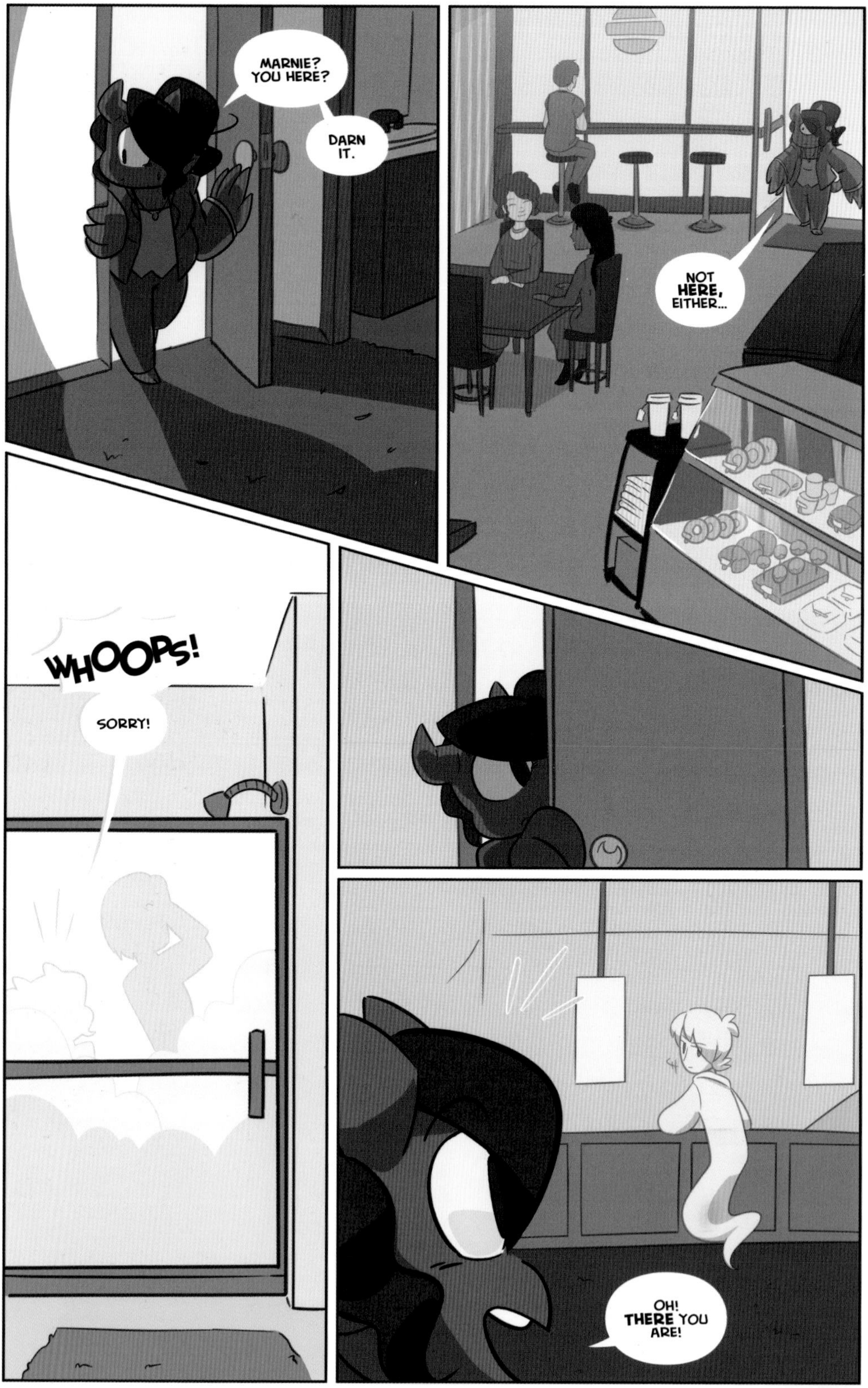
MARNIE? YOU HERE?
DARN IT.
NOT HERE, EITHER...
WHOOPS!
SORRY!
OH! THERE YOU ARE!

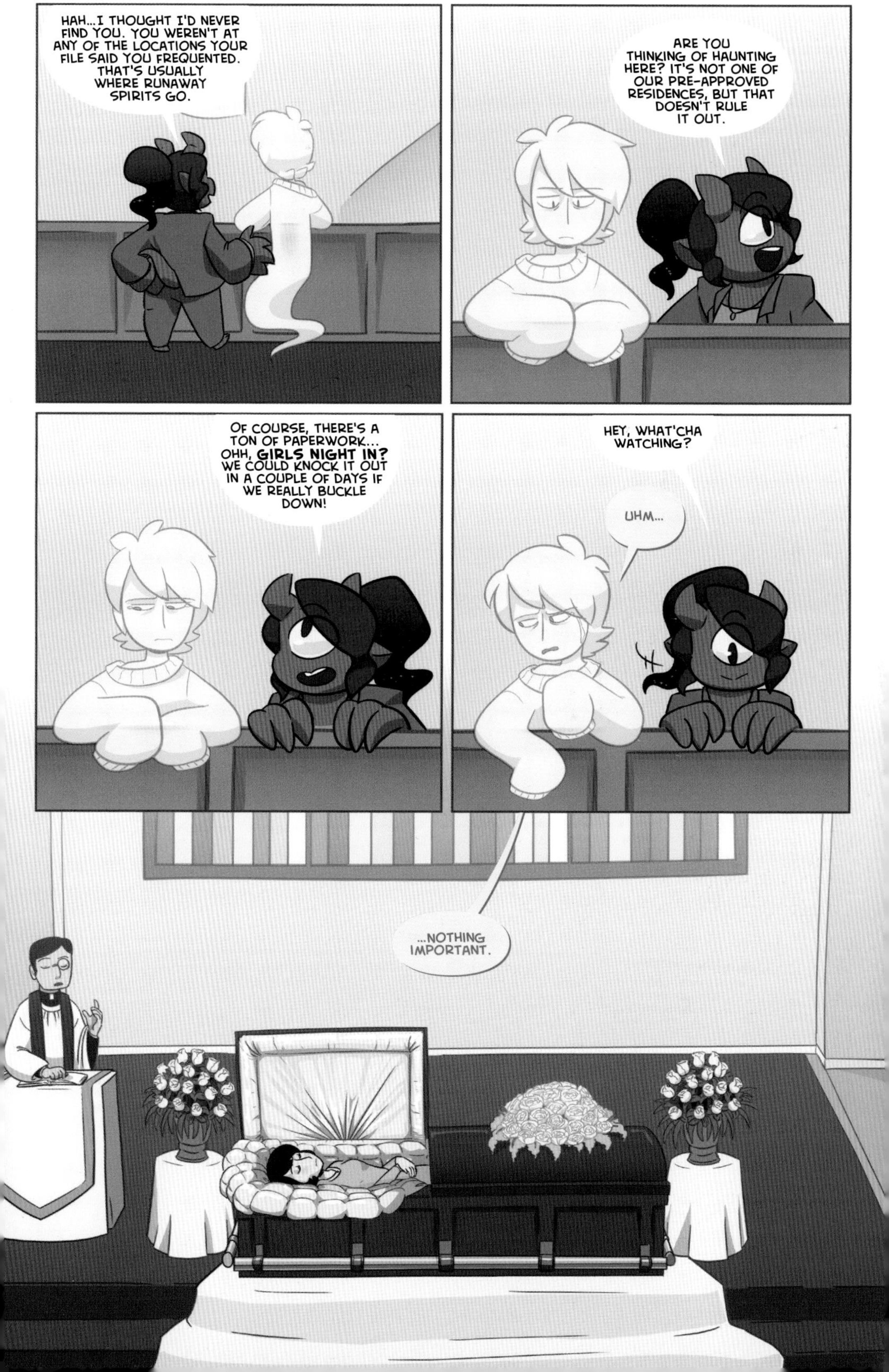
HAH...I THOUGHT I'D NEVER FIND YOU. YOU WEREN'T AT ANY OF THE LOCATIONS YOUR FILE SAID YOU FREQUENTED. THAT'S USUALLY WHERE RUNAWAY SPIRITS GO.
ARE YOU THINKING OF HAUNTING HERE? IT'S NOT ONE OF OUR PRE-APPROVED RESIDENCES, BUT THAT DOESN'T RULE IT OUT.
OF COURSE, THERE'S A TON OF PAPERWORK... OHH, **GIRLS NIGHT IN?** WE COULD KNOCK IT OUT IN A COUPLE OF DAYS IF WE REALLY BUCKLE DOWN!
HEY, WHAT'CHA WATCHING?
UHM...
...NOTHING IMPORTANT.

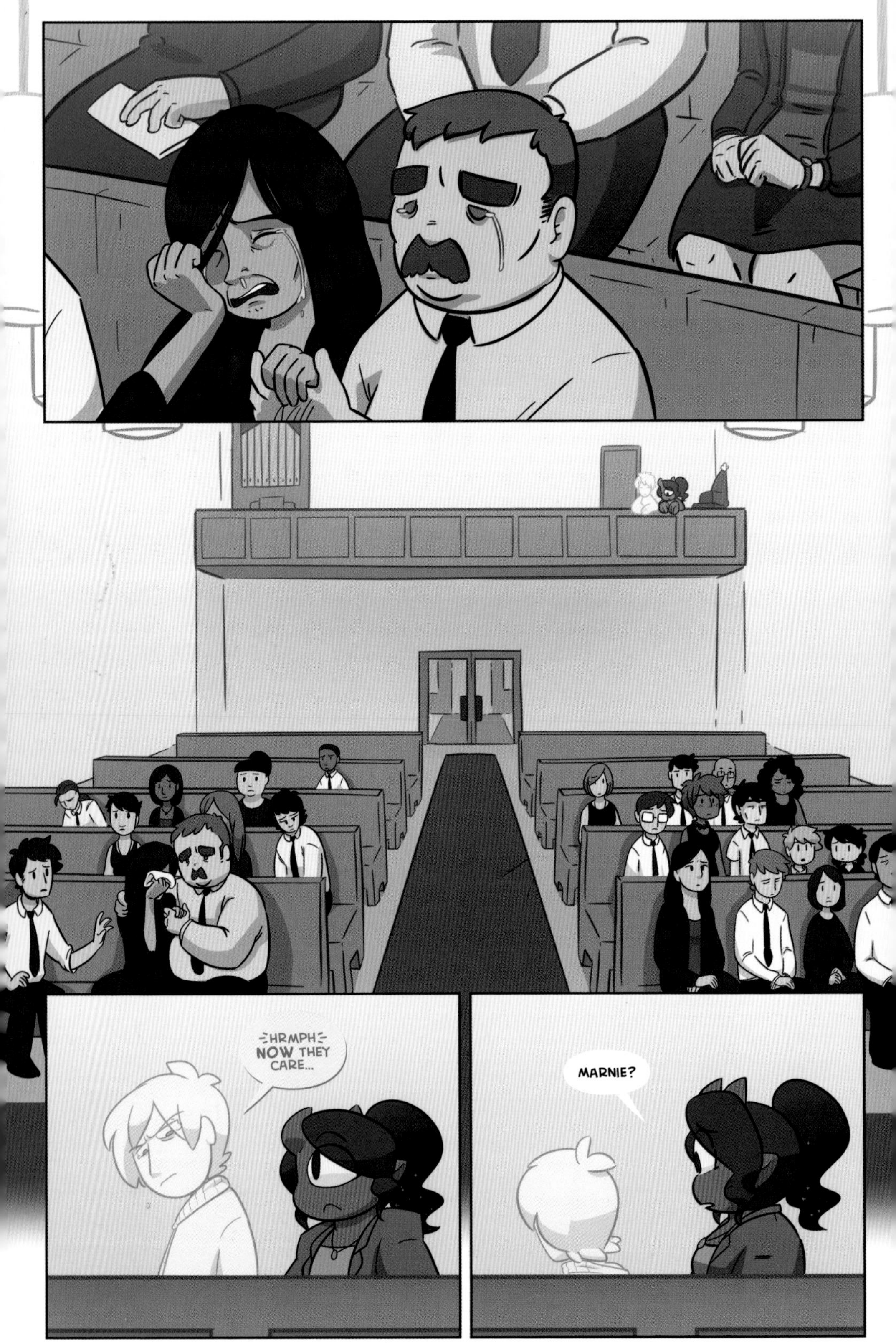
HRMPH NOW THEY CARE...
MARNIE?

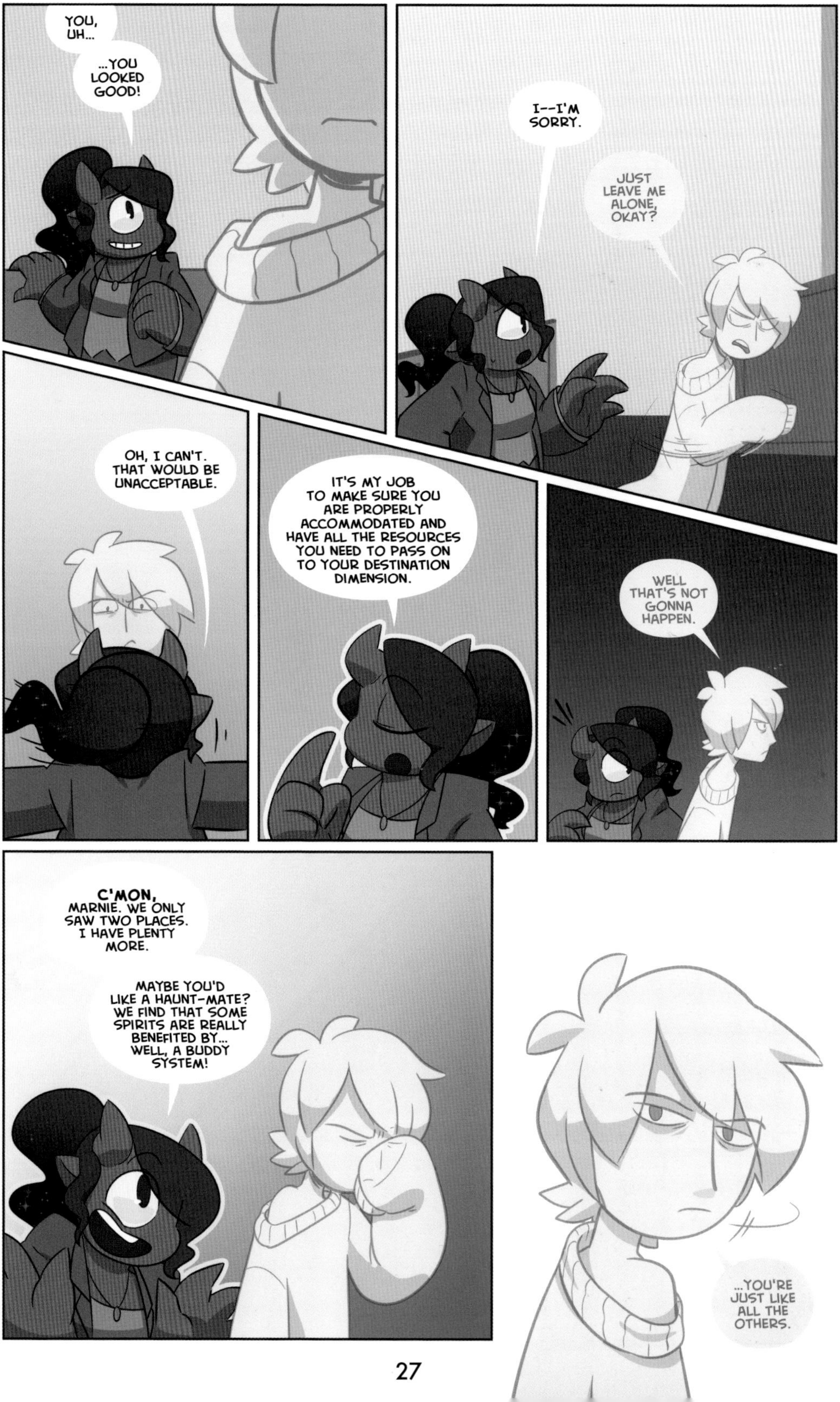
YOU, UH...
...YOU LOOKED GOOD!
I--I'M SORRY.
JUST LEAVE ME ALONE, OKAY?
OH, I CAN'T. THAT WOULD BE UNACCEPTABLE.
IT'S MY JOB TO MAKE SURE YOU ARE PROPERLY ACCOMMODATED AND HAVE ALL THE RESOURCES YOU NEED TO PASS ON TO YOUR DESTINATION DIMENSION.
WELL THAT'S NOT GONNA HAPPEN.
C'MON, MARNIE. WE ONLY SAW TWO PLACES. I HAVE PLENTY MORE.
MAYBE YOU'D LIKE A HAUNT-MATE? WE FIND THAT SOME SPIRITS ARE REALLY BENEFITED BY... WELL, A BUDDY SYSTEM!
...YOU'RE JUST LIKE ALL THE OTHERS.

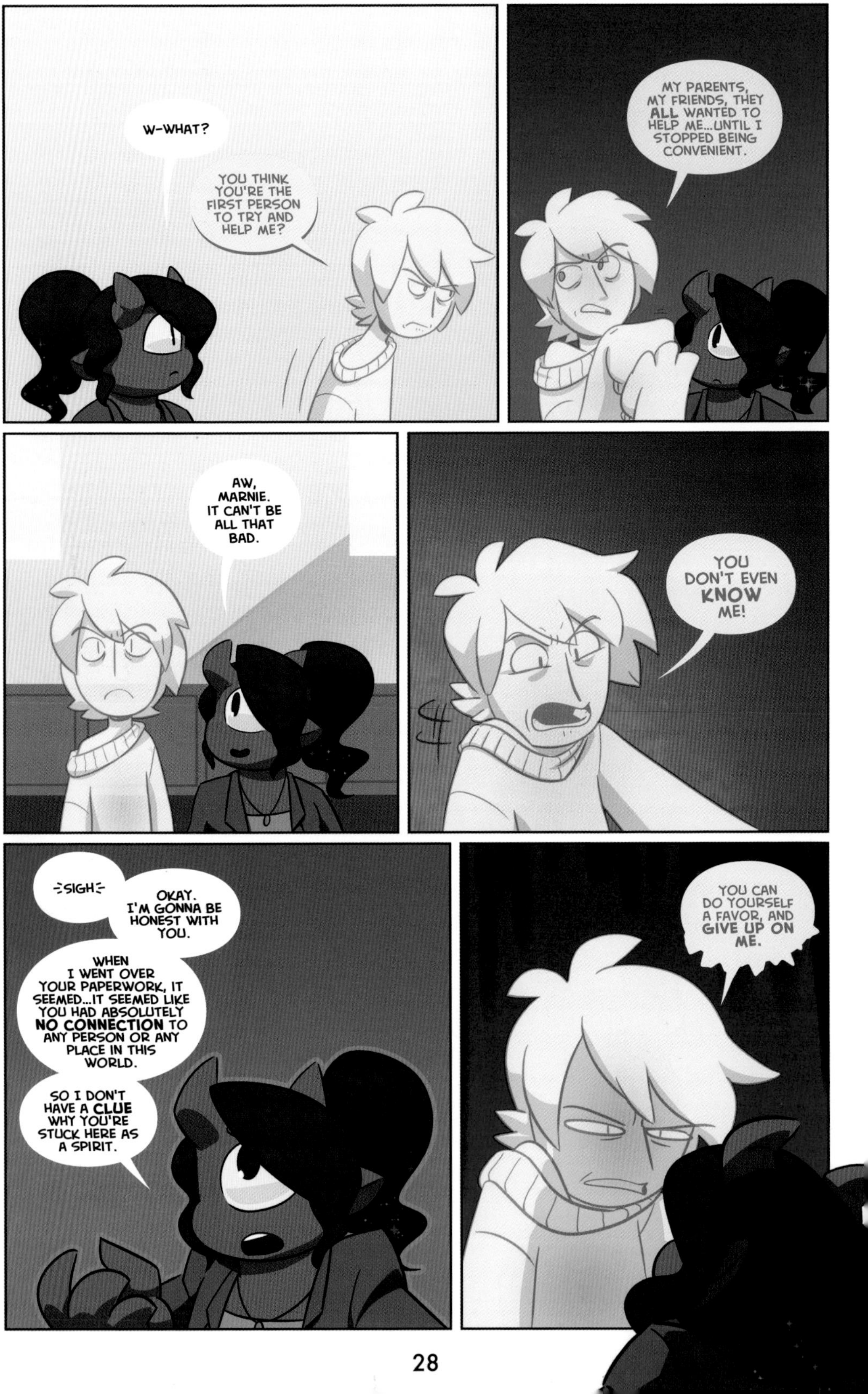
W-WHAT?
YOU THINK YOU'RE THE FIRST PERSON TO TRY AND HELP ME?
MY PARENTS, MY FRIENDS, THEY ALL WANTED TO HELP ME...UNTIL I STOPPED BEING CONVENIENT.
AW, MARNIE. IT CAN'T BE ALL THAT BAD.
YOU DON'T EVEN KNOW ME!
SIGH
OKAY. I'M GONNA BE HONEST WITH YOU.
WHEN I WENT OVER YOUR PAPERWORK, IT SEEMED...IT SEEMED LIKE YOU HAD ABSOLUTELY NO CONNECTION TO ANY PERSON OR ANY PLACE IN THIS WORLD.
SO I DON'T HAVE A CLUE WHY YOU'RE STUCK HERE AS A SPIRIT.
YOU CAN DO YOURSELF A FAVOR, AND GIVE UP ON ME.

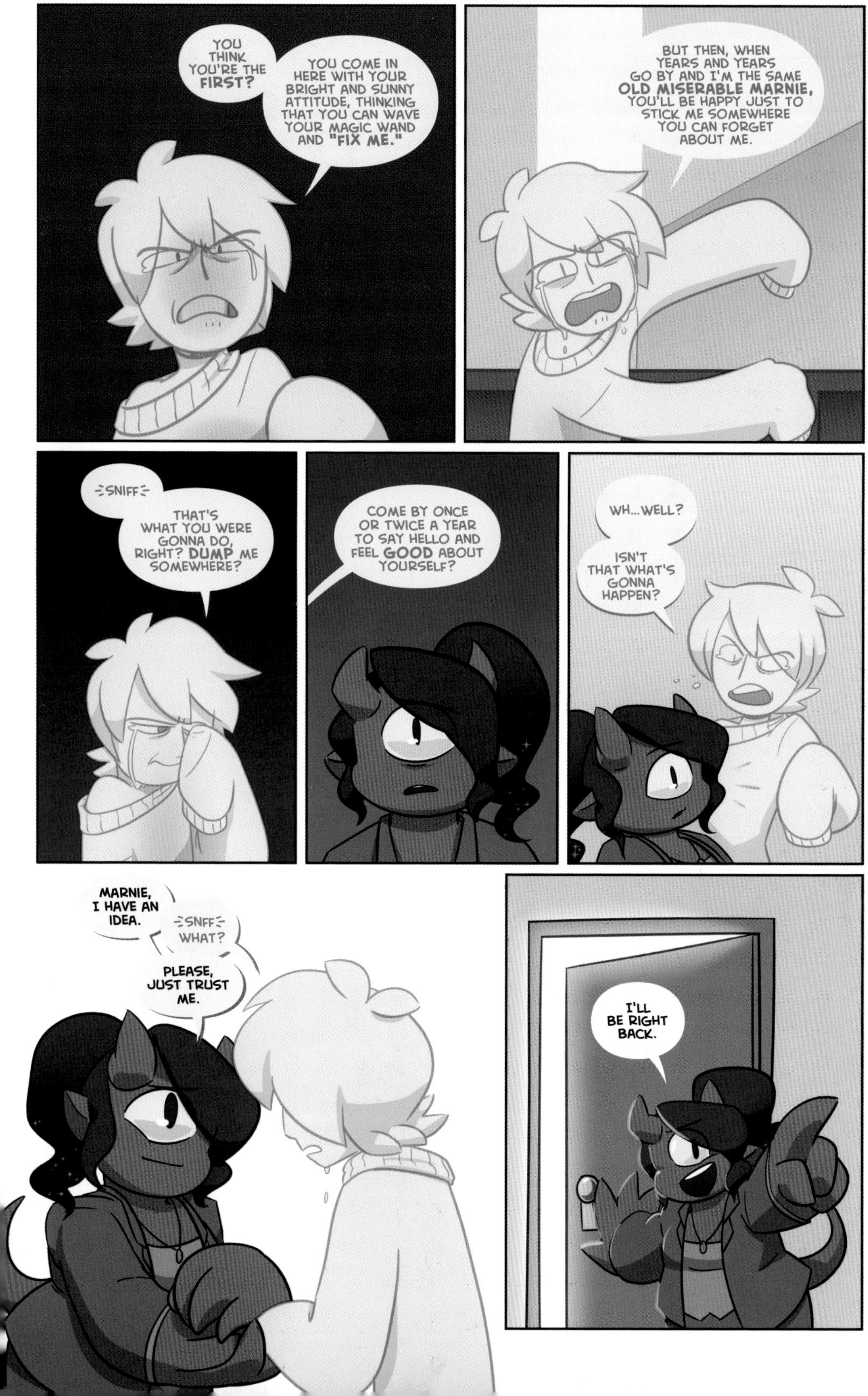
YOU THINK YOU'RE THE FIRST?
YOU COME IN HERE WITH YOUR BRIGHT AND SUNNY ATTITUDE, THINKING THAT YOU CAN WAVE YOUR MAGIC WAND AND "FIX ME."
BUT THEN, WHEN YEARS AND YEARS GO BY AND I'M THE SAME OLD MISERABLE MARNIE, YOU'LL BE HAPPY JUST TO STICK ME SOMEWHERE YOU CAN FORGET ABOUT ME.
SNIFF
THAT'S WHAT YOU WERE GONNA DO, RIGHT? DUMP ME SOMEWHERE?
COME BY ONCE OR TWICE A YEAR TO SAY HELLO AND FEEL GOOD ABOUT YOURSELF?
WH...WELL?
ISN'T THAT WHAT'S GONNA HAPPEN?
MARNIE, I HAVE AN IDEA.
SNFF WHAT?
PLEASE, JUST TRUST ME.
I'LL BE RIGHT BACK.

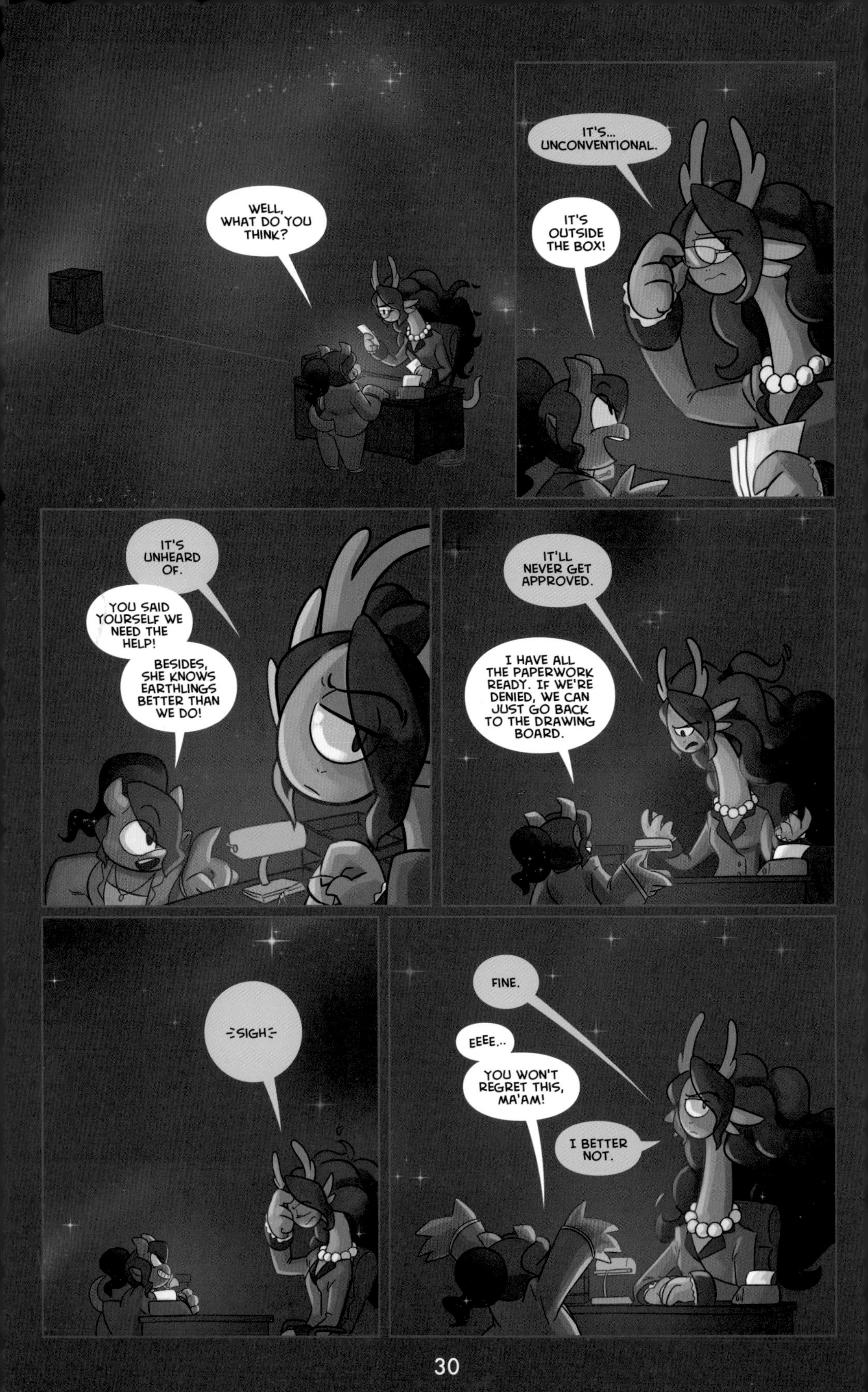
WELL, WHAT DO YOU THINK?
IT'S... UNCONVENTIONAL.
IT'S OUTSIDE THE BOX!
IT'S UNHEARD OF.
YOU SAID YOURSELF WE NEED THE HELP!
BESIDES, SHE KNOWS EARTHLINGS BETTER THAN WE DO!
IT'LL NEVER GET APPROVED.
I HAVE ALL THE PAPERWORK READY. IF WE'RE DENIED, WE CAN JUST GO BACK TO THE DRAWING BOARD.
=SIGH=
FINE.
EEEE...
YOU WON'T REGRET THIS, MA'AM!
I BETTER NOT.

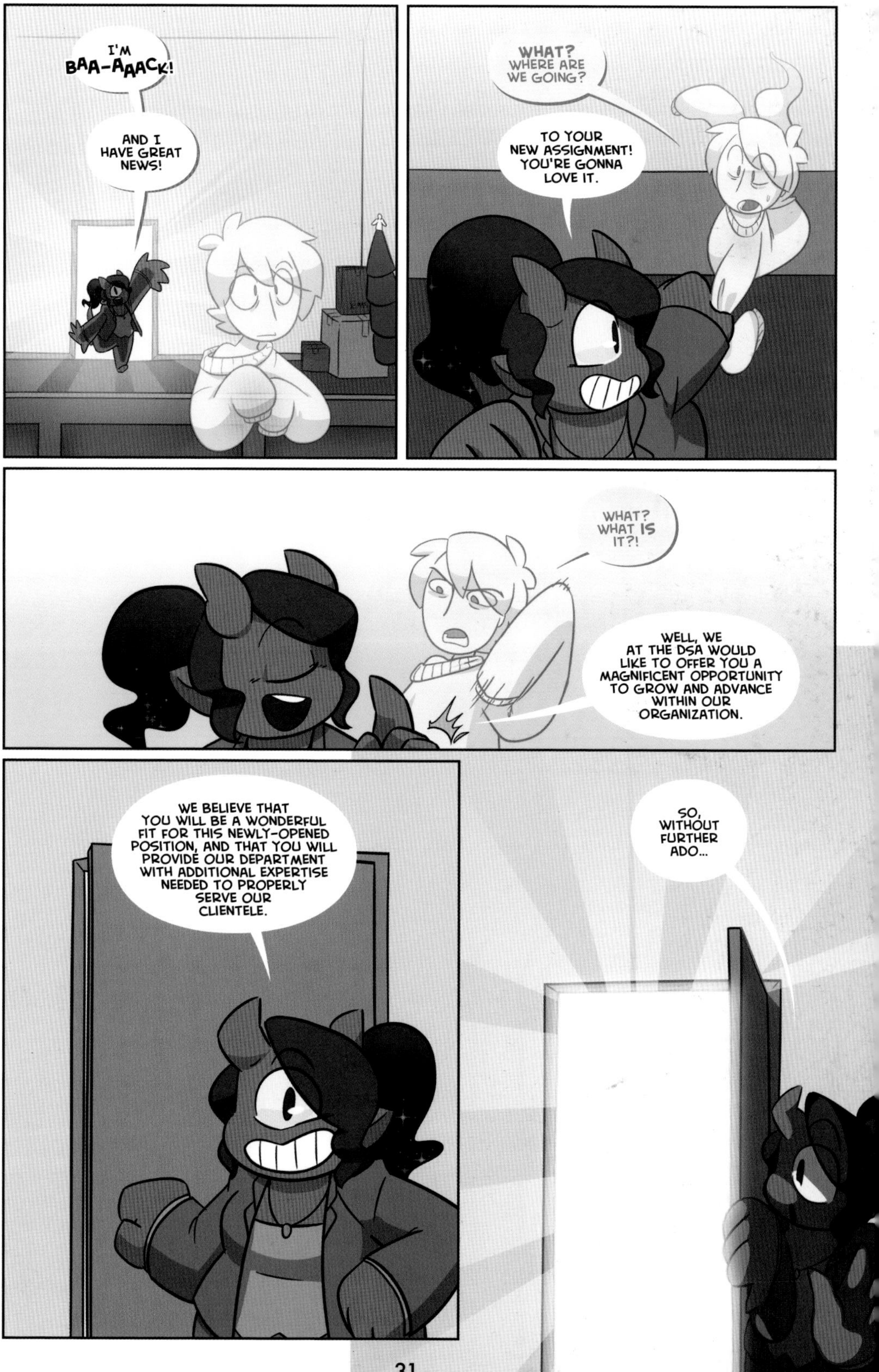
I'M BAA-AAACK!
AND I HAVE GREAT NEWS!
WHAT? WHERE ARE WE GOING?
TO YOUR NEW ASSIGNMENT! YOU'RE GONNA LOVE IT.
WHAT? WHAT IS IT?!
WELL, WE AT THE DSA WOULD LIKE TO OFFER YOU A MAGNIFICENT OPPORTUNITY TO GROW AND ADVANCE WITHIN OUR ORGANIZATION.
WE BELIEVE THAT YOU WILL BE A WONDERFUL FIT FOR THIS NEWLY-OPENED POSITION, AND THAT YOU WILL PROVIDE OUR DEPARTMENT WITH ADDITIONAL EXPERTISE NEEDED TO PROPERLY SERVE OUR CLIENTELE.
SO, WITHOUT FURTHER ADO...

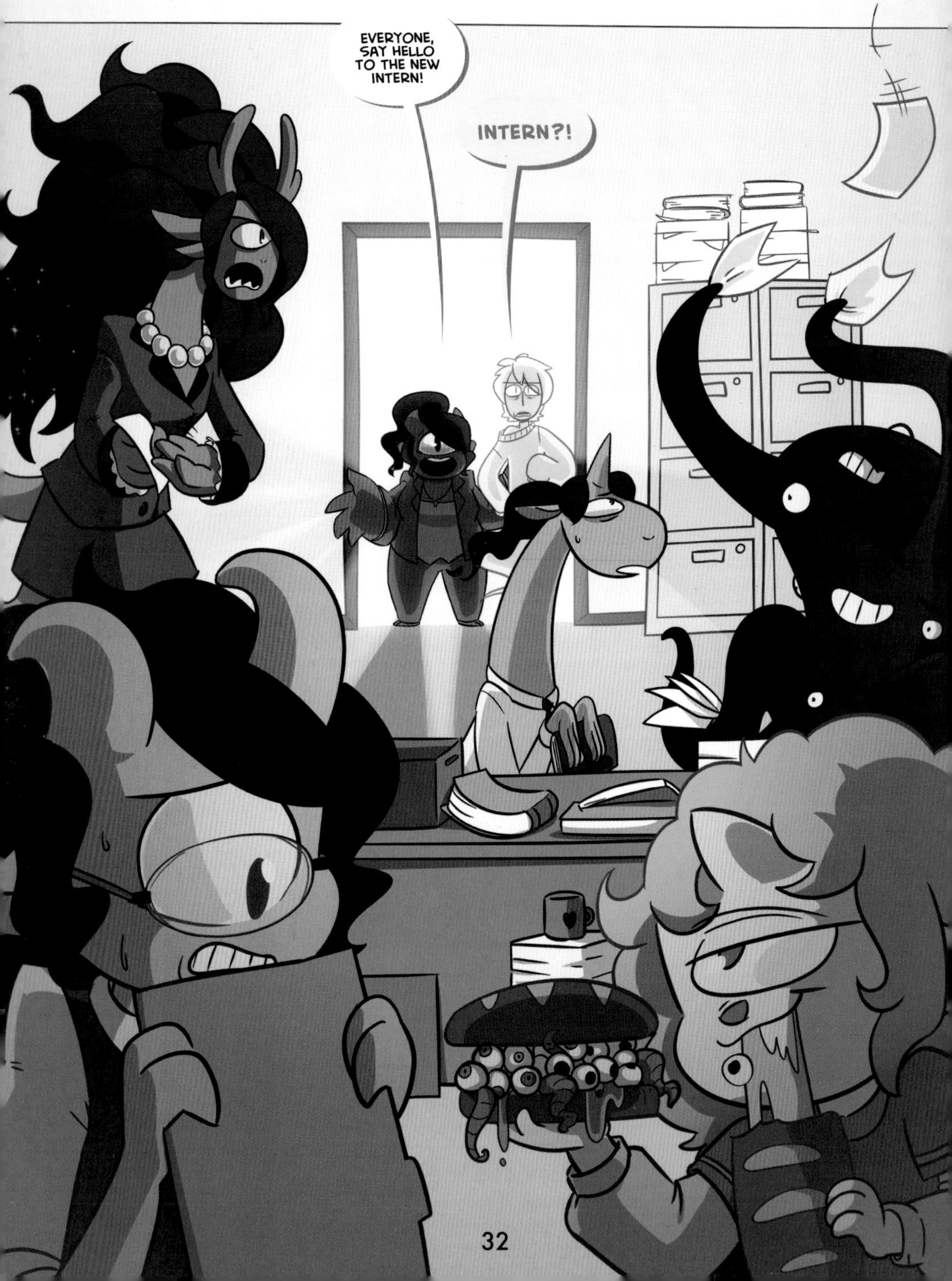
EVERYONE, SAY HELLO TO THE NEW INTERN!
INTERN?!

Department
of
Spectral Affairs

D'vrrah

Chapter 2

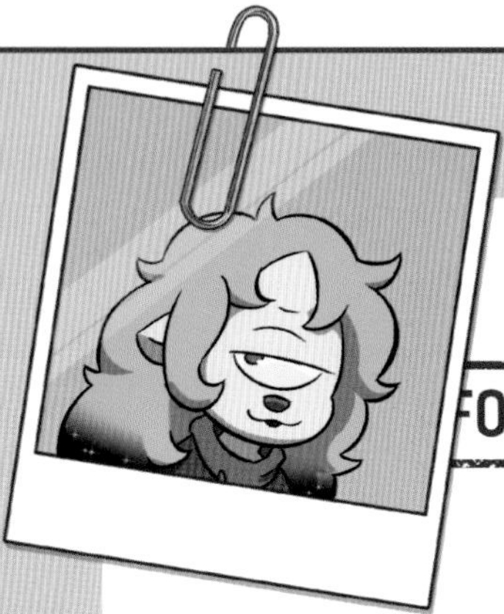

FOR OFFICIAL USE ONLY

Name: D'vrrah

Pronunciation: Dev-Rah

Pronouns: she/her

Age: ∞

Position: case worker

Likes: Food, days off, kickin' it, making piles of stuff.

Dislikes: Cleaning, paperwork, the RULES!

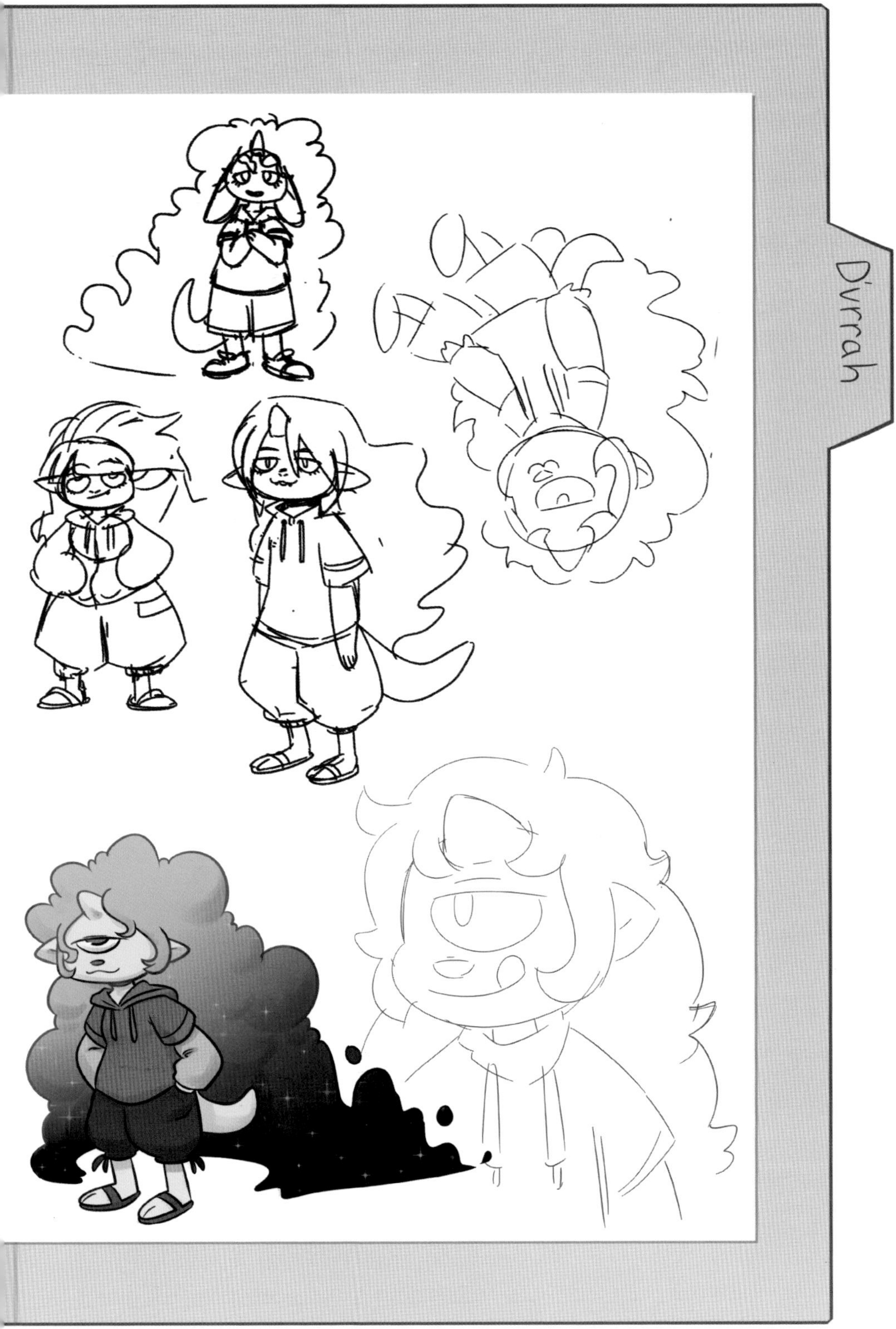
Dirrah

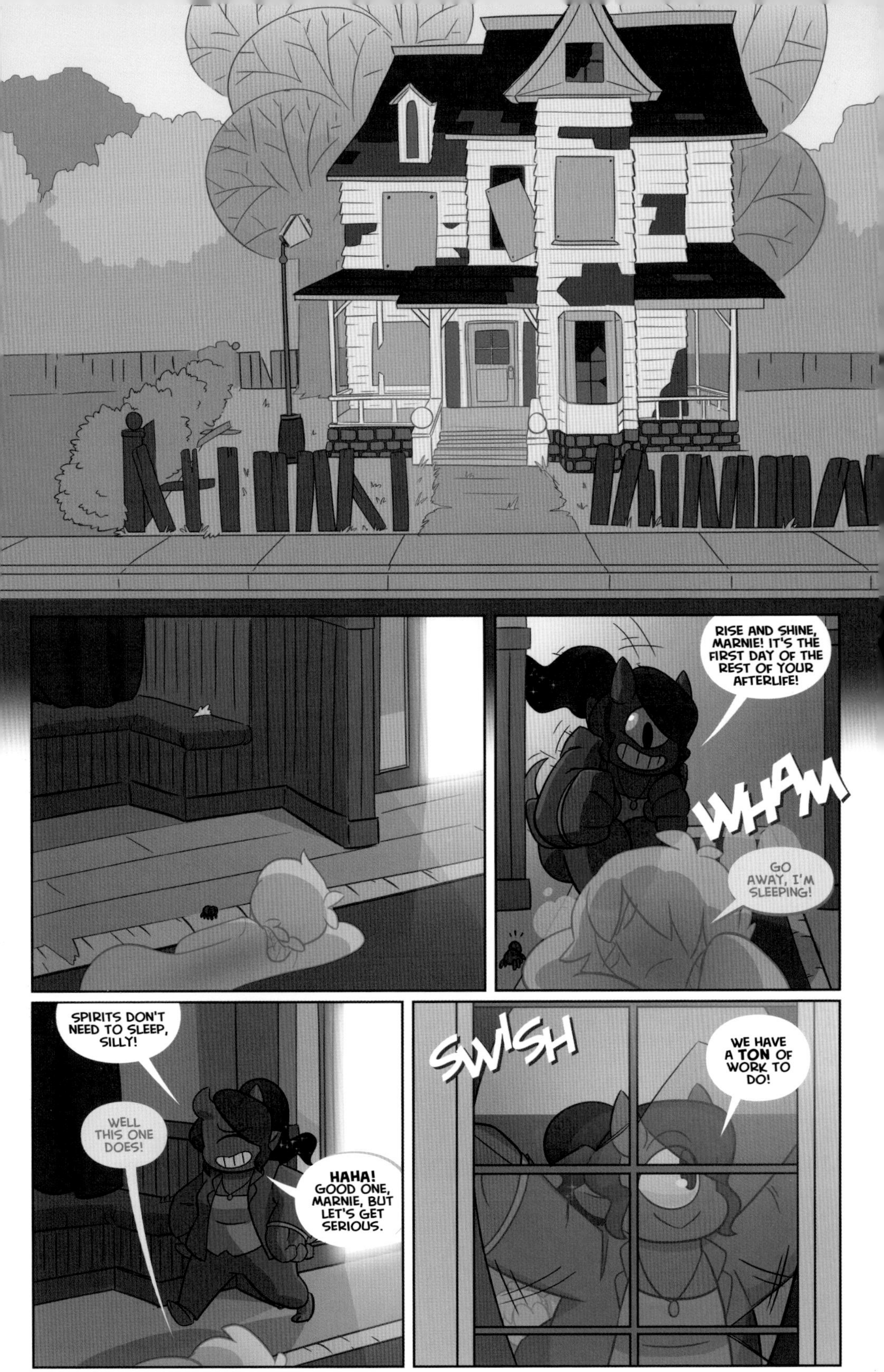
RISE AND SHINE, MARNIE! IT'S THE FIRST DAY OF THE REST OF YOUR AFTERLIFE!
WHAM
GO AWAY, I'M SLEEPING!
SPIRITS DON'T NEED TO SLEEP, SILLY!
WELL THIS ONE DOES!
HAHA! GOOD ONE, MARNIE, BUT LET'S GET SERIOUS.
SWISH
WE HAVE A TON OF WORK TO DO!

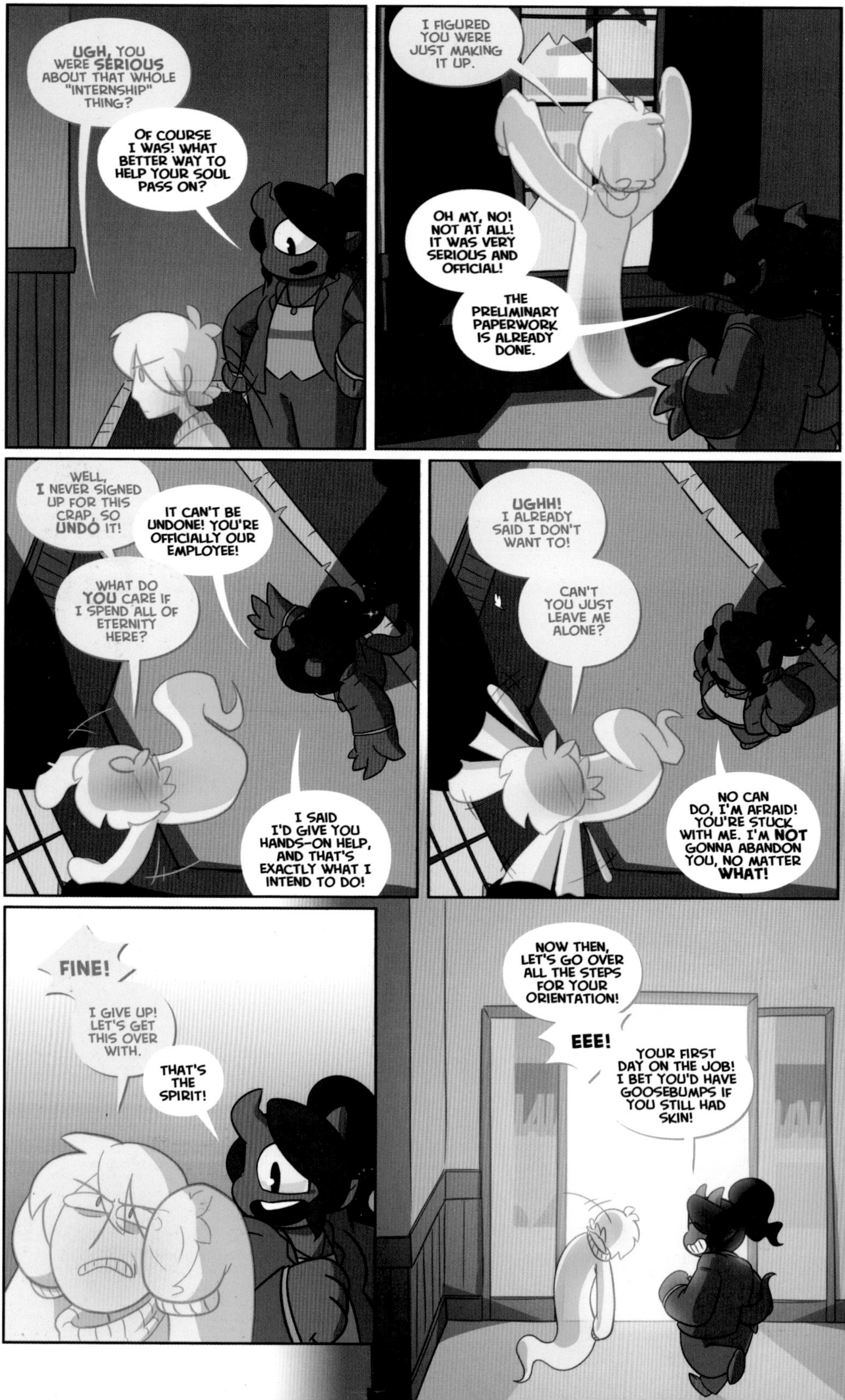
UGH, YOU WERE SERIOUS ABOUT THAT WHOLE "INTERNSHIP" THING?
OF COURSE I WAS! WHAT BETTER WAY TO HELP YOUR SOUL PASS ON?
I FIGURED YOU WERE JUST MAKING IT UP.
OH MY, NO! NOT AT ALL! IT WAS VERY SERIOUS AND OFFICIAL!
THE PRELIMINARY PAPERWORK IS ALREADY DONE.
WELL, I NEVER SIGNED UP FOR THIS CRAP, SO UNDO IT!
IT CAN'T BE UNDONE! YOU'RE OFFICIALLY OUR EMPLOYEE!
WHAT DO YOU CARE IF I SPEND ALL OF ETERNITY HERE?
I SAID I'D GIVE YOU HANDS-ON HELP, AND THAT'S EXACTLY WHAT I INTEND TO DO!
UGHH! I ALREADY SAID I DON'T WANT TO!
CAN'T YOU JUST LEAVE ME ALONE?
NO CAN DO, I'M AFRAID! YOU'RE STUCK WITH ME. I'M NOT GONNA ABANDON YOU, NO MATTER WHAT!
FINE!
I GIVE UP! LET'S GET THIS OVER WITH.
THAT'S THE SPIRIT!
NOW THEN, LET'S GO OVER ALL THE STEPS FOR YOUR ORIENTATION!
EEE!
YOUR FIRST DAY ON THE JOB! I BET YOU'D HAVE GOOSEBUMPS IF YOU STILL HAD SKIN!

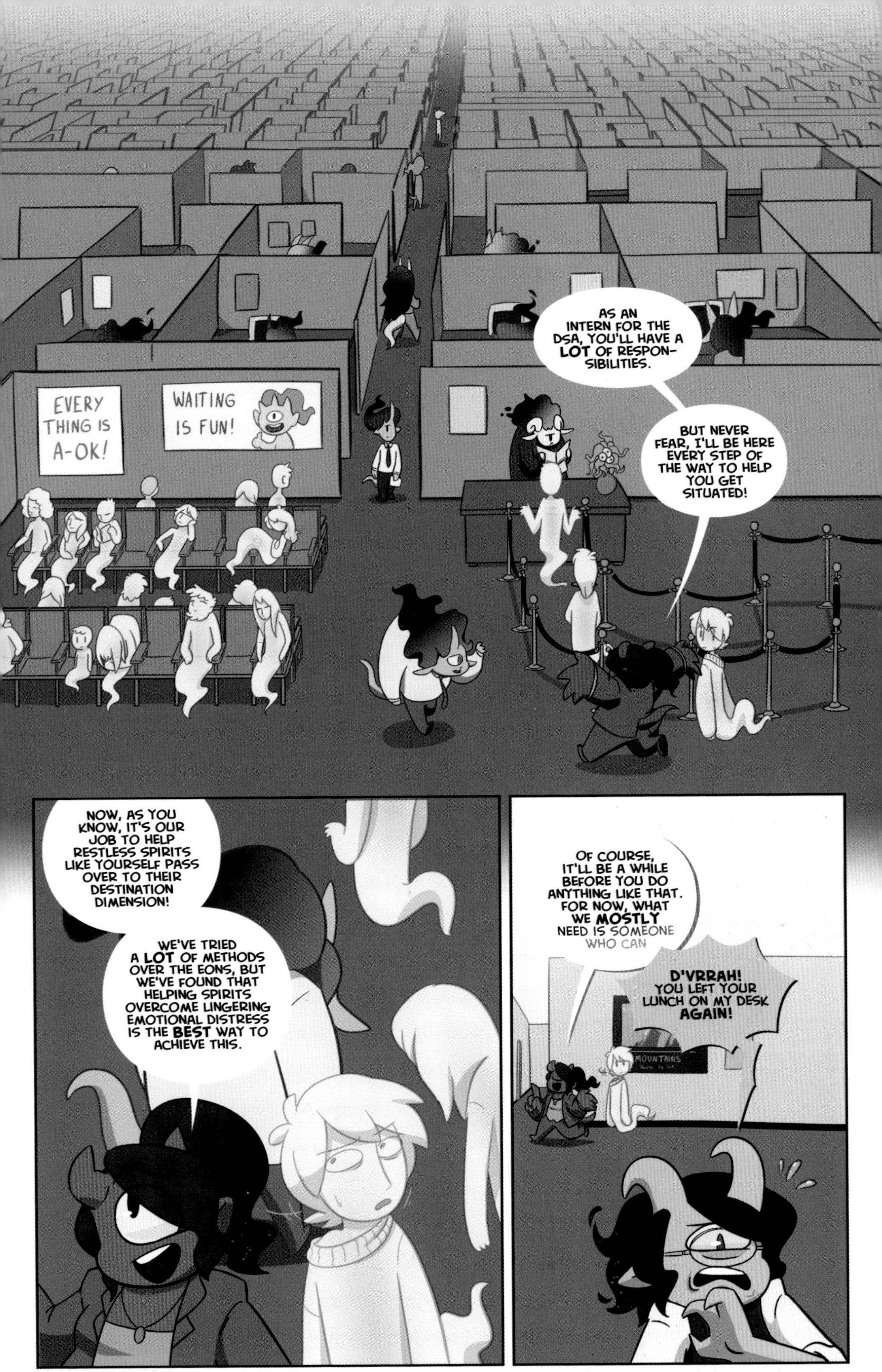
EVERY THING IS A-OK!
WAITING IS FUN!
AS AN INTERN FOR THE DSA, YOU'LL HAVE A **LOT** OF RESPON-SIBILITIES.
BUT NEVER FEAR, I'LL BE HERE EVERY STEP OF THE WAY TO HELP YOU GET SITUATED!
NOW, AS YOU KNOW, IT'S OUR JOB TO HELP RESTLESS SPIRITS LIKE YOURSELF PASS OVER TO THEIR DESTINATION DIMENSION!
WE'VE TRIED A **LOT** OF METHODS OVER THE EONS, BUT WE'VE FOUND THAT HELPING SPIRITS OVERCOME LINGERING EMOTIONAL DISTRESS IS THE **BEST** WAY TO ACHIEVE THIS.
OF COURSE, IT'LL BE A WHILE BEFORE YOU DO ANYTHING LIKE THAT. FOR NOW, WHAT WE **MOSTLY** NEED IS SOMEONE WHO CAN
D'VRRAH! YOU LEFT YOUR LUNCH ON MY DESK **AGAIN!**
MOUNTAINS

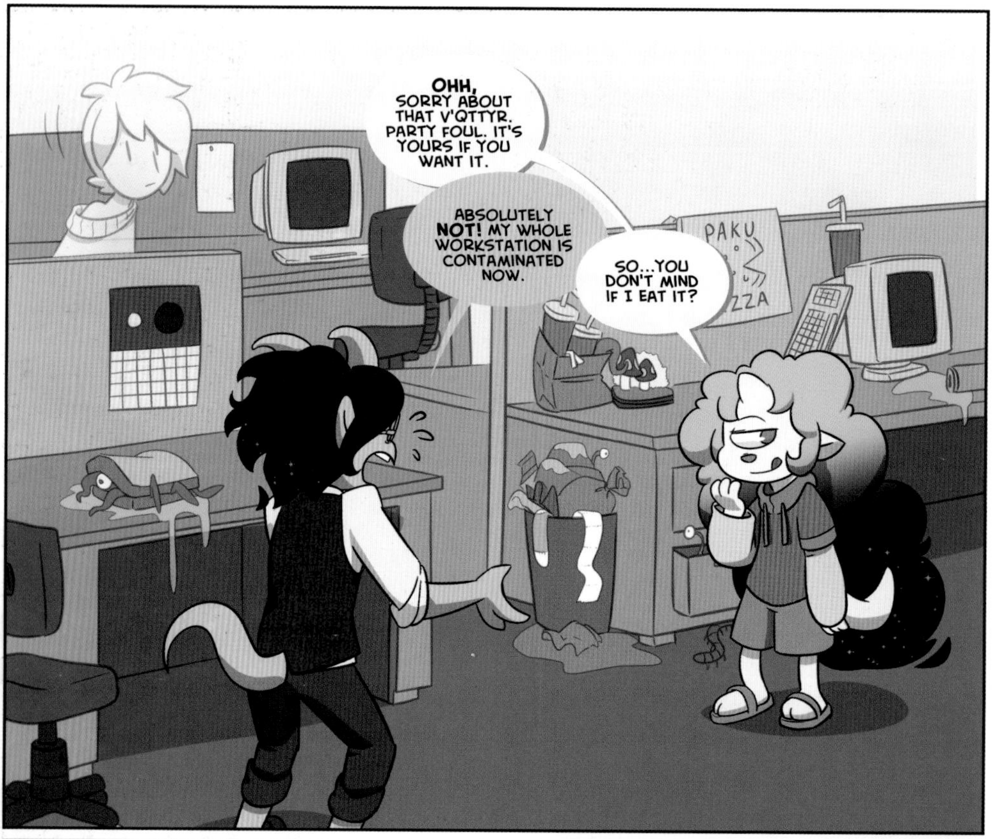
OHH, SORRY ABOUT THAT V'QTTYR. PARTY FOUL. IT'S YOURS IF YOU WANT IT.
ABSOLUTELY NOT! MY WHOLE WORKSTATION IS CONTAMINATED NOW.
SO...YOU DON'T MIND IF I EAT IT?
PAKU
ZZA

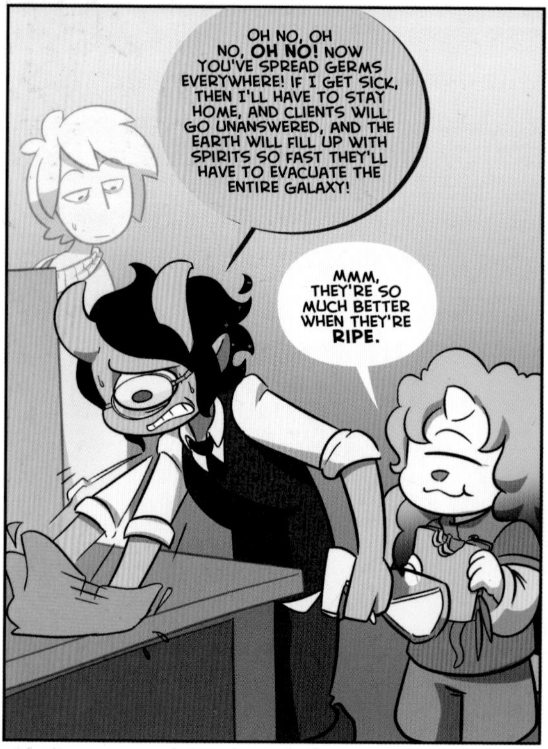
OH NO, OH NO, OH NO! NOW YOU'VE SPREAD GERMS EVERYWHERE! IF I GET SICK, THEN I'LL HAVE TO STAY HOME, AND CLIENTS WILL GO UNANSWERED, AND THE EARTH WILL FILL UP WITH SPIRITS SO FAST THEY'LL HAVE TO EVACUATE THE ENTIRE GALAXY!
MMM, THEY'RE SO MUCH BETTER WHEN THEY'RE RIPE.

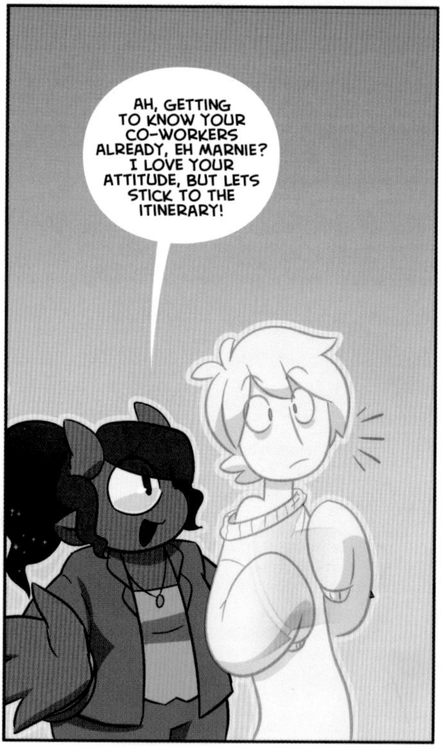
AH, GETTING TO KNOW YOUR CO-WORKERS ALREADY, EH MARNIE? I LOVE YOUR ATTITUDE, BUT LETS STICK TO THE ITINERARY!

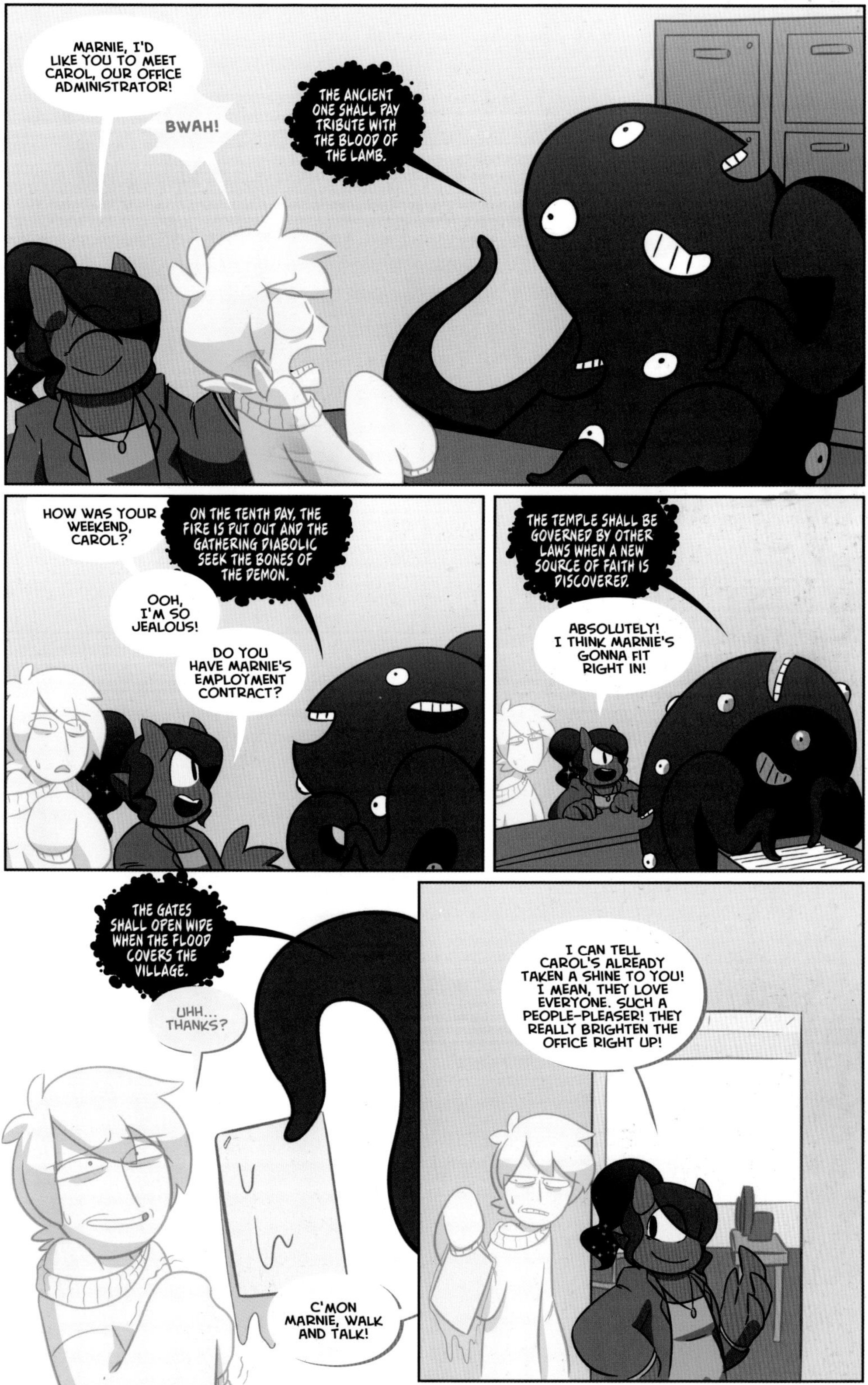
MARNIE, I'D LIKE YOU TO MEET CAROL, OUR OFFICE ADMINISTRATOR!
BWAH!
THE ANCIENT ONE SHALL PAY TRIBUTE WITH THE BLOOD OF THE LAMB.
HOW WAS YOUR WEEKEND, CAROL?
ON THE TENTH DAY, THE FIRE IS PUT OUT AND THE GATHERING DIABOLIC SEEK THE BONES OF THE DEMON.
OOH, I'M SO JEALOUS!
DO YOU HAVE MARNIE'S EMPLOYMENT CONTRACT?
THE TEMPLE SHALL BE GOVERNED BY OTHER LAWS WHEN A NEW SOURCE OF FAITH IS DISCOVERED.
ABSOLUTELY! I THINK MARNIE'S GONNA FIT RIGHT IN!
THE GATES SHALL OPEN WIDE WHEN THE FLOOD COVERS THE VILLAGE.
UHH... THANKS?
C'MON MARNIE, WALK AND TALK!
I CAN TELL CAROL'S ALREADY TAKEN A SHINE TO YOU! I MEAN, THEY LOVE EVERYONE. SUCH A PEOPLE-PLEASER! THEY REALLY BRIGHTEN THE OFFICE RIGHT UP!

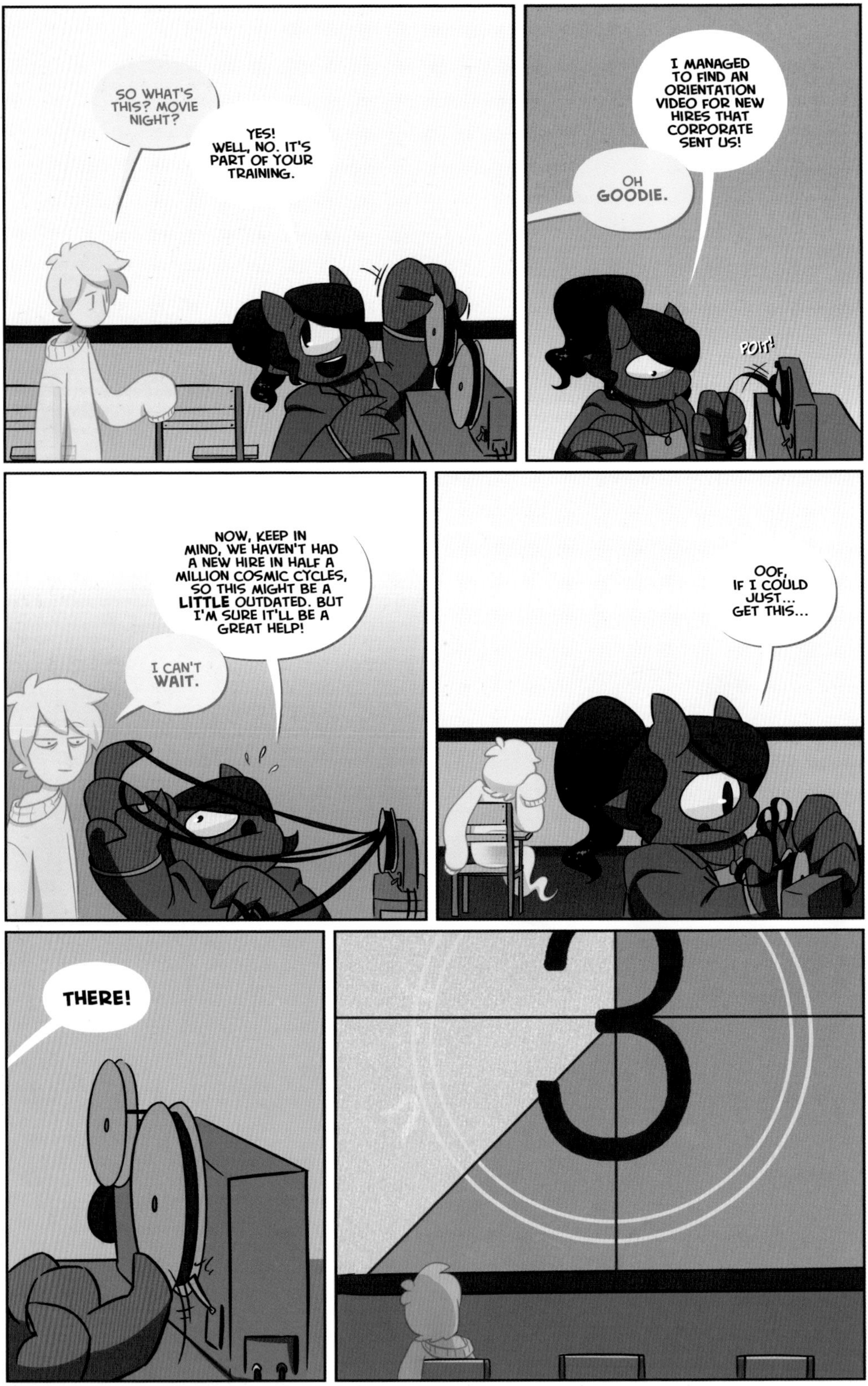
SO WHAT'S THIS? MOVIE NIGHT?
YES! WELL, NO. IT'S PART OF YOUR TRAINING.
I MANAGED TO FIND AN ORIENTATION VIDEO FOR NEW HIRES THAT CORPORATE SENT US!
OH GOODIE.
POIT!
NOW, KEEP IN MIND, WE HAVEN'T HAD A NEW HIRE IN HALF A MILLION COSMIC CYCLES, SO THIS MIGHT BE A LITTLE OUTDATED. BUT I'M SURE IT'LL BE A GREAT HELP!
I CAN'T WAIT.
OOF, IF I COULD JUST... GET THIS...
THERE!
3

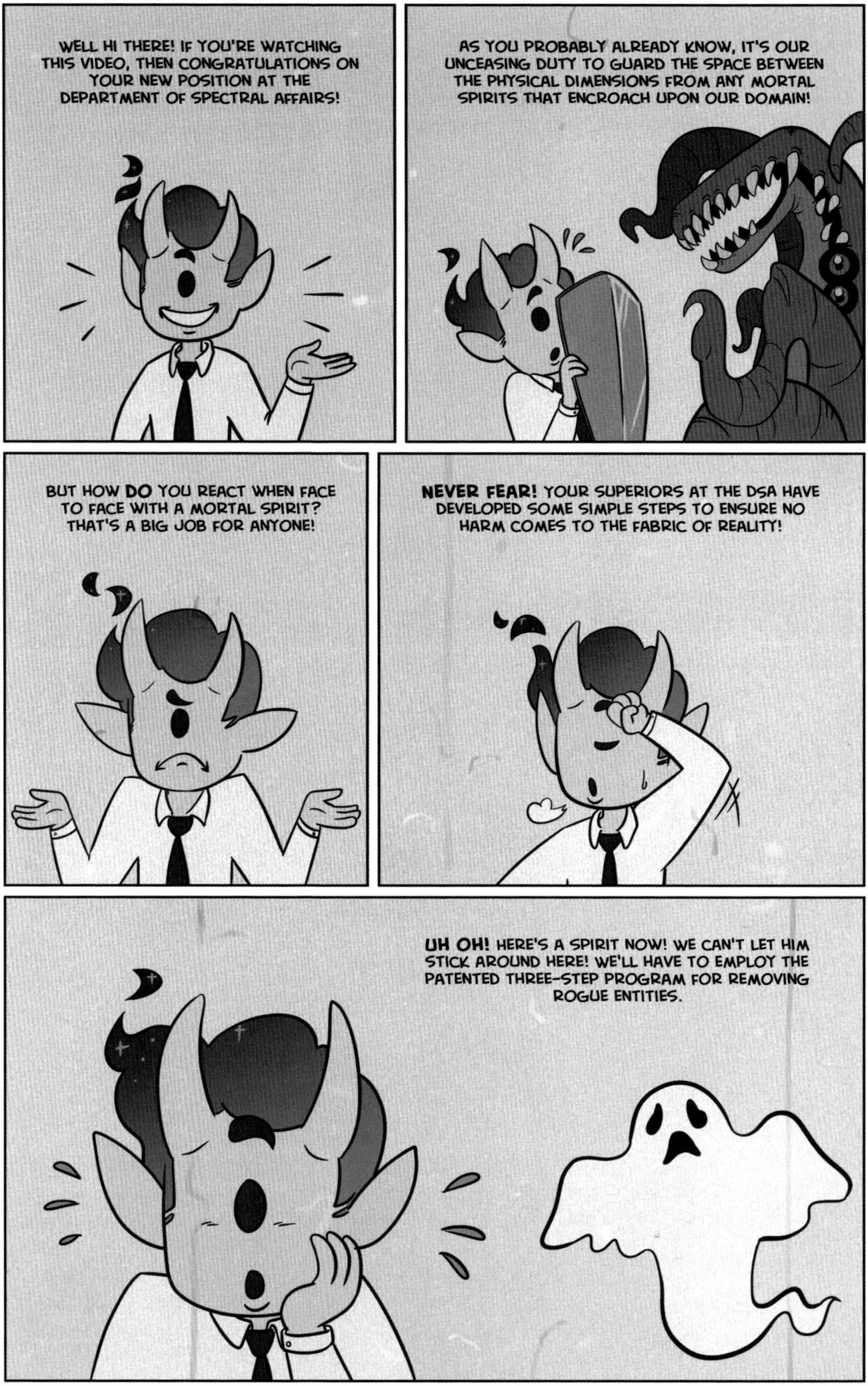
WELL HI THERE! IF YOU'RE WATCHING THIS VIDEO, THEN CONGRATULATIONS ON YOUR NEW POSITION AT THE DEPARTMENT OF SPECTRAL AFFAIRS!
AS YOU PROBABLY ALREADY KNOW, IT'S OUR UNCEASING DUTY TO GUARD THE SPACE BETWEEN THE PHYSICAL DIMENSIONS FROM ANY MORTAL SPIRITS THAT ENCROACH UPON OUR DOMAIN!
BUT HOW **DO** YOU REACT WHEN FACE TO FACE WITH A MORTAL SPIRIT? THAT'S A BIG JOB FOR ANYONE!
NEVER FEAR! YOUR SUPERIORS AT THE DSA HAVE DEVELOPED SOME SIMPLE STEPS TO ENSURE NO HARM COMES TO THE FABRIC OF REALITY!
UH OH! HERE'S A SPIRIT NOW! WE CAN'T LET HIM STICK AROUND HERE! WE'LL HAVE TO EMPLOY THE PATENTED THREE-STEP PROGRAM FOR REMOVING ROGUE ENTITIES.

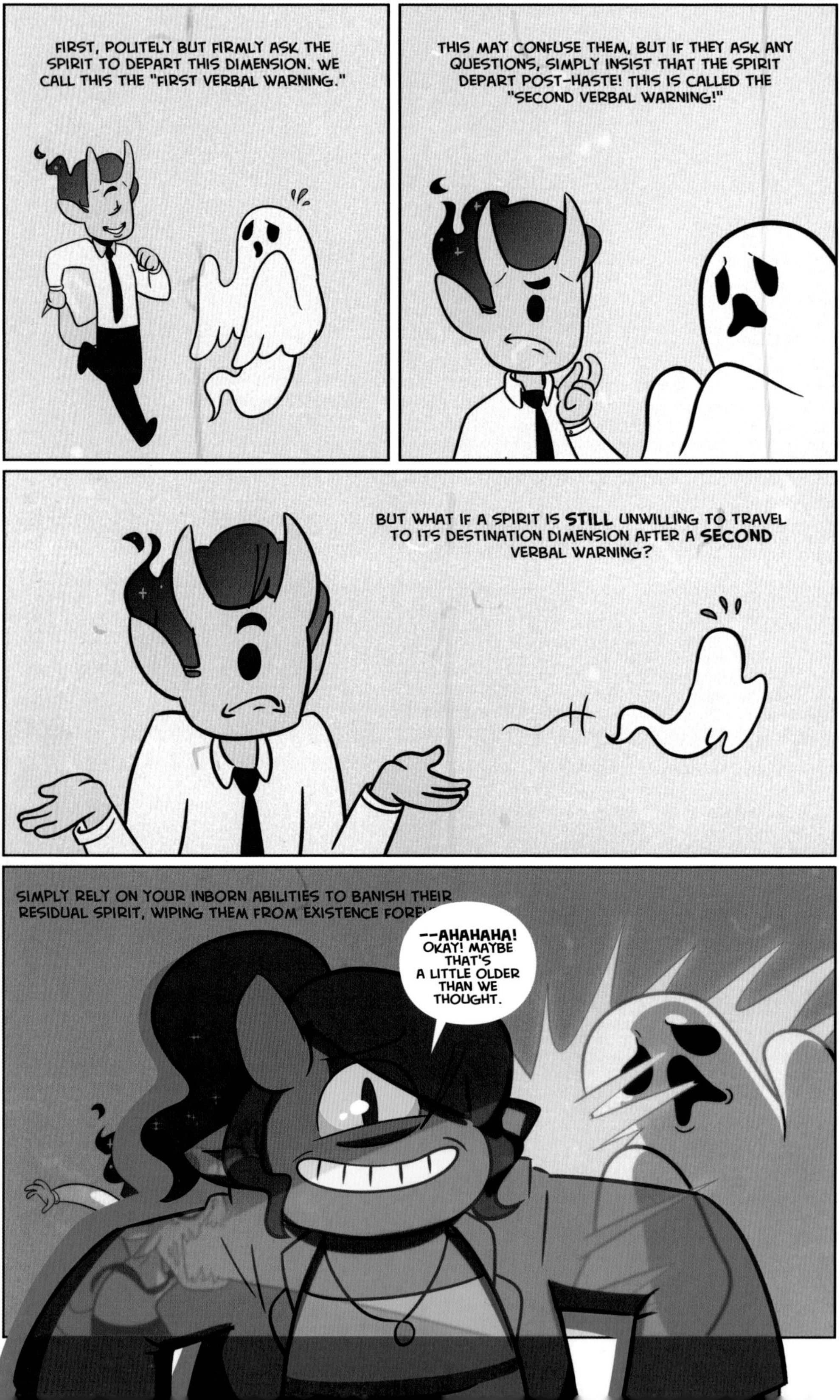
FIRST, POLITELY BUT FIRMLY ASK THE SPIRIT TO DEPART THIS DIMENSION. WE CALL THIS THE "FIRST VERBAL WARNING."
THIS MAY CONFUSE THEM, BUT IF THEY ASK ANY QUESTIONS, SIMPLY INSIST THAT THE SPIRIT DEPART POST-HASTE! THIS IS CALLED THE "SECOND VERBAL WARNING!"
BUT WHAT IF A SPIRIT IS **STILL** UNWILLING TO TRAVEL TO ITS DESTINATION DIMENSION AFTER A **SECOND** VERBAL WARNING?
SIMPLY RELY ON YOUR INBORN ABILITIES TO BANISH THEIR RESIDUAL SPIRIT, WIPING THEM FROM EXISTENCE FORE
--AHAHAHA! OKAY! MAYBE THAT'S A LITTLE OLDER THAN WE THOUGHT.

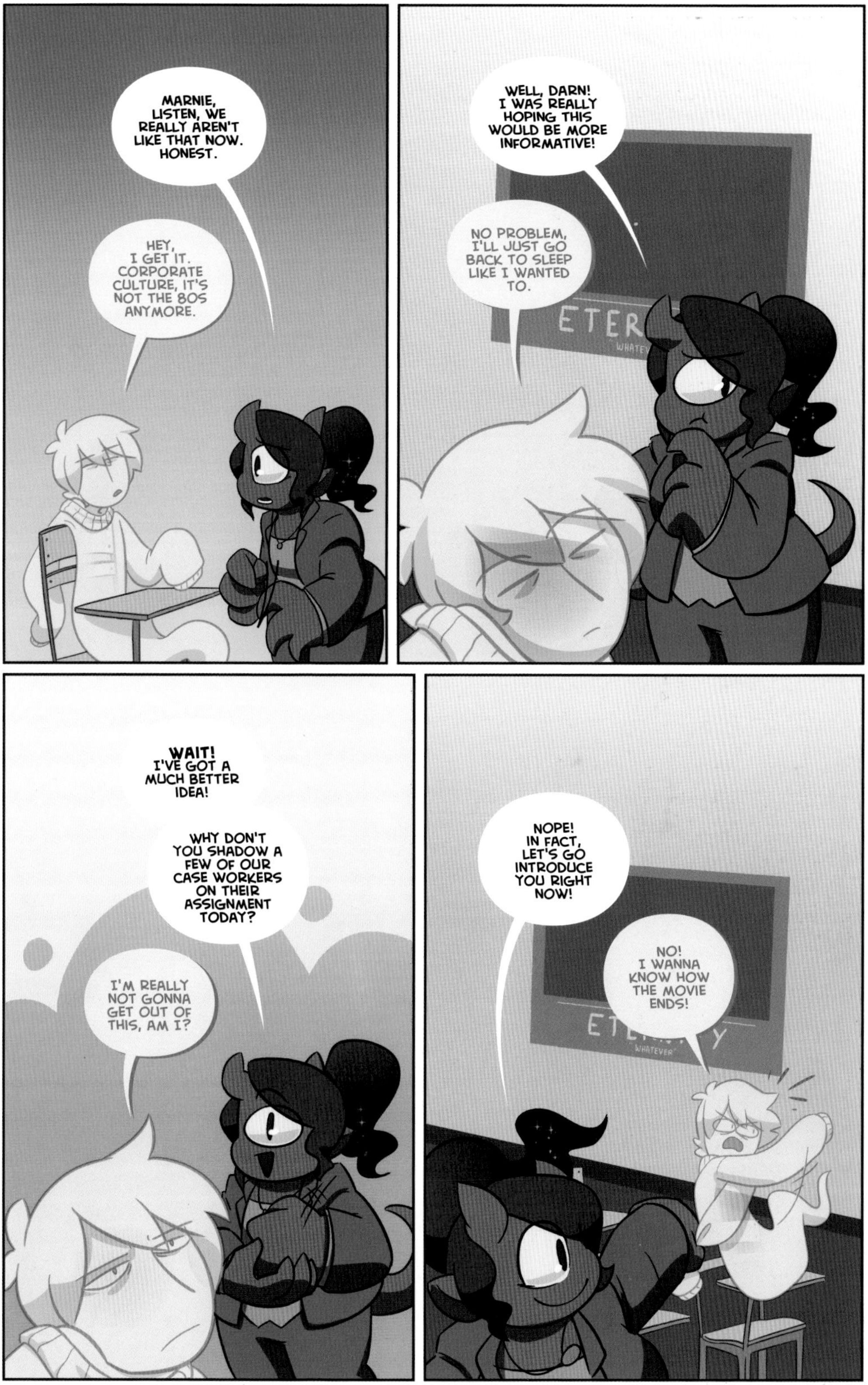
MARNIE, LISTEN, WE REALLY AREN'T LIKE THAT NOW. HONEST.
HEY, I GET IT. CORPORATE CULTURE, IT'S NOT THE 80S ANYMORE.
WELL, DARN! I WAS REALLY HOPING THIS WOULD BE MORE INFORMATIVE!
NO PROBLEM, I'LL JUST GO BACK TO SLEEP LIKE I WANTED TO.
WAIT! I'VE GOT A MUCH BETTER IDEA!
WHY DON'T YOU SHADOW A FEW OF OUR CASE WORKERS ON THEIR ASSIGNMENT TODAY?
I'M REALLY NOT GONNA GET OUT OF THIS, AM I?
NOPE! IN FACT, LET'S GO INTRODUCE YOU RIGHT NOW!
NO! I WANNA KNOW HOW THE MOVIE ENDS!

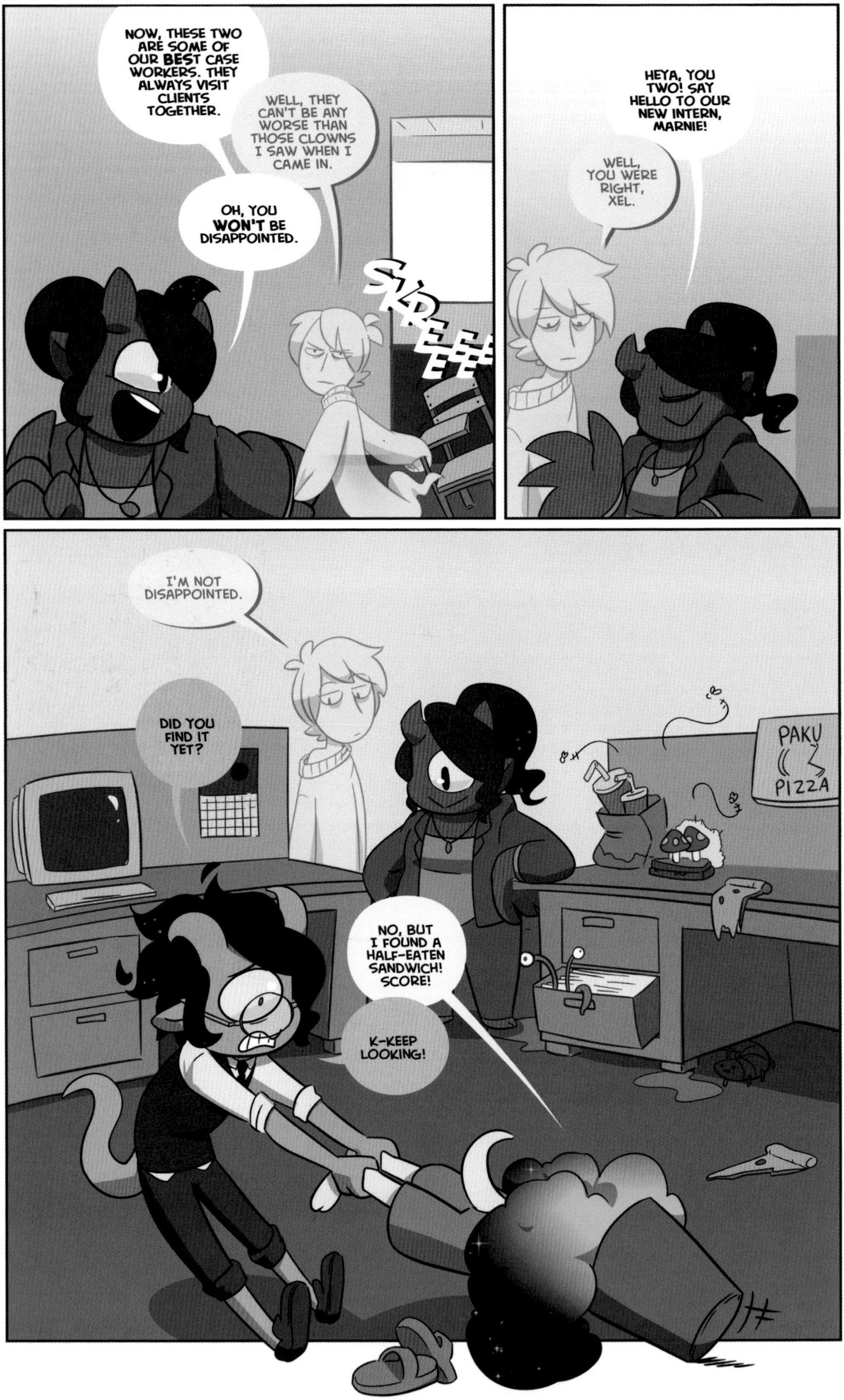
NOW, THESE TWO ARE SOME OF OUR BEST CASE WORKERS. THEY ALWAYS VISIT CLIENTS TOGETHER.
WELL, THEY CAN'T BE ANY WORSE THAN THOSE CLOWNS I SAW WHEN I CAME IN.
OH, YOU WON'T BE DISAPPOINTED.
SKREEEEE
HEYA, YOU TWO! SAY HELLO TO OUR NEW INTERN, MARNIE!
WELL, YOU WERE RIGHT, XEL.
I'M NOT DISAPPOINTED.
DID YOU FIND IT YET?
PAKU PIZZA
NO, BUT I FOUND A HALF-EATEN SANDWICH! SCORE!
K-KEEP LOOKING!

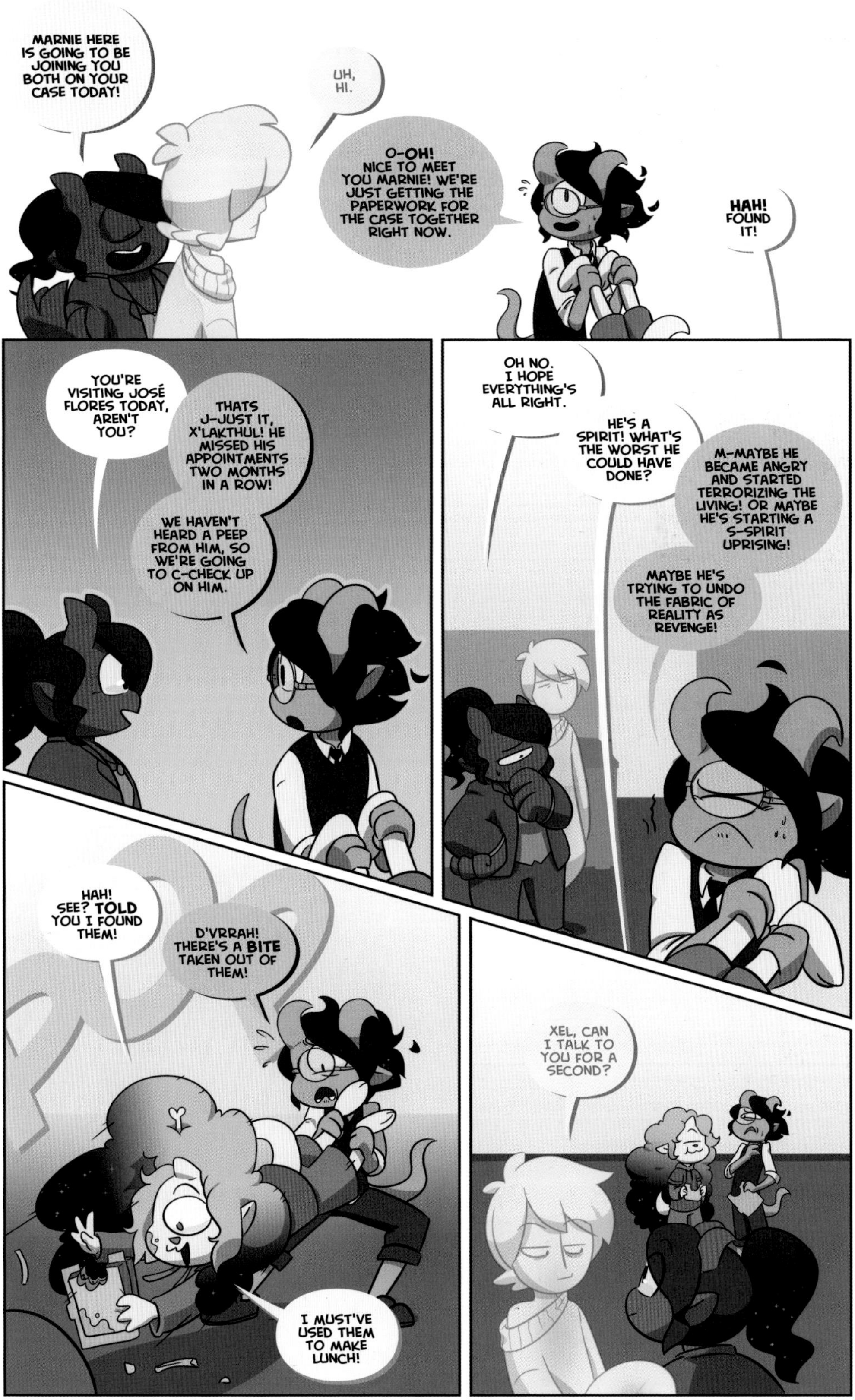
MARNIE HERE IS GOING TO BE JOINING YOU BOTH ON YOUR CASE TODAY!
UH, HI.
O-OH! NICE TO MEET YOU MARNIE! WE'RE JUST GETTING THE PAPERWORK FOR THE CASE TOGETHER RIGHT NOW.
HAH! FOUND IT!
YOU'RE VISITING JOSÉ FLORES TODAY, AREN'T YOU?
THATS J-JUST IT, X'LAKTHUL! HE MISSED HIS APPOINTMENTS TWO MONTHS IN A ROW!
WE HAVEN'T HEARD A PEEP FROM HIM, SO WE'RE GOING TO C-CHECK UP ON HIM.
OH NO. I HOPE EVERYTHING'S ALL RIGHT.
HE'S A SPIRIT! WHAT'S THE WORST HE COULD HAVE DONE?
M-MAYBE HE BECAME ANGRY AND STARTED TERRORIZING THE LIVING! OR MAYBE HE'S STARTING A S-SPIRIT UPRISING!
MAYBE HE'S TRYING TO UNDO THE FABRIC OF REALITY AS REVENGE!
HAH! SEE? TOLD YOU I FOUND THEM!
D'VRRAH! THERE'S A BITE TAKEN OUT OF THEM!
I MUST'VE USED THEM TO MAKE LUNCH!
XEL, CAN I TALK TO YOU FOR A SECOND?

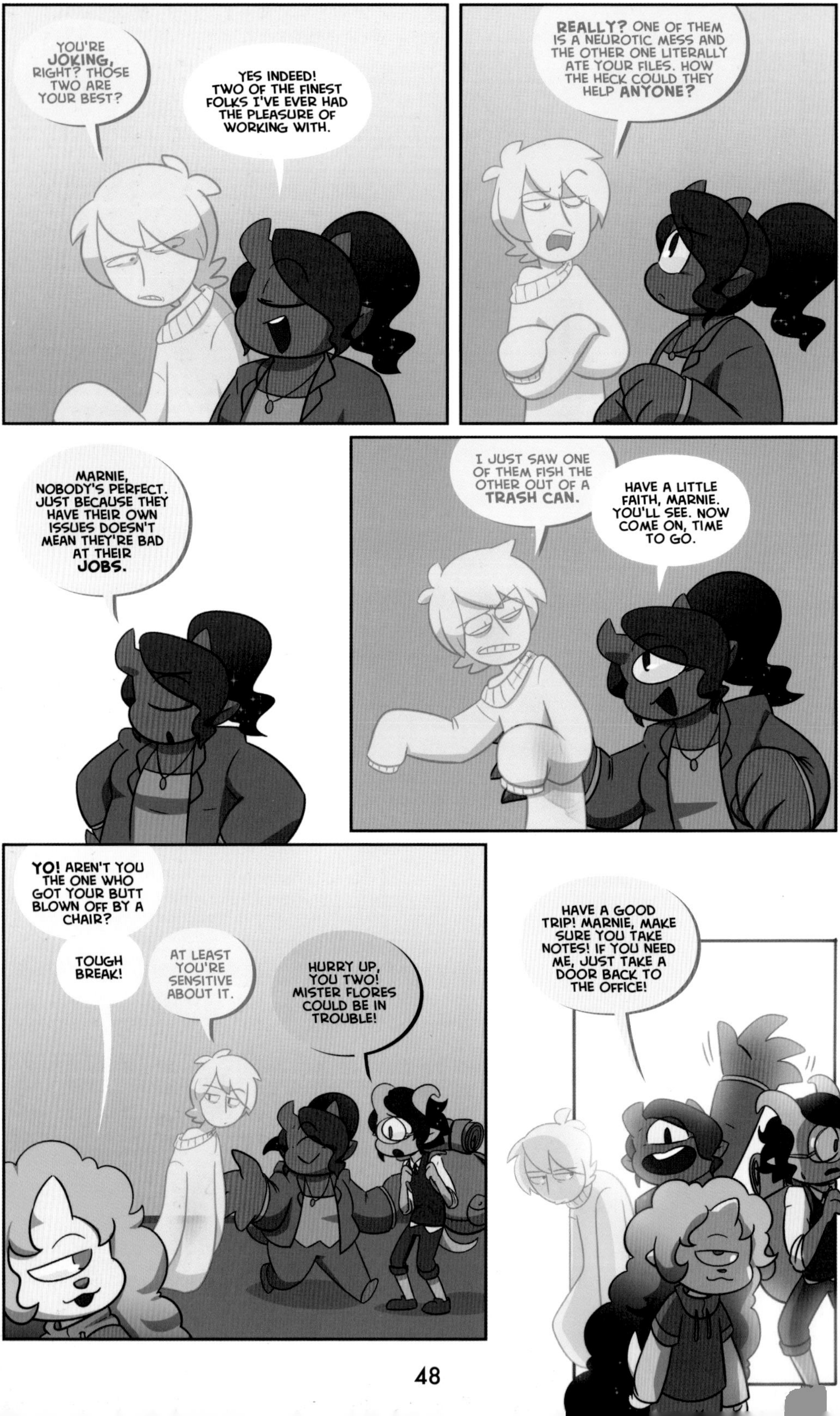
YOU'RE JOKING, RIGHT? THOSE TWO ARE YOUR BEST?
YES INDEED! TWO OF THE FINEST FOLKS I'VE EVER HAD THE PLEASURE OF WORKING WITH.
REALLY? ONE OF THEM IS A NEUROTIC MESS AND THE OTHER ONE LITERALLY ATE YOUR FILES. HOW THE HECK COULD THEY HELP ANYONE?
MARNIE, NOBODY'S PERFECT. JUST BECAUSE THEY HAVE THEIR OWN ISSUES DOESN'T MEAN THEY'RE BAD AT THEIR JOBS.
I JUST SAW ONE OF THEM FISH THE OTHER OUT OF A TRASH CAN.
HAVE A LITTLE FAITH, MARNIE. YOU'LL SEE. NOW COME ON, TIME TO GO.
YO! AREN'T YOU THE ONE WHO GOT YOUR BUTT BLOWN OFF BY A CHAIR?
TOUGH BREAK!
AT LEAST YOU'RE SENSITIVE ABOUT IT.
HURRY UP, YOU TWO! MISTER FLORES COULD BE IN TROUBLE!
HAVE A GOOD TRIP! MARNIE, MAKE SURE YOU TAKE NOTES! IF YOU NEED ME, JUST TAKE A DOOR BACK TO THE OFFICE!

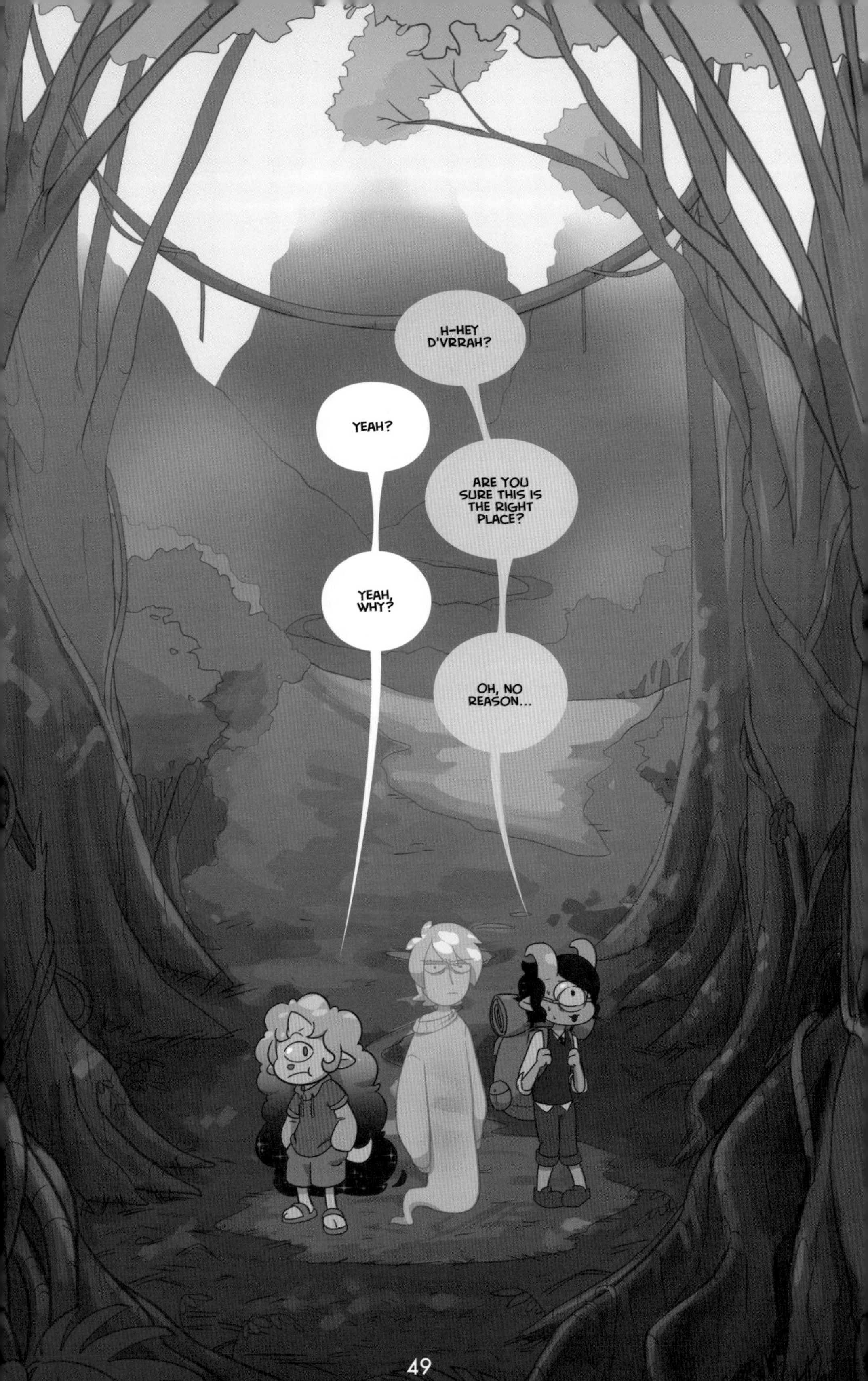
H-HEY D'VRRAH?
YEAH?
ARE YOU SURE THIS IS THE RIGHT PLACE?
YEAH, WHY?
OH, NO REASON...

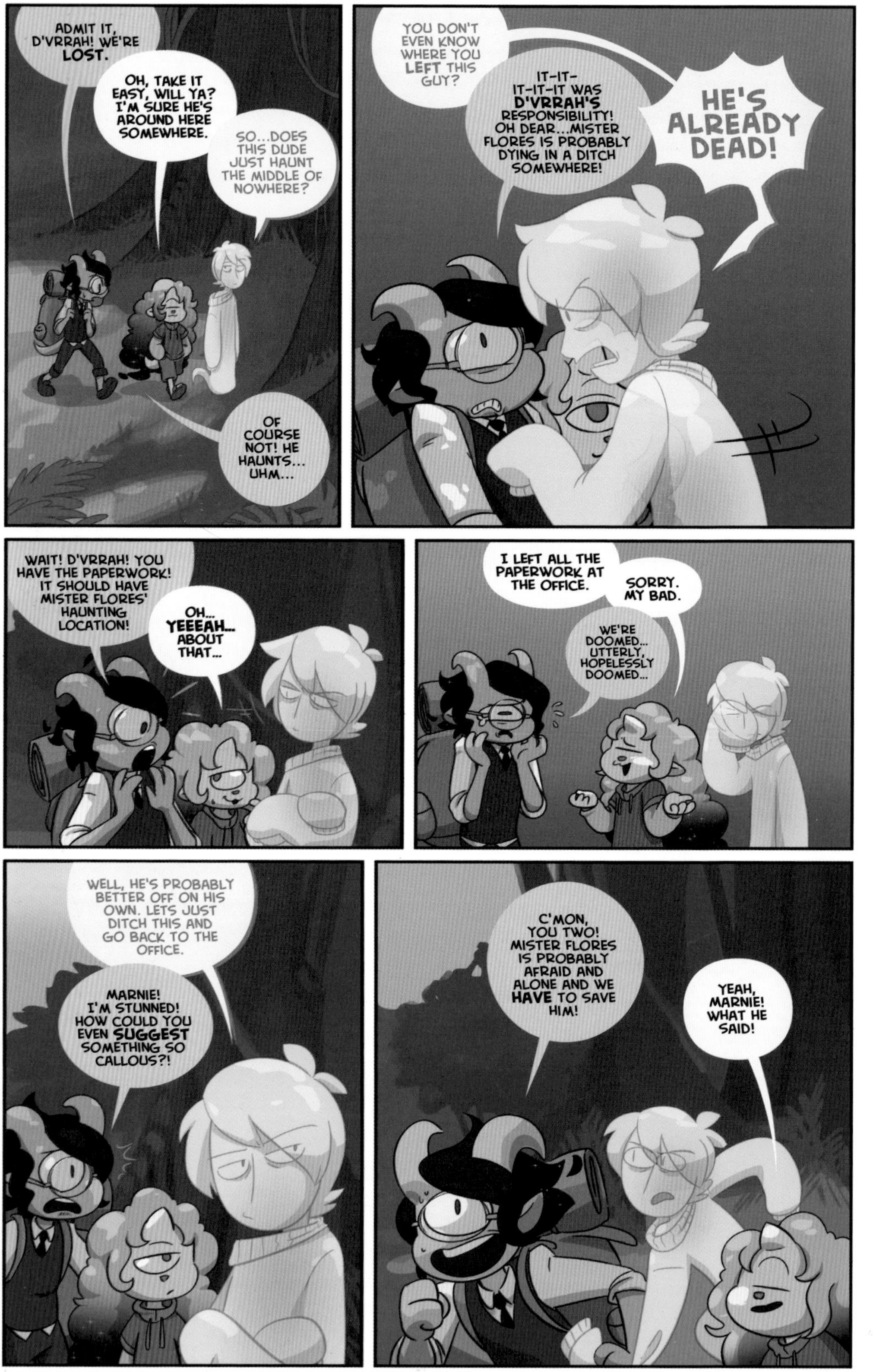
ADMIT IT, D'VRRAH! WE'RE LOST.
OH, TAKE IT EASY, WILL YA? I'M SURE HE'S AROUND HERE SOMEWHERE.
SO...DOES THIS DUDE JUST HAUNT THE MIDDLE OF NOWHERE?
OF COURSE NOT! HE HAUNTS... UHM...
YOU DON'T EVEN KNOW WHERE YOU LEFT THIS GUY?
IT-IT-IT-IT-IT WAS D'VRRAH'S RESPONSIBILITY! OH DEAR...MISTER FLORES IS PROBABLY DYING IN A DITCH SOMEWHERE!
HE'S ALREADY DEAD!
WAIT! D'VRRAH! YOU HAVE THE PAPERWORK! IT SHOULD HAVE MISTER FLORES' HAUNTING LOCATION!
OH... YEEEAH... ABOUT THAT...
I LEFT ALL THE PAPERWORK AT THE OFFICE.
SORRY. MY BAD.
WE'RE DOOMED... UTTERLY, HOPELESSLY DOOMED...
WELL, HE'S PROBABLY BETTER OFF ON HIS OWN. LETS JUST DITCH THIS AND GO BACK TO THE OFFICE.
MARNIE! I'M STUNNED! HOW COULD YOU EVEN SUGGEST SOMETHING SO CALLOUS?!
C'MON, YOU TWO! MISTER FLORES IS PROBABLY AFRAID AND ALONE AND WE HAVE TO SAVE HIM!
YEAH, MARNIE! WHAT HE SAID!

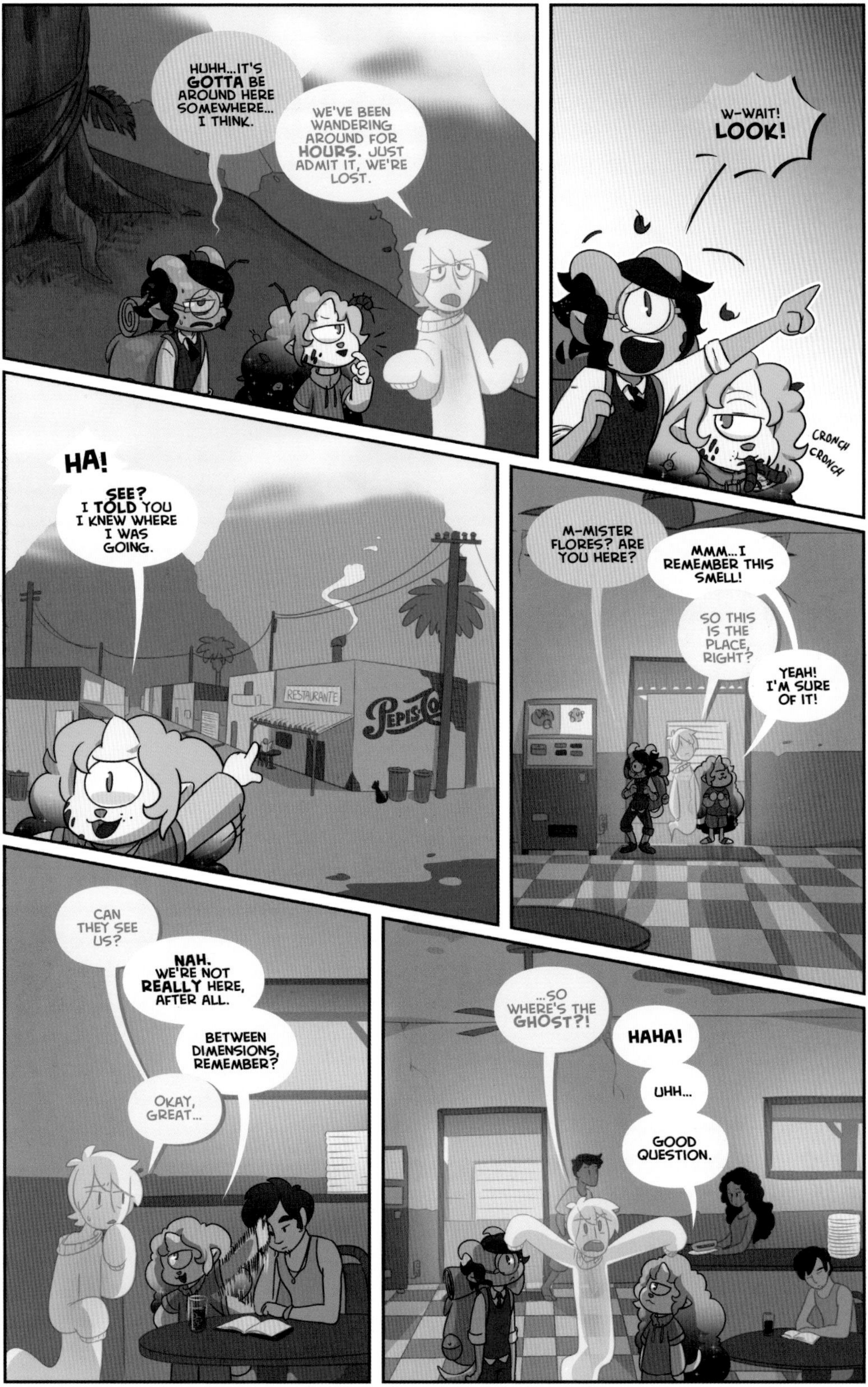
HUHH...IT'S GOTTA BE AROUND HERE SOMEWHERE... I THINK.
WE'VE BEEN WANDERING AROUND FOR HOURS. JUST ADMIT IT, WE'RE LOST.
W-WAIT! LOOK!
CRONCH
CRONCH
HA!
SEE? I TOLD YOU I KNEW WHERE I WAS GOING.
RESTAURANTE
PEPSI-COLA
M-MISTER FLORES? ARE YOU HERE?
MMM...I REMEMBER THIS SMELL!
SO THIS IS THE PLACE, RIGHT?
YEAH! I'M SURE OF IT!
CAN THEY SEE US?
NAH. WE'RE NOT REALLY HERE, AFTER ALL.
BETWEEN DIMENSIONS, REMEMBER?
OKAY, GREAT...
...SO WHERE'S THE GHOST?!
HAHA!
UHH...
GOOD QUESTION.

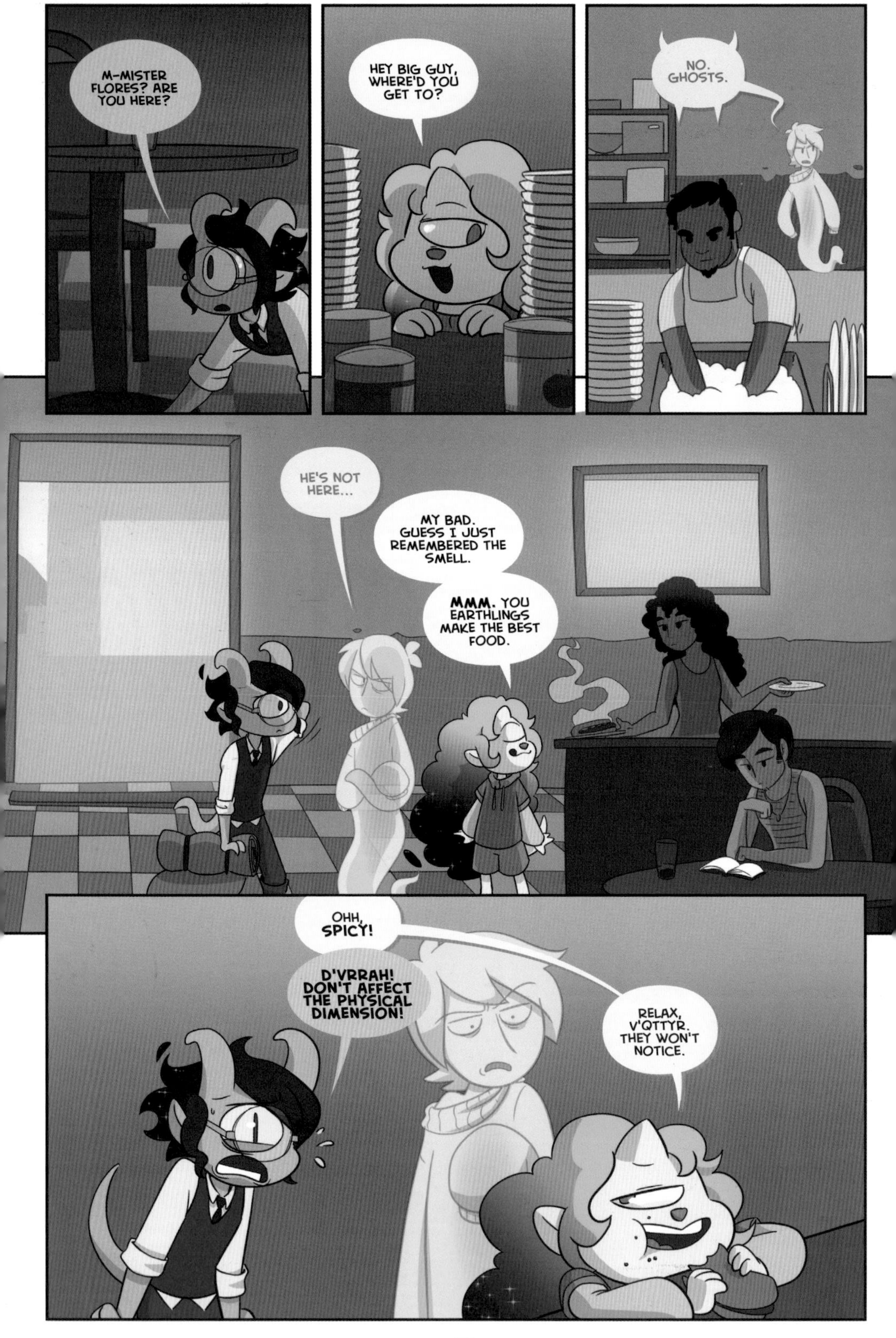
M-MISTER FLORES? ARE YOU HERE?
HEY BIG GUY, WHERE'D YOU GET TO?
NO. GHOSTS.
HE'S NOT HERE...
MY BAD. GUESS I JUST REMEMBERED THE SMELL.
MMM. YOU EARTHLINGS MAKE THE BEST FOOD.
OHH, SPICY!
D'VRRAH! DON'T AFFECT THE PHYSICAL DIMENSION!
RELAX, V'QTTYR. THEY WON'T NOTICE.

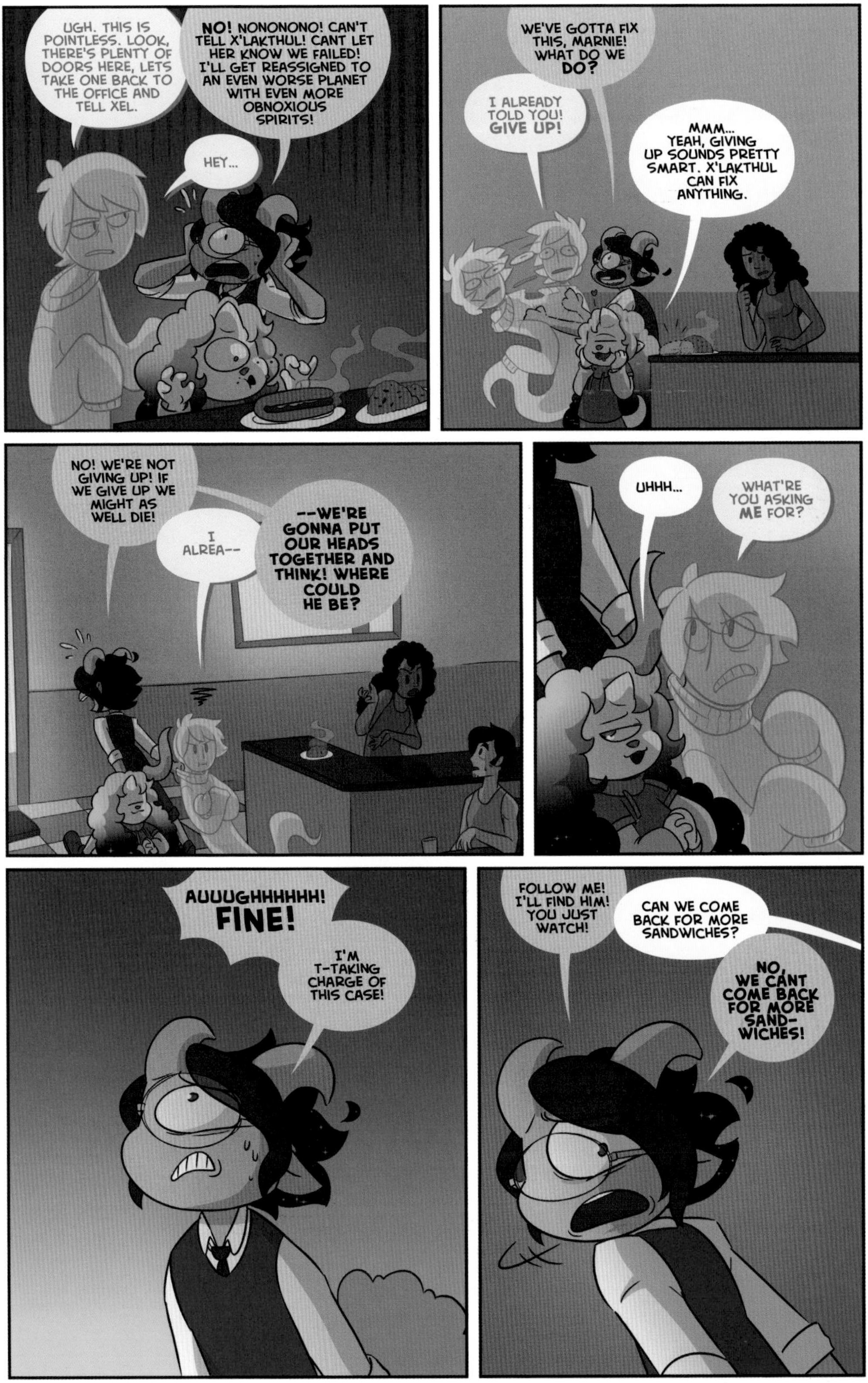
UGH. THIS IS POINTLESS. LOOK, THERE'S PLENTY OF DOORS HERE, LETS TAKE ONE BACK TO THE OFFICE AND TELL XEL.
NO! NONONONO! CAN'T TELL X'LAKTHUL! CANT LET HER KNOW WE FAILED! I'LL GET REASSIGNED TO AN EVEN WORSE PLANET WITH EVEN MORE OBNOXIOUS SPIRITS!
HEY...
WE'VE GOTTA FIX THIS, MARNIE! WHAT DO WE DO?
I ALREADY TOLD YOU! GIVE UP!
MMM... YEAH, GIVING UP SOUNDS PRETTY SMART. X'LAKTHUL CAN FIX ANYTHING.
NO! WE'RE NOT GIVING UP! IF WE GIVE UP WE MIGHT AS WELL DIE!
I ALREA--
--WE'RE GONNA PUT OUR HEADS TOGETHER AND THINK! WHERE COULD HE BE?
UHHH...
WHAT'RE YOU ASKING ME FOR?
AUUUGHHHHHH! FINE!
I'M T-TAKING CHARGE OF THIS CASE!
FOLLOW ME! I'LL FIND HIM! YOU JUST WATCH!
CAN WE COME BACK FOR MORE SANDWICHES?
NO, WE CANT COME BACK FOR MORE SAND-WICHES!

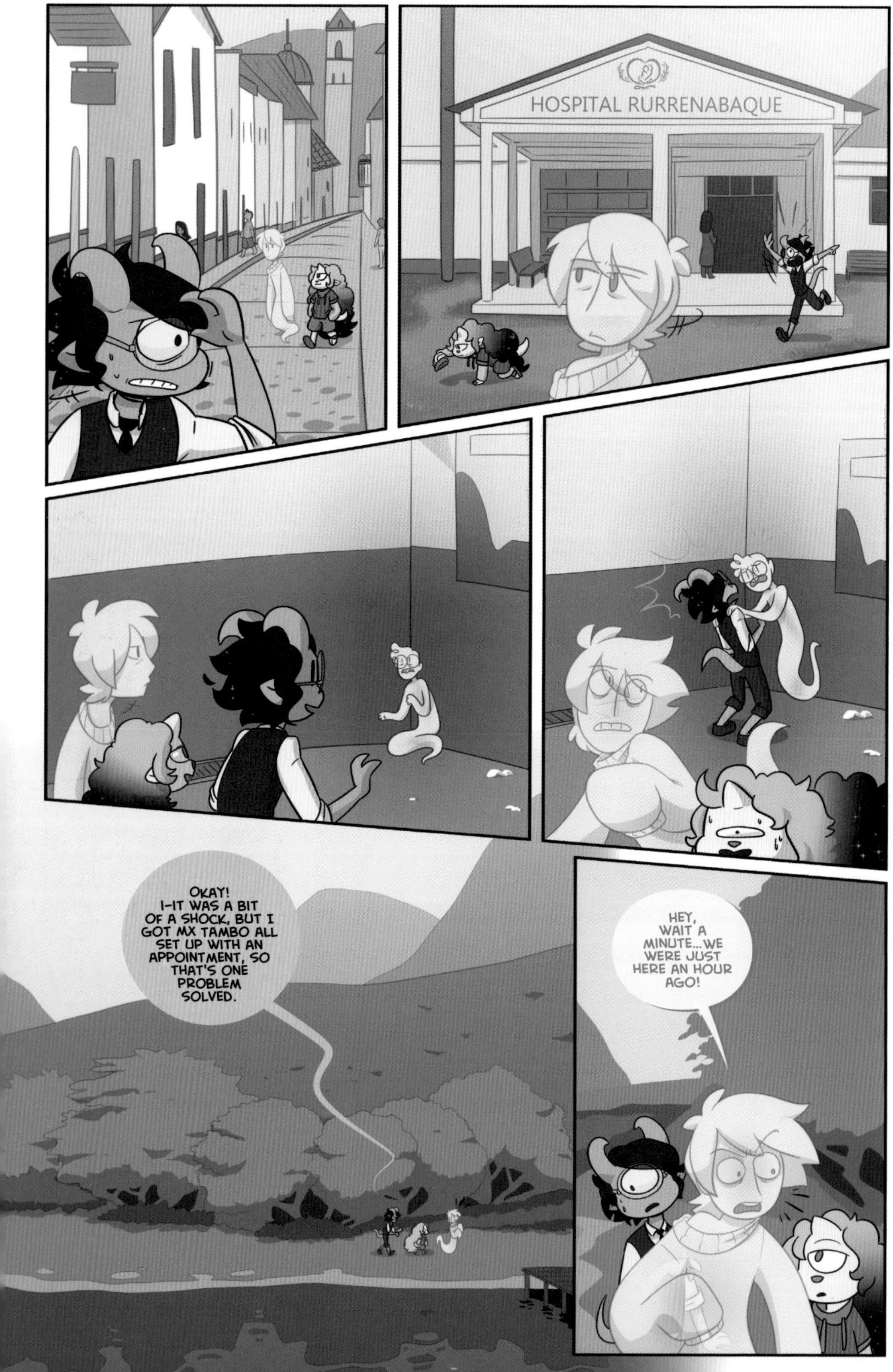
HOSPITAL RURRENABAQUE
OKAY! I-IT WAS A BIT OF A SHOCK, BUT I GOT MX TAMBO ALL SET UP WITH AN APPOINTMENT, SO THAT'S ONE PROBLEM SOLVED.
HEY, WAIT A MINUTE... WE WERE JUST HERE AN HOUR AGO!

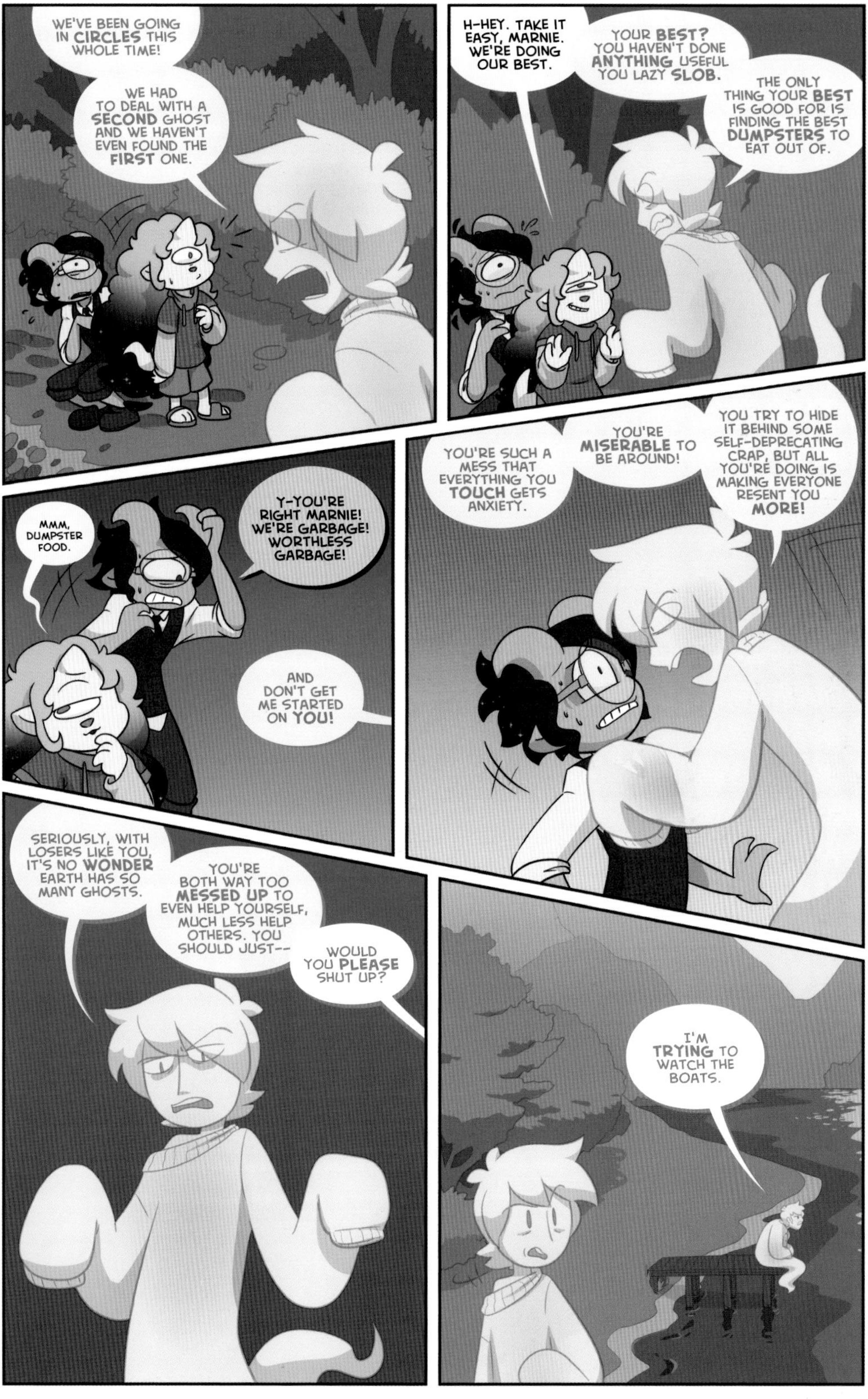
WE'VE BEEN GOING IN CIRCLES THIS WHOLE TIME!
WE HAD TO DEAL WITH A SECOND GHOST AND WE HAVEN'T EVEN FOUND THE FIRST ONE.
H-HEY. TAKE IT EASY, MARNIE. WE'RE DOING OUR BEST.
YOUR BEST? YOU HAVEN'T DONE ANYTHING USEFUL YOU LAZY SLOB.
THE ONLY THING YOUR BEST IS GOOD FOR IS FINDING THE BEST DUMPSTERS TO EAT OUT OF.
MMM, DUMPSTER FOOD.
Y-YOU'RE RIGHT MARNIE! WE'RE GARBAGE! WORTHLESS GARBAGE!
AND DON'T GET ME STARTED ON YOU!
YOU'RE SUCH A MESS THAT EVERYTHING YOU TOUCH GETS ANXIETY.
YOU'RE MISERABLE TO BE AROUND!
YOU TRY TO HIDE IT BEHIND SOME SELF-DEPRECATING CRAP, BUT ALL YOU'RE DOING IS MAKING EVERYONE RESENT YOU MORE!
SERIOUSLY, WITH LOSERS LIKE YOU, IT'S NO WONDER EARTH HAS SO MANY GHOSTS.
YOU'RE BOTH WAY TOO MESSED UP TO EVEN HELP YOURSELF, MUCH LESS HELP OTHERS. YOU SHOULD JUST--
WOULD YOU PLEASE SHUT UP?
I'M TRYING TO WATCH THE BOATS.

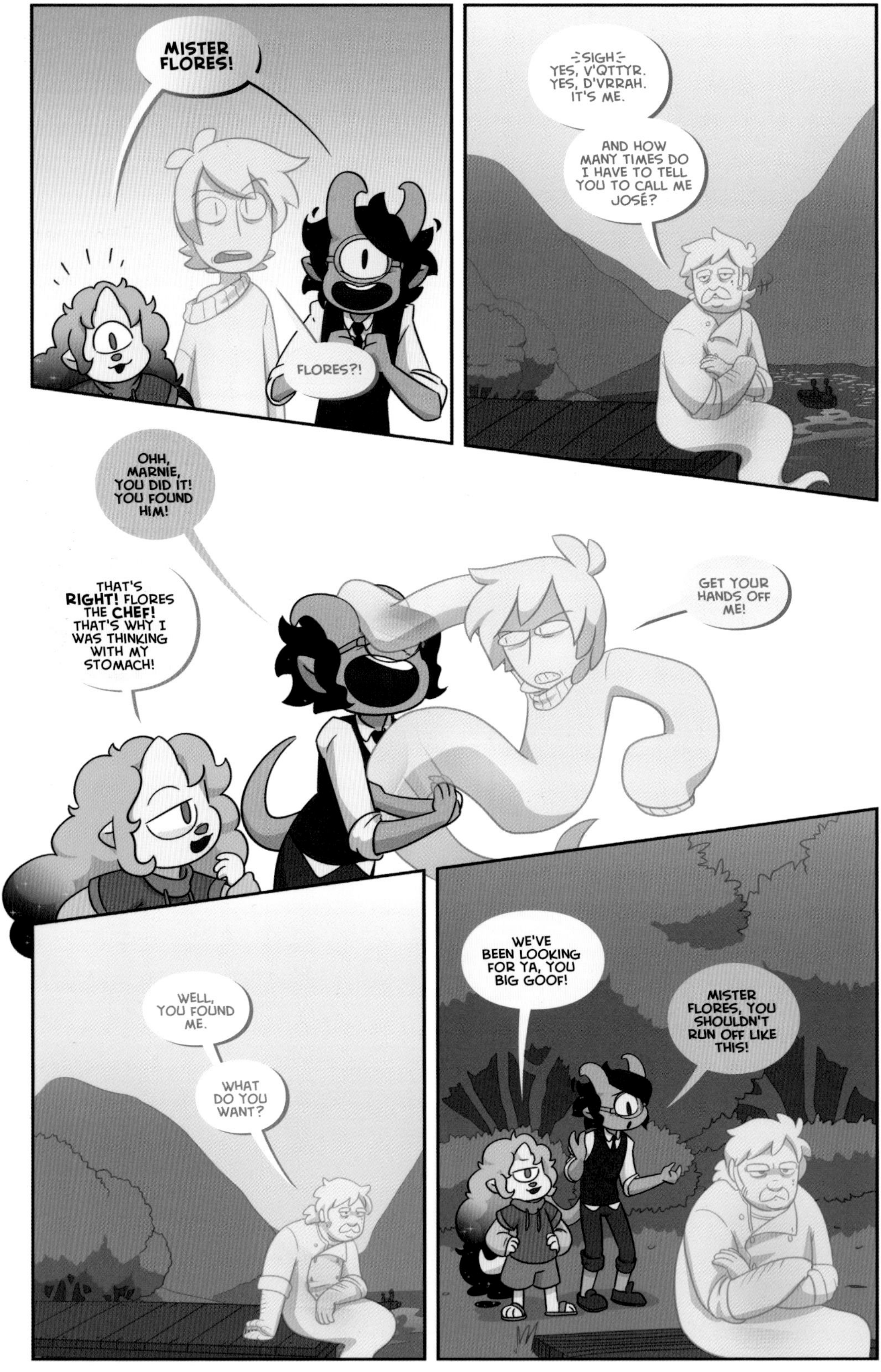
MISTER FLORES!
FLORES?!
=SIGH= YES, V'QTTYR. YES, D'VRRAH. IT'S ME.
AND HOW MANY TIMES DO I HAVE TO TELL YOU TO CALL ME JOSÉ?
OHH, MARNIE, YOU DID IT! YOU FOUND HIM!
THAT'S RIGHT! FLORES THE CHEF! THAT'S WHY I WAS THINKING WITH MY STOMACH!
GET YOUR HANDS OFF ME!
WELL, YOU FOUND ME.
WHAT DO YOU WANT?
WE'VE BEEN LOOKING FOR YA, YOU BIG GOOF!
MISTER FLORES, YOU SHOULDN'T RUN OFF LIKE THIS!

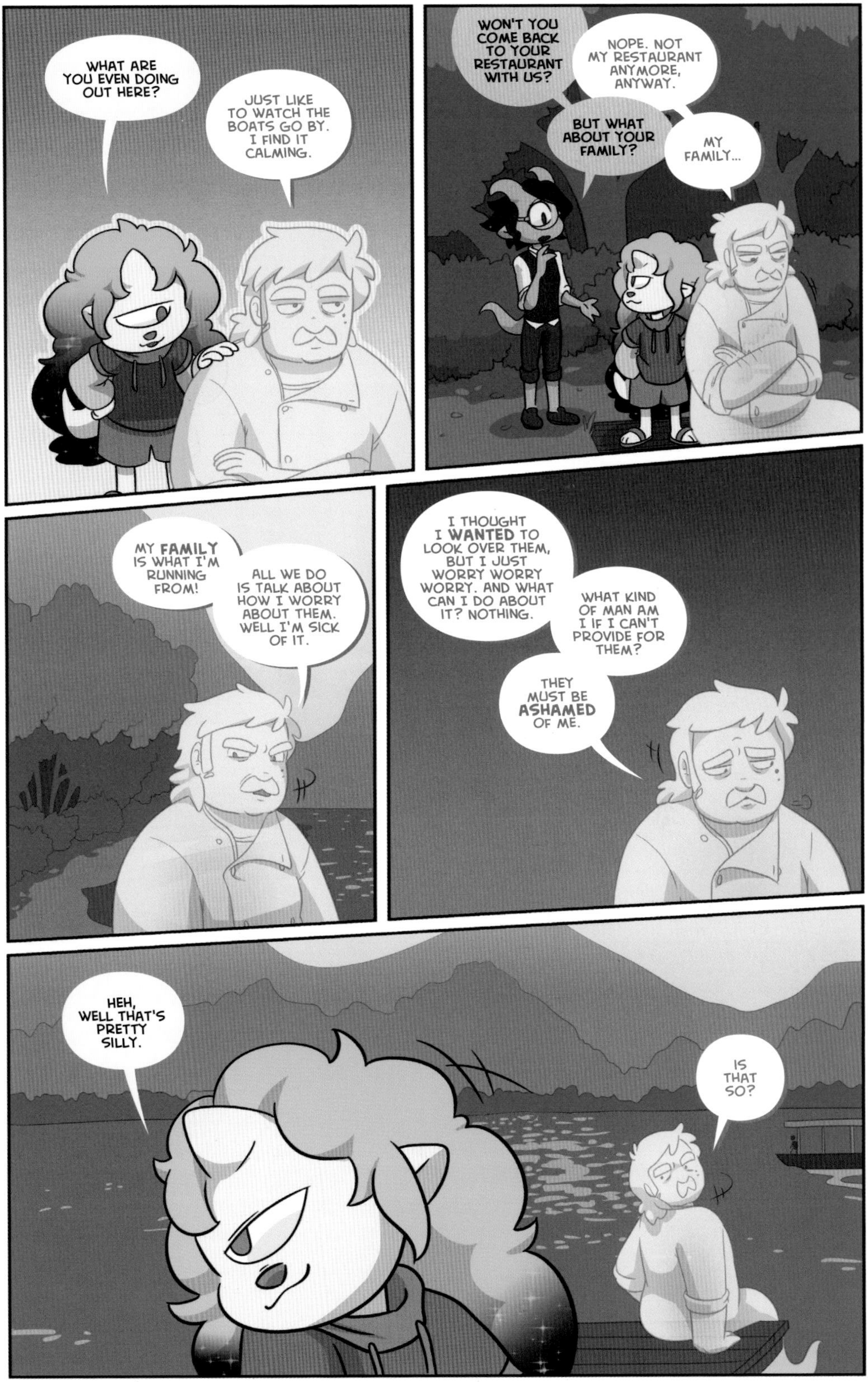
WHAT ARE YOU EVEN DOING OUT HERE?
JUST LIKE TO WATCH THE BOATS GO BY. I FIND IT CALMING.
WON'T YOU COME BACK TO YOUR RESTAURANT WITH US?
NOPE. NOT MY RESTAURANT ANYMORE, ANYWAY.
BUT WHAT ABOUT YOUR FAMILY?
MY FAMILY...
MY FAMILY IS WHAT I'M RUNNING FROM!
ALL WE DO IS TALK ABOUT HOW I WORRY ABOUT THEM. WELL I'M SICK OF IT.
I THOUGHT I WANTED TO LOOK OVER THEM, BUT I JUST WORRY WORRY WORRY. AND WHAT CAN I DO ABOUT IT? NOTHING.
WHAT KIND OF MAN AM I IF I CAN'T PROVIDE FOR THEM?
THEY MUST BE ASHAMED OF ME.
HEH, WELL THAT'S PRETTY SILLY.
IS THAT SO?

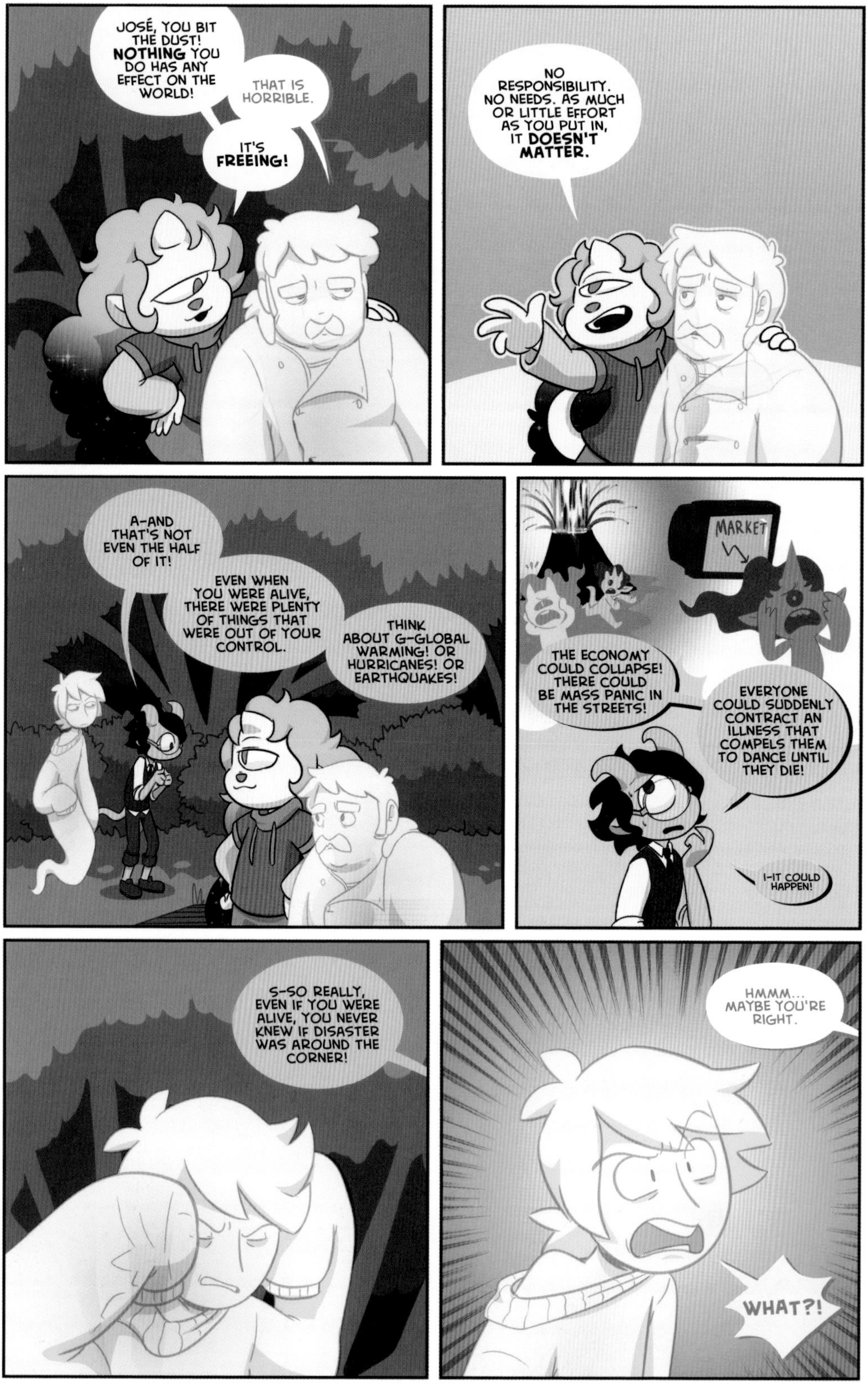
JOSÉ, YOU BIT THE DUST! **NOTHING** YOU DO HAS ANY EFFECT ON THE WORLD!
THAT IS HORRIBLE.
IT'S **FREEING!**
NO RESPONSIBILITY. NO NEEDS. AS MUCH OR LITTLE EFFORT AS YOU PUT IN, IT **DOESN'T MATTER.**
A-AND THAT'S NOT EVEN THE HALF OF IT!
EVEN WHEN YOU WERE ALIVE, THERE WERE PLENTY OF THINGS THAT WERE OUT OF YOUR CONTROL.
THINK ABOUT G-GLOBAL WARMING! OR HURRICANES! OR EARTHQUAKES!
MARKET
THE ECONOMY COULD COLLAPSE! THERE COULD BE MASS PANIC IN THE STREETS!
EVERYONE COULD SUDDENLY CONTRACT AN ILLNESS THAT COMPELS THEM TO DANCE UNTIL THEY DIE!
I-IT COULD HAPPEN!
S-SO REALLY, EVEN IF YOU WERE ALIVE, YOU NEVER KNEW IF DISASTER WAS AROUND THE CORNER!
HMMM... MAYBE YOU'RE RIGHT.
WHAT?!

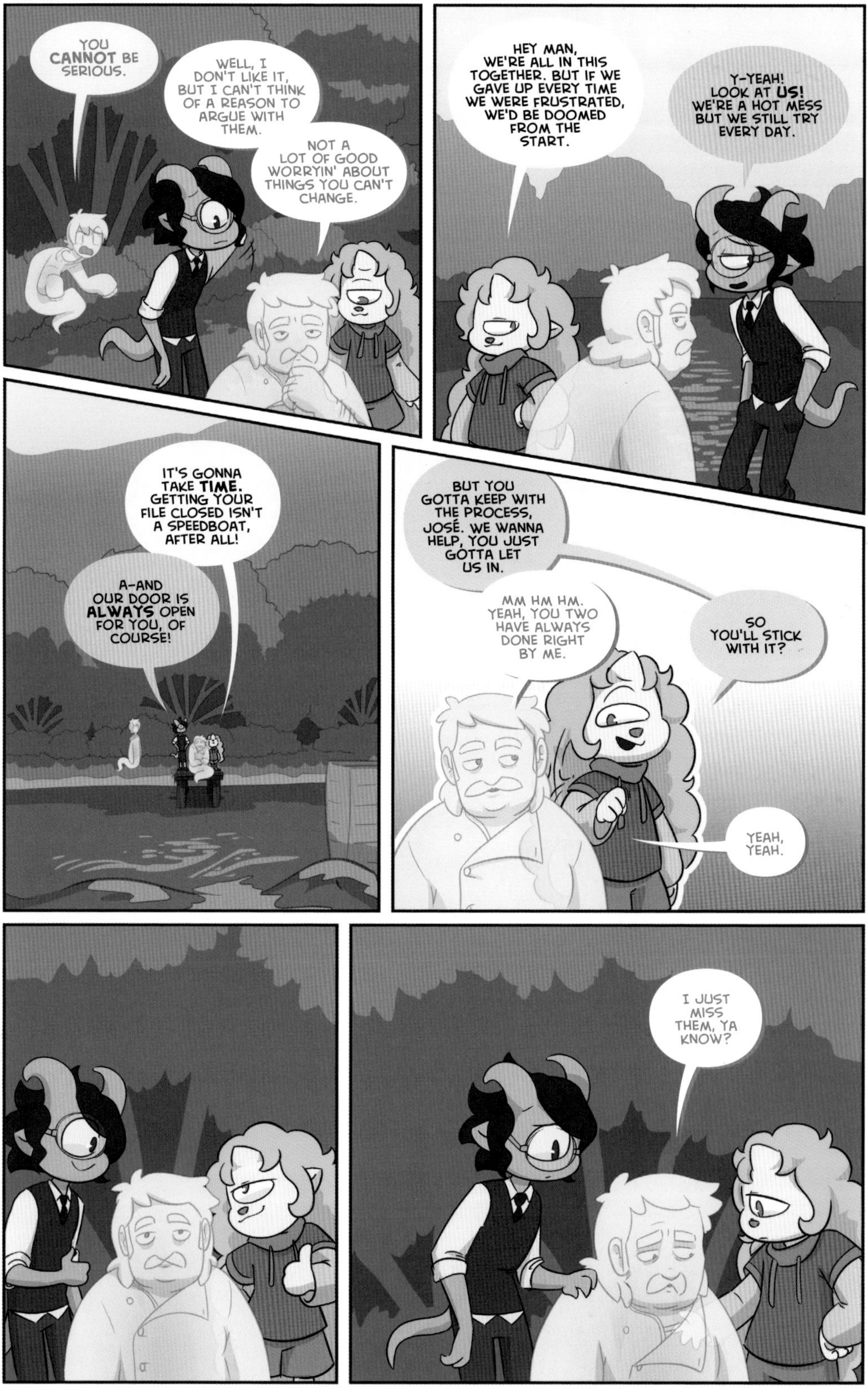
YOU CANNOT BE SERIOUS.
WELL, I DON'T LIKE IT, BUT I CAN'T THINK OF A REASON TO ARGUE WITH THEM.
NOT A LOT OF GOOD WORRYIN' ABOUT THINGS YOU CAN'T CHANGE.
HEY MAN, WE'RE ALL IN THIS TOGETHER. BUT IF WE GAVE UP EVERY TIME WE WERE FRUSTRATED, WE'D BE DOOMED FROM THE START.
Y-YEAH! LOOK AT US! WE'RE A HOT MESS BUT WE STILL TRY EVERY DAY.
IT'S GONNA TAKE TIME. GETTING YOUR FILE CLOSED ISN'T A SPEEDBOAT, AFTER ALL!
A-AND OUR DOOR IS ALWAYS OPEN FOR YOU, OF COURSE!
BUT YOU GOTTA KEEP WITH THE PROCESS, JOSÉ. WE WANNA HELP, YOU JUST GOTTA LET US IN.
MM HM HM. YEAH, YOU TWO HAVE ALWAYS DONE RIGHT BY ME.
SO YOU'LL STICK WITH IT?
YEAH, YEAH.
I JUST MISS THEM, YA KNOW?

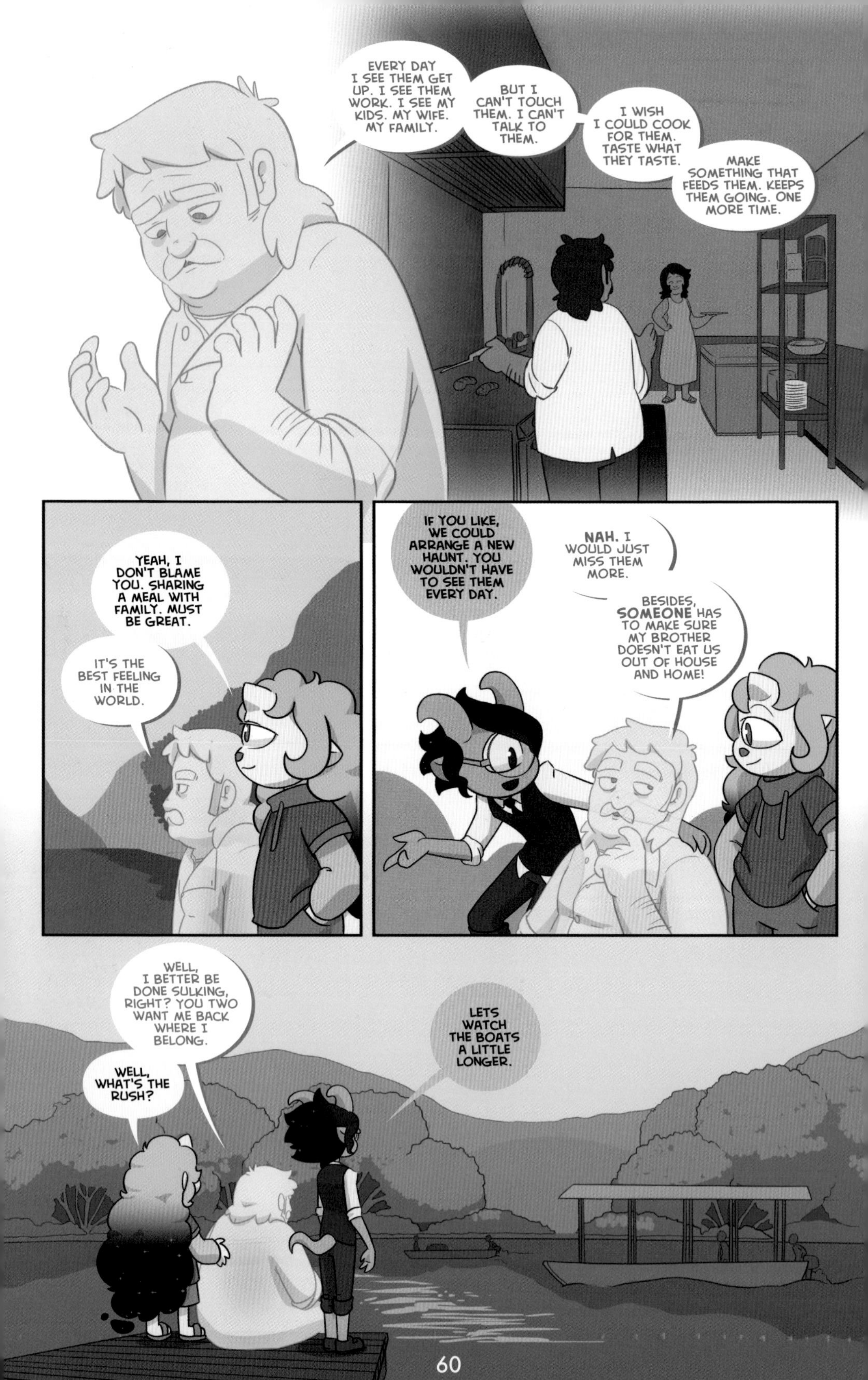

EVERY DAY I SEE THEM GET UP. I SEE THEM WORK. I SEE MY KIDS. MY WIFE. MY FAMILY.
BUT I CAN'T TOUCH THEM. I CAN'T TALK TO THEM.
I WISH I COULD COOK FOR THEM. TASTE WHAT THEY TASTE.
MAKE SOMETHING THAT FEEDS THEM. KEEPS THEM GOING. ONE MORE TIME.
YEAH, I DON'T BLAME YOU. SHARING A MEAL WITH FAMILY. MUST BE GREAT.
IT'S THE BEST FEELING IN THE WORLD.
IF YOU LIKE, WE COULD ARRANGE A NEW HAUNT. YOU WOULDN'T HAVE TO SEE THEM EVERY DAY.
NAH. I WOULD JUST MISS THEM MORE.
BESIDES, SOMEONE HAS TO MAKE SURE MY BROTHER DOESN'T EAT US OUT OF HOUSE AND HOME!
WELL, I BETTER BE DONE SULKING, RIGHT? YOU TWO WANT ME BACK WHERE I BELONG.
WELL, WHAT'S THE RUSH?
LETS WATCH THE BOATS A LITTLE LONGER.

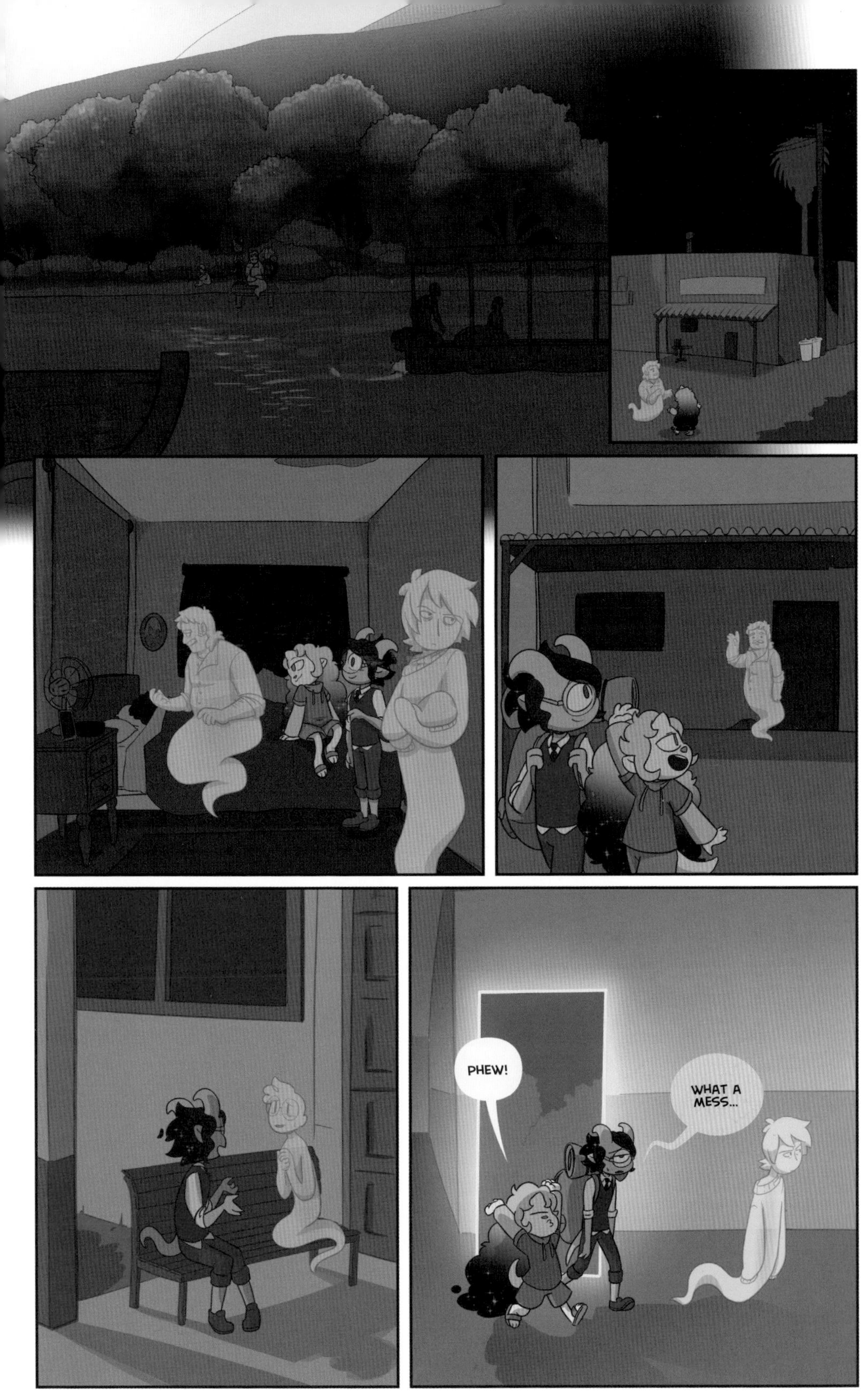
PHEW!
WHAT A MESS...

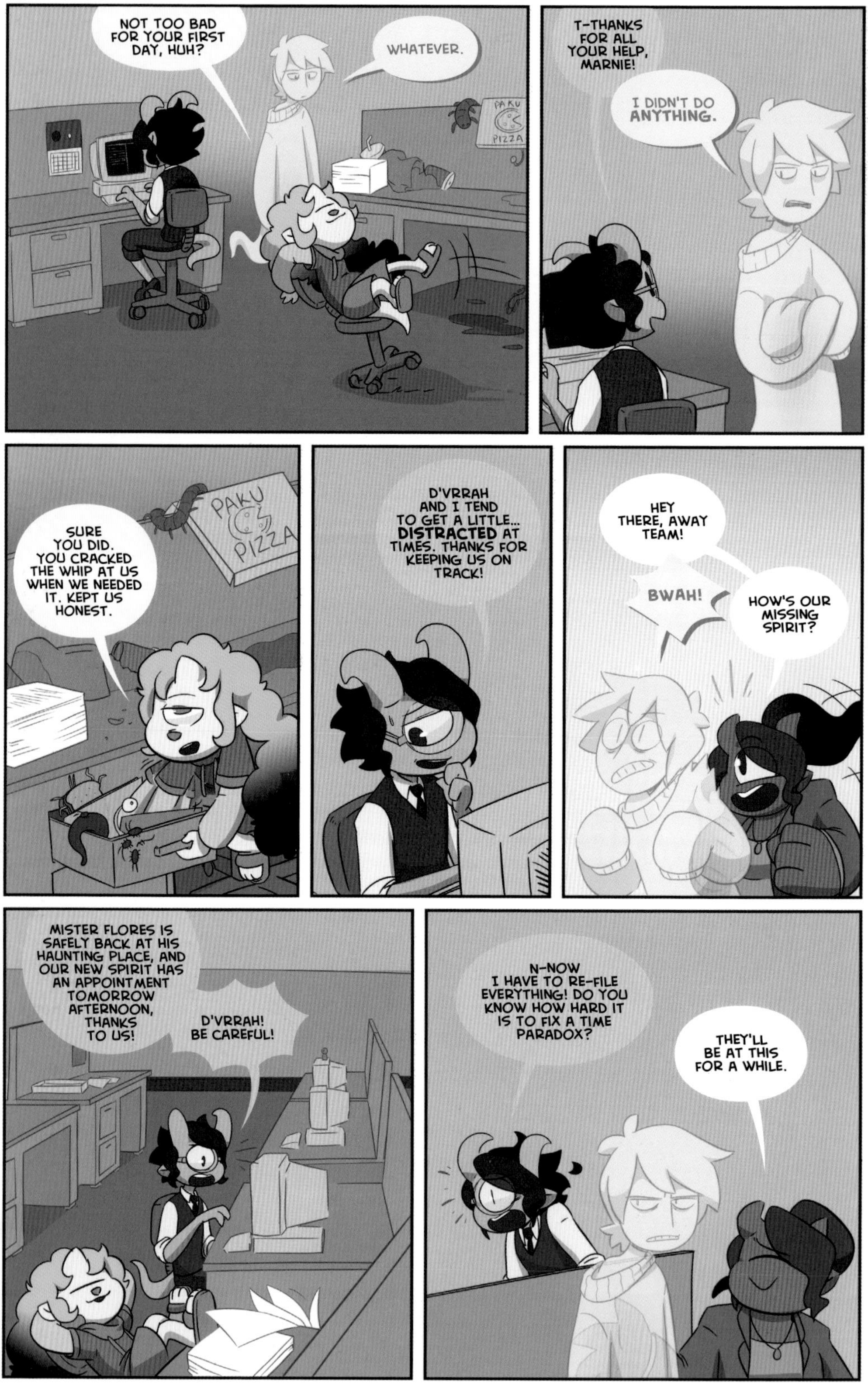
NOT TOO BAD FOR YOUR FIRST DAY, HUH?
WHATEVER.
PAKU PIZZA
T-THANKS FOR ALL YOUR HELP, MARNIE!
I DIDN'T DO **ANYTHING.**
PAKU PIZZA
SURE YOU DID. YOU CRACKED THE WHIP AT US WHEN WE NEEDED IT. KEPT US HONEST.
D'VRRAH AND I TEND TO GET A LITTLE... **DISTRACTED** AT TIMES. THANKS FOR KEEPING US ON TRACK!
HEY THERE, AWAY TEAM!
BWAH!
HOW'S OUR MISSING SPIRIT?
MISTER FLORES IS SAFELY BACK AT HIS HAUNTING PLACE, AND OUR NEW SPIRIT HAS AN APPOINTMENT TOMORROW AFTERNOON, THANKS TO US!
D'VRRAH! BE CAREFUL!
N-NOW I HAVE TO RE-FILE EVERYTHING! DO YOU KNOW HOW HARD IT IS TO FIX A TIME PARADOX?
THEY'LL BE AT THIS FOR A WHILE.

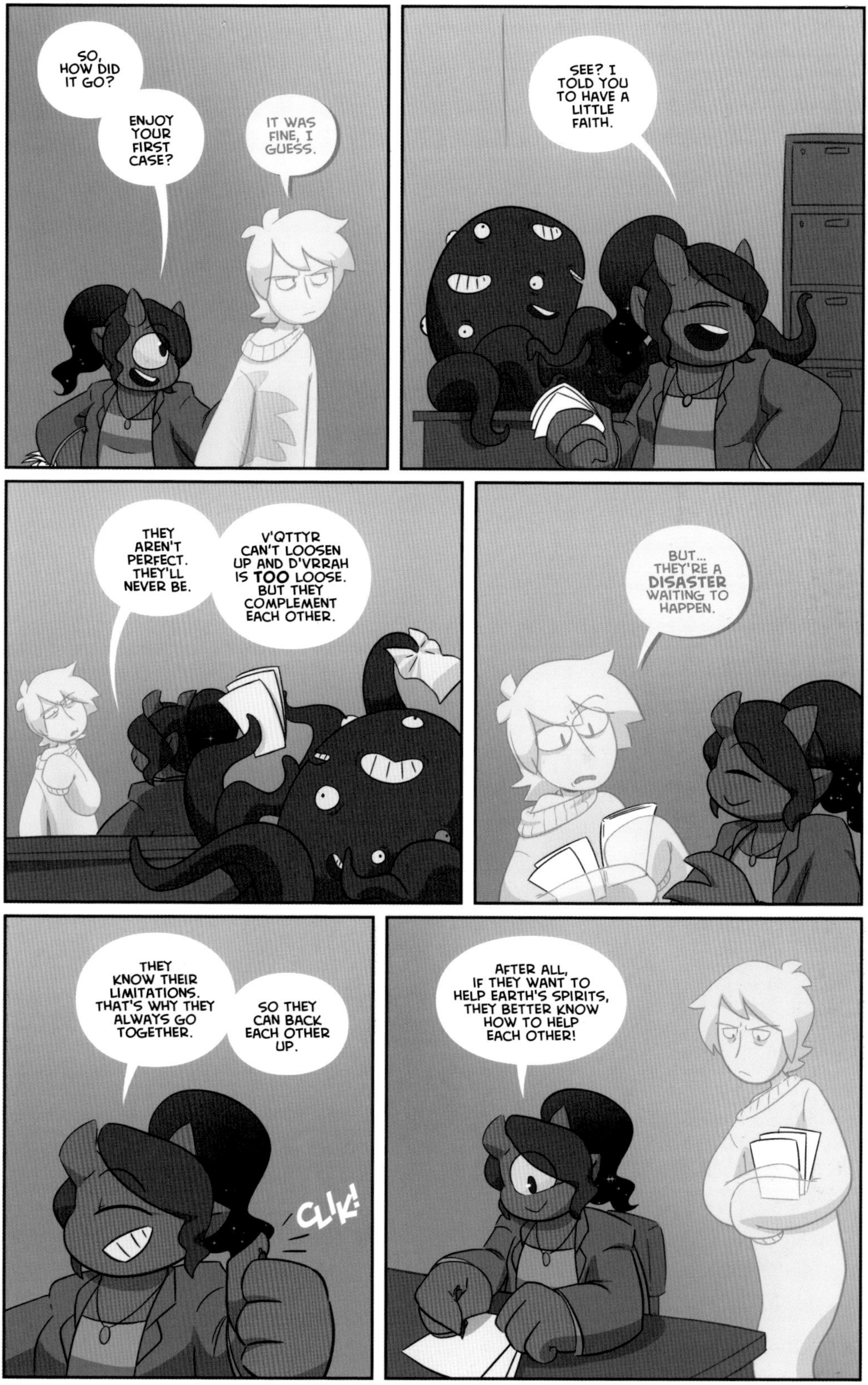
SO, HOW DID IT GO?
ENJOY YOUR FIRST CASE?
IT WAS FINE, I GUESS.
SEE? I TOLD YOU TO HAVE A LITTLE FAITH.
THEY AREN'T PERFECT. THEY'LL NEVER BE.
V'QTTYR CAN'T LOOSEN UP AND D'VRRAH IS **TOO** LOOSE. BUT THEY COMPLEMENT EACH OTHER.
BUT... THEY'RE A **DISASTER** WAITING TO HAPPEN.
THEY KNOW THEIR LIMITATIONS. THAT'S WHY THEY ALWAYS GO TOGETHER.
SO THEY CAN BACK EACH OTHER UP.
CLIK!
AFTER ALL, IF THEY WANT TO HELP EARTH'S SPIRITS, THEY BETTER KNOW HOW TO HELP EACH OTHER!

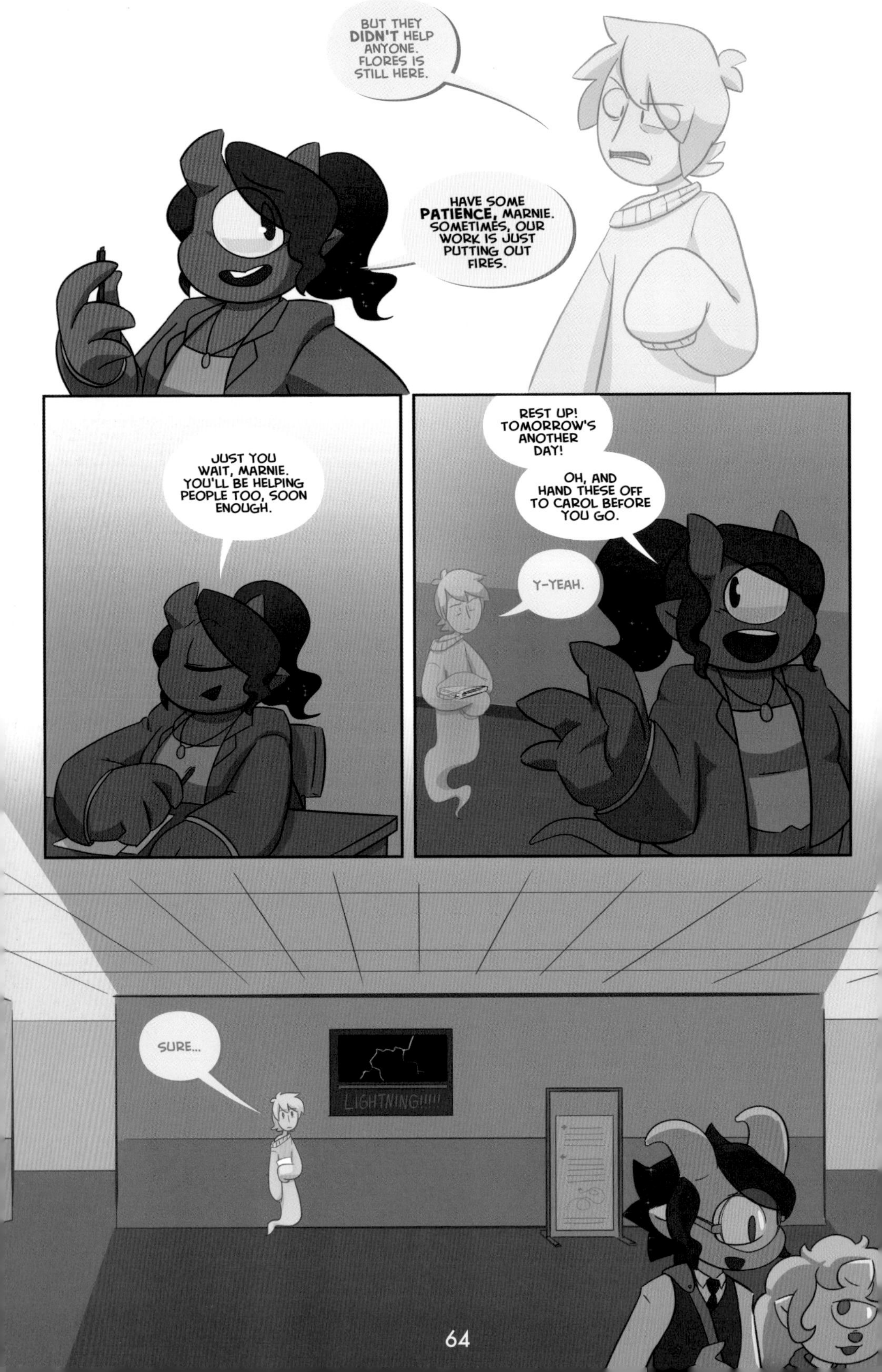

BUT THEY DIDN'T HELP ANYONE. FLORES IS STILL HERE.
HAVE SOME PATIENCE, MARNIE. SOMETIMES, OUR WORK IS JUST PUTTING OUT FIRES.
JUST YOU WAIT, MARNIE. YOU'LL BE HELPING PEOPLE TOO, SOON ENOUGH.
REST UP! TOMORROW'S ANOTHER DAY!
OH, AND HAND THESE OFF TO CAROL BEFORE YOU GO.
Y-YEAH.
SURE...
LIGHTNING!!!!!

Department of Spectral Affairs

Chapter 3

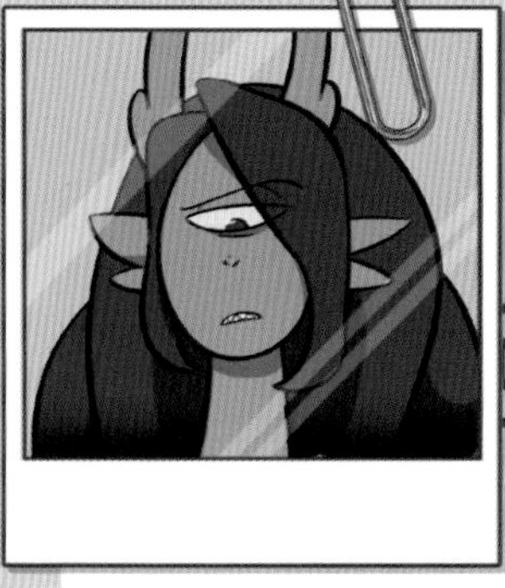

OR OFFICIAL USE ONLY

Name: C'tharla

Pronunciation: Kith-Are-Lah

Pronouns: she/her

Age: ∞

Position: Branch manager

Likes: Efficiency, loyalty, duty, a chain of command.

Dislikes: Being told no, self-doubt, insubordination.

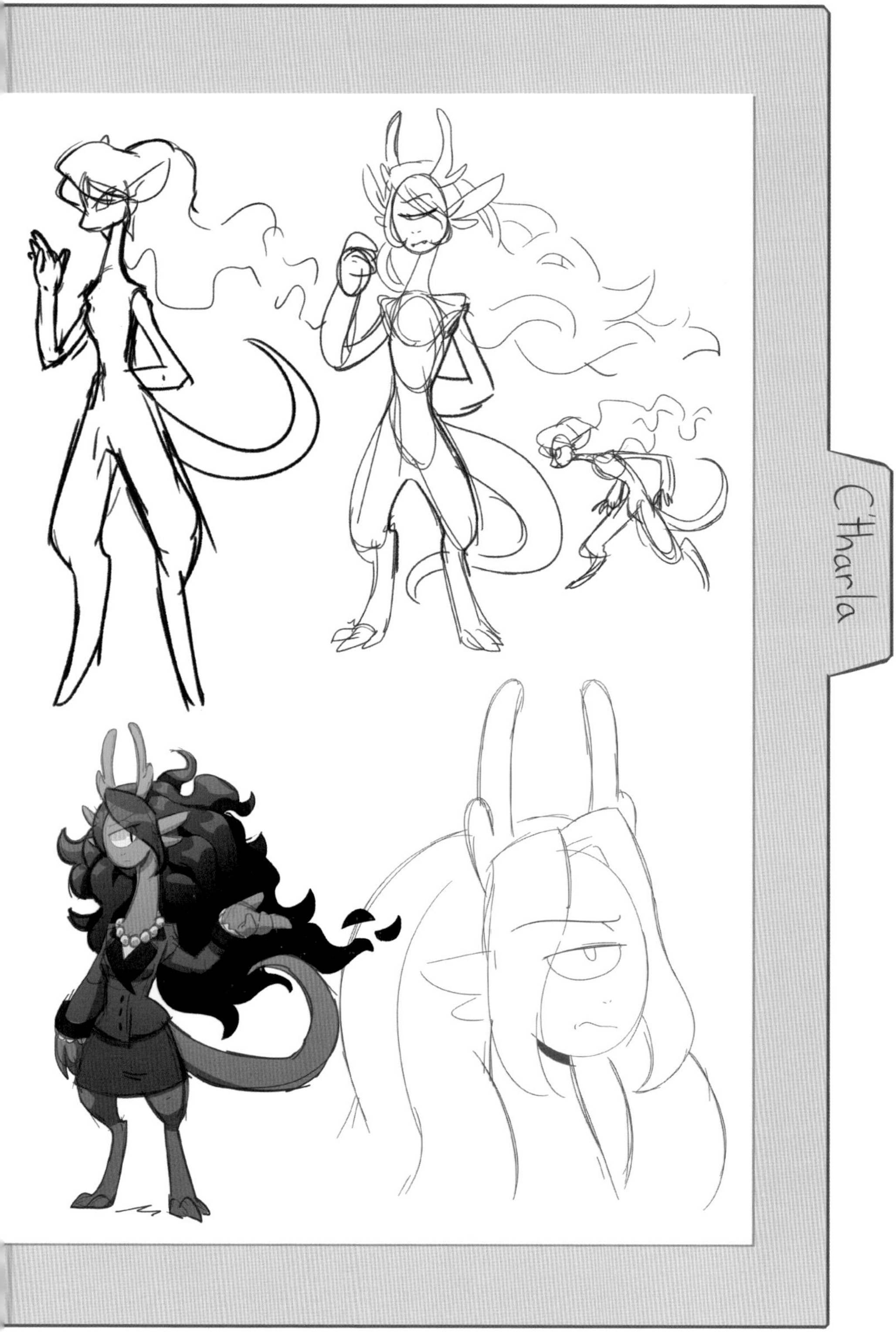
C'tharla

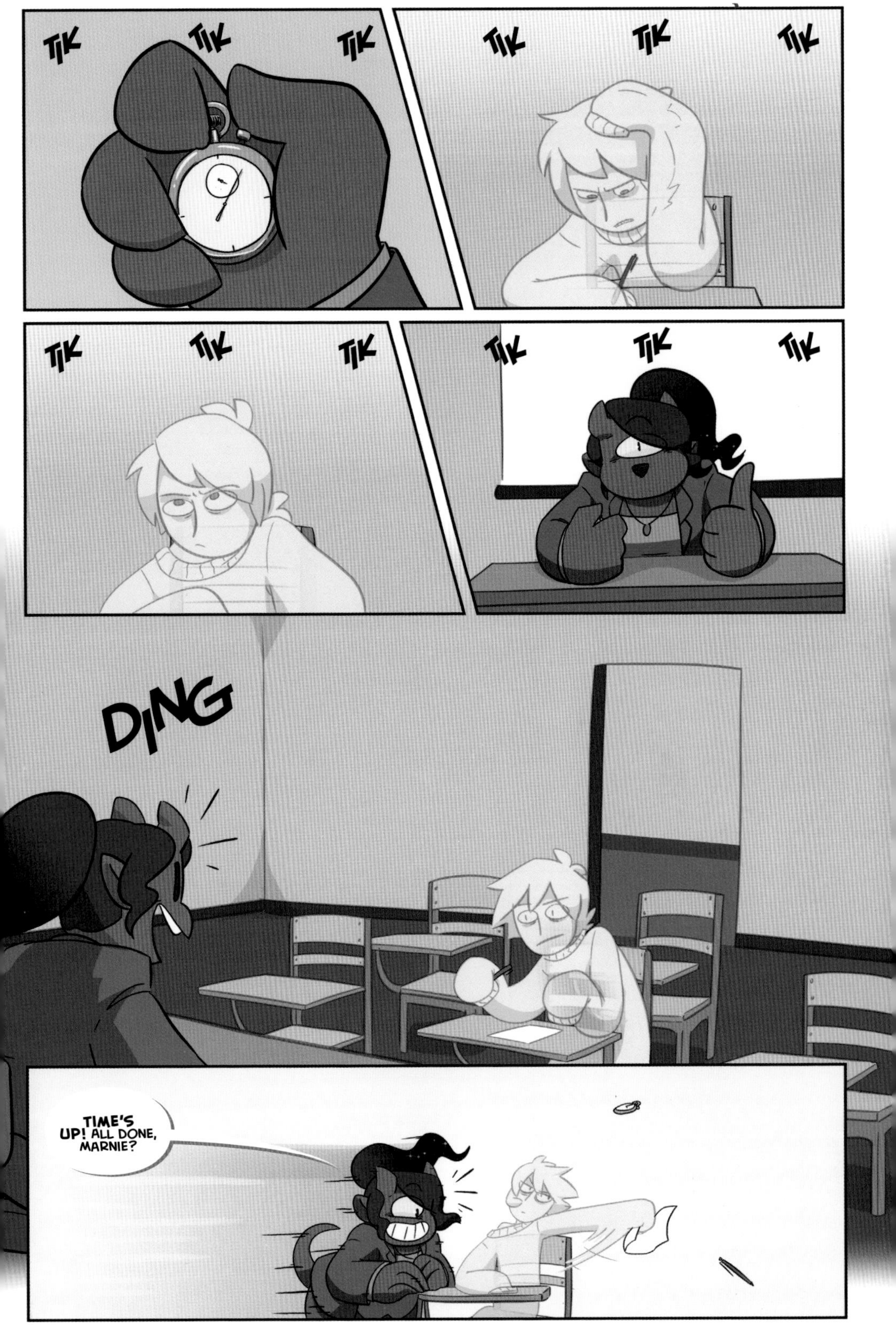
TIK TIK TIK
TIK TIK TIK
TIK TIK TIK
TIK TIK TIK
DING
TIME'S UP! ALL DONE, MARNIE?

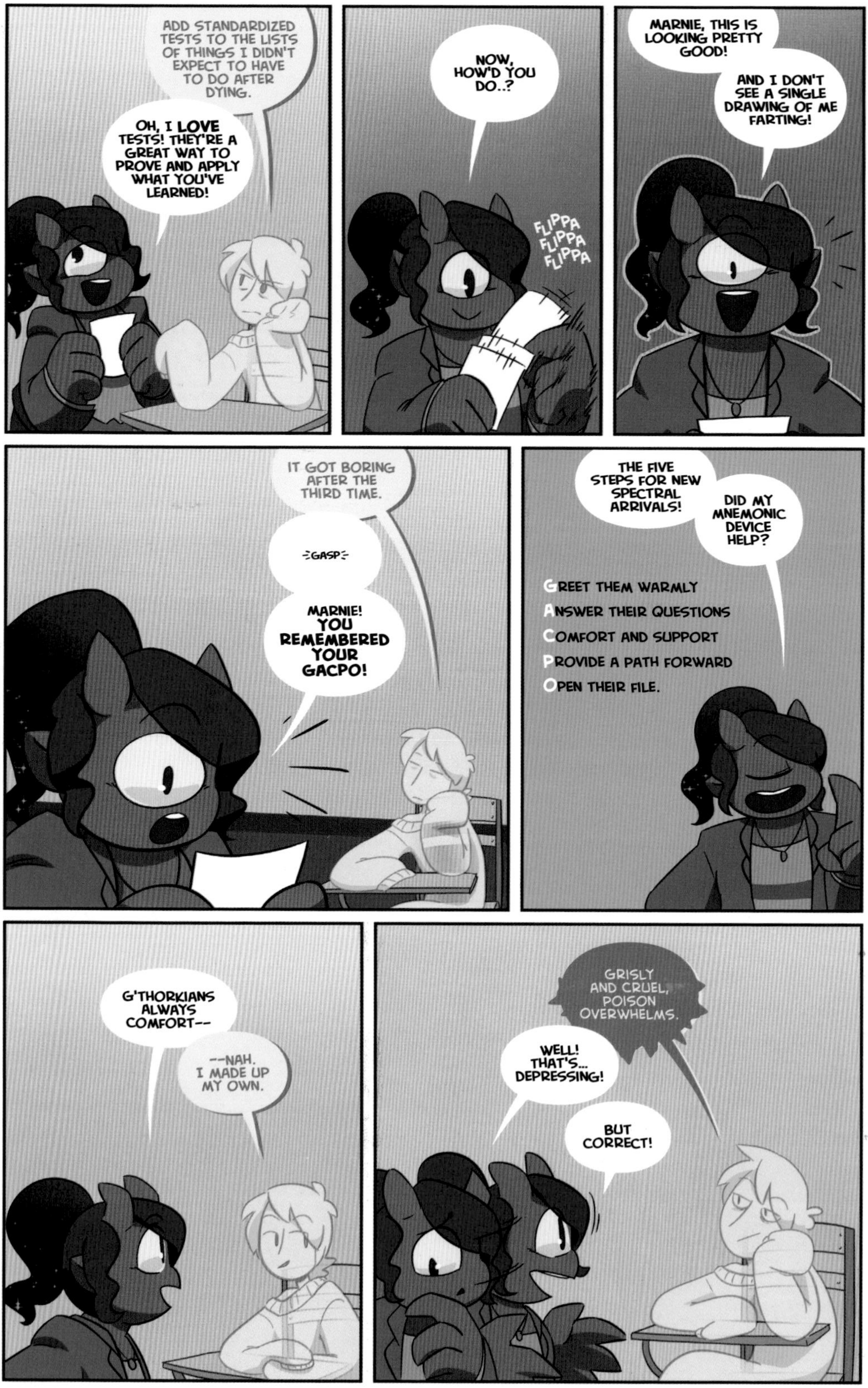
ADD STANDARDIZED TESTS TO THE LISTS OF THINGS I DIDN'T EXPECT TO HAVE TO DO AFTER DYING.
OH, I LOVE TESTS! THEY'RE A GREAT WAY TO PROVE AND APPLY WHAT YOU'VE LEARNED!
NOW, HOW'D YOU DO..?
FLIPPA FLIPPA FLIPPA
MARNIE, THIS IS LOOKING PRETTY GOOD!
AND I DON'T SEE A SINGLE DRAWING OF ME FARTING!
IT GOT BORING AFTER THE THIRD TIME.
GASP
MARNIE! YOU REMEMBERED YOUR GACPO!
THE FIVE STEPS FOR NEW SPECTRAL ARRIVALS!
DID MY MNEMONIC DEVICE HELP?
GREET THEM WARMLY
ANSWER THEIR QUESTIONS
COMFORT AND SUPPORT
PROVIDE A PATH FORWARD
OPEN THEIR FILE.
G'THORKIANS ALWAYS COMFORT--
--NAH. I MADE UP MY OWN.
GRISLY AND CRUEL, POISON OVERWHELMS.
WELL! THAT'S... DEPRESSING!
BUT CORRECT!

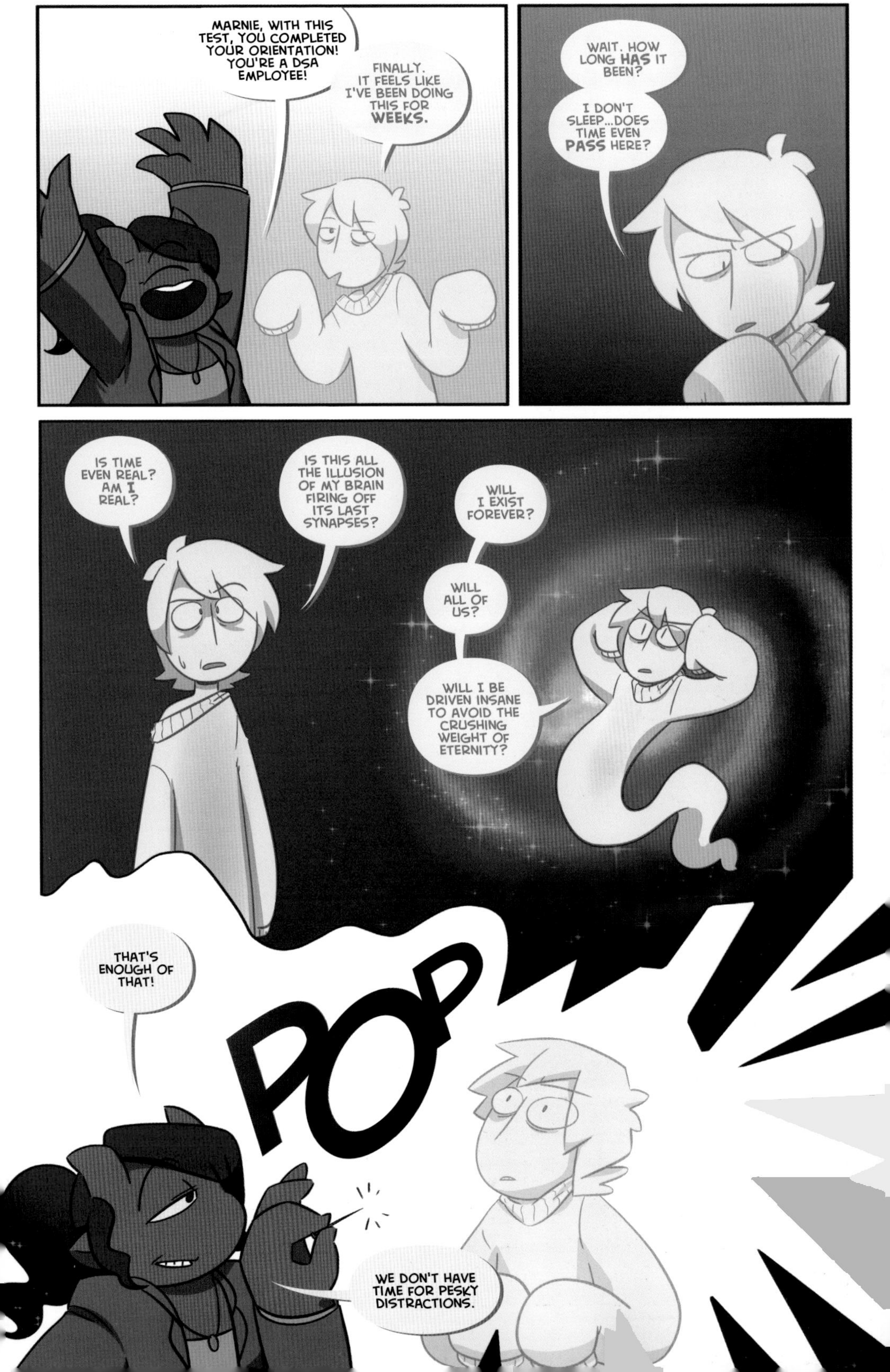
MARNIE, WITH THIS TEST, YOU COMPLETED YOUR ORIENTATION! YOU'RE A DSA EMPLOYEE!
FINALLY. IT FEELS LIKE I'VE BEEN DOING THIS FOR **WEEKS.**
WAIT. HOW LONG **HAS** IT BEEN?
I DON'T SLEEP...DOES TIME EVEN **PASS** HERE?
IS TIME EVEN REAL? AM **I** REAL?
IS THIS ALL THE ILLUSION OF MY BRAIN FIRING OFF ITS LAST SYNAPSES?
WILL I EXIST FOREVER?
WILL ALL OF US?
WILL I BE DRIVEN INSANE TO AVOID THE CRUSHING WEIGHT OF ETERNITY?
THAT'S ENOUGH OF THAT!
POP
WE DON'T HAVE TIME FOR PESKY DISTRACTIONS.

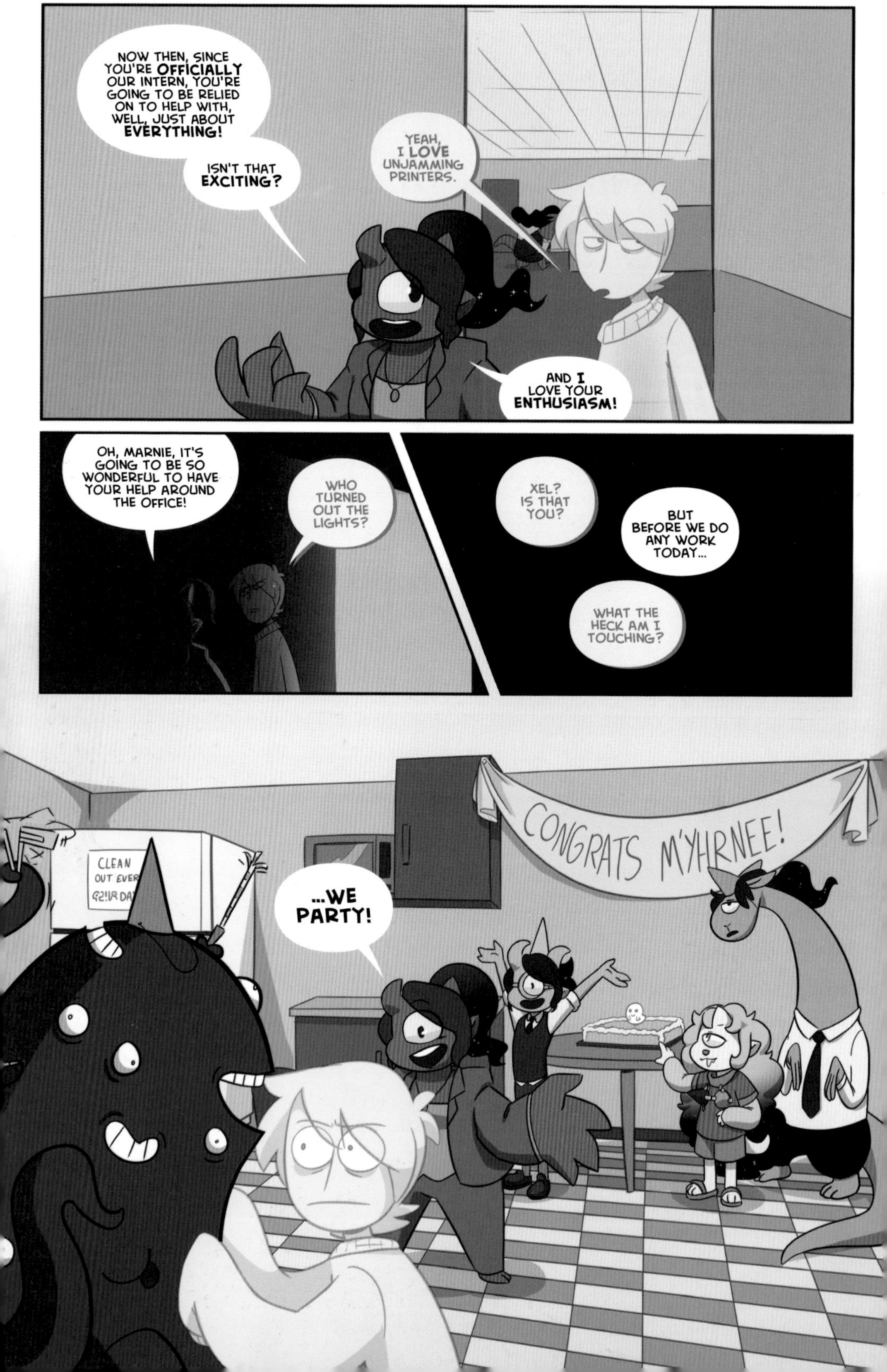
NOW THEN, SINCE YOU'RE **OFFICIALLY** OUR INTERN, YOU'RE GOING TO BE RELIED ON TO HELP WITH, WELL, JUST ABOUT **EVERYTHING!**
ISN'T THAT **EXCITING?**
YEAH, I **LOVE** UNJAMMING PRINTERS.
AND **I** LOVE YOUR **ENTHUSIASM!**
OH, MARNIE, IT'S GOING TO BE SO WONDERFUL TO HAVE YOUR HELP AROUND THE OFFICE!
WHO TURNED OUT THE LIGHTS?
XEL? IS THAT YOU?
BUT BEFORE WE DO ANY WORK TODAY...
WHAT THE HECK AM I TOUCHING?
CONGRATS M'YHRNEE!
...**WE PARTY!**

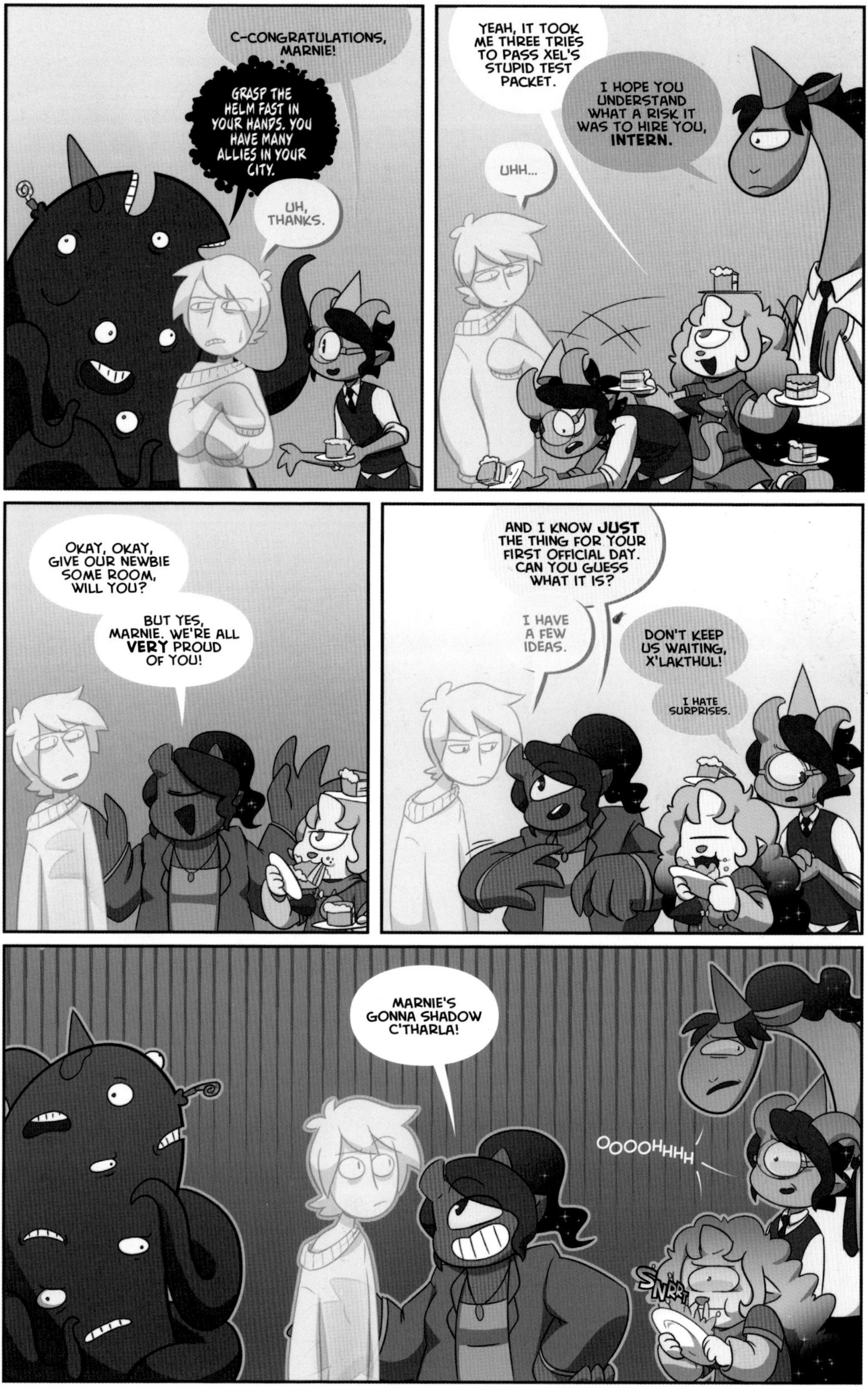
C-CONGRATULATIONS, MARNIE!
GRASP THE HELM FAST IN YOUR HANDS. YOU HAVE MANY ALLIES IN YOUR CITY.
UH, THANKS.
YEAH, IT TOOK ME THREE TRIES TO PASS XEL'S STUPID TEST PACKET.
I HOPE YOU UNDERSTAND WHAT A RISK IT WAS TO HIRE YOU, **INTERN.**
UHH...
OKAY, OKAY, GIVE OUR NEWBIE SOME ROOM, WILL YOU?
BUT YES, MARNIE. WE'RE ALL **VERY** PROUD OF YOU!
AND I KNOW **JUST** THE THING FOR YOUR FIRST OFFICIAL DAY. CAN YOU GUESS WHAT IT IS?
I HAVE A FEW IDEAS.
DON'T KEEP US WAITING, X'LAKTHUL!
I HATE SURPRISES.
MARNIE'S GONNA SHADOW C'THARLA!
OOOOHHHH
SNRRT

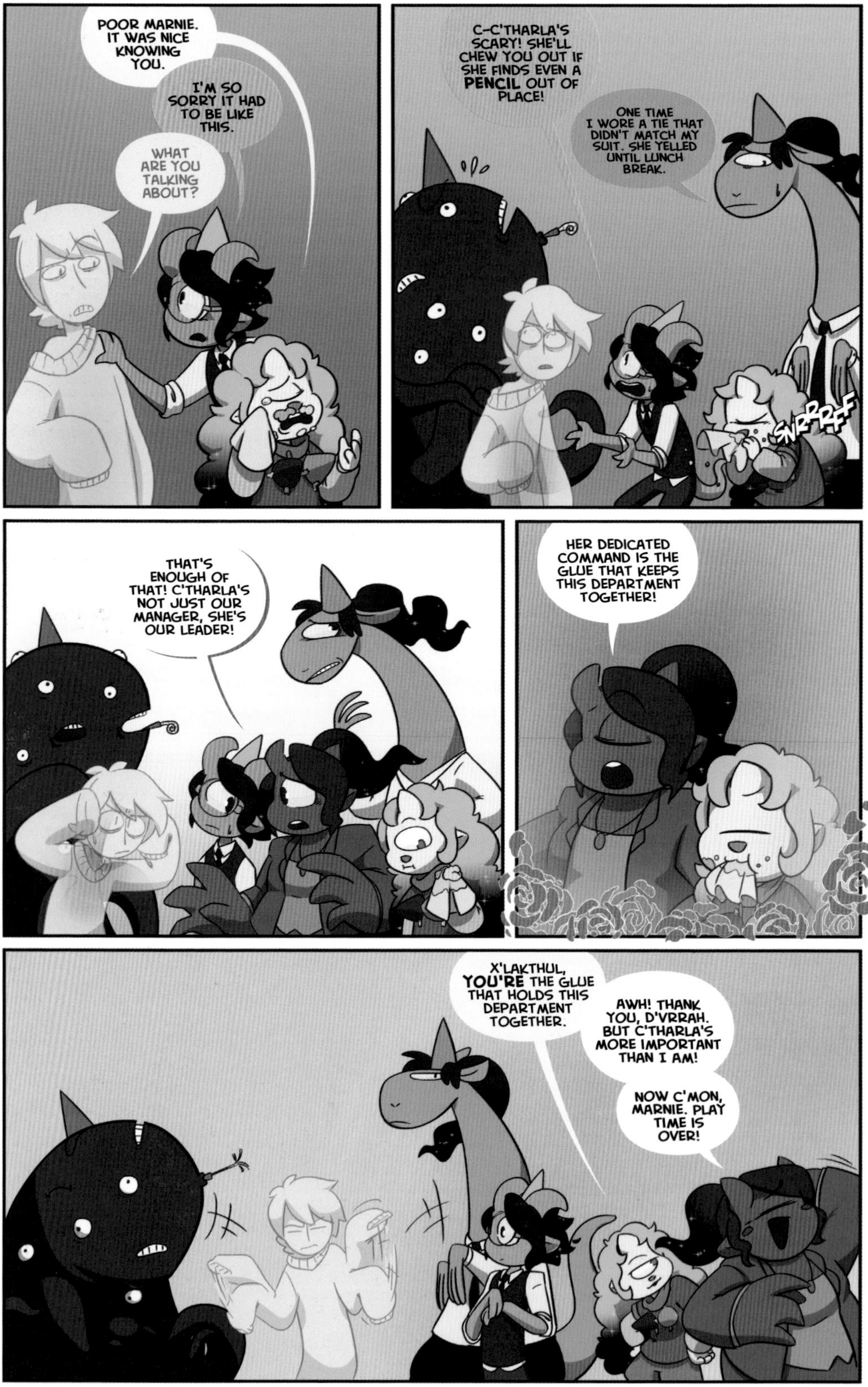
POOR MARNIE. IT WAS NICE KNOWING YOU.
I'M SO SORRY IT HAD TO BE LIKE THIS.
WHAT ARE YOU TALKING ABOUT?
C-C'THARLA'S SCARY! SHE'LL CHEW YOU OUT IF SHE FINDS EVEN A **PENCIL** OUT OF PLACE!
ONE TIME I WORE A TIE THAT DIDN'T MATCH MY SUIT. SHE YELLED UNTIL LUNCH BREAK.
SNRRRFF
THAT'S ENOUGH OF THAT! C'THARLA'S NOT JUST OUR MANAGER, SHE'S OUR LEADER!
HER DEDICATED COMMAND IS THE GLUE THAT KEEPS THIS DEPARTMENT TOGETHER!
X'LAKTHUL, **YOU'RE** THE GLUE THAT HOLDS THIS DEPARTMENT TOGETHER.
AWH! THANK YOU, D'VRRAH. BUT C'THARLA'S MORE IMPORTANT THAN I AM!
NOW C'MON, MARNIE. PLAY TIME IS OVER!

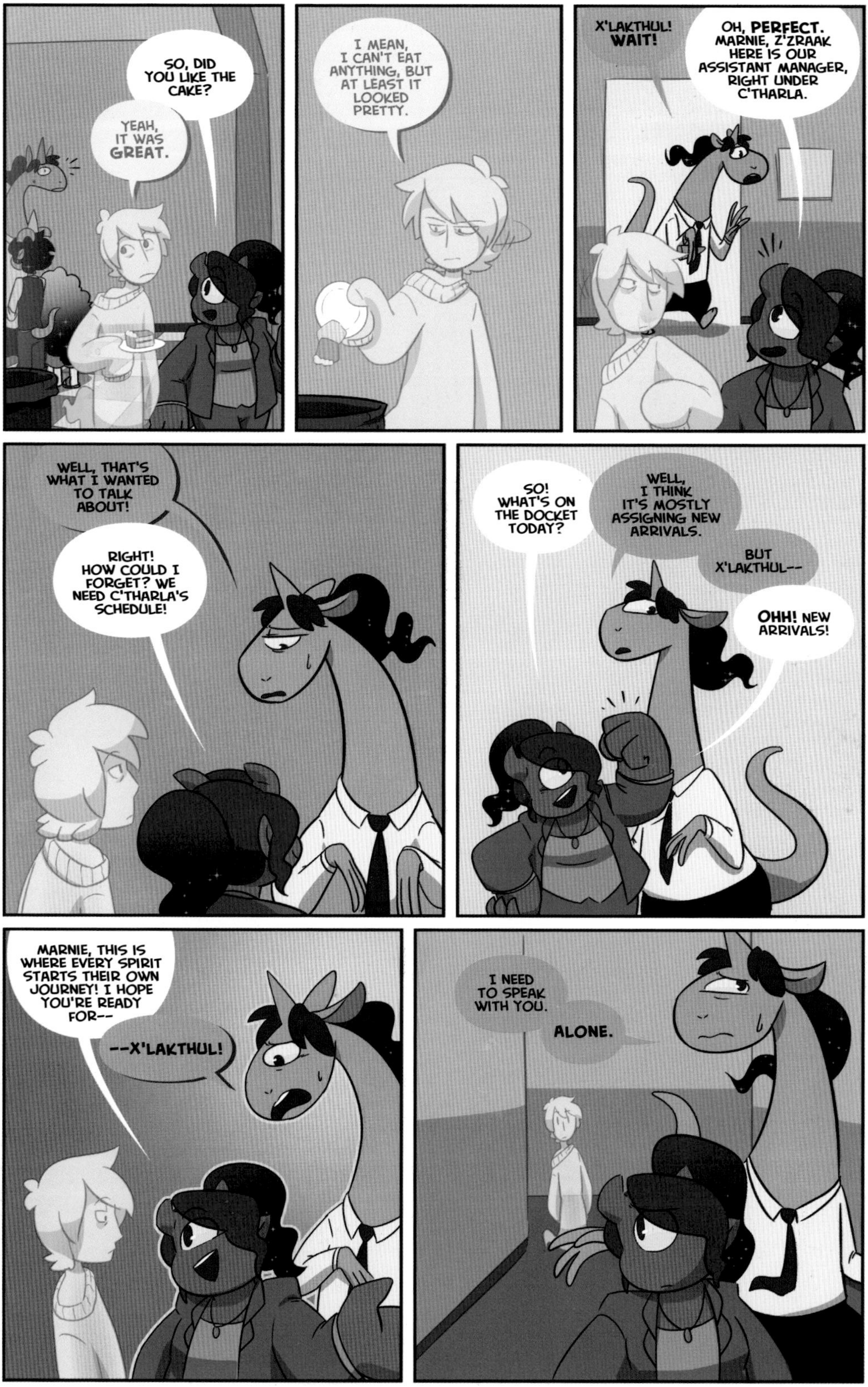
SO, DID YOU LIKE THE CAKE?
YEAH, IT WAS GREAT.
I MEAN, I CAN'T EAT ANYTHING, BUT AT LEAST IT LOOKED PRETTY.
X'LAKTHUL! WAIT!
OH, PERFECT. MARNIE, Z'ZRAAK HERE IS OUR ASSISTANT MANAGER, RIGHT UNDER C'THARLA.
WELL, THAT'S WHAT I WANTED TO TALK ABOUT!
RIGHT! HOW COULD I FORGET? WE NEED C'THARLA'S SCHEDULE!
SO! WHAT'S ON THE DOCKET TODAY?
WELL, I THINK IT'S MOSTLY ASSIGNING NEW ARRIVALS.
BUT X'LAKTHUL--
OHH! NEW ARRIVALS!
MARNIE, THIS IS WHERE EVERY SPIRIT STARTS THEIR OWN JOURNEY! I HOPE YOU'RE READY FOR--
--X'LAKTHUL!
I NEED TO SPEAK WITH YOU.
ALONE.

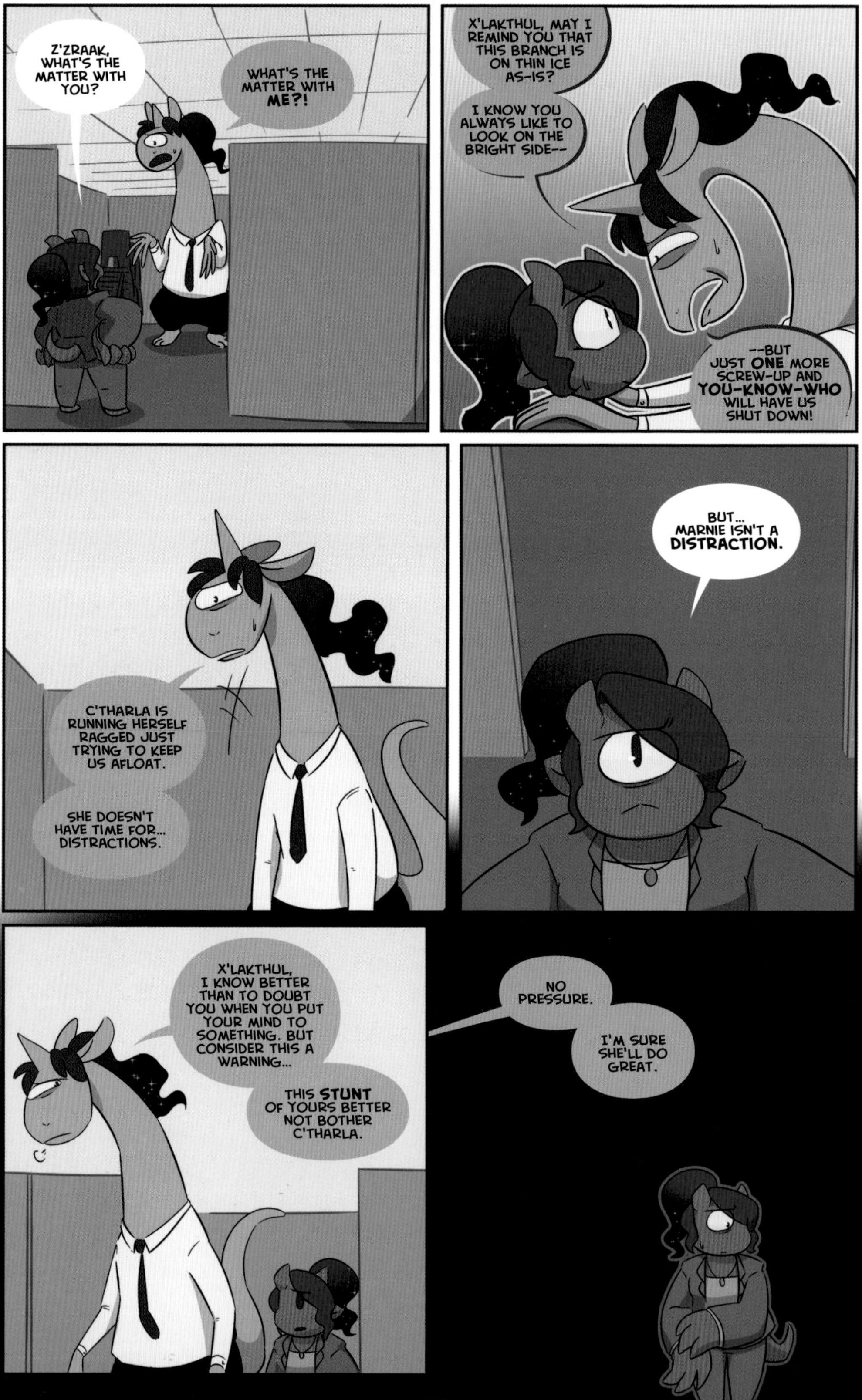
Z'ZRAAK, WHAT'S THE MATTER WITH YOU?
WHAT'S THE MATTER WITH ME?!
X'LAKTHUL, MAY I REMIND YOU THAT THIS BRANCH IS ON THIN ICE AS-IS?
I KNOW YOU ALWAYS LIKE TO LOOK ON THE BRIGHT SIDE--
--BUT JUST ONE MORE SCREW-UP AND YOU-KNOW-WHO WILL HAVE US SHUT DOWN!
C'THARLA IS RUNNING HERSELF RAGGED JUST TRYING TO KEEP US AFLOAT.
SHE DOESN'T HAVE TIME FOR... DISTRACTIONS.
BUT... MARNIE ISN'T A DISTRACTION.
X'LAKTHUL, I KNOW BETTER THAN TO DOUBT YOU WHEN YOU PUT YOUR MIND TO SOMETHING. BUT CONSIDER THIS A WARNING...
THIS STUNT OF YOURS BETTER NOT BOTHER C'THARLA.
NO PRESSURE.
I'M SURE SHE'LL DO GREAT.

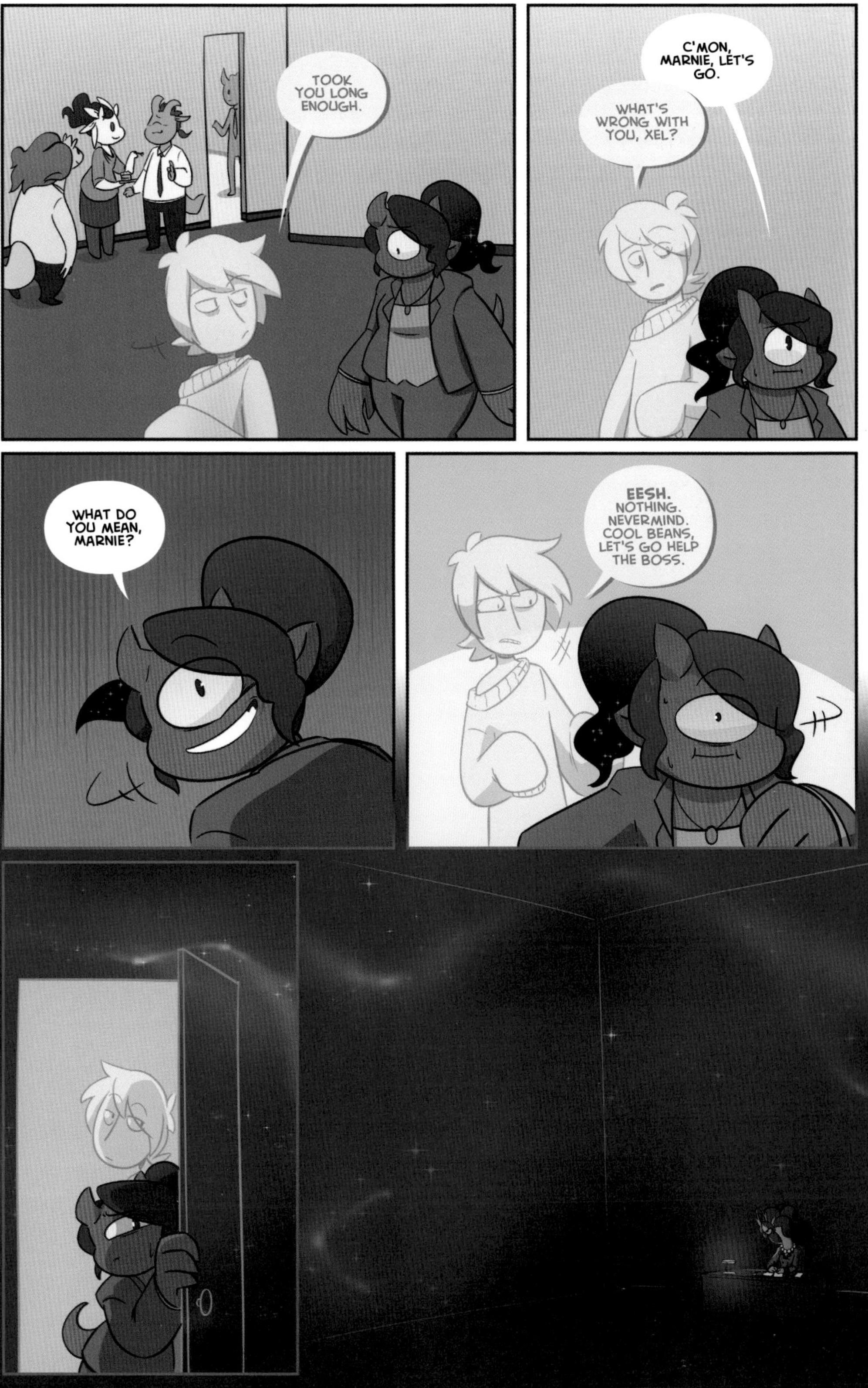
TOOK YOU LONG ENOUGH.
C'MON, MARNIE, LET'S GO.
WHAT'S WRONG WITH YOU, XEL?
WHAT DO YOU MEAN, MARNIE?
EESH. NOTHING. NEVERMIND. COOL BEANS, LET'S GO HELP THE BOSS.

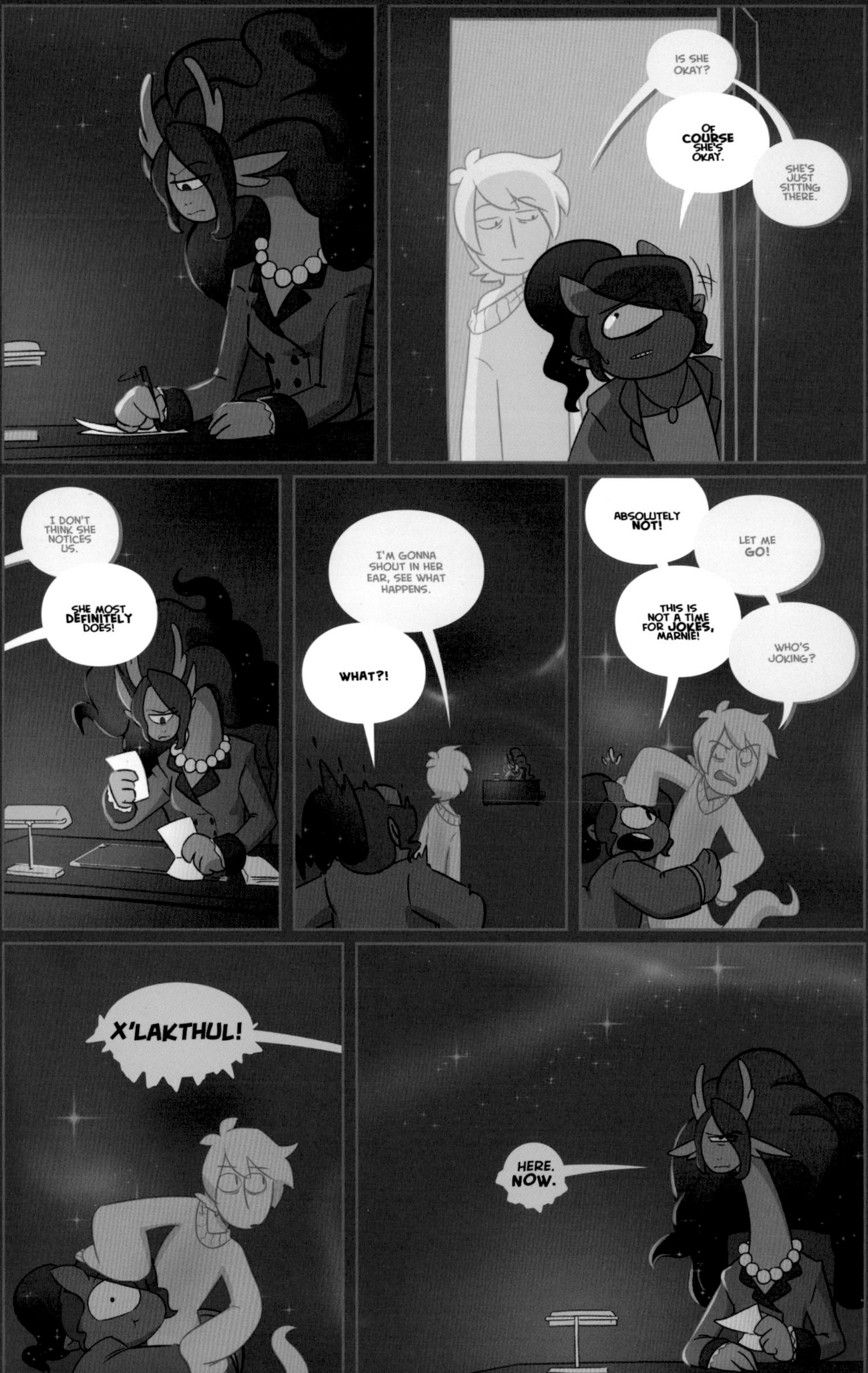
IS SHE OKAY?
OF COURSE SHE'S OKAY.
SHE'S JUST SITTING THERE.
I DON'T THINK SHE NOTICES US.
SHE MOST DEFINITELY DOES!
I'M GONNA SHOUT IN HER EAR, SEE WHAT HAPPENS.
WHAT?!
ABSOLUTELY NOT!
LET ME GO!
THIS IS NOT A TIME FOR JOKES, MARNIE!
WHO'S JOKING?
X'LAKTHUL!
HERE. NOW.

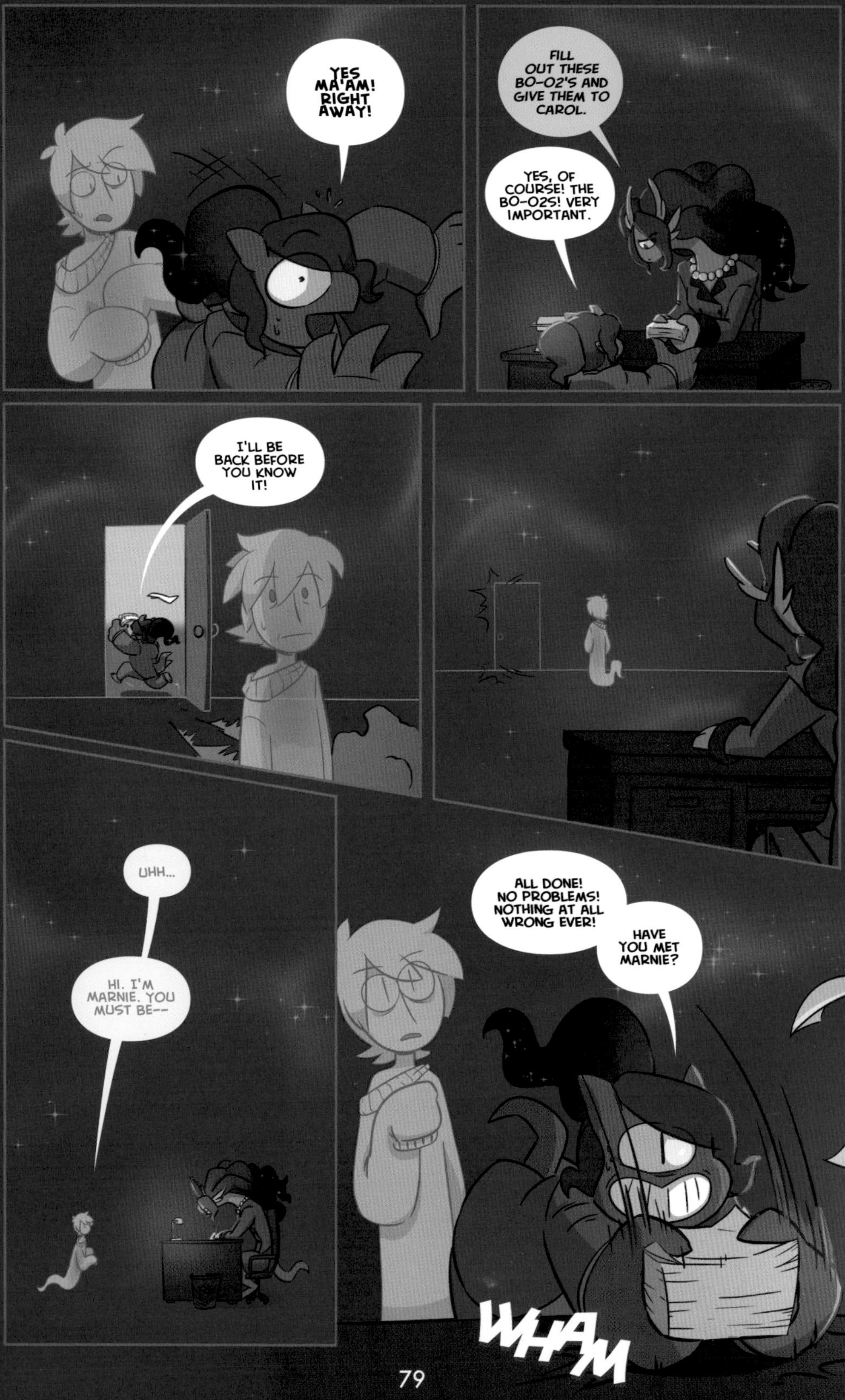
YES MA'AM! RIGHT AWAY!
FILL OUT THESE BO-02'S AND GIVE THEM TO CAROL.
YES, OF COURSE! THE BO-02S! VERY IMPORTANT.
I'LL BE BACK BEFORE YOU KNOW IT!
UHH...
HI. I'M MARNIE. YOU MUST BE--
ALL DONE! NO PROBLEMS! NOTHING AT ALL WRONG EVER!
HAVE YOU MET MARNIE?
WHAM

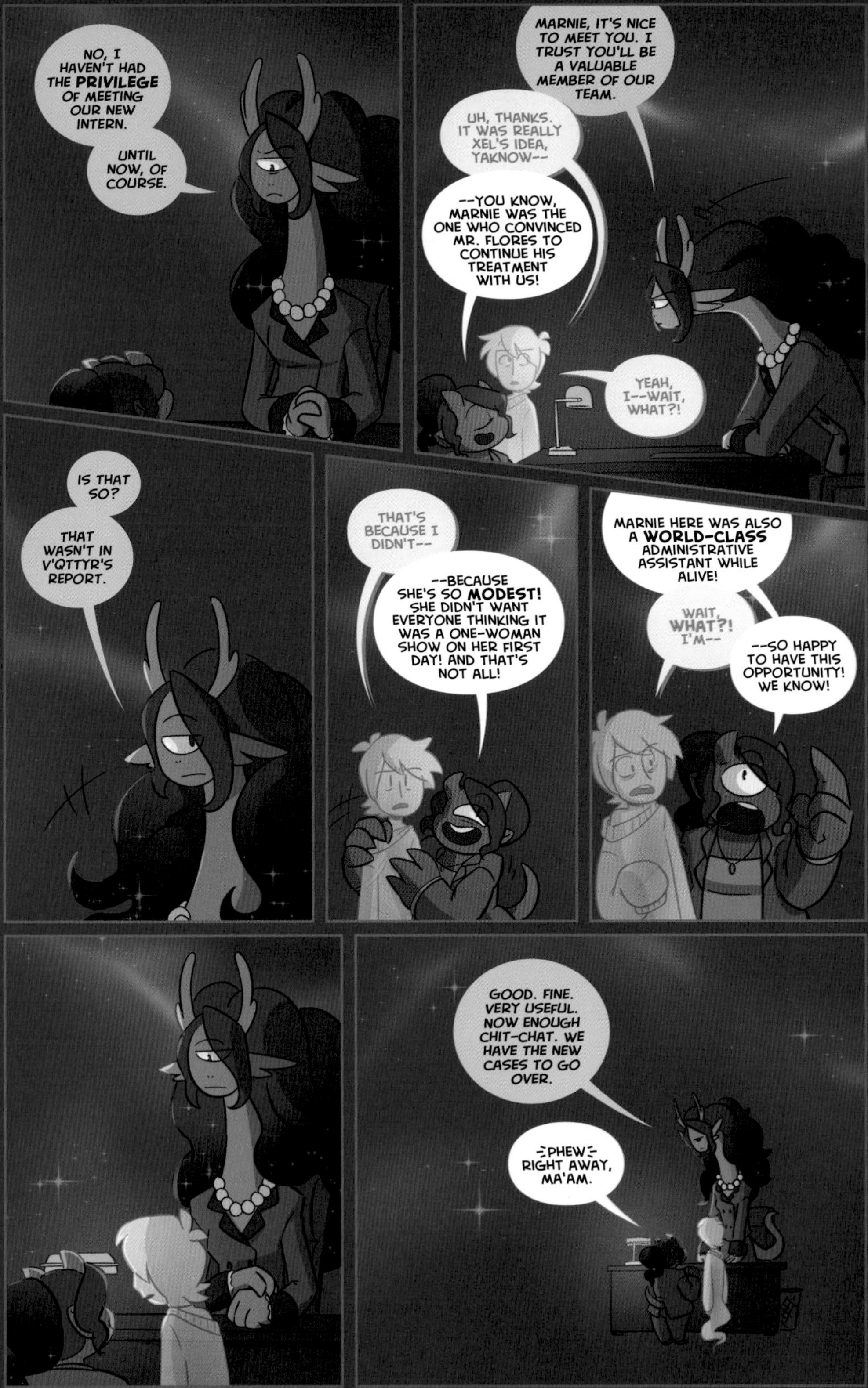
NO, I HAVEN'T HAD THE **PRIVILEGE** OF MEETING OUR NEW INTERN.
UNTIL NOW, OF COURSE.
MARNIE, IT'S NICE TO MEET YOU. I TRUST YOU'LL BE A VALUABLE MEMBER OF OUR TEAM.
UH, THANKS. IT WAS REALLY XEL'S IDEA, YAKNOW--
--YOU KNOW, MARNIE WAS THE ONE WHO CONVINCED MR. FLORES TO CONTINUE HIS TREATMENT WITH US!
YEAH, I--WAIT, WHAT?!
IS THAT SO?
THAT WASN'T IN V'QTTYR'S REPORT.
THAT'S BECAUSE I DIDN'T--
--BECAUSE SHE'S SO **MODEST!** SHE DIDN'T WANT EVERYONE THINKING IT WAS A ONE-WOMAN SHOW ON HER FIRST DAY! AND THAT'S NOT ALL!
MARNIE HERE WAS ALSO A **WORLD-CLASS** ADMINISTRATIVE ASSISTANT WHILE ALIVE!
WAIT, **WHAT?!** I'M--
--SO HAPPY TO HAVE THIS OPPORTUNITY! WE KNOW!
GOOD. FINE. VERY USEFUL. NOW ENOUGH CHIT-CHAT. WE HAVE THE NEW CASES TO GO OVER.
=PHEW= RIGHT AWAY, MA'AM.

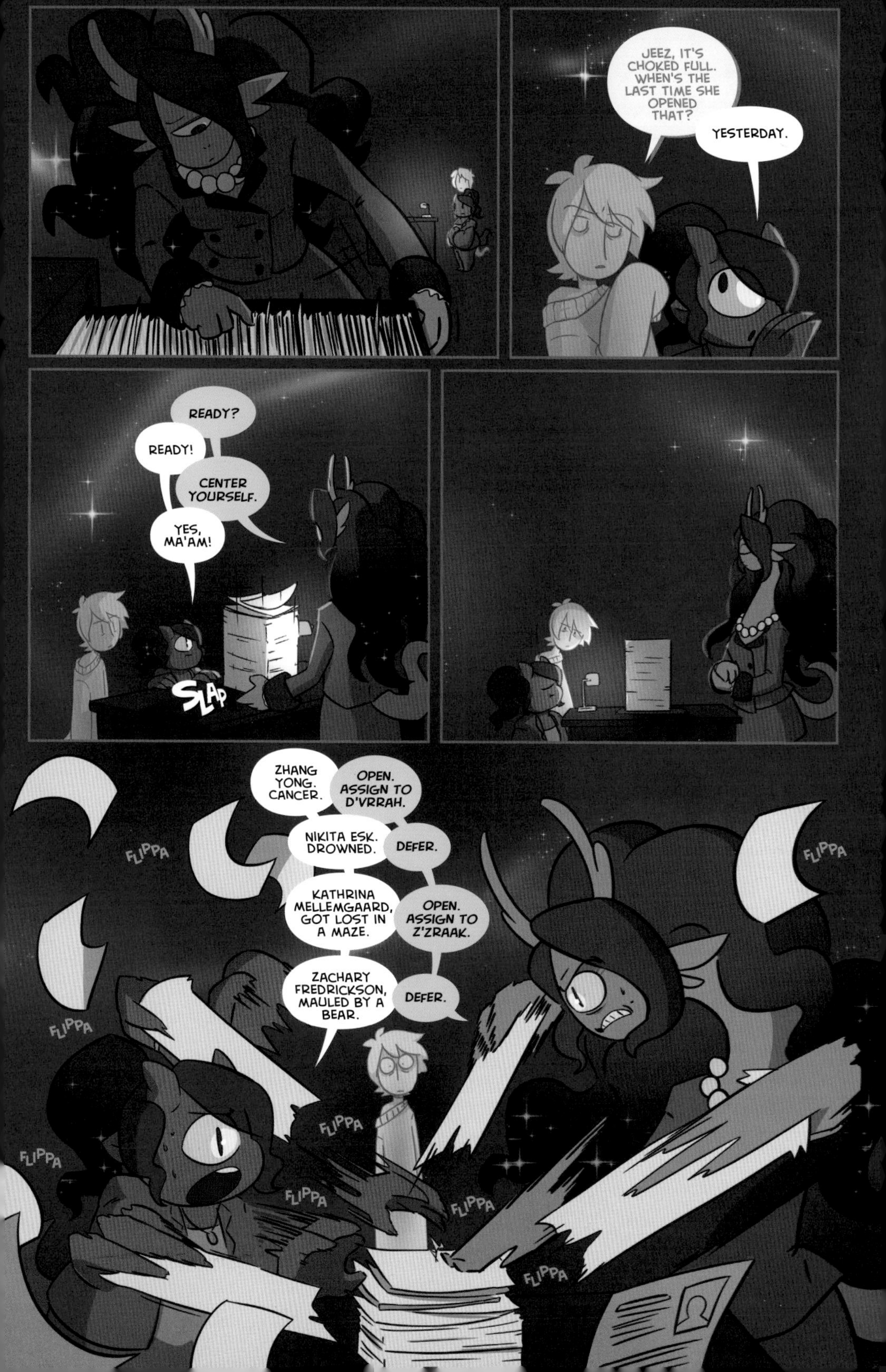
JEEZ, IT'S CHOKED FULL. WHEN'S THE LAST TIME SHE OPENED THAT?
YESTERDAY.
READY?
READY!
CENTER YOURSELF.
YES, MA'AM!
SLAP
ZHANG YONG. CANCER.
OPEN. ASSIGN TO D'VRRAH.
NIKITA ESK. DROWNED.
DEFER.
KATHRINA MELLEMGAARD, GOT LOST IN A MAZE.
OPEN. ASSIGN TO Z'ZRAAK.
ZACHARY FREDRICKSON, MAULED BY A BEAR.
DEFER.
FLIPPA
FLIPPA
FLIPPA
FLIPPA
FLIPPA
FLIPPA
FLIPPA
FLIPPA

SHALINI SENTHIL. HIT BY A BUS.

DEFER.

ADRIANNA SANTOS. HEART FAILURE.

OPEN. ASSIGN TO D'VRRAH.

FLIPPA FLIPPA FLIPPA FLIPPA FLIPPA FLIPPA FLIPPA

CARL SAMIS. PAPER CUT GOT INFECTED.

OPEN. ASSIGN TO V'QTTYR.

JENNI BATT. SANK IN A SWAMP.

OPEN. ASSIGN TO YOURSELF.

FLIPPA FLIPPA FLIPPA FLIPPA FLIPPA

CHLOE RITTER. FELL OFF A BUILDING.

DEFER.

CHANTELLE COETZEE. TRIED TO EAT A LIGHT BULB.

DEFER.

FLIPPA FLIPPA

GRACE--

HEY!!

HOW THE **HECK** CAN YOU GO THROUGH PEOPLE'S **LIVES**--ER, **DEATHS**--SO QUICKLY?

IS THIS HOW I WAS ASSIGNED TO XEL?

MMFFHR!

SLAP!

FLIPPA

FLIPPA

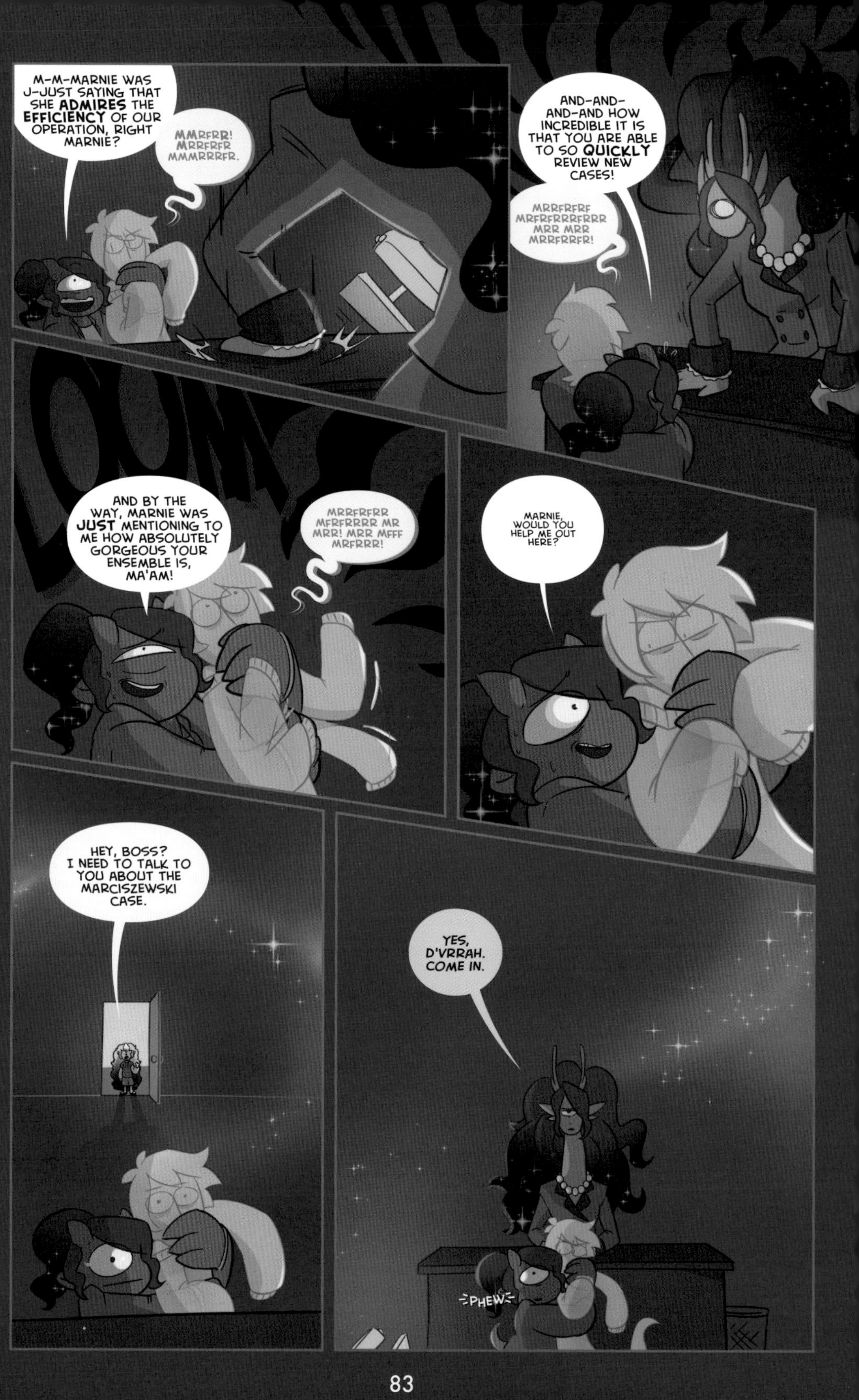
M-M-MARNIE WAS J-JUST SAYING THAT SHE **ADMIRES** THE **EFFICIENCY** OF OUR OPERATION, RIGHT MARNIE?
MMRFRR! MRRFRFR MMMRRRFR.
AND-AND-AND-AND HOW INCREDIBLE IT IS THAT YOU ARE ABLE TO SO **QUICKLY** REVIEW NEW CASES!
MRRFRFRF MRFRFRRRRFRRR MRR MRR MRRFRRFR!
AND BY THE WAY, MARNIE WAS **JUST** MENTIONING TO ME HOW ABSOLUTELY GORGEOUS YOUR ENSEMBLE IS, MA'AM!
MRRFRFRR MFRFRRRR MR MRR! MRR MFFF MRFRRR!
MARNIE, WOULD YOU HELP ME OUT HERE?
HEY, BOSS? I NEED TO TALK TO YOU ABOUT THE MARCISZEWSKI CASE.
YES, D'VRRAH. COME IN.
PHEW

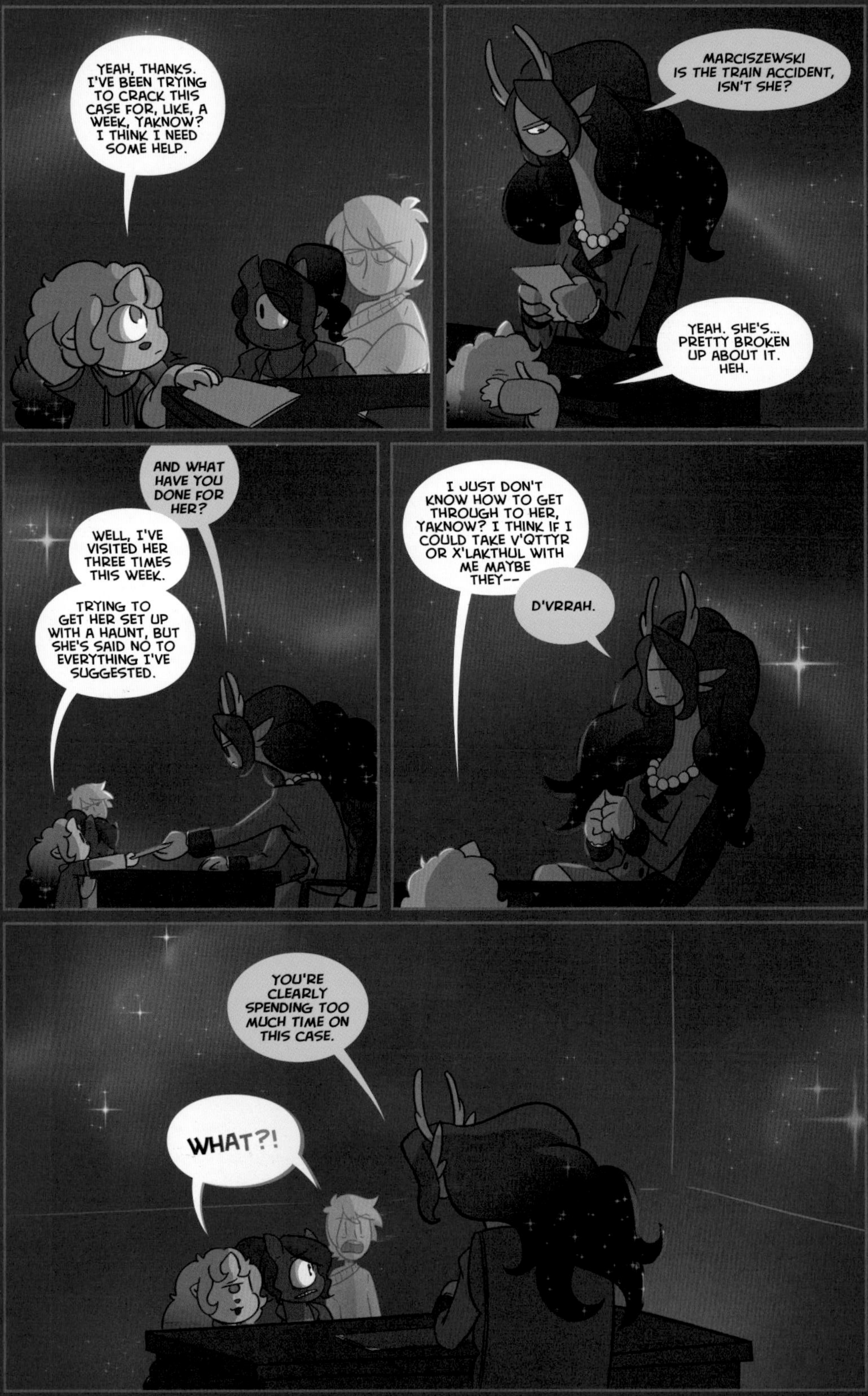
YEAH, THANKS. I'VE BEEN TRYING TO CRACK THIS CASE FOR, LIKE, A WEEK, YAKNOW? I THINK I NEED SOME HELP.
MARCISZEWSKI IS THE TRAIN ACCIDENT, ISN'T SHE?
YEAH. SHE'S... PRETTY BROKEN UP ABOUT IT. HEH.
AND WHAT HAVE YOU DONE FOR HER?
WELL, I'VE VISITED HER THREE TIMES THIS WEEK.
TRYING TO GET HER SET UP WITH A HAUNT, BUT SHE'S SAID NO TO EVERYTHING I'VE SUGGESTED.
I JUST DON'T KNOW HOW TO GET THROUGH TO HER, YAKNOW? I THINK IF I COULD TAKE V'QTTYR OR X'LAKTHUL WITH ME MAYBE THEY--
D'VRRAH.
YOU'RE CLEARLY SPENDING TOO MUCH TIME ON THIS CASE.
WHAT?!

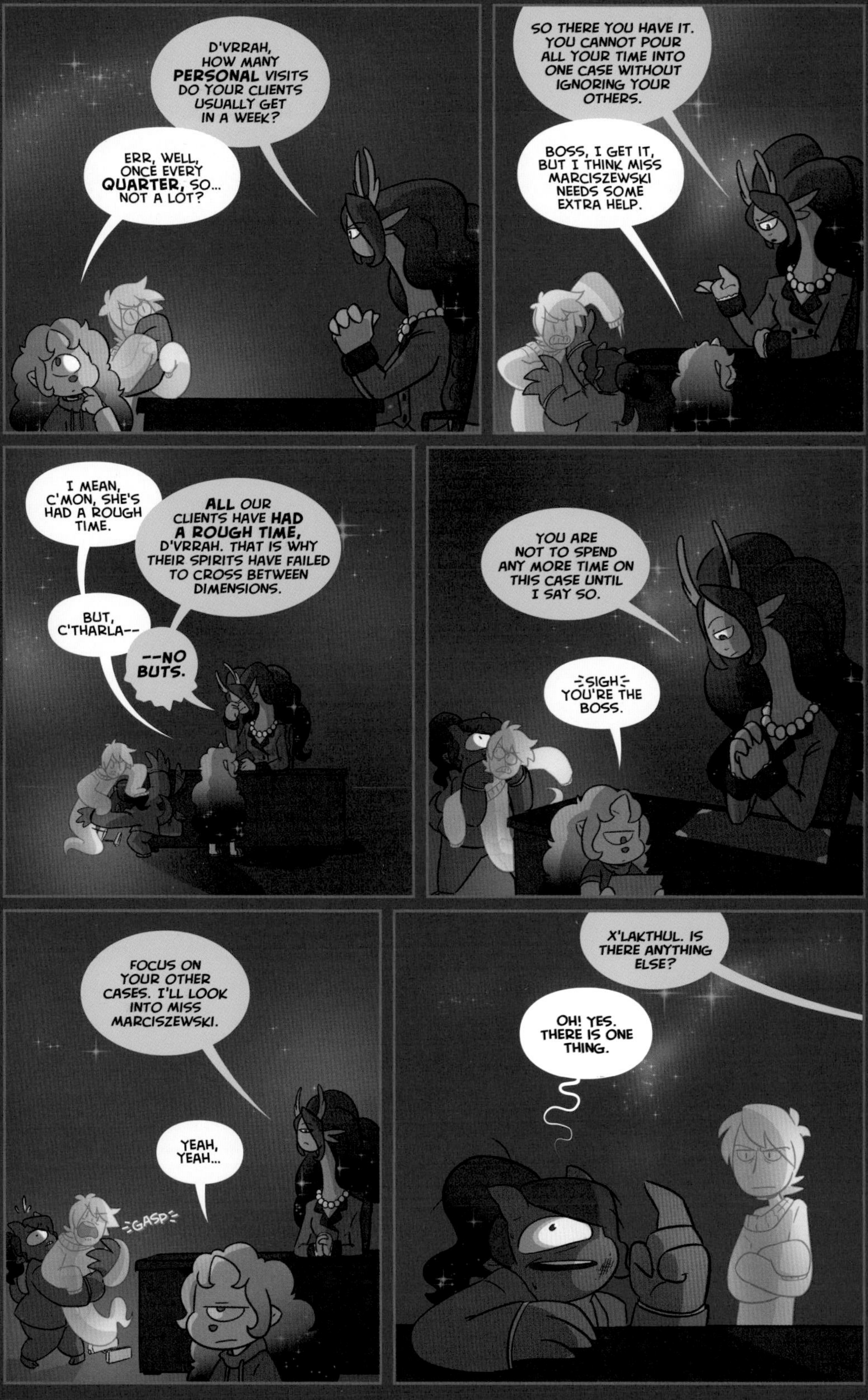
D'VRRAH, HOW MANY **PERSONAL** VISITS DO YOUR CLIENTS USUALLY GET IN A WEEK?
ERR, WELL, ONCE EVERY **QUARTER,** SO... NOT A LOT?
SO THERE YOU HAVE IT. YOU CANNOT POUR ALL YOUR TIME INTO ONE CASE WITHOUT IGNORING YOUR OTHERS.
BOSS, I GET IT, BUT I THINK MISS MARCISZEWSKI NEEDS SOME EXTRA HELP.
I MEAN, C'MON, SHE'S HAD A ROUGH TIME.
ALL OUR CLIENTS HAVE **HAD A ROUGH TIME,** D'VRRAH. THAT IS WHY THEIR SPIRITS HAVE FAILED TO CROSS BETWEEN DIMENSIONS.
BUT, C'THARLA--
--NO BUTS.
YOU ARE NOT TO SPEND ANY MORE TIME ON THIS CASE UNTIL I SAY SO.
SIGH YOU'RE THE BOSS.
FOCUS ON YOUR OTHER CASES. I'LL LOOK INTO MISS MARCISZEWSKI.
YEAH, YEAH...
GASP
X'LAKTHUL. IS THERE ANYTHING ELSE?
OH! YES. THERE IS ONE THING.

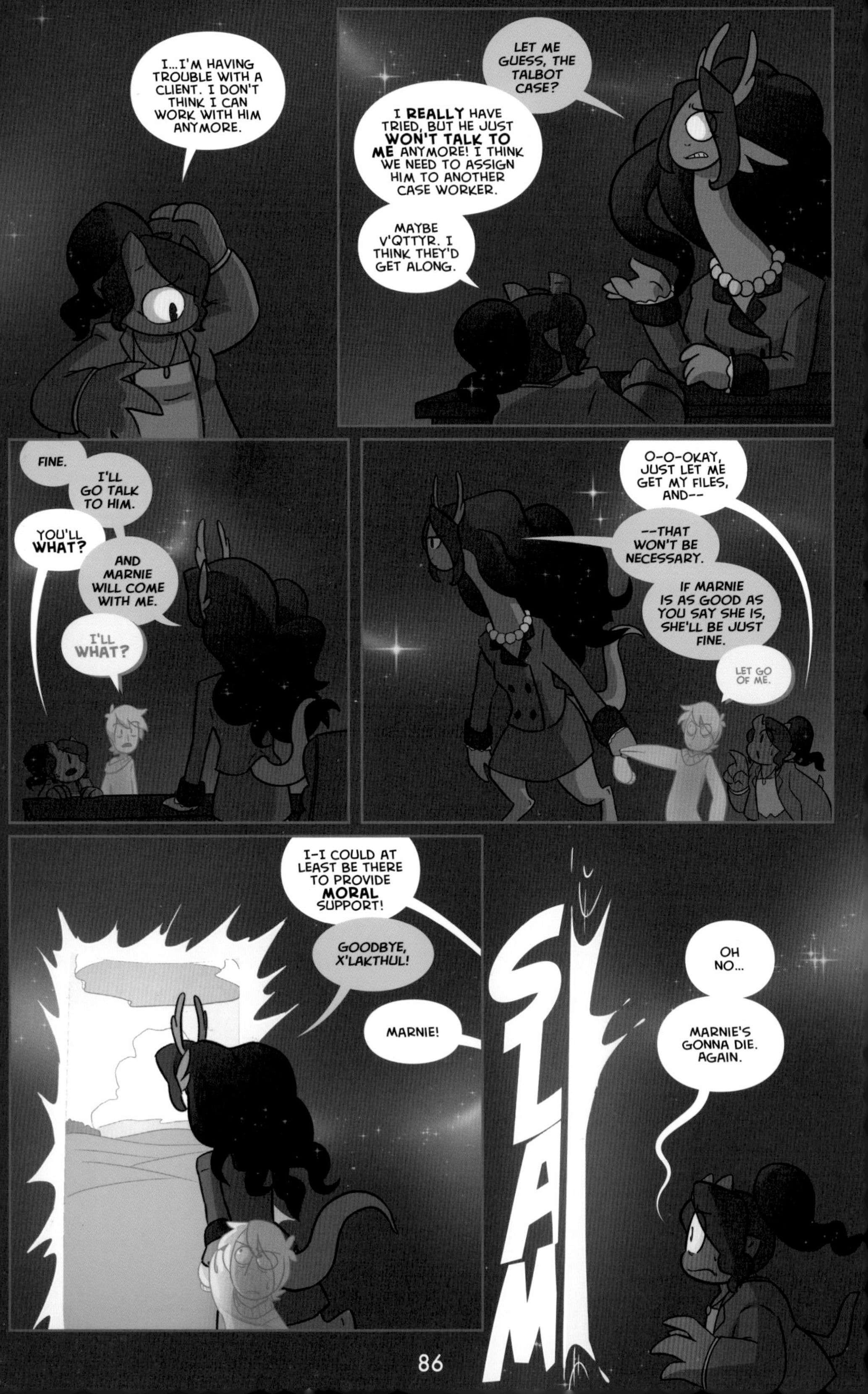
I...I'M HAVING TROUBLE WITH A CLIENT. I DON'T THINK I CAN WORK WITH HIM ANYMORE.
LET ME GUESS, THE TALBOT CASE?
I **REALLY** HAVE TRIED, BUT HE JUST **WON'T TALK TO ME** ANYMORE! I THINK WE NEED TO ASSIGN HIM TO ANOTHER CASE WORKER.
MAYBE V'QTTYR. I THINK THEY'D GET ALONG.
FINE.
I'LL GO TALK TO HIM.
YOU'LL **WHAT?**
AND MARNIE WILL COME WITH ME.
I'LL **WHAT?**
O-O-OKAY, JUST LET ME GET MY FILES, AND--
--THAT WON'T BE NECESSARY.
IF MARNIE IS AS GOOD AS YOU SAY SHE IS, SHE'LL BE JUST FINE.
LET GO OF ME.
I-I COULD AT LEAST BE THERE TO PROVIDE **MORAL** SUPPORT!
GOODBYE, X'LAKTHUL!
MARNIE!
SLAM
OH NO...
MARNIE'S GONNA DIE. AGAIN.

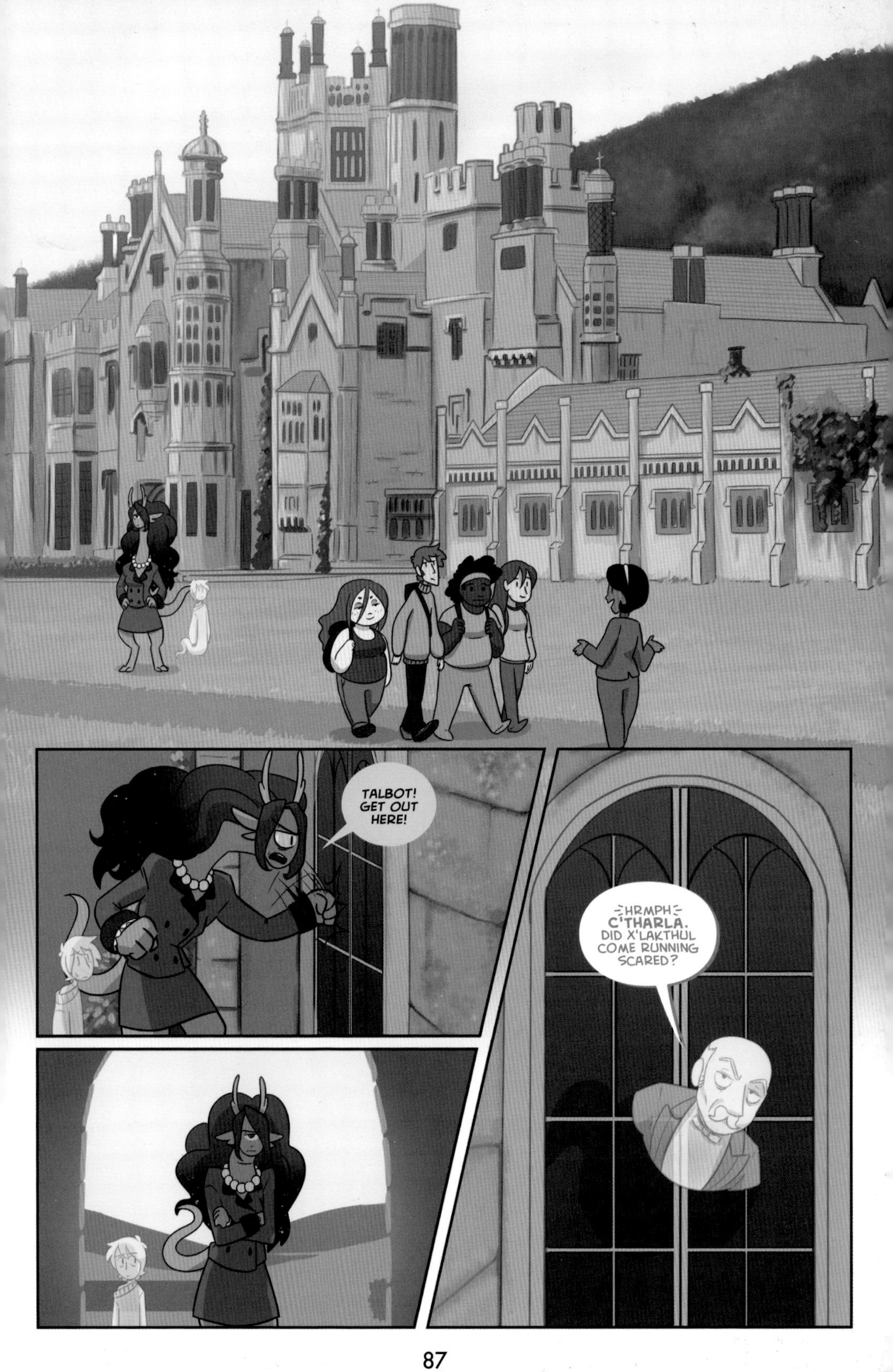
TALBOT! GET OUT HERE!
HRMPH C'THARLA. DID X'LAKTHUL COME RUNNING SCARED?

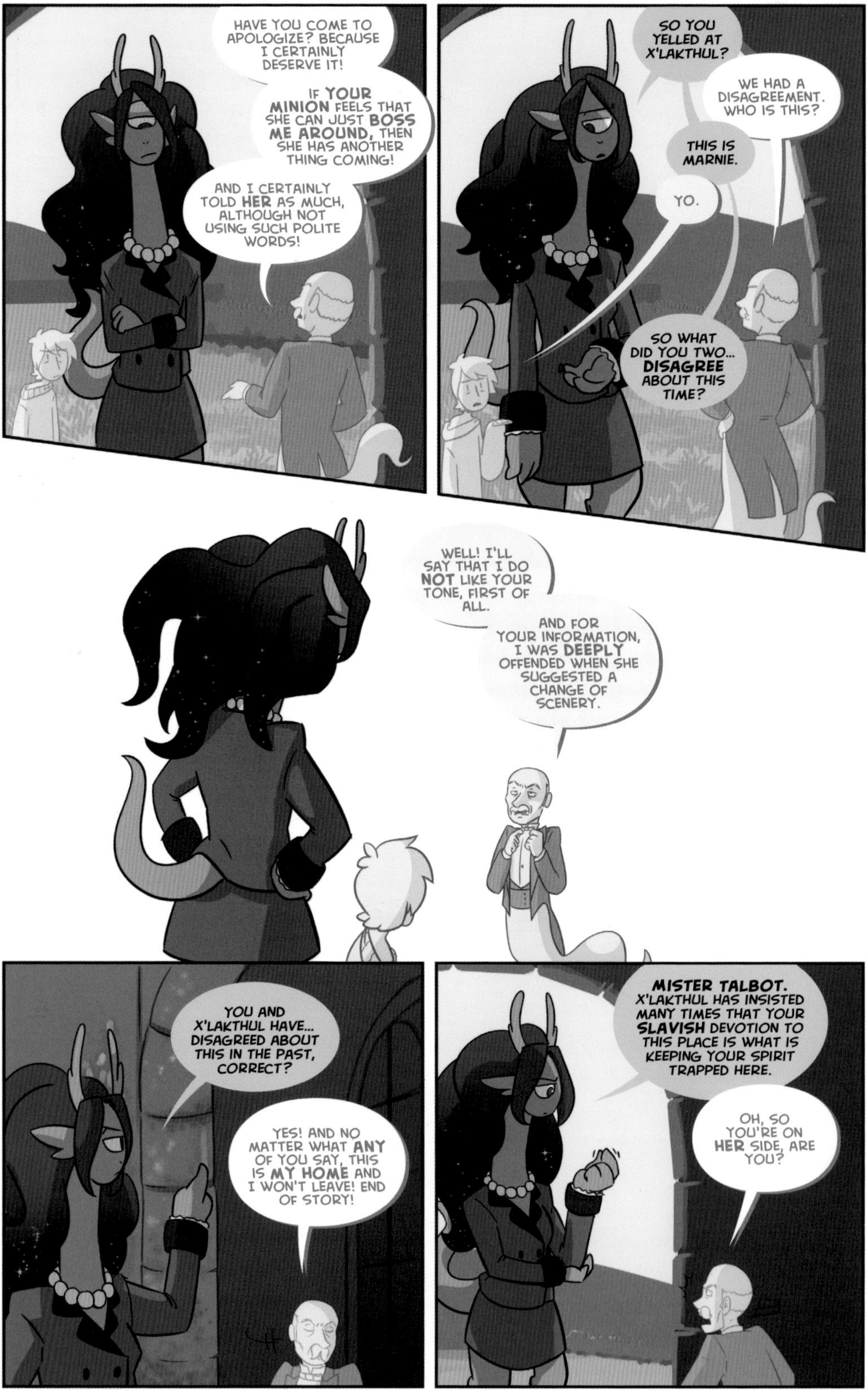
HAVE YOU COME TO APOLOGIZE? BECAUSE I CERTAINLY DESERVE IT!
IF YOUR MINION FEELS THAT SHE CAN JUST BOSS ME AROUND, THEN SHE HAS ANOTHER THING COMING!
AND I CERTAINLY TOLD HER AS MUCH, ALTHOUGH NOT USING SUCH POLITE WORDS!
SO YOU YELLED AT X'LAKTHUL?
WE HAD A DISAGREEMENT. WHO IS THIS?
THIS IS MARNIE.
YO.
SO WHAT DID YOU TWO... DISAGREE ABOUT THIS TIME?
WELL! I'LL SAY THAT I DO NOT LIKE YOUR TONE, FIRST OF ALL.
AND FOR YOUR INFORMATION, I WAS DEEPLY OFFENDED WHEN SHE SUGGESTED A CHANGE OF SCENERY.
YOU AND X'LAKTHUL HAVE... DISAGREED ABOUT THIS IN THE PAST, CORRECT?
YES! AND NO MATTER WHAT ANY OF YOU SAY, THIS IS MY HOME AND I WON'T LEAVE! END OF STORY!
MISTER TALBOT. X'LAKTHUL HAS INSISTED MANY TIMES THAT YOUR SLAVISH DEVOTION TO THIS PLACE IS WHAT IS KEEPING YOUR SPIRIT TRAPPED HERE.
OH, SO YOU'RE ON HER SIDE, ARE YOU?

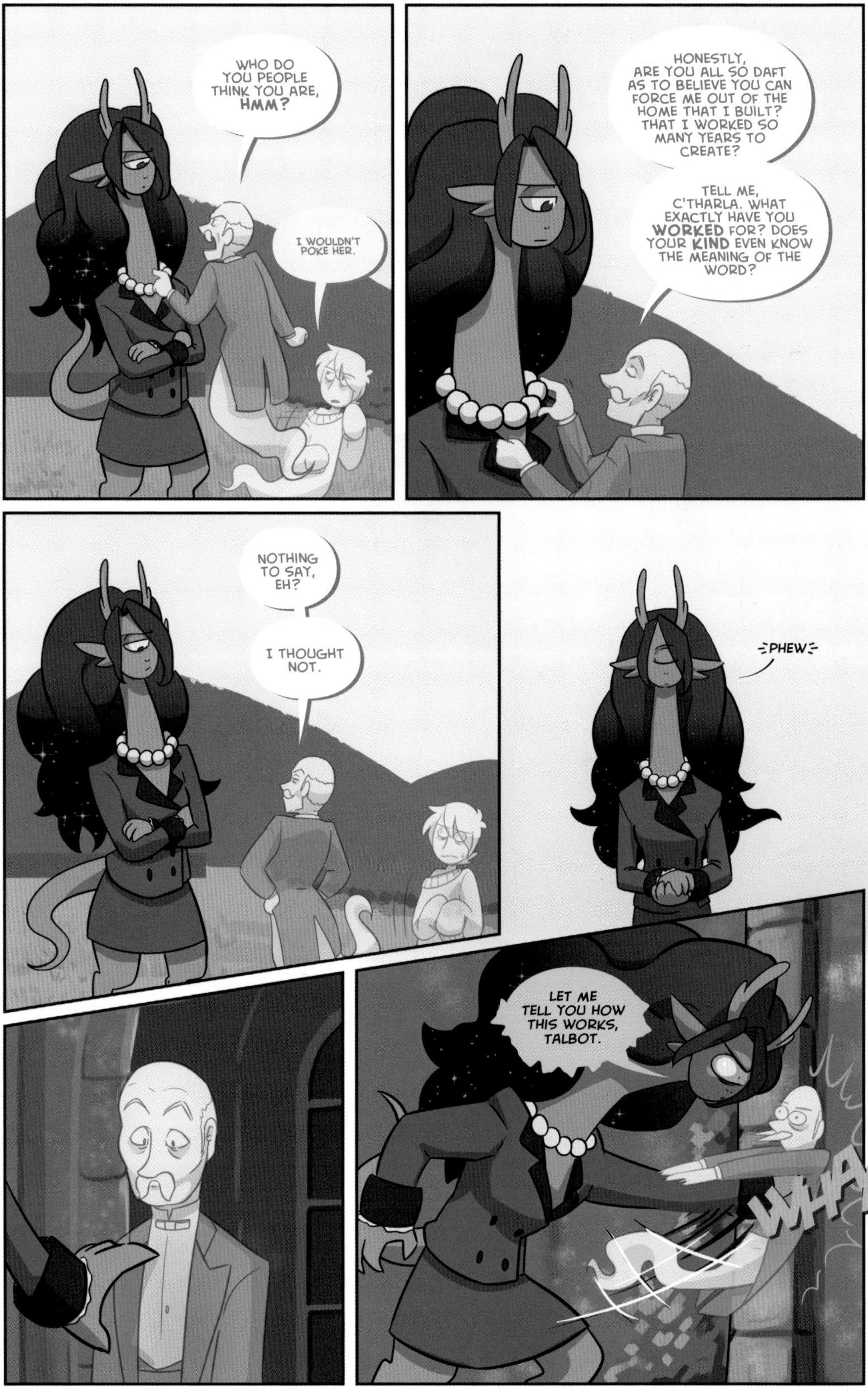
WHO DO YOU PEOPLE THINK YOU ARE, HMM?
I WOULDN'T POKE HER.
HONESTLY, ARE YOU ALL SO DAFT AS TO BELIEVE YOU CAN FORCE ME OUT OF THE HOME THAT I BUILT? THAT I WORKED SO MANY YEARS TO CREATE?
TELL ME, C'THARLA. WHAT EXACTLY HAVE YOU WORKED FOR? DOES YOUR KIND EVEN KNOW THE MEANING OF THE WORD?
NOTHING TO SAY, EH?
I THOUGHT NOT.
PHEW
LET ME TELL YOU HOW THIS WORKS, TALBOT.
WHAM

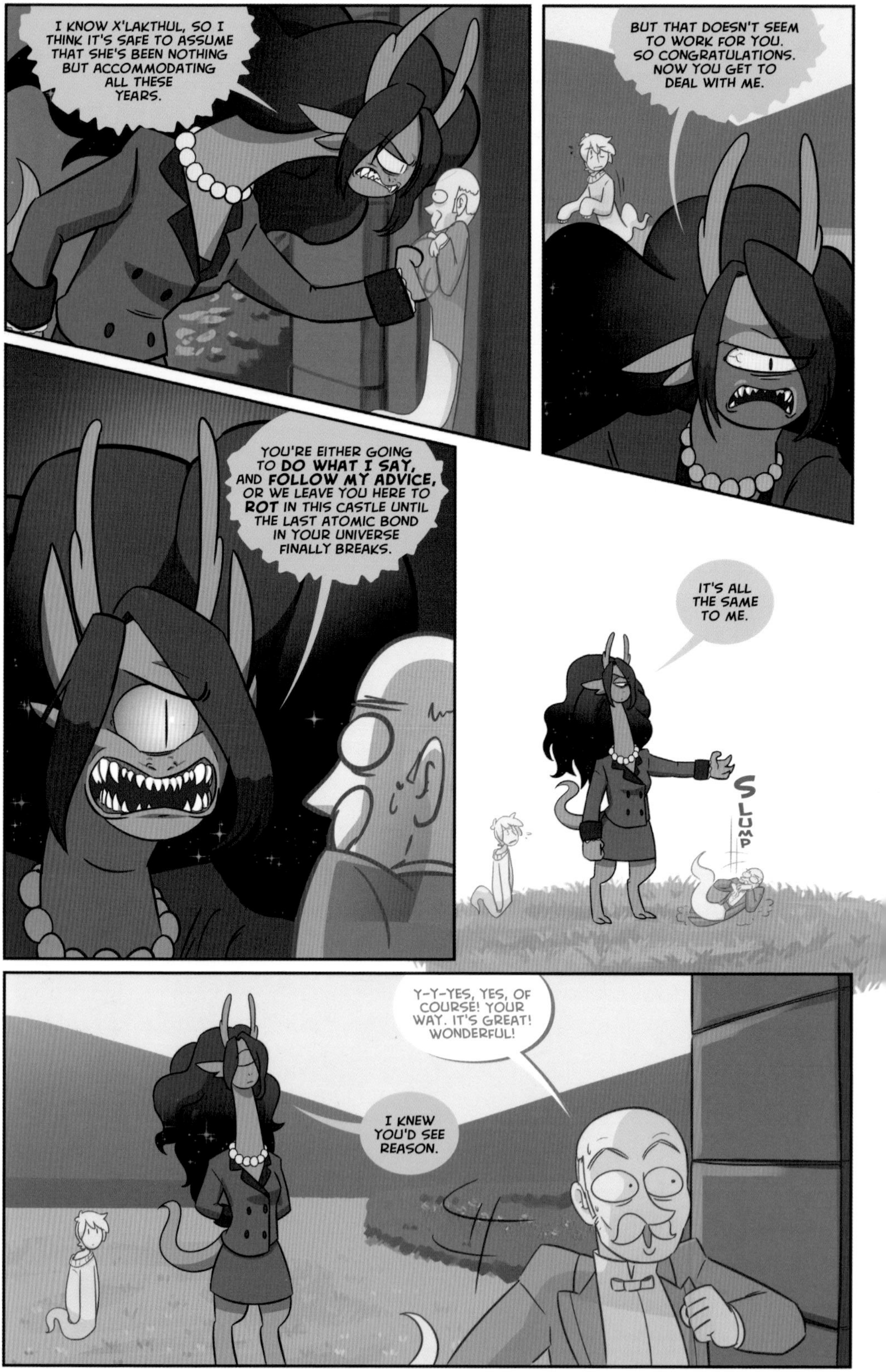
I KNOW X'LAKTHUL, SO I THINK IT'S SAFE TO ASSUME THAT SHE'S BEEN NOTHING BUT ACCOMMODATING ALL THESE YEARS.
BUT THAT DOESN'T SEEM TO WORK FOR YOU. SO CONGRATULATIONS. NOW YOU GET TO DEAL WITH ME.
YOU'RE EITHER GOING TO DO WHAT I SAY, AND FOLLOW MY ADVICE, OR WE LEAVE YOU HERE TO ROT IN THIS CASTLE UNTIL THE LAST ATOMIC BOND IN YOUR UNIVERSE FINALLY BREAKS.
IT'S ALL THE SAME TO ME.
SLUMP
Y-Y-YES, YES, OF COURSE! YOUR WAY. IT'S GREAT! WONDERFUL!
I KNEW YOU'D SEE REASON.

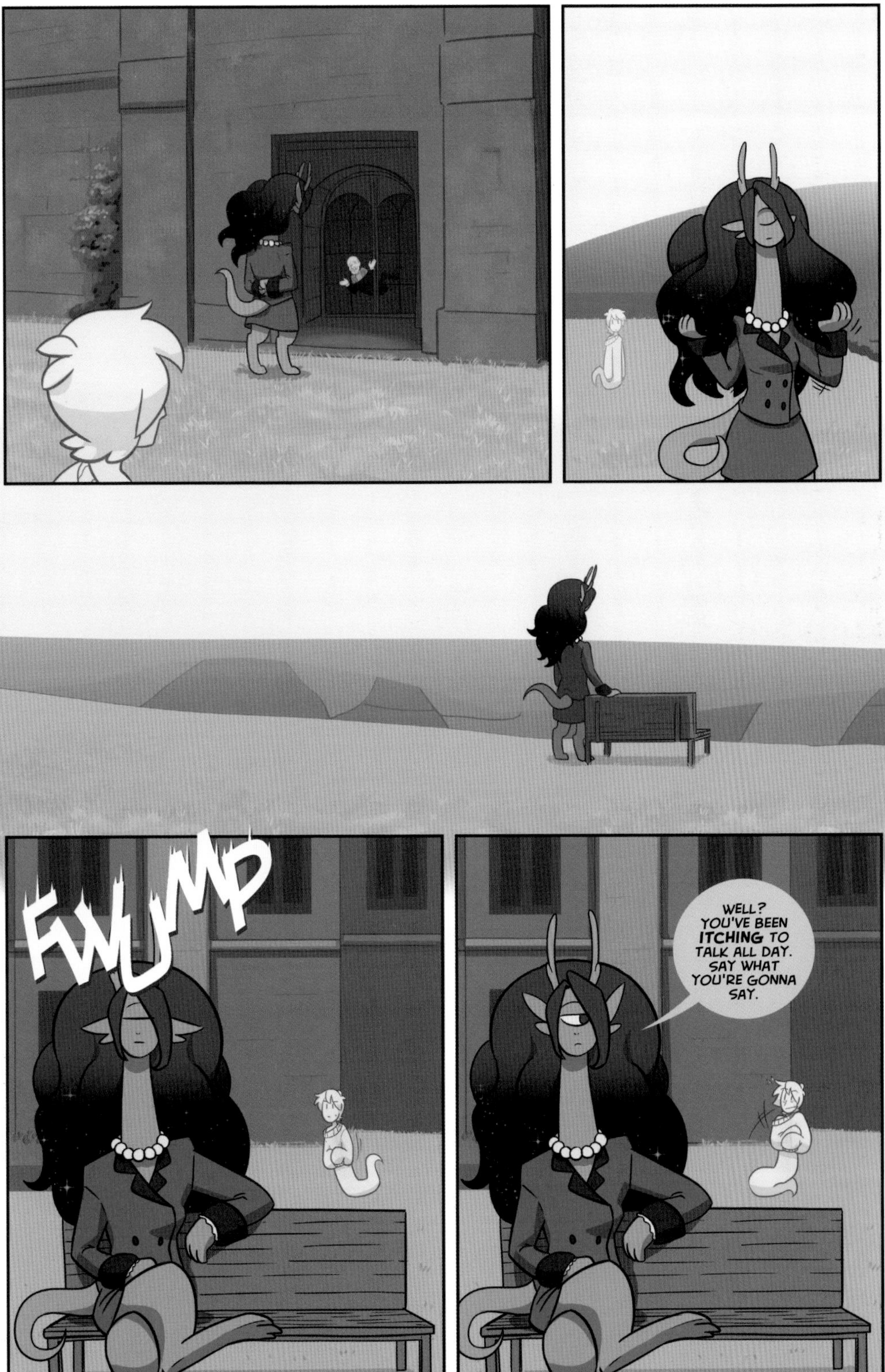
FWUMP
WELL? YOU'VE BEEN ITCHING TO TALK ALL DAY. SAY WHAT YOU'RE GONNA SAY.

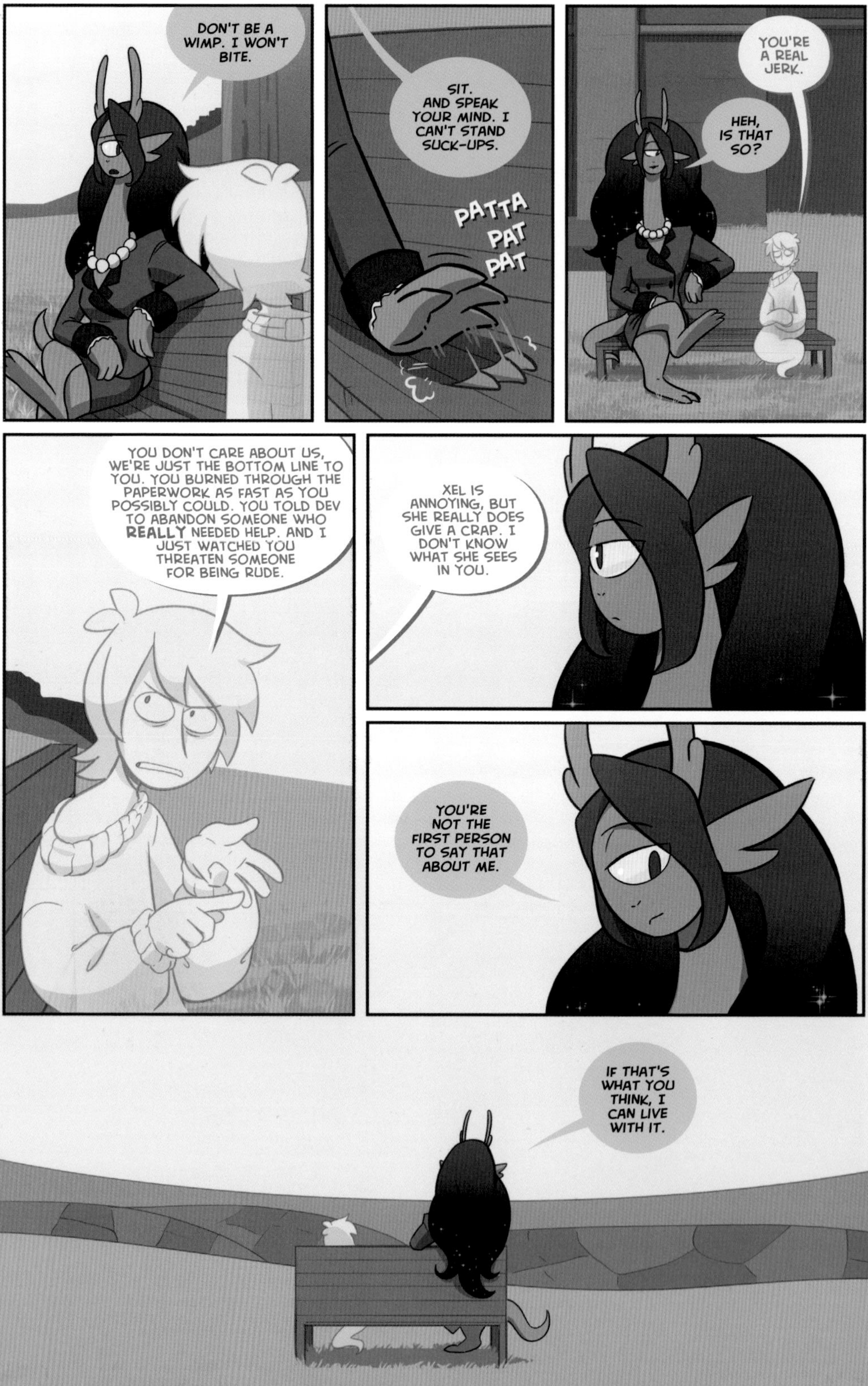
DON'T BE A WIMP. I WON'T BITE.
SIT. AND SPEAK YOUR MIND. I CAN'T STAND SUCK-UPS.
PATTA PAT PAT
YOU'RE A REAL JERK.
HEH, IS THAT SO?
YOU DON'T CARE ABOUT US, WE'RE JUST THE BOTTOM LINE TO YOU. YOU BURNED THROUGH THE PAPERWORK AS FAST AS YOU POSSIBLY COULD. YOU TOLD DEV TO ABANDON SOMEONE WHO REALLY NEEDED HELP. AND I JUST WATCHED YOU THREATEN SOMEONE FOR BEING RUDE.
XEL IS ANNOYING, BUT SHE REALLY DOES GIVE A CRAP. I DON'T KNOW WHAT SHE SEES IN YOU.
YOU'RE NOT THE FIRST PERSON TO SAY THAT ABOUT ME.
IF THAT'S WHAT YOU THINK, I CAN LIVE WITH IT.

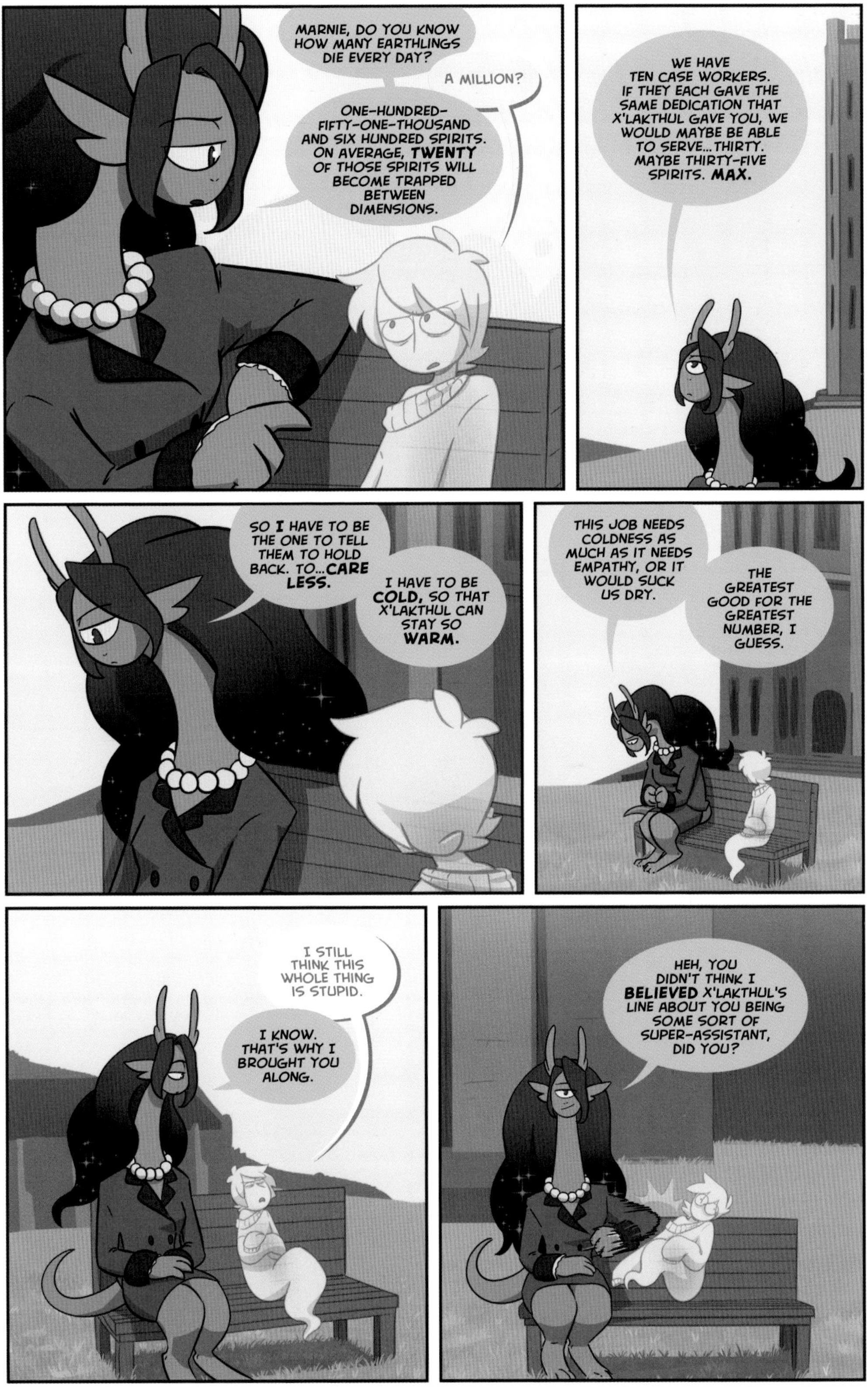
MARNIE, DO YOU KNOW HOW MANY EARTHLINGS DIE EVERY DAY?
A MILLION?
ONE-HUNDRED-FIFTY-ONE-THOUSAND AND SIX HUNDRED SPIRITS. ON AVERAGE, **TWENTY** OF THOSE SPIRITS WILL BECOME TRAPPED BETWEEN DIMENSIONS.
WE HAVE TEN CASE WORKERS. IF THEY EACH GAVE THE SAME DEDICATION THAT X'LAKTHUL GAVE YOU, WE WOULD MAYBE BE ABLE TO SERVE... THIRTY. MAYBE THIRTY-FIVE SPIRITS. **MAX.**
SO **I** HAVE TO BE THE ONE TO TELL THEM TO HOLD BACK. TO... **CARE LESS.**
I HAVE TO BE **COLD,** SO THAT X'LAKTHUL CAN STAY SO **WARM.**
THIS JOB NEEDS COLDNESS AS MUCH AS IT NEEDS EMPATHY, OR IT WOULD SUCK US DRY.
THE GREATEST GOOD FOR THE GREATEST NUMBER, I GUESS.
I STILL THINK THIS WHOLE THING IS STUPID.
I KNOW. THAT'S WHY I BROUGHT YOU ALONG.
HEH, YOU DIDN'T THINK I **BELIEVED** X'LAKTHUL'S LINE ABOUT YOU BEING SOME SORT OF SUPER-ASSISTANT, DID YOU?

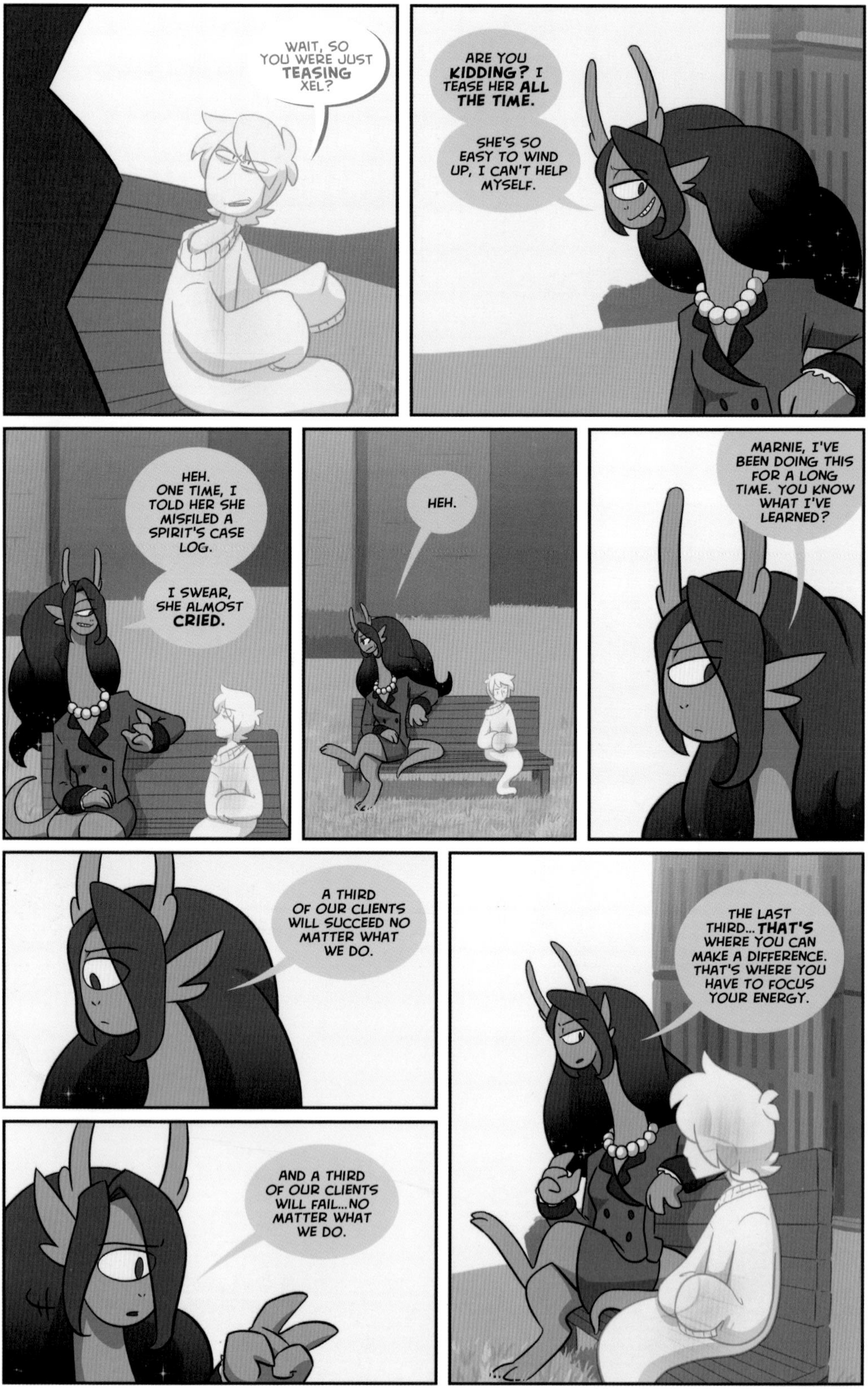
WAIT, SO YOU WERE JUST **TEASING** XEL?
ARE YOU **KIDDING?** I TEASE HER **ALL THE TIME.**
SHE'S SO EASY TO WIND UP, I CAN'T HELP MYSELF.
HEH. ONE TIME, I TOLD HER SHE MISFILED A SPIRIT'S CASE LOG.
I SWEAR, SHE ALMOST **CRIED.**
HEH.
MARNIE, I'VE BEEN DOING THIS FOR A LONG TIME. YOU KNOW WHAT I'VE LEARNED?
A THIRD OF OUR CLIENTS WILL SUCCEED NO MATTER WHAT WE DO.
AND A THIRD OF OUR CLIENTS WILL FAIL...NO MATTER WHAT WE DO.
THE LAST THIRD... **THAT'S** WHERE YOU CAN MAKE A DIFFERENCE. THAT'S WHERE YOU HAVE TO FOCUS YOUR ENERGY.

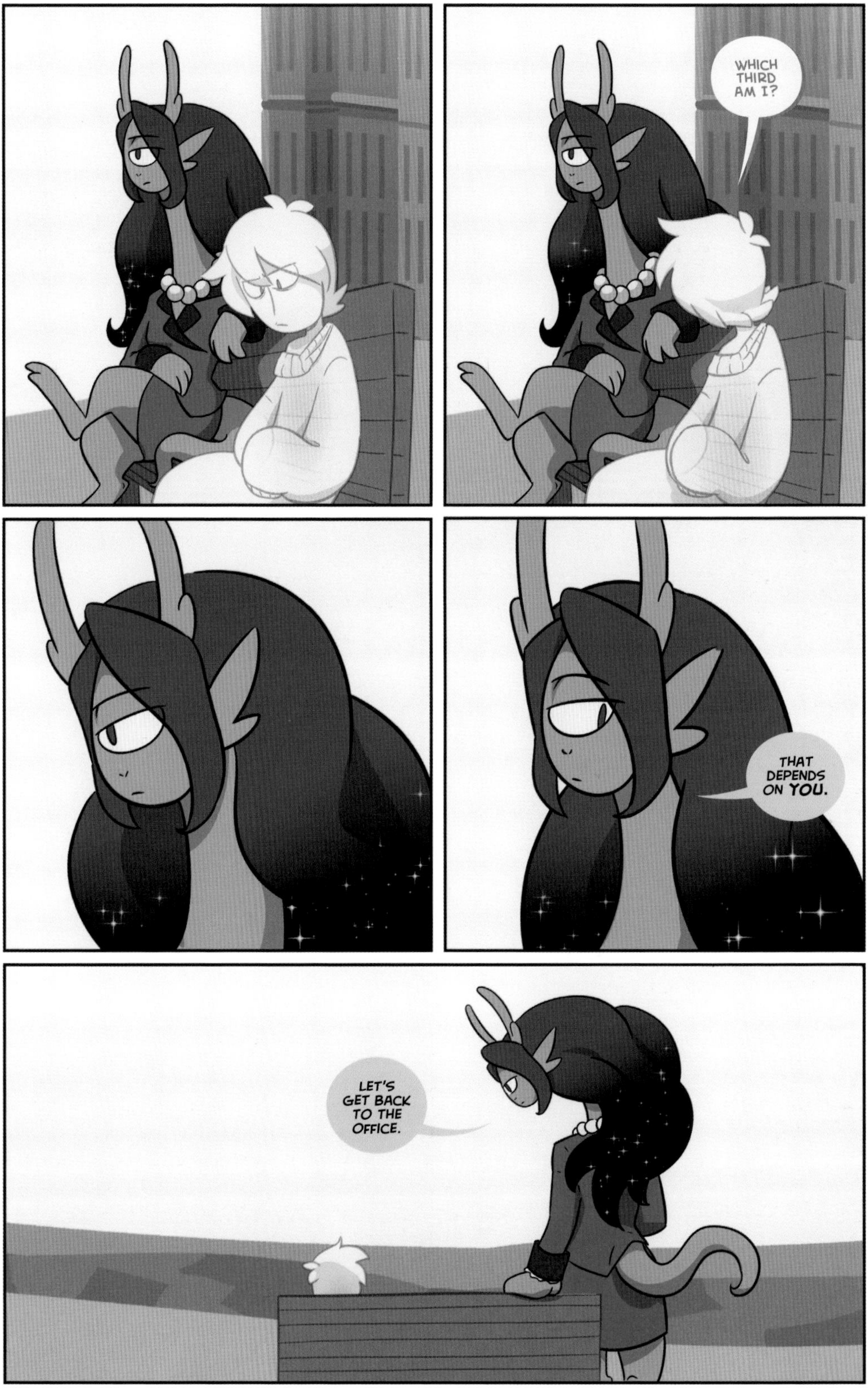
WHICH THIRD AM I?
THAT DEPENDS ON **YOU.**
LET'S GET BACK TO THE OFFICE.

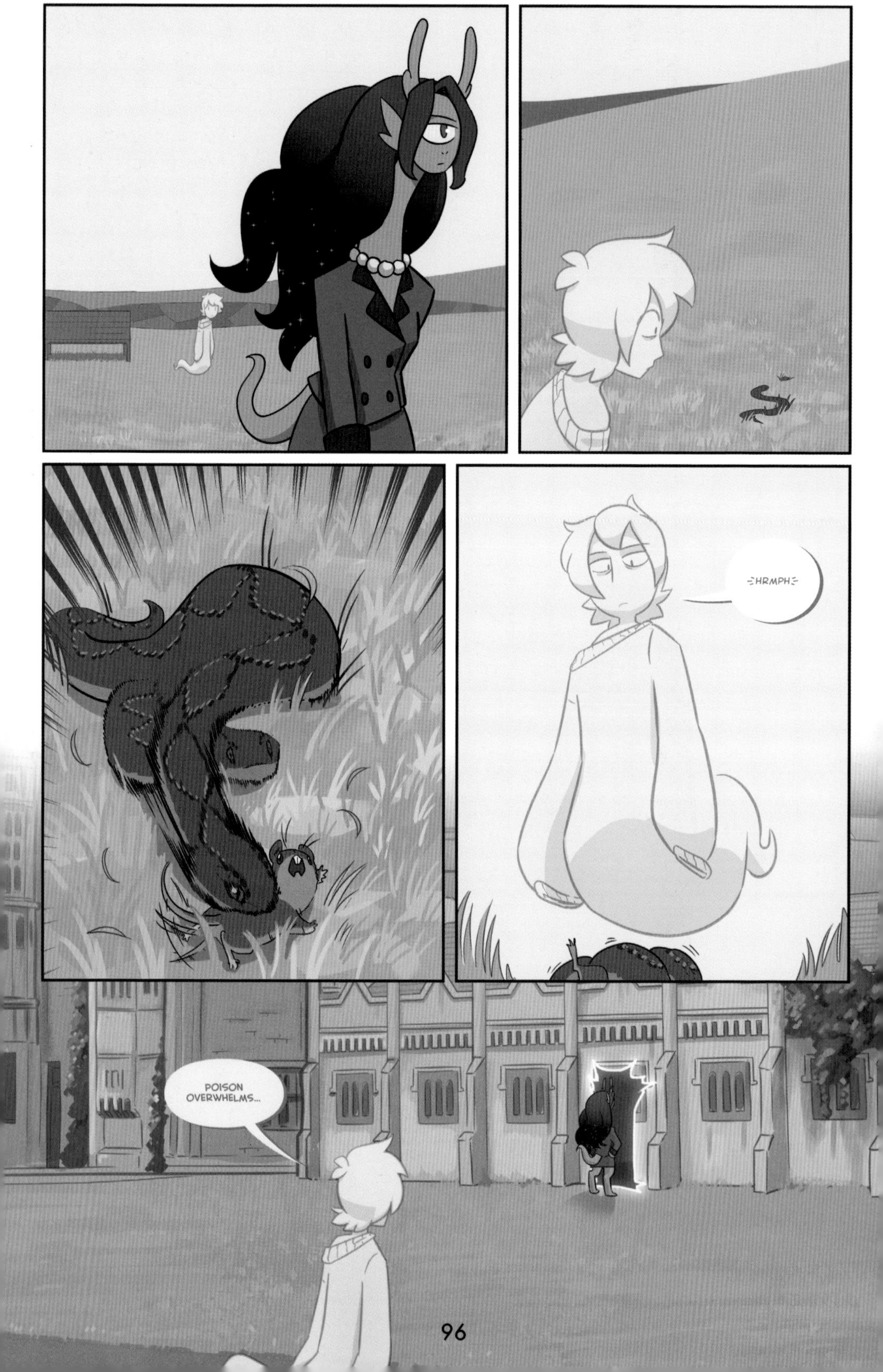
HRMPH
POISON OVERWHELMS...

Department
of
Spectral Affairs

Chapter 4

Carol

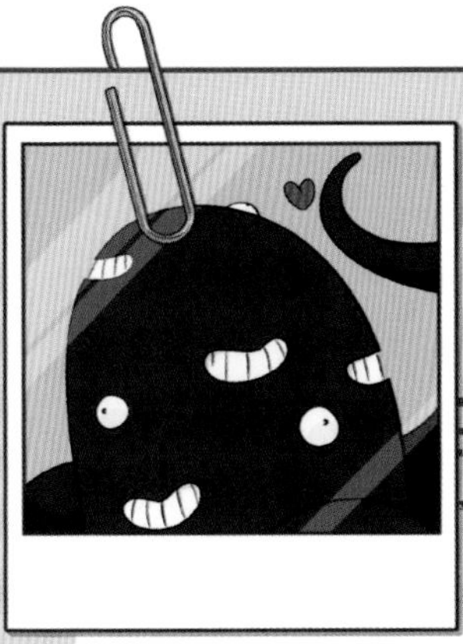

FOR OFFICIAL USE ONLY

Name: Carol

Pronunciation: Care-ol

Pronouns: they/them

Age: 500,001

Position: Office administrator

Likes: Weekend barbecues, long slithers on the beach, romance, small talk.

Dislikes: Scary movies

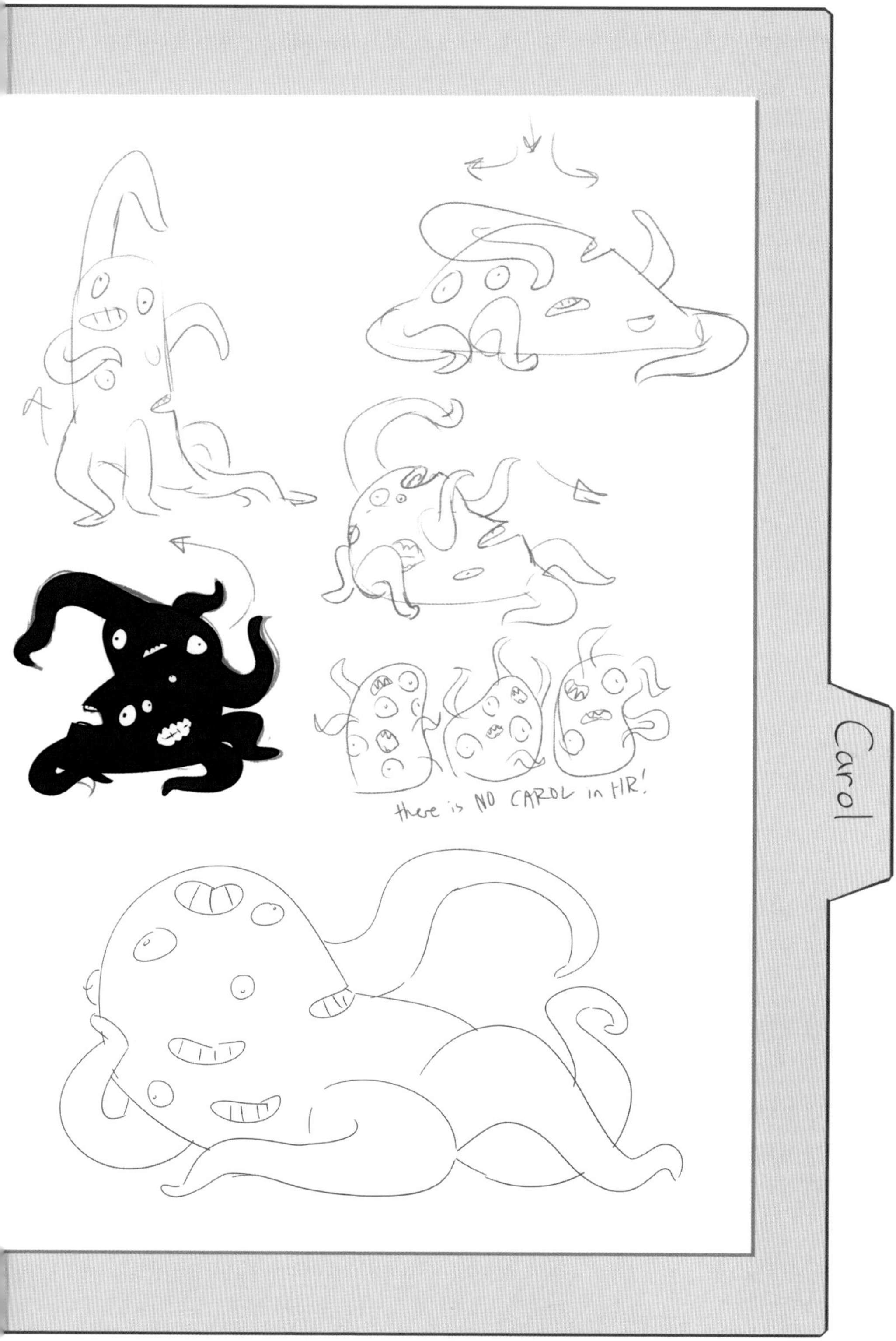
there is NO CAROL in HR!
Carol

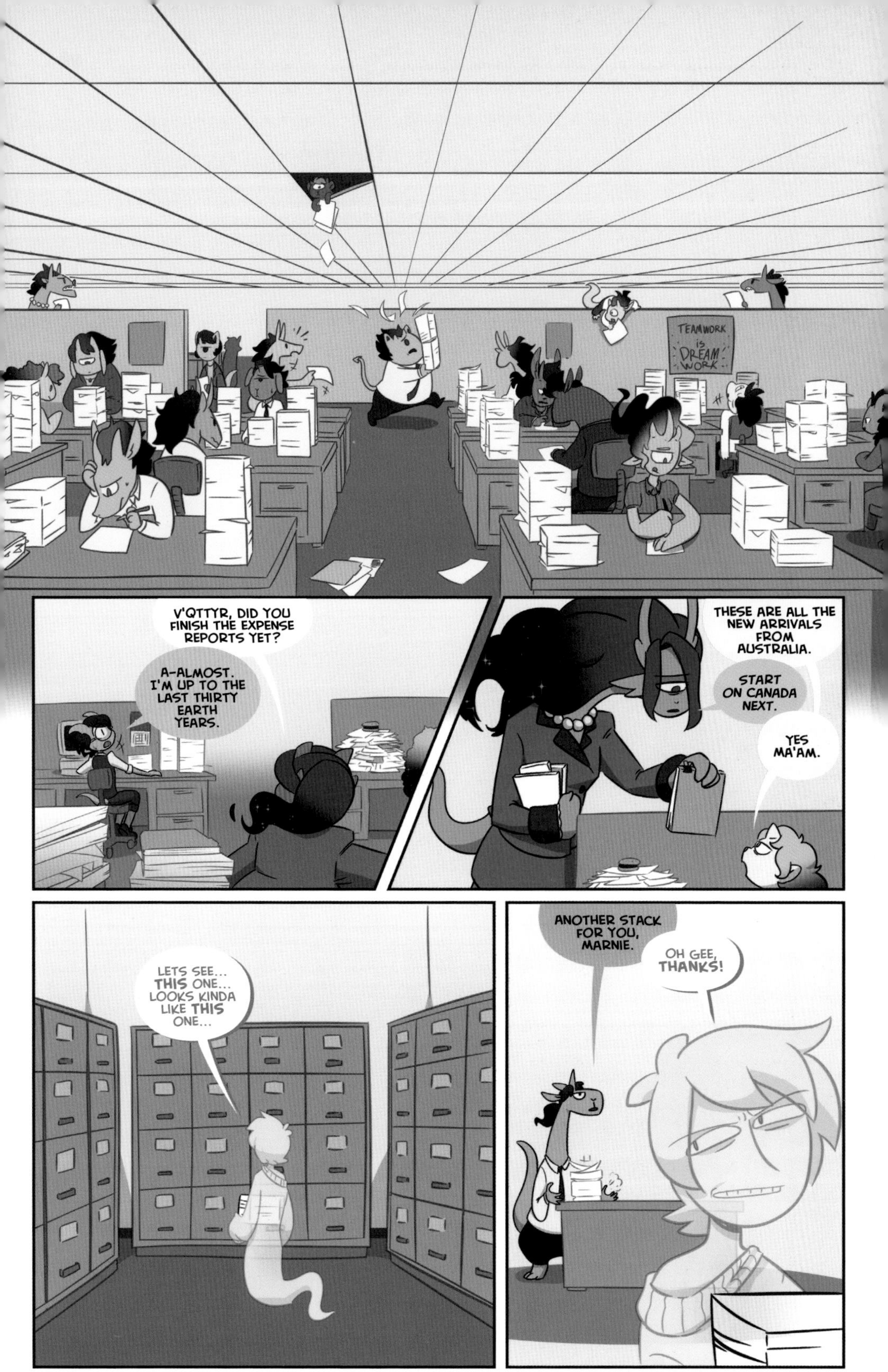
TEAMWORK is DREAM WORK
V'QTTYR, DID YOU FINISH THE EXPENSE REPORTS YET?
A-ALMOST. I'M UP TO THE LAST THIRTY EARTH YEARS.
THESE ARE ALL THE NEW ARRIVALS FROM AUSTRALIA.
START ON CANADA NEXT.
YES MA'AM.
LETS SEE... THIS ONE... LOOKS KINDA LIKE THIS ONE...
ANOTHER STACK FOR YOU, MARNIE.
OH GEE, THANKS!

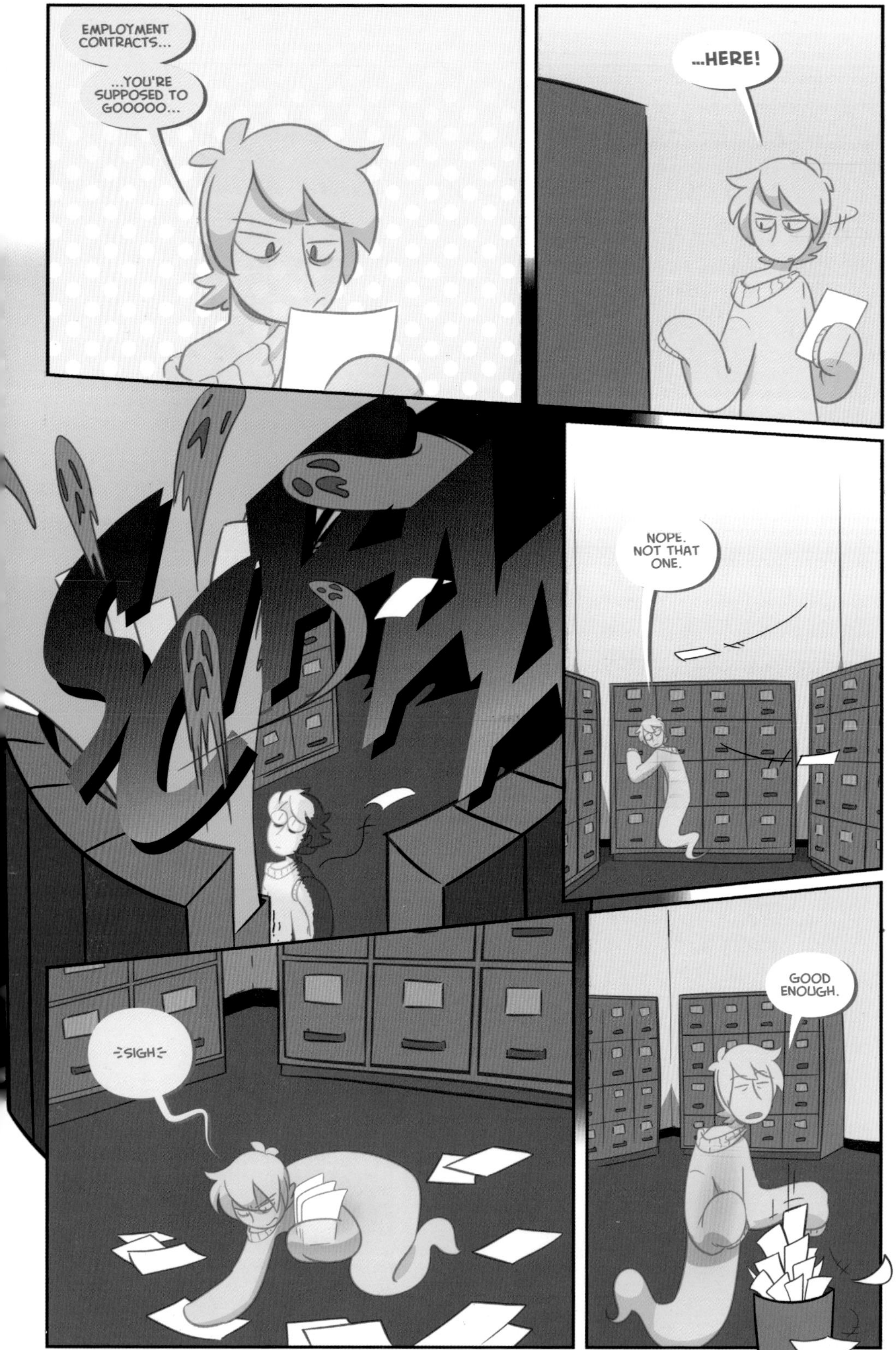
EMPLOYMENT CONTRACTS...
...YOU'RE SUPPOSED TO GOOOOO...
...HERE!
NOPE. NOT THAT ONE.
SIGH
GOOD ENOUGH.

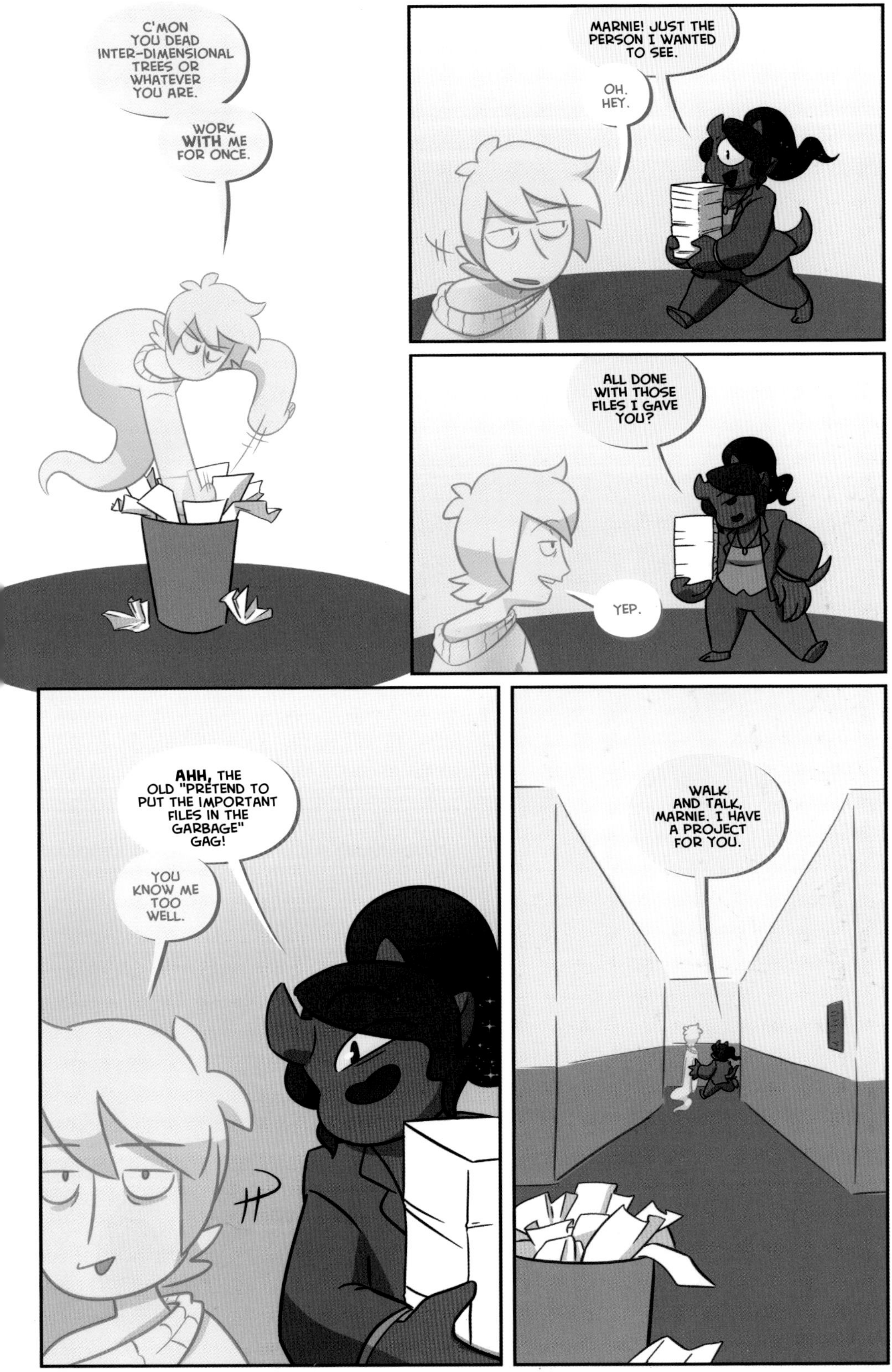
C'MON YOU DEAD INTER-DIMENSIONAL TREES OR WHATEVER YOU ARE.
WORK **WITH** ME FOR ONCE.
MARNIE! JUST THE PERSON I WANTED TO SEE.
OH. HEY.
ALL DONE WITH THOSE FILES I GAVE YOU?
YEP.
AHH, THE OLD "PRETEND TO PUT THE IMPORTANT FILES IN THE GARBAGE" GAG!
YOU KNOW ME TOO WELL.
WALK AND TALK, MARNIE. I HAVE A PROJECT FOR YOU.

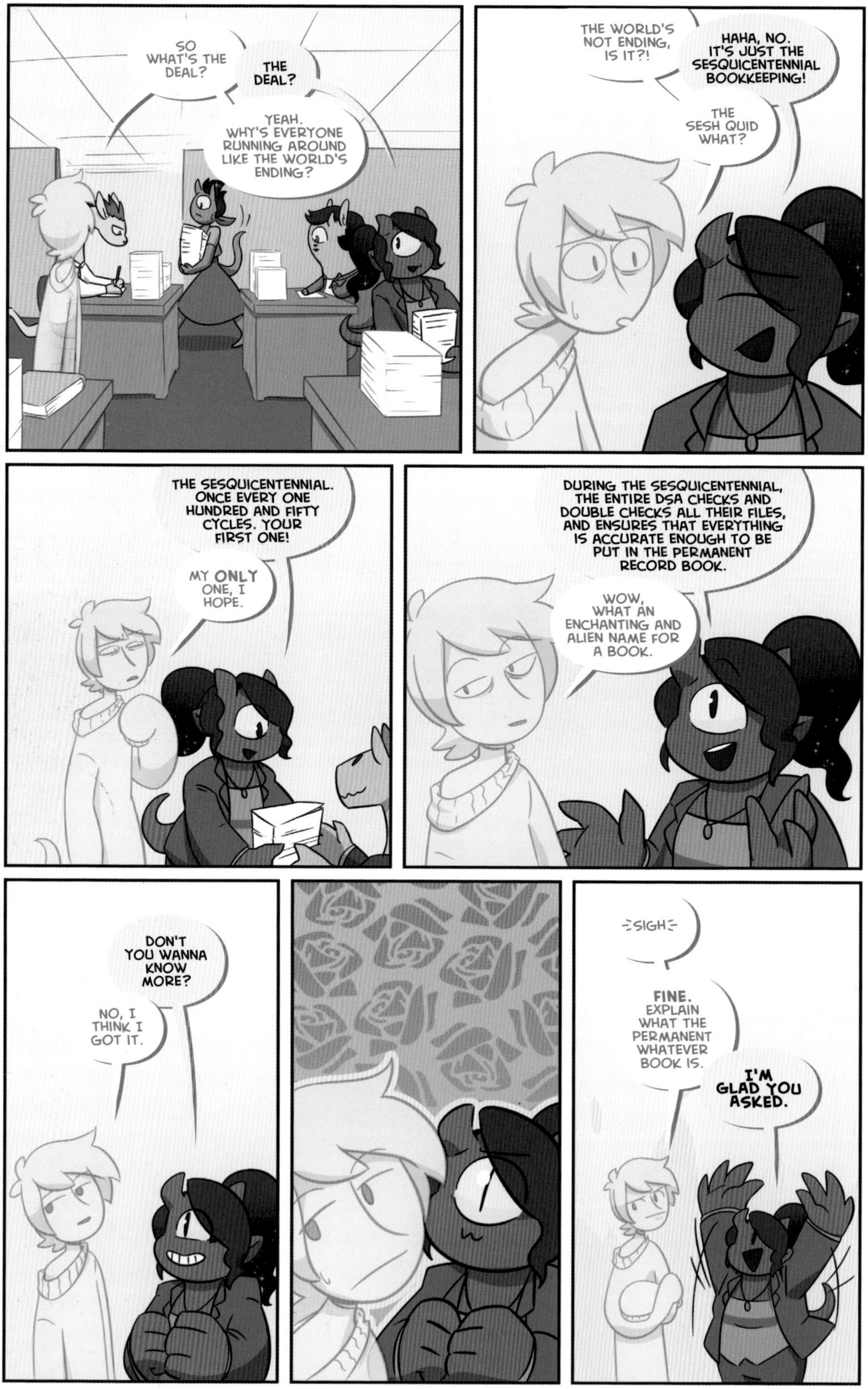
SO WHAT'S THE DEAL?
THE DEAL?
YEAH. WHY'S EVERYONE RUNNING AROUND LIKE THE WORLD'S ENDING?
THE WORLD'S NOT ENDING, IS IT?!
HAHA, NO. IT'S JUST THE SESQUICENTENNIAL BOOKKEEPING!
THE SESH QUID WHAT?
THE SESQUICENTENNIAL. ONCE EVERY ONE HUNDRED AND FIFTY CYCLES. YOUR FIRST ONE!
MY ONLY ONE, I HOPE.
DURING THE SESQUICENTENNIAL, THE ENTIRE DSA CHECKS AND DOUBLE CHECKS ALL THEIR FILES, AND ENSURES THAT EVERYTHING IS ACCURATE ENOUGH TO BE PUT IN THE PERMANENT RECORD BOOK.
WOW, WHAT AN ENCHANTING AND ALIEN NAME FOR A BOOK.
DON'T YOU WANNA KNOW MORE?
NO, I THINK I GOT IT.
SIGH
FINE. EXPLAIN WHAT THE PERMANENT WHATEVER BOOK IS.
I'M GLAD YOU ASKED.

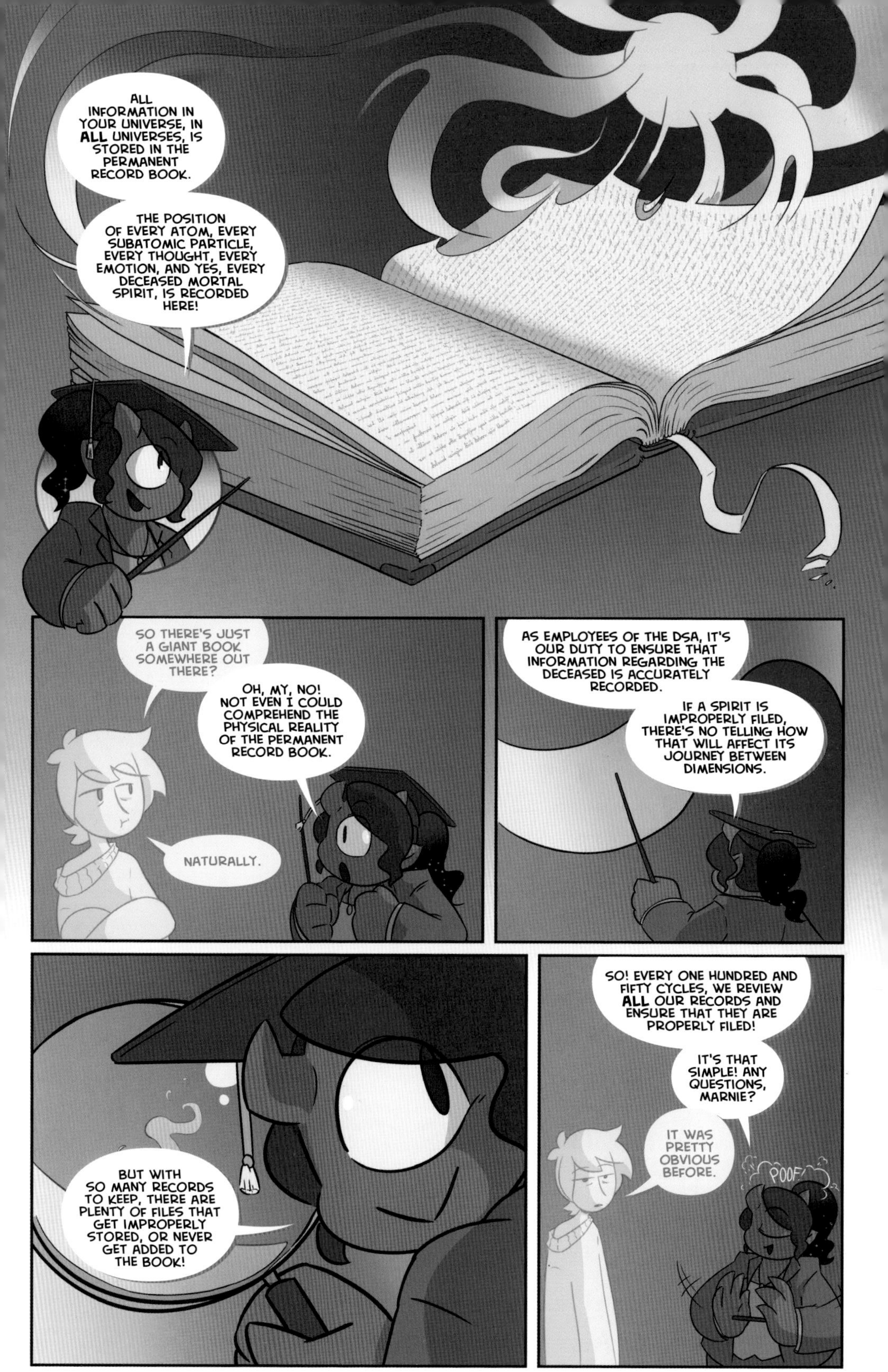
ALL INFORMATION IN YOUR UNIVERSE, IN **ALL** UNIVERSES, IS STORED IN THE PERMANENT RECORD BOOK.
THE POSITION OF EVERY ATOM, EVERY SUBATOMIC PARTICLE, EVERY THOUGHT, EVERY EMOTION, AND YES, EVERY DECEASED MORTAL SPIRIT, IS RECORDED HERE!
SO THERE'S JUST A GIANT BOOK SOMEWHERE OUT THERE?
OH, MY, NO! NOT EVEN I COULD COMPREHEND THE PHYSICAL REALITY OF THE PERMANENT RECORD BOOK.
NATURALLY.
AS EMPLOYEES OF THE DSA, IT'S OUR DUTY TO ENSURE THAT INFORMATION REGARDING THE DECEASED IS ACCURATELY RECORDED.
IF A SPIRIT IS IMPROPERLY FILED, THERE'S NO TELLING HOW THAT WILL AFFECT ITS JOURNEY BETWEEN DIMENSIONS.
BUT WITH SO MANY RECORDS TO KEEP, THERE ARE PLENTY OF FILES THAT GET IMPROPERLY STORED, OR NEVER GET ADDED TO THE BOOK!
SO! EVERY ONE HUNDRED AND FIFTY CYCLES, WE REVIEW **ALL** OUR RECORDS AND ENSURE THAT THEY ARE PROPERLY FILED!
IT'S THAT SIMPLE! ANY QUESTIONS, MARNIE?
IT WAS PRETTY OBVIOUS BEFORE.
POOF!

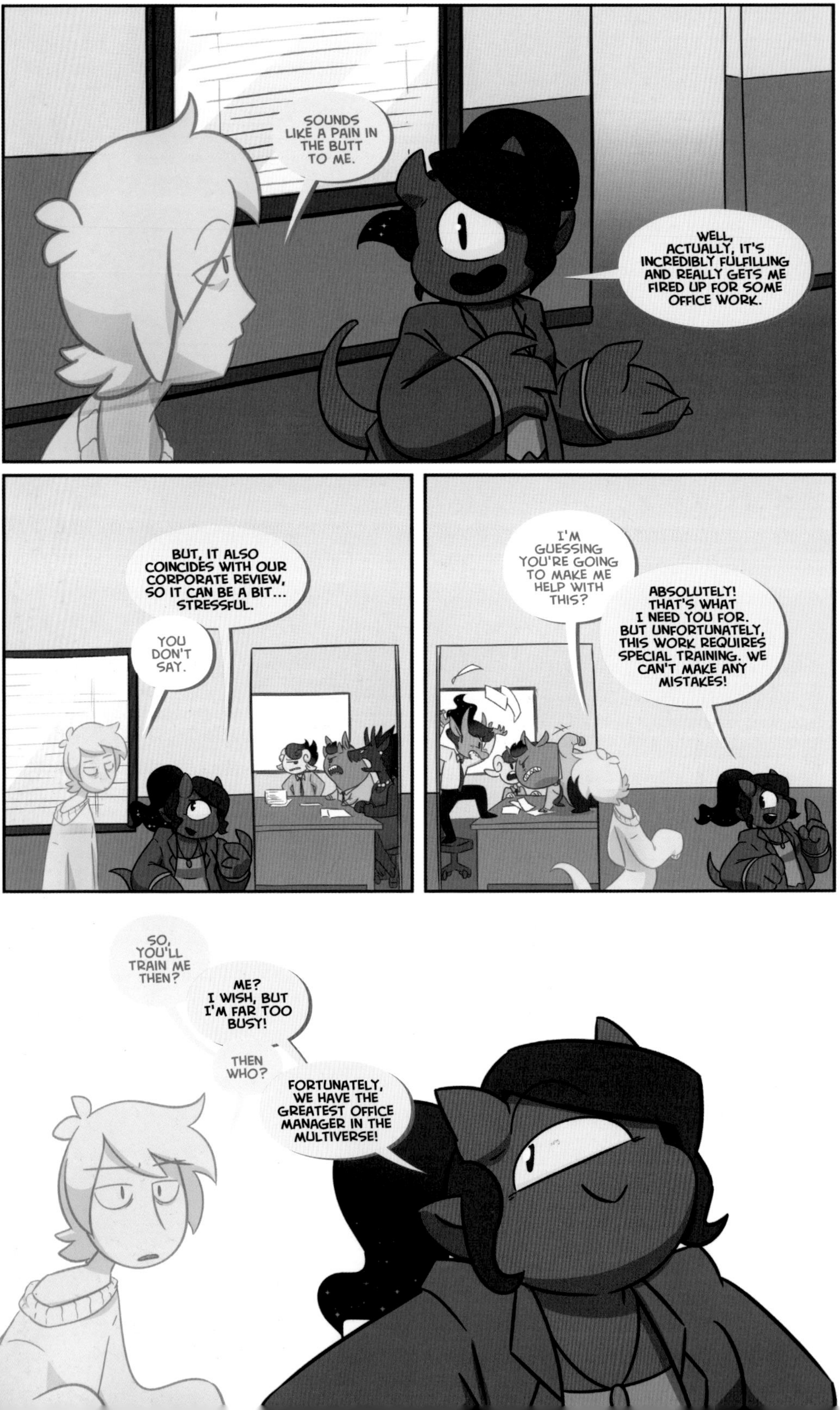
SOUNDS LIKE A PAIN IN THE BUTT TO ME.
WELL, ACTUALLY, IT'S INCREDIBLY FULFILLING AND REALLY GETS ME FIRED UP FOR SOME OFFICE WORK.
BUT, IT ALSO COINCIDES WITH OUR CORPORATE REVIEW, SO IT CAN BE A BIT... STRESSFUL.
YOU DON'T SAY.
I'M GUESSING YOU'RE GOING TO MAKE ME HELP WITH THIS?
ABSOLUTELY! THAT'S WHAT I NEED YOU FOR. BUT UNFORTUNATELY, THIS WORK REQUIRES SPECIAL TRAINING. WE CAN'T MAKE ANY MISTAKES!
SO, YOU'LL TRAIN ME THEN?
ME? I WISH, BUT I'M FAR TOO BUSY!
THEN WHO?
FORTUNATELY, WE HAVE THE GREATEST OFFICE MANAGER IN THE MULTIVERSE!

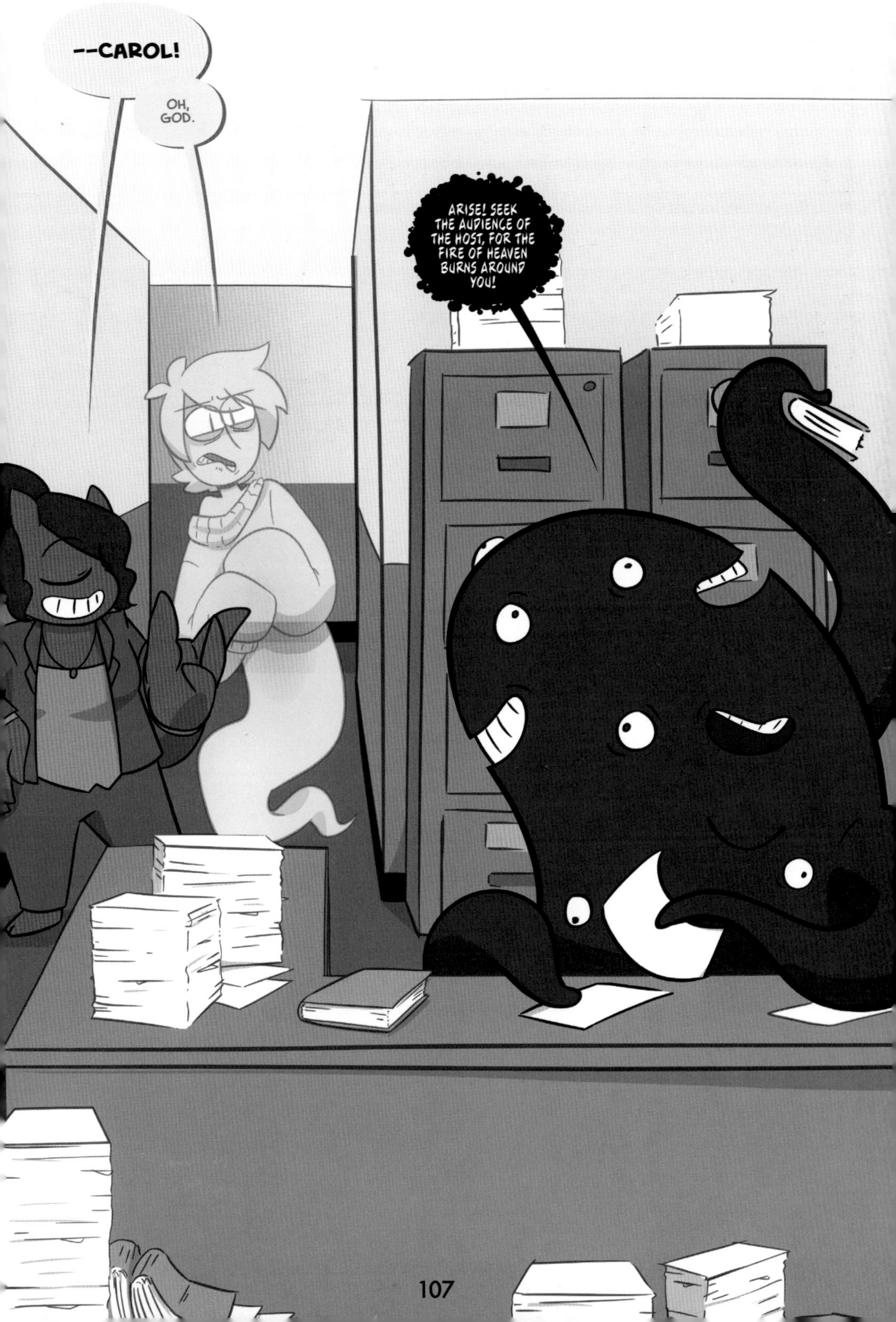
--CAROL!
OH, GOD.
ARISE! SEEK THE AUDIENCE OF THE HOST, FOR THE FIRE OF HEAVEN BURNS AROUND YOU!

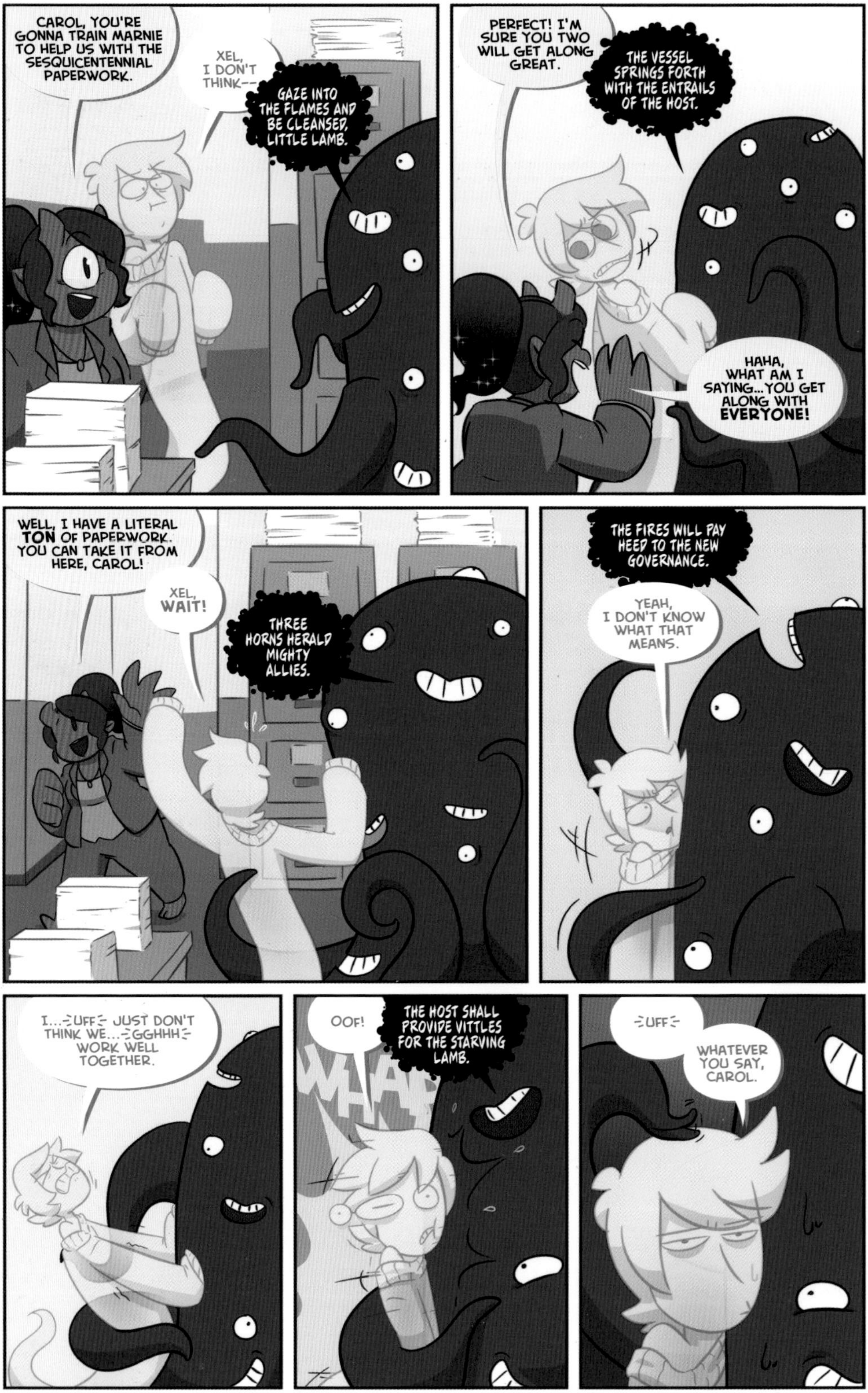
CAROL, YOU'RE GONNA TRAIN MARNIE TO HELP US WITH THE SESQUICENTENNIAL PAPERWORK.
XEL, I DON'T THINK--
GAZE INTO THE FLAMES AND BE CLEANSED, LITTLE LAMB.
PERFECT! I'M SURE YOU TWO WILL GET ALONG GREAT.
THE VESSEL SPRINGS FORTH WITH THE ENTRAILS OF THE HOST.
HAHA, WHAT AM I SAYING...YOU GET ALONG WITH EVERYONE!
WELL, I HAVE A LITERAL TON OF PAPERWORK. YOU CAN TAKE IT FROM HERE, CAROL!
XEL, WAIT!
THREE HORNS HERALD MIGHTY ALLIES.
THE FIRES WILL PAY HEED TO THE NEW GOVERNANCE.
YEAH, I DON'T KNOW WHAT THAT MEANS.
I... UFF JUST DON'T THINK WE... GGHHH WORK WELL TOGETHER.
OOF!
THE HOST SHALL PROVIDE VITTLES FOR THE STARVING LAMB.
UFF
WHATEVER YOU SAY, CAROL.

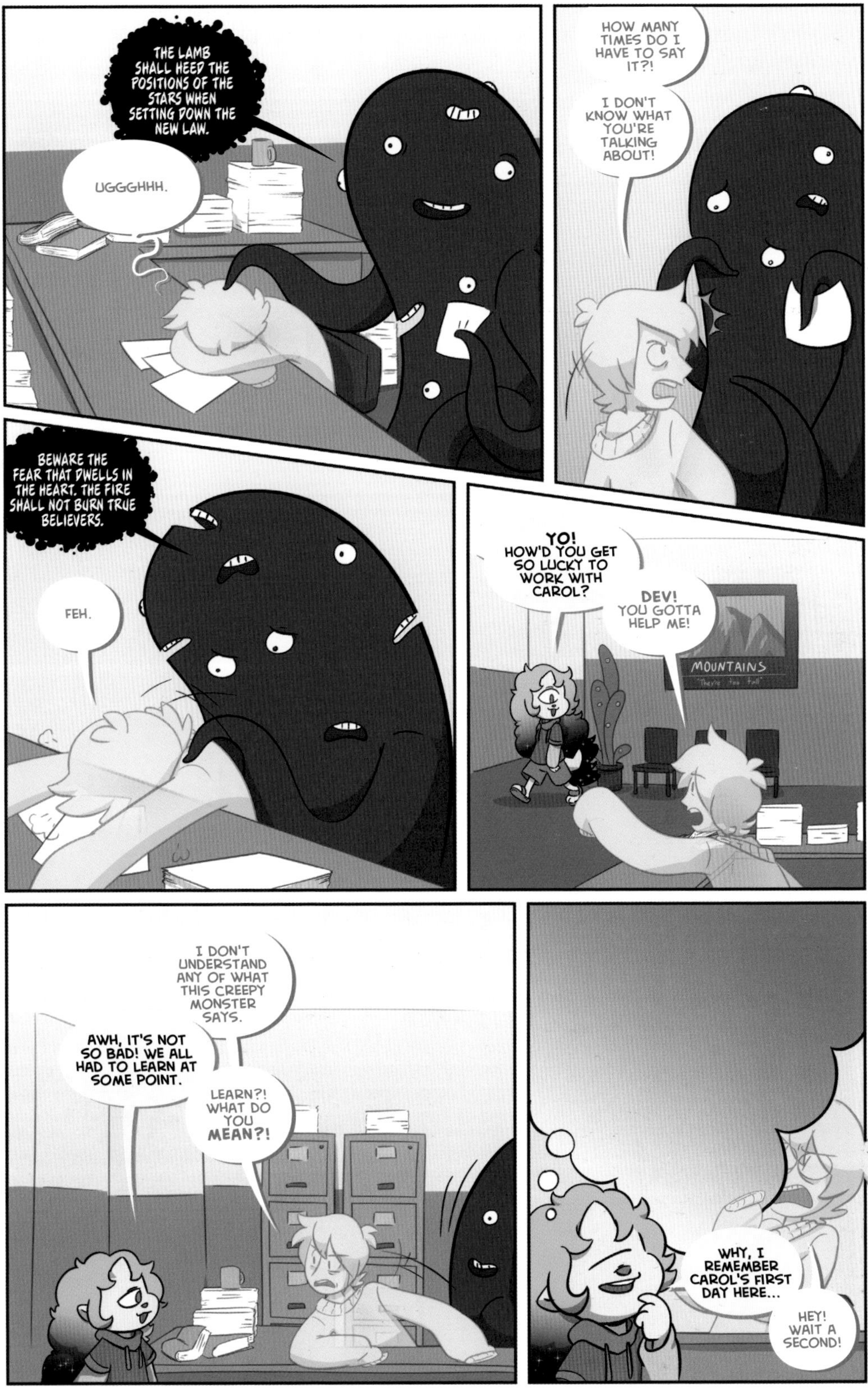
THE LAMB SHALL HEED THE POSITIONS OF THE STARS WHEN SETTING DOWN THE NEW LAW.
UGGGHHH.
HOW MANY TIMES DO I HAVE TO SAY IT?!
I DON'T KNOW WHAT YOU'RE TALKING ABOUT!
BEWARE THE FEAR THAT DWELLS IN THE HEART. THE FIRE SHALL NOT BURN TRUE BELIEVERS.
FEH.
YO! HOW'D YOU GET SO LUCKY TO WORK WITH CAROL?
DEV! YOU GOTTA HELP ME!
MOUNTAINS
I DON'T UNDERSTAND ANY OF WHAT THIS CREEPY MONSTER SAYS.
AWH, IT'S NOT SO BAD! WE ALL HAD TO LEARN AT SOME POINT.
LEARN?! WHAT DO YOU MEAN?!
WHY, I REMEMBER CAROL'S FIRST DAY HERE...
HEY! WAIT A SECOND!

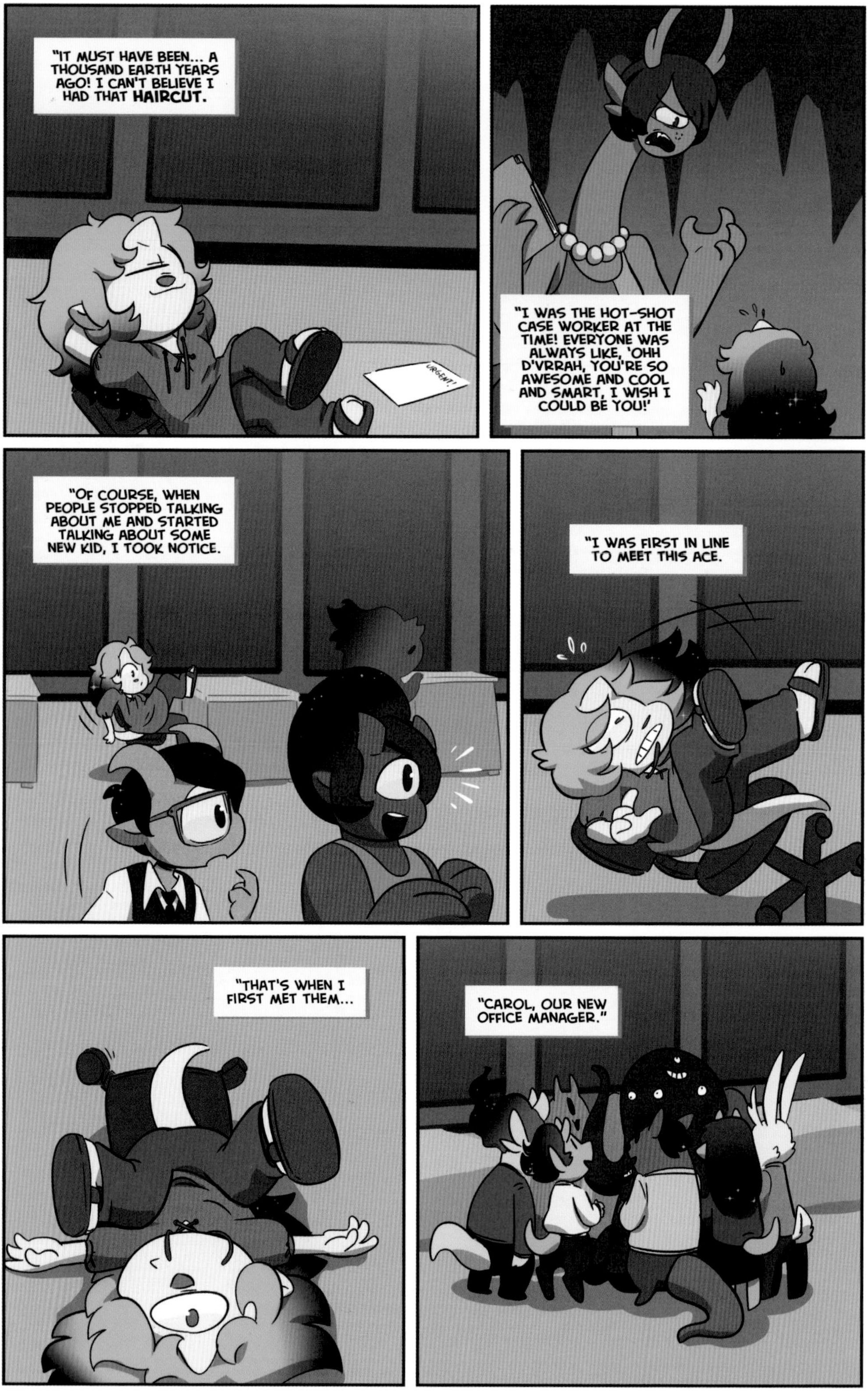
"IT MUST HAVE BEEN... A THOUSAND EARTH YEARS AGO! I CAN'T BELIEVE I HAD THAT HAIRCUT.
URGENT!
"I WAS THE HOT-SHOT CASE WORKER AT THE TIME! EVERYONE WAS ALWAYS LIKE, 'OHH D'VRRAH, YOU'RE SO AWESOME AND COOL AND SMART, I WISH I COULD BE YOU!'
"OF COURSE, WHEN PEOPLE STOPPED TALKING ABOUT ME AND STARTED TALKING ABOUT SOME NEW KID, I TOOK NOTICE.
"I WAS FIRST IN LINE TO MEET THIS ACE.
"THAT'S WHEN I FIRST MET THEM...
"CAROL, OUR NEW OFFICE MANAGER."

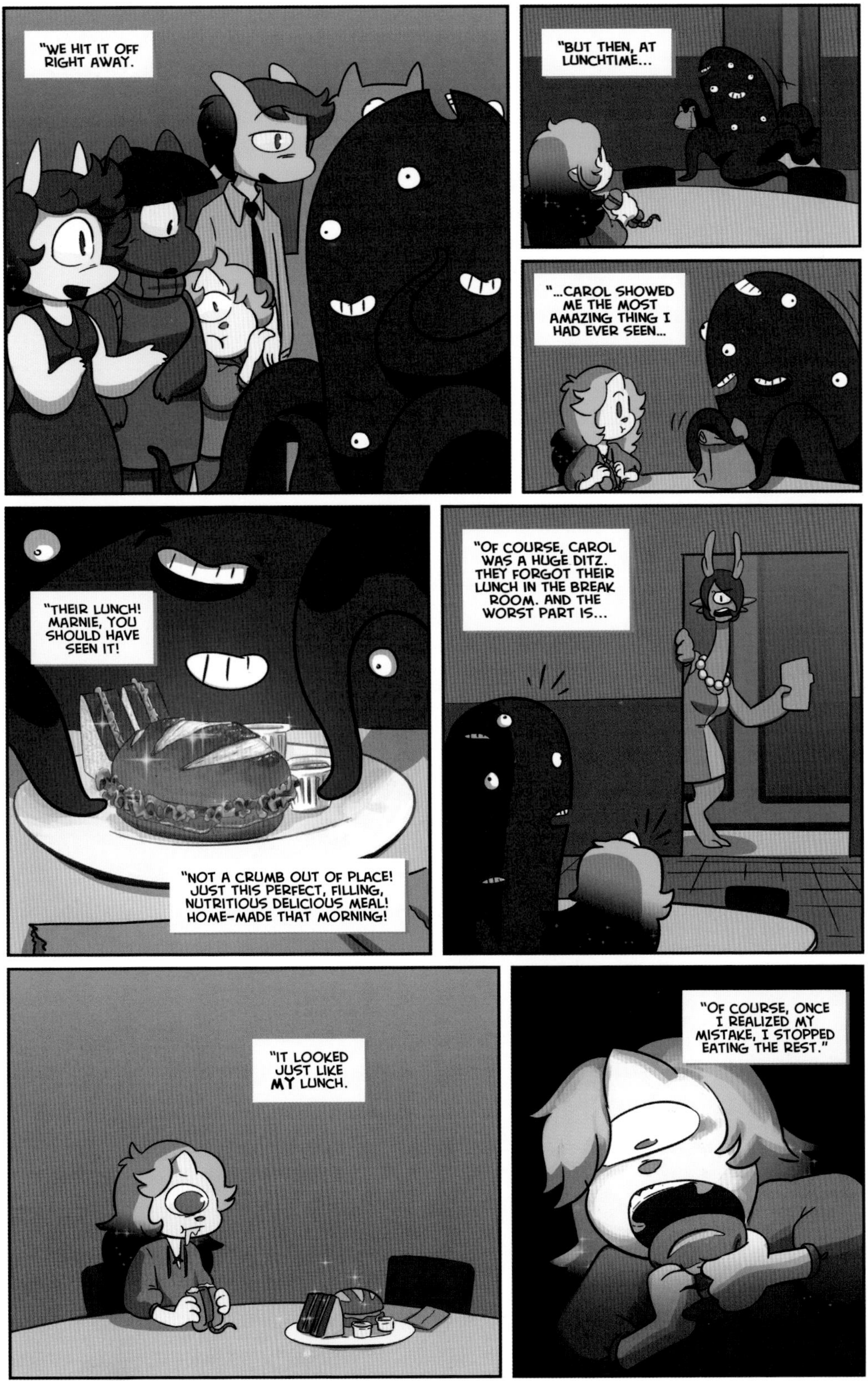
"WE HIT IT OFF RIGHT AWAY.
"BUT THEN, AT LUNCHTIME...
"...CAROL SHOWED ME THE MOST AMAZING THING I HAD EVER SEEN...
"THEIR LUNCH! MARNIE, YOU SHOULD HAVE SEEN IT!
"NOT A CRUMB OUT OF PLACE! JUST THIS PERFECT, FILLING, NUTRITIOUS DELICIOUS MEAL! HOME-MADE THAT MORNING!
"OF COURSE, CAROL WAS A HUGE DITZ. THEY FORGOT THEIR LUNCH IN THE BREAK ROOM. AND THE WORST PART IS...
"IT LOOKED JUST LIKE MY LUNCH.
"OF COURSE, ONCE I REALIZED MY MISTAKE, I STOPPED EATING THE REST."

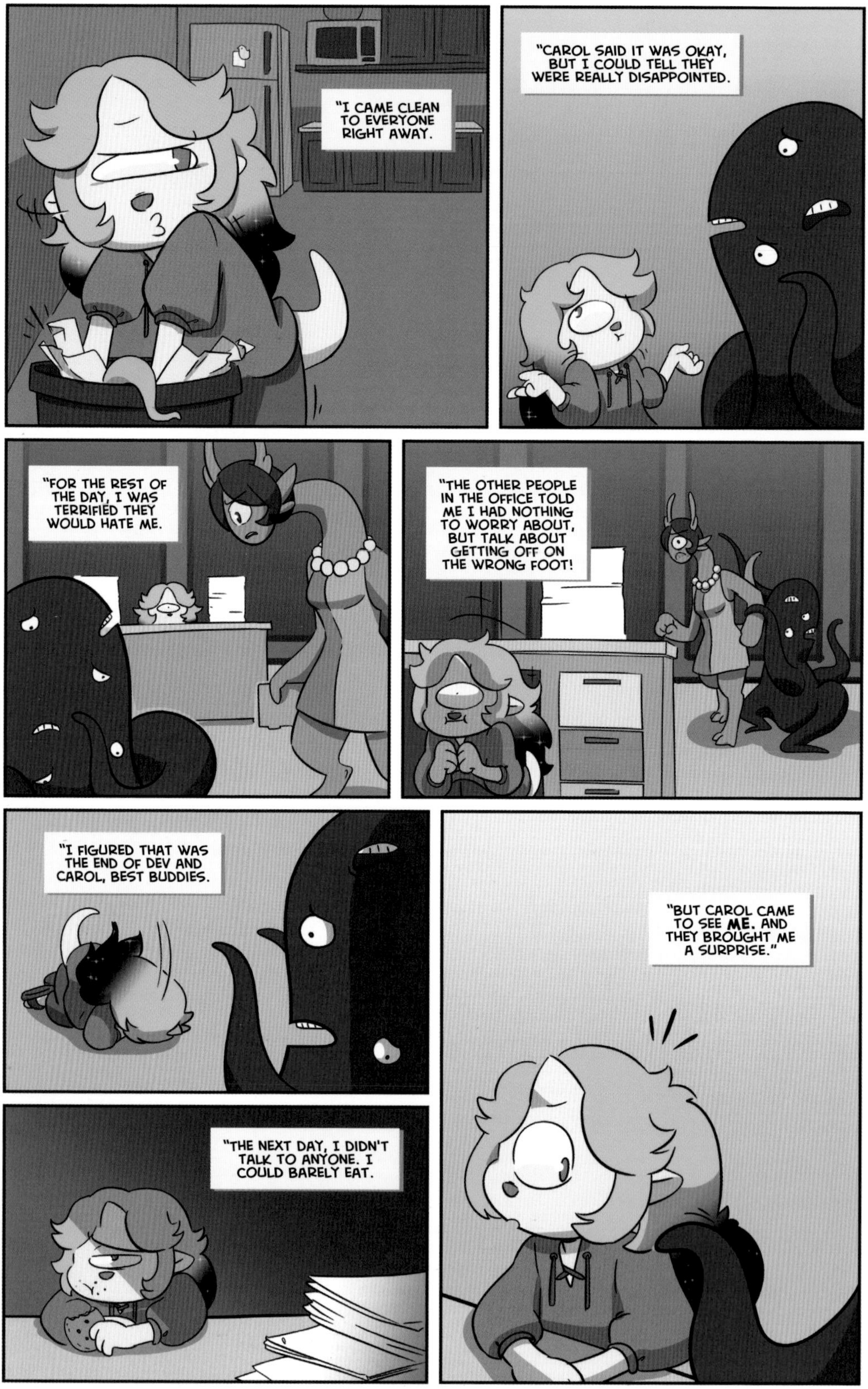
"I CAME CLEAN TO EVERYONE RIGHT AWAY.
"CAROL SAID IT WAS OKAY, BUT I COULD TELL THEY WERE REALLY DISAPPOINTED.
"FOR THE REST OF THE DAY, I WAS TERRIFIED THEY WOULD HATE ME.
"THE OTHER PEOPLE IN THE OFFICE TOLD ME I HAD NOTHING TO WORRY ABOUT, BUT TALK ABOUT GETTING OFF ON THE WRONG FOOT!
"I FIGURED THAT WAS THE END OF DEV AND CAROL, BEST BUDDIES.
"THE NEXT DAY, I DIDN'T TALK TO ANYONE. I COULD BARELY EAT.
"BUT CAROL CAME TO SEE **ME.** AND THEY BROUGHT ME A SURPRISE."

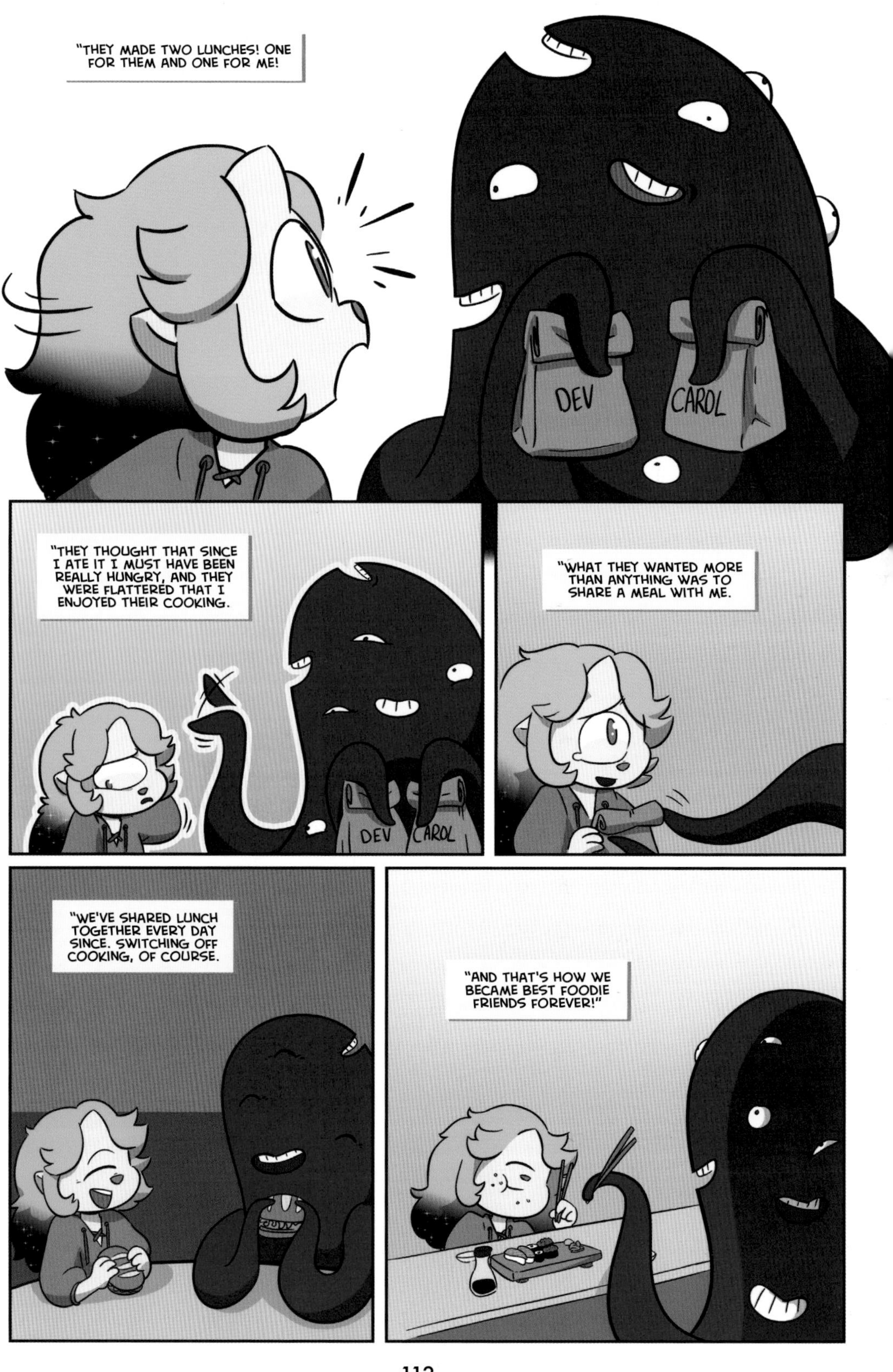
"THEY MADE TWO LUNCHES! ONE FOR THEM AND ONE FOR ME!
DEV
CAROL
"THEY THOUGHT THAT SINCE I ATE IT I MUST HAVE BEEN REALLY HUNGRY, AND THEY WERE FLATTERED THAT I ENJOYED THEIR COOKING.
DEV
CAROL
"WHAT THEY WANTED MORE THAN ANYTHING WAS TO SHARE A MEAL WITH ME.
"WE'VE SHARED LUNCH TOGETHER EVERY DAY SINCE. SWITCHING OFF COOKING, OF COURSE.
"AND THAT'S HOW WE BECAME BEST FOODIE FRIENDS FOREVER!"

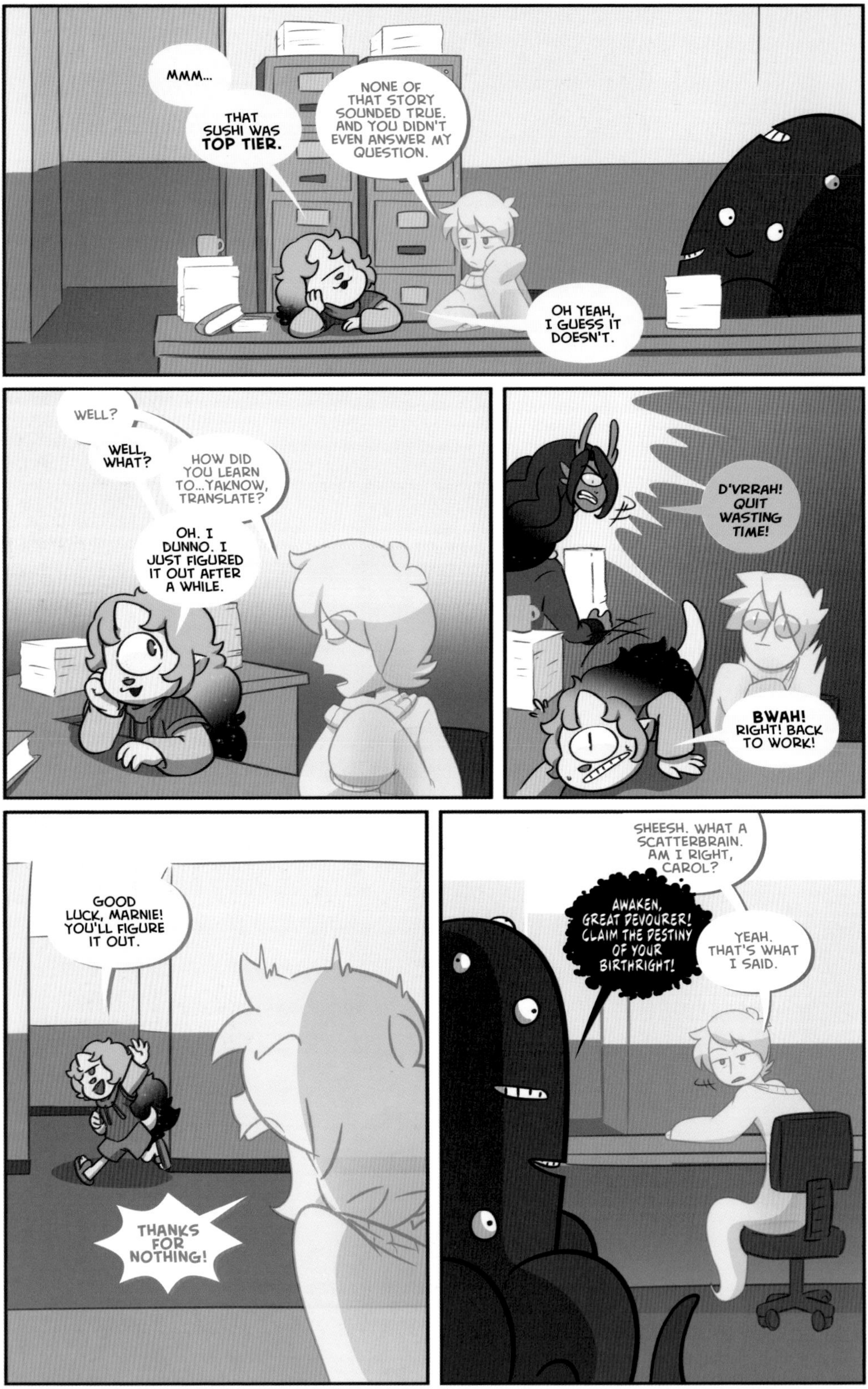
MMM...
THAT SUSHI WAS TOP TIER.
NONE OF THAT STORY SOUNDED TRUE. AND YOU DIDN'T EVEN ANSWER MY QUESTION.
OH YEAH, I GUESS IT DOESN'T.
WELL?
WELL, WHAT?
HOW DID YOU LEARN TO...YAKNOW, TRANSLATE?
OH. I DUNNO. I JUST FIGURED IT OUT AFTER A WHILE.
D'VRRAH! QUIT WASTING TIME!
BWAH! RIGHT! BACK TO WORK!
GOOD LUCK, MARNIE! YOU'LL FIGURE IT OUT.
THANKS FOR NOTHING!
SHEESH. WHAT A SCATTERBRAIN. AM I RIGHT, CAROL?
AWAKEN, GREAT DEVOURER! CLAIM THE DESTINY OF YOUR BIRTHRIGHT!
YEAH. THAT'S WHAT I SAID.

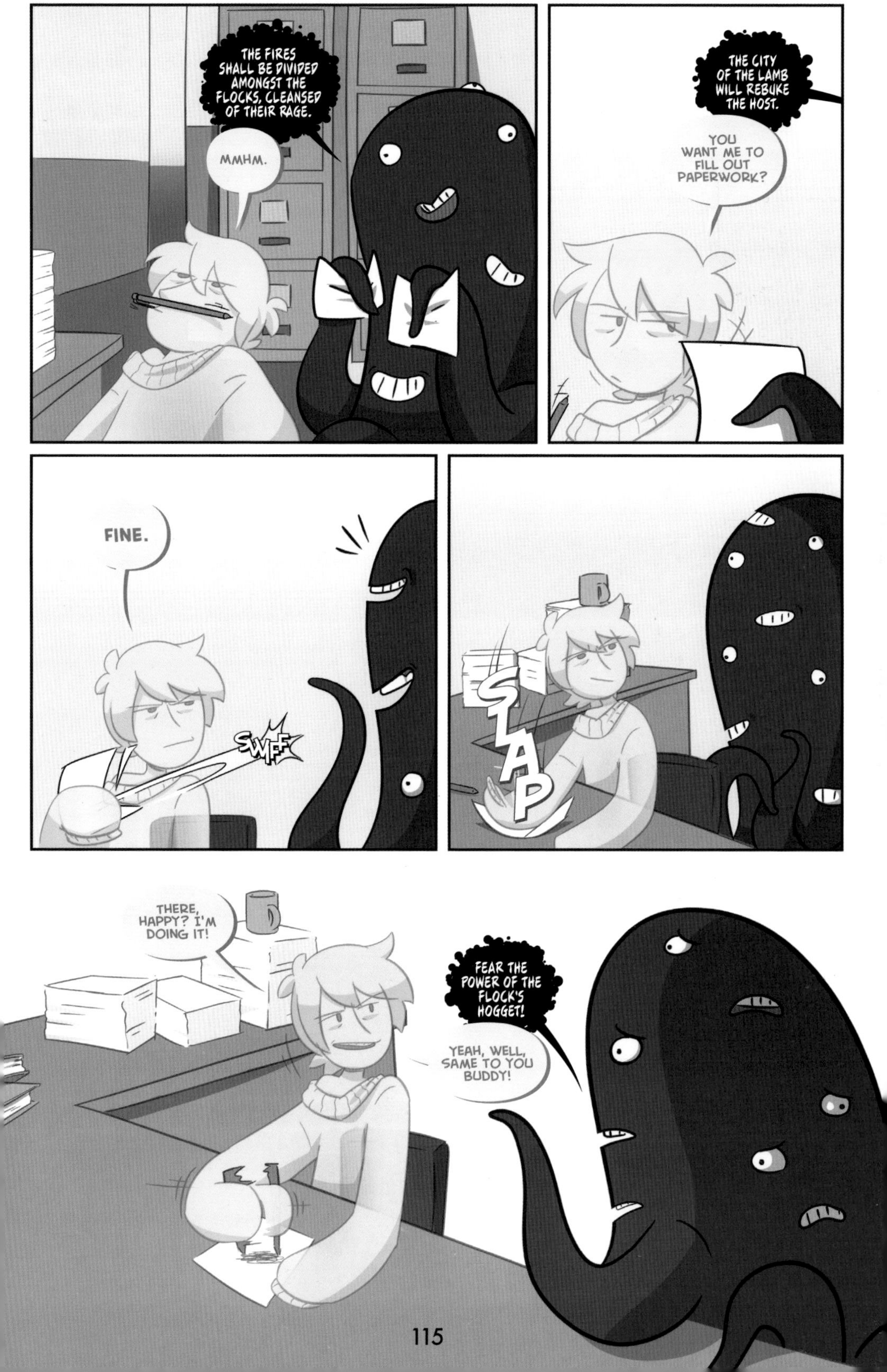
THE FIRES SHALL BE DIVIDED AMONGST THE FLOCKS, CLEANSED OF THEIR RAGE.
MMHM.
THE CITY OF THE LAMB WILL REBUKE THE HOST.
YOU WANT ME TO FILL OUT PAPERWORK?
FINE.
SWFF
SLAP
THERE, HAPPY? I'M DOING IT!
FEAR THE POWER OF THE FLOCK'S HOGGET!
YEAH, WELL, SAME TO YOU BUDDY!

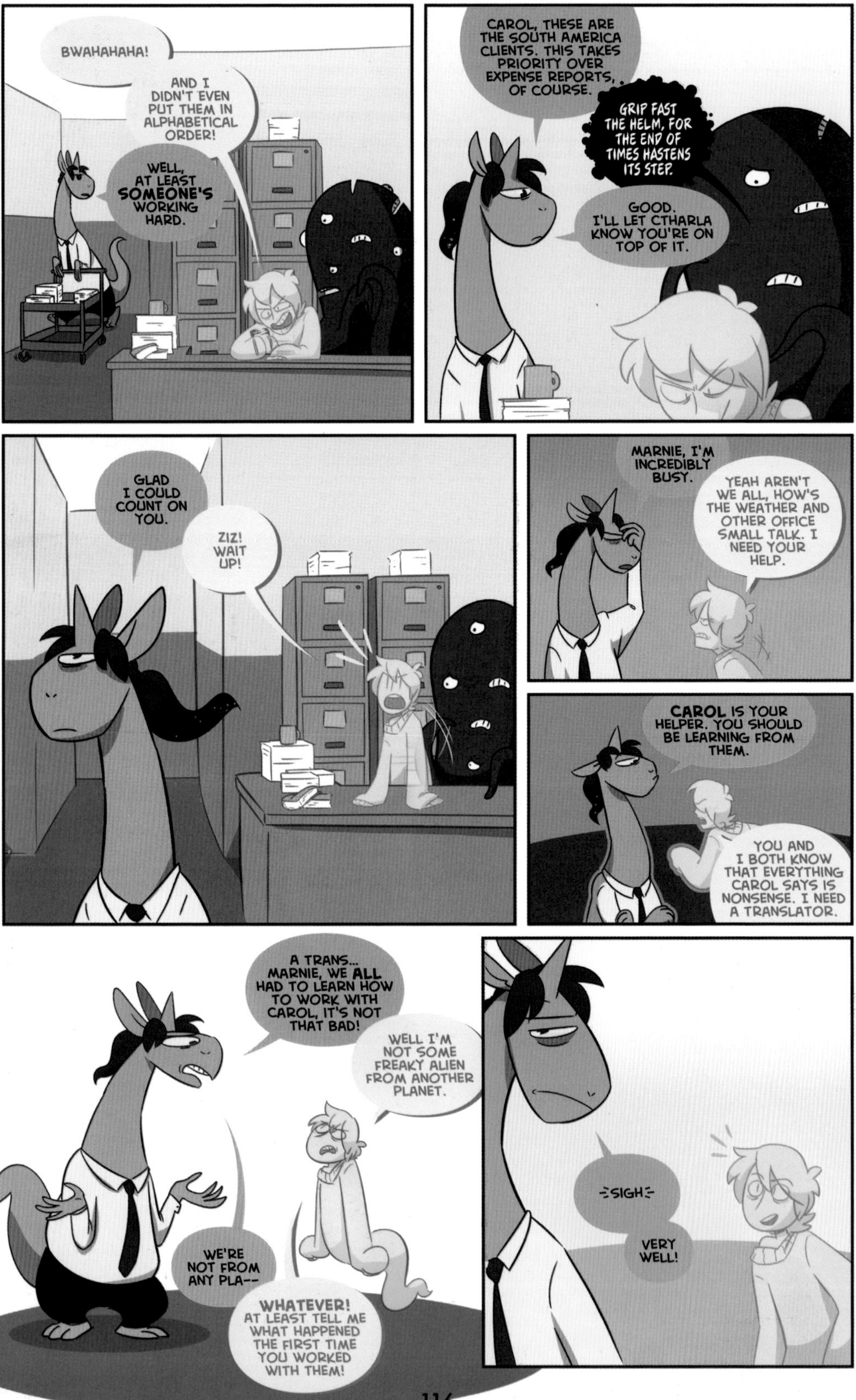
BWAHAHAHA!
AND I DIDN'T EVEN PUT THEM IN ALPHABETICAL ORDER!
WELL, AT LEAST **SOMEONE'S** WORKING HARD.
CAROL, THESE ARE THE SOUTH AMERICA CLIENTS. THIS TAKES PRIORITY OVER EXPENSE REPORTS, OF COURSE.
GRIP FAST THE HELM, FOR THE END OF TIMES HASTENS ITS STEP.
GOOD. I'LL LET CTHARLA KNOW YOU'RE ON TOP OF IT.
GLAD I COULD COUNT ON YOU.
ZIZ! WAIT UP!
MARNIE, I'M INCREDIBLY BUSY.
YEAH AREN'T WE ALL, HOW'S THE WEATHER AND OTHER OFFICE SMALL TALK. I NEED YOUR HELP.
CAROL IS YOUR HELPER. YOU SHOULD BE LEARNING FROM THEM.
YOU AND I BOTH KNOW THAT EVERYTHING CAROL SAYS IS NONSENSE. I NEED A TRANSLATOR.
A TRANS... MARNIE, WE **ALL** HAD TO LEARN HOW TO WORK WITH CAROL, IT'S NOT THAT BAD!
WELL I'M NOT SOME FREAKY ALIEN FROM ANOTHER PLANET.
WE'RE NOT FROM ANY PLA--
WHATEVER! AT LEAST TELL ME WHAT HAPPENED THE FIRST TIME YOU WORKED WITH THEM!
-SIGH-
VERY WELL!

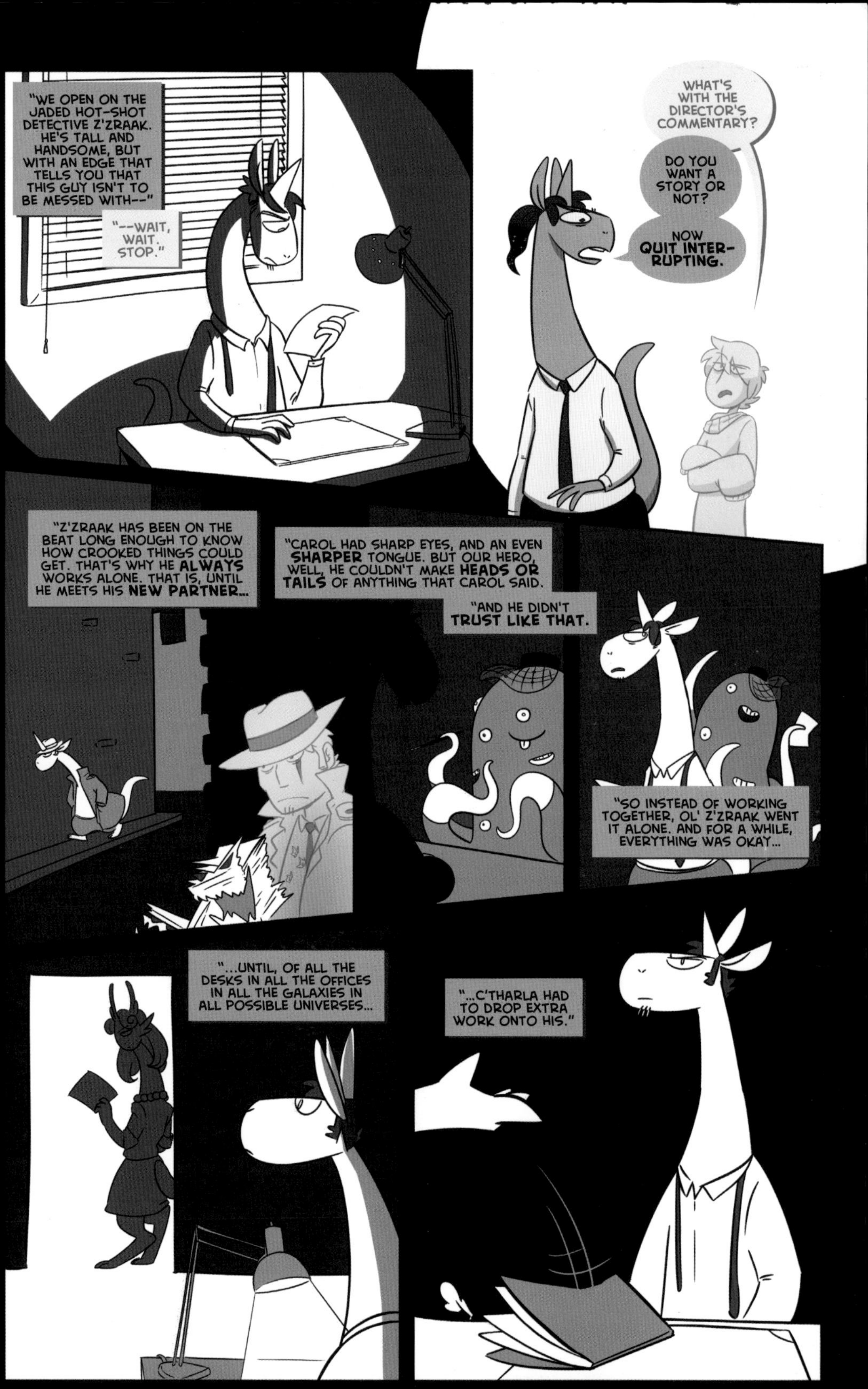
"WE OPEN ON THE JADED HOT-SHOT DETECTIVE Z'ZRAAK. HE'S TALL AND HANDSOME, BUT WITH AN EDGE THAT TELLS YOU THAT THIS GUY ISN'T TO BE MESSED WITH--"
"--WAIT, WAIT. STOP."
WHAT'S WITH THE DIRECTOR'S COMMENTARY?
DO YOU WANT A STORY OR NOT?
NOW QUIT INTER-RUPTING.
"Z'ZRAAK HAS BEEN ON THE BEAT LONG ENOUGH TO KNOW HOW CROOKED THINGS COULD GET. THAT'S WHY HE ALWAYS WORKS ALONE. THAT IS, UNTIL HE MEETS HIS NEW PARTNER...
"CAROL HAD SHARP EYES, AND AN EVEN SHARPER TONGUE. BUT OUR HERO, WELL, HE COULDN'T MAKE HEADS OR TAILS OF ANYTHING THAT CAROL SAID.
"AND HE DIDN'T TRUST LIKE THAT.
"SO INSTEAD OF WORKING TOGETHER, OL' Z'ZRAAK WENT IT ALONE. AND FOR A WHILE, EVERYTHING WAS OKAY...
"...UNTIL, OF ALL THE DESKS IN ALL THE OFFICES IN ALL THE GALAXIES IN ALL POSSIBLE UNIVERSES...
"...C'THARLA HAD TO DROP EXTRA WORK ONTO HIS."

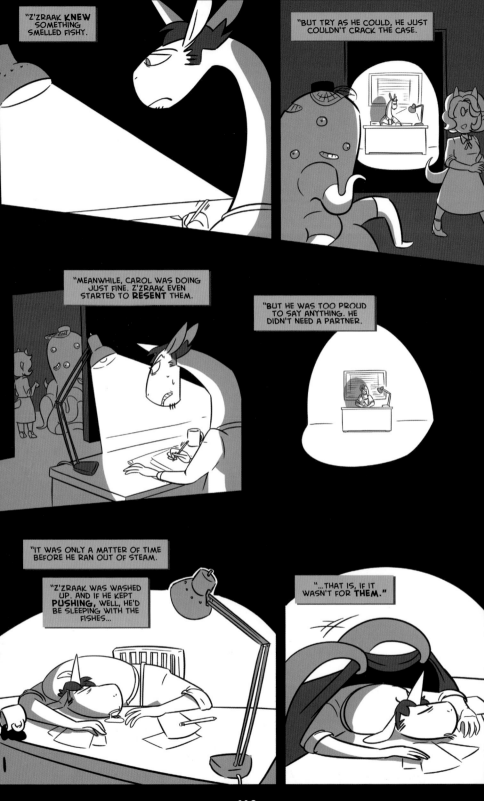

"Z'ZRAAK **KNEW** SOMETHING SMELLED FISHY.

"BUT TRY AS HE COULD, HE JUST COULDN'T CRACK THE CASE.

"MEANWHILE, CAROL WAS DOING JUST FINE. Z'ZRAAK EVEN STARTED TO **RESENT** THEM.

"BUT HE WAS TOO PROUD TO SAY ANYTHING. HE DIDN'T NEED A PARTNER.

"IT WAS ONLY A MATTER OF TIME BEFORE HE RAN OUT OF STEAM.

"Z'ZRAAK WAS WASHED UP. AND IF HE KEPT **PUSHING**, WELL, HE'D BE SLEEPING WITH THE FISHES...

"...THAT IS, IF IT WASN'T FOR **THEM**."

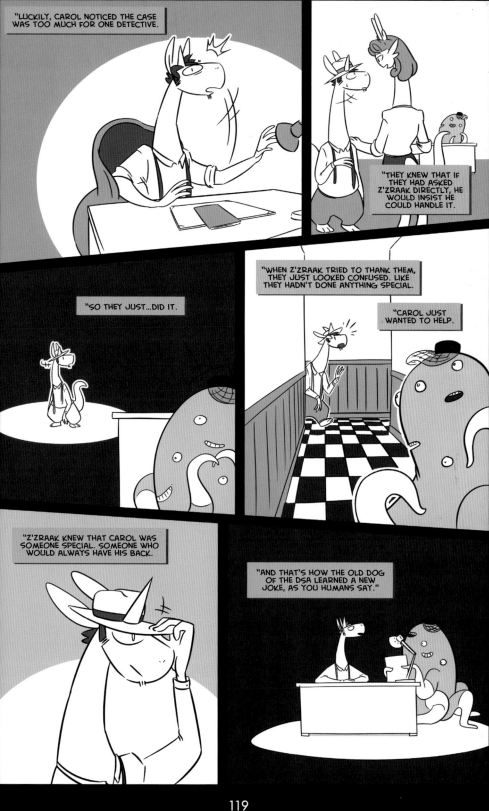

"LUCKILY, CAROL NOTICED THE CASE WAS TOO MUCH FOR ONE DETECTIVE.

"THEY KNEW THAT IF THEY HAD ASKED Z'ZRAAK DIRECTLY, HE WOULD INSIST HE COULD HANDLE IT.

"SO THEY JUST...DID IT.

"WHEN Z'ZRAAK TRIED TO THANK THEM, THEY JUST LOOKED CONFUSED. LIKE THEY HADN'T DONE ANYTHING SPECIAL.

"CAROL JUST WANTED TO HELP.

"Z'ZRAAK KNEW THAT CAROL WAS SOMEONE SPECIAL. SOMEONE WHO WOULD ALWAYS HAVE HIS BACK.

"AND THAT'S HOW THE OLD DOG OF THE DSA LEARNED A NEW JOKE, AS YOU HUMANS SAY."

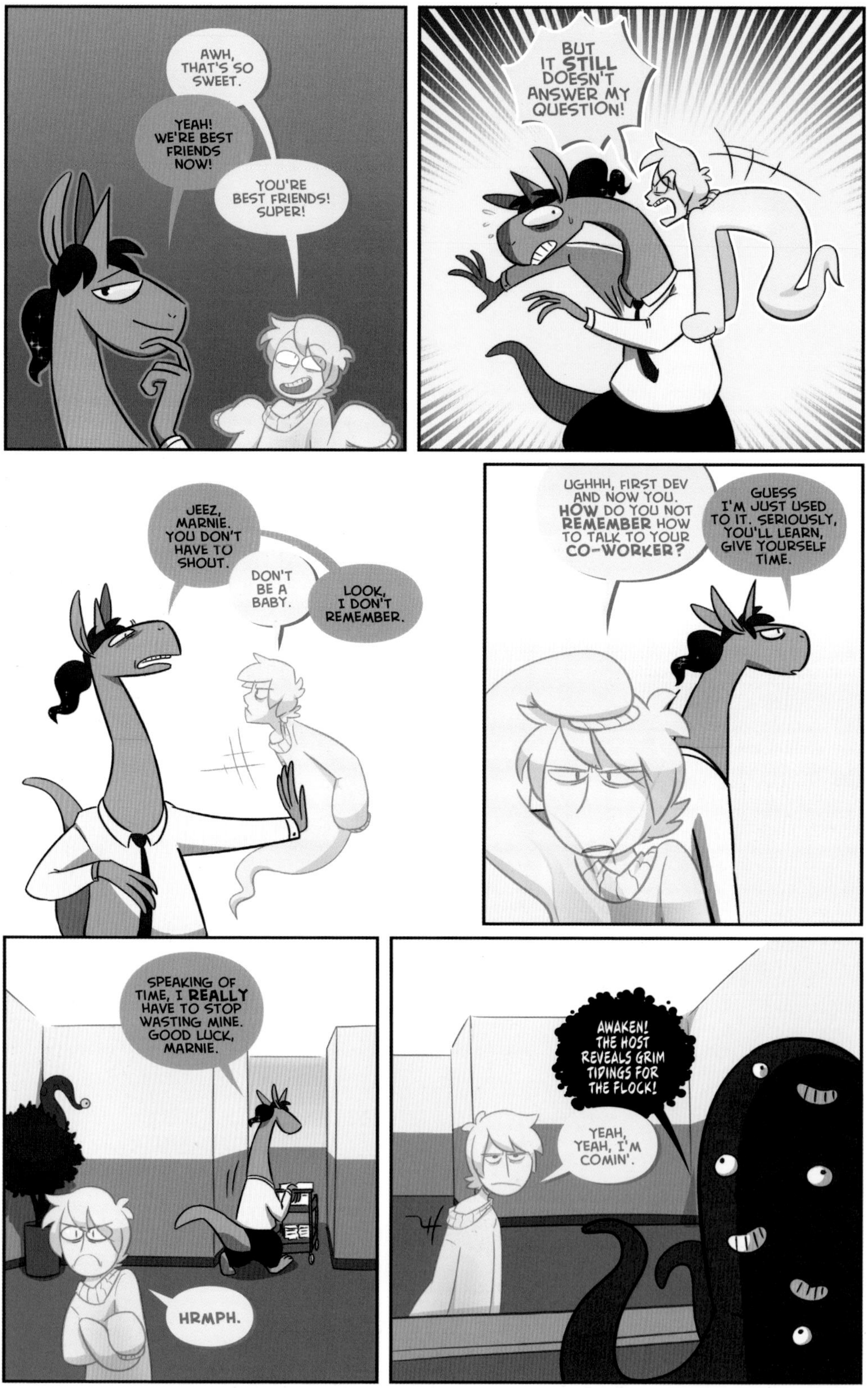
AWH, THAT'S SO SWEET.
YEAH! WE'RE BEST FRIENDS NOW!
YOU'RE BEST FRIENDS! SUPER!
BUT IT STILL DOESN'T ANSWER MY QUESTION!
JEEZ, MARNIE. YOU DON'T HAVE TO SHOUT.
DON'T BE A BABY.
LOOK, I DON'T REMEMBER.
UGHHH, FIRST DEV AND NOW YOU. HOW DO YOU NOT REMEMBER HOW TO TALK TO YOUR CO-WORKER?
GUESS I'M JUST USED TO IT. SERIOUSLY, YOU'LL LEARN, GIVE YOURSELF TIME.
SPEAKING OF TIME, I REALLY HAVE TO STOP WASTING MINE. GOOD LUCK, MARNIE.
HRMPH.
AWAKEN! THE HOST REVEALS GRIM TIDINGS FOR THE FLOCK!
YEAH, YEAH, I'M COMIN'.

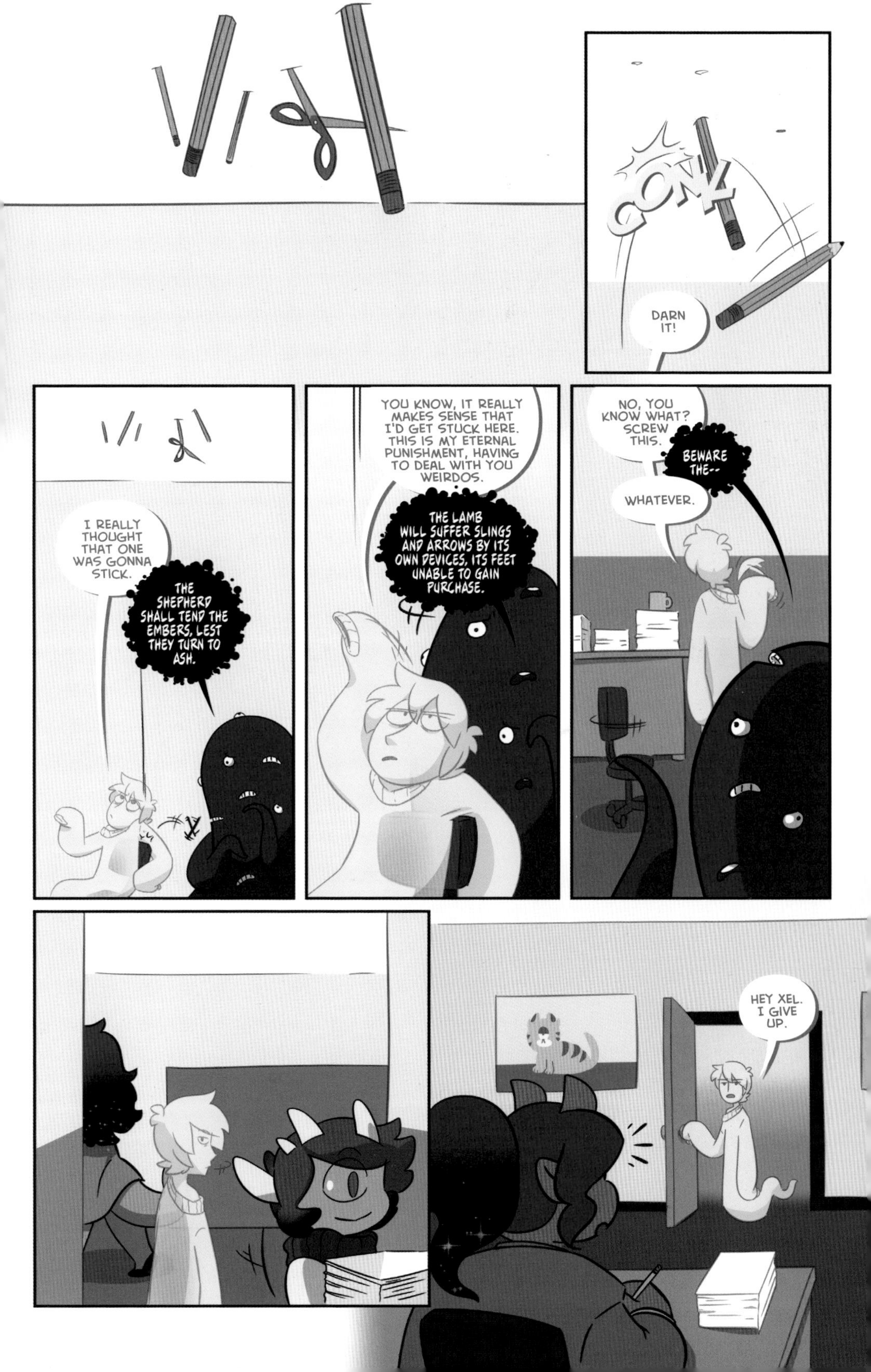
CONK
DARN IT!
I REALLY THOUGHT THAT ONE WAS GONNA STICK.
THE SHEPHERD SHALL TEND THE EMBERS, LEST THEY TURN TO ASH.
YOU KNOW, IT REALLY MAKES SENSE THAT I'D GET STUCK HERE. THIS IS MY ETERNAL PUNISHMENT, HAVING TO DEAL WITH YOU WEIRDOS.
THE LAMB WILL SUFFER SLINGS AND ARROWS BY ITS OWN DEVICES, ITS FEET UNABLE TO GAIN PURCHASE.
NO, YOU KNOW WHAT? SCREW THIS.
BEWARE THE--
WHATEVER.
HEY XEL. I GIVE UP.

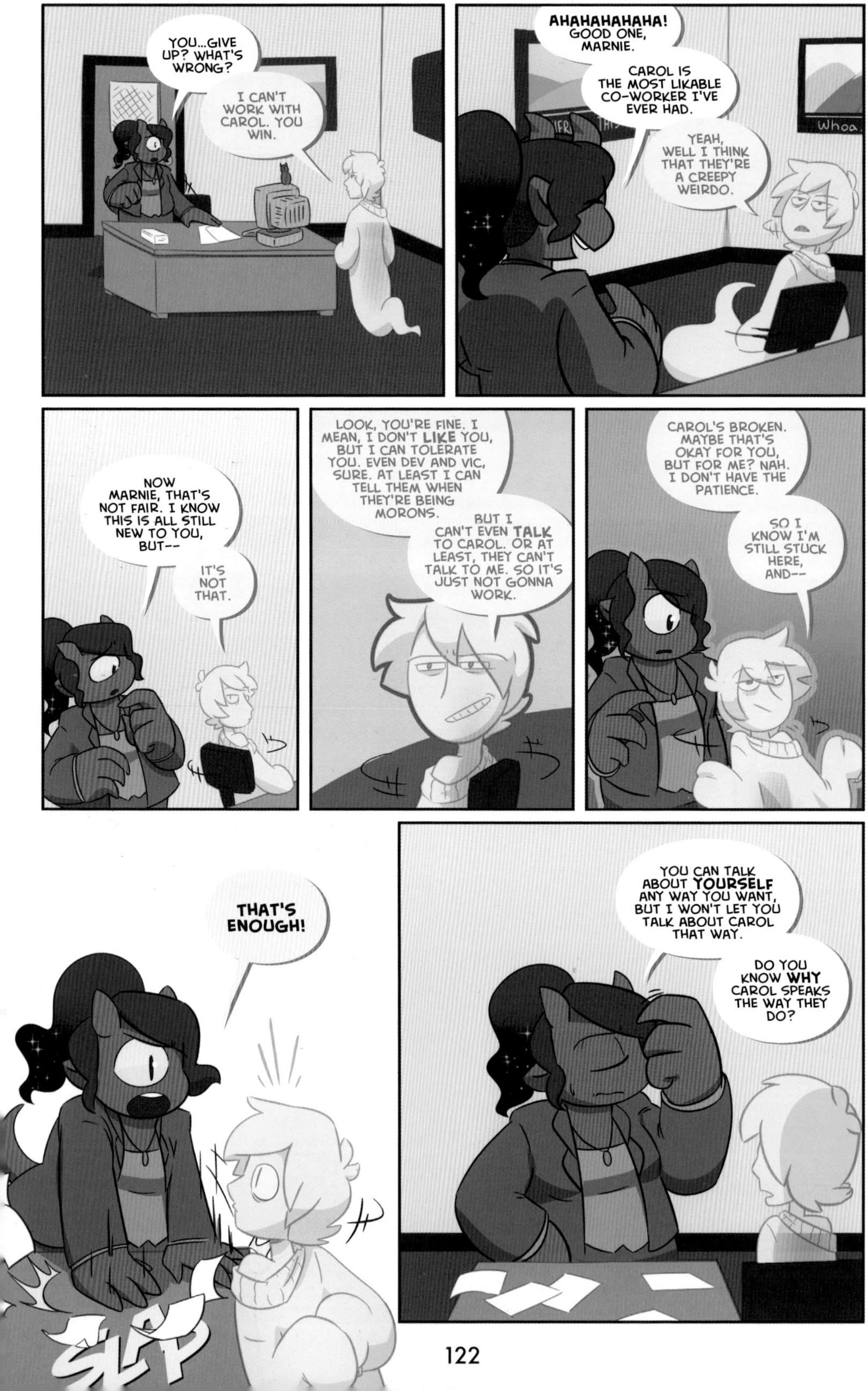
YOU...GIVE UP? WHAT'S WRONG?
I CAN'T WORK WITH CAROL. YOU WIN.
AHAHAHAHAHA! GOOD ONE, MARNIE.
CAROL IS THE MOST LIKABLE CO-WORKER I'VE EVER HAD.
YEAH, WELL I THINK THAT THEY'RE A CREEPY WEIRDO.
NOW MARNIE, THAT'S NOT FAIR. I KNOW THIS IS ALL STILL NEW TO YOU, BUT--
IT'S NOT THAT.
LOOK, YOU'RE FINE. I MEAN, I DON'T LIKE YOU, BUT I CAN TOLERATE YOU. EVEN DEV AND VIC, SURE. AT LEAST I CAN TELL THEM WHEN THEY'RE BEING MORONS.
BUT I CAN'T EVEN TALK TO CAROL. OR AT LEAST, THEY CAN'T TALK TO ME. SO IT'S JUST NOT GONNA WORK.
CAROL'S BROKEN. MAYBE THAT'S OKAY FOR YOU, BUT FOR ME? NAH. I DON'T HAVE THE PATIENCE.
SO I KNOW I'M STILL STUCK HERE, AND--
THAT'S ENOUGH!
YOU CAN TALK ABOUT YOURSELF ANY WAY YOU WANT, BUT I WON'T LET YOU TALK ABOUT CAROL THAT WAY.
DO YOU KNOW WHY CAROL SPEAKS THE WAY THEY DO?

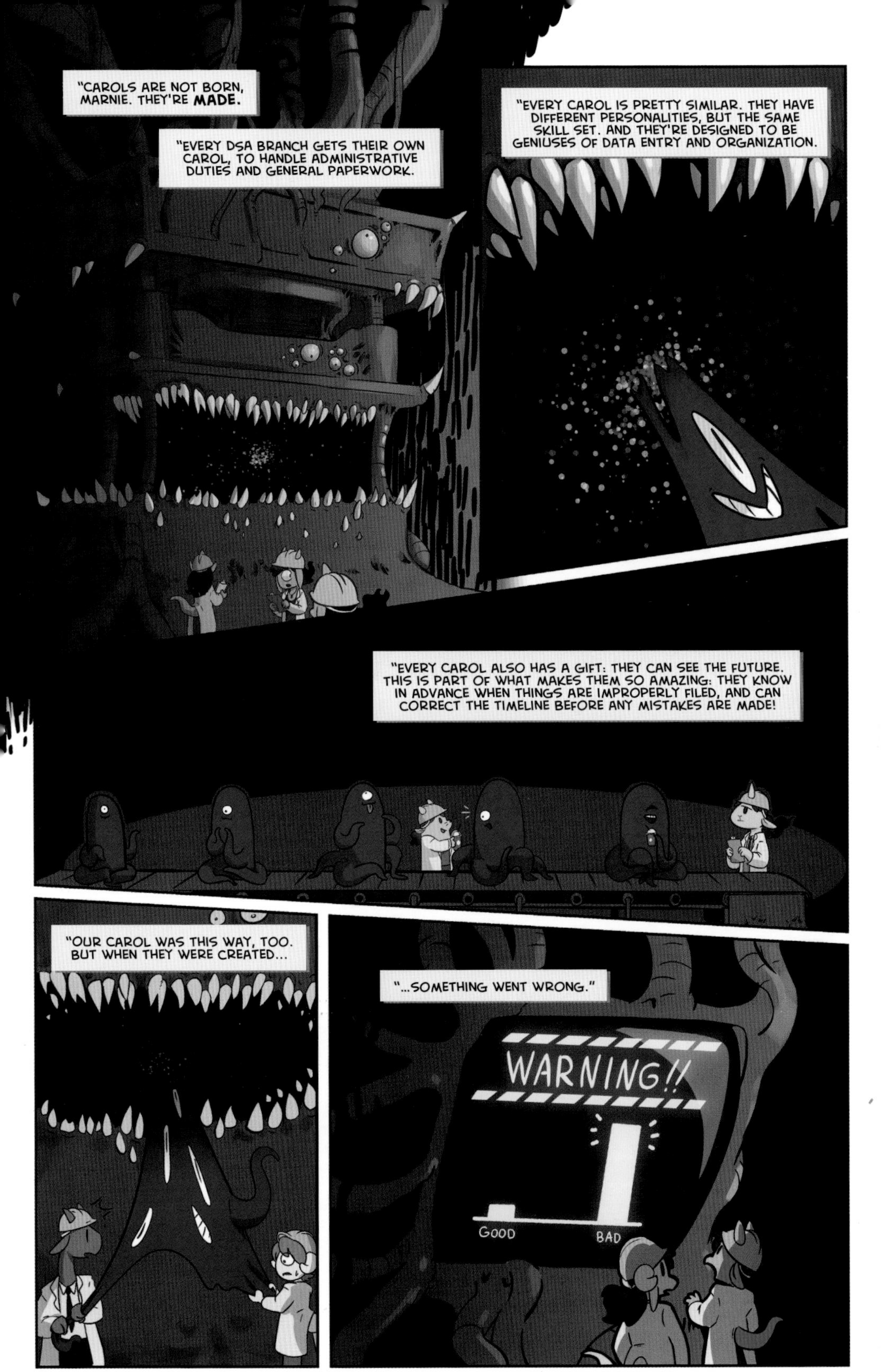
"CAROLS ARE NOT BORN, MARNIE. THEY'RE **MADE.**
"EVERY DSA BRANCH GETS THEIR OWN CAROL, TO HANDLE ADMINISTRATIVE DUTIES AND GENERAL PAPERWORK.
"EVERY CAROL IS PRETTY SIMILAR. THEY HAVE DIFFERENT PERSONALITIES, BUT THE SAME SKILL SET. AND THEY'RE DESIGNED TO BE GENIUSES OF DATA ENTRY AND ORGANIZATION.
"EVERY CAROL ALSO HAS A GIFT: THEY CAN SEE THE FUTURE. THIS IS PART OF WHAT MAKES THEM SO AMAZING: THEY KNOW IN ADVANCE WHEN THINGS ARE IMPROPERLY FILED, AND CAN CORRECT THE TIMELINE BEFORE ANY MISTAKES ARE MADE!
"OUR CAROL WAS THIS WAY, TOO. BUT WHEN THEY WERE CREATED...
"...SOMETHING WENT WRONG."
WARNING!!
GOOD
BAD

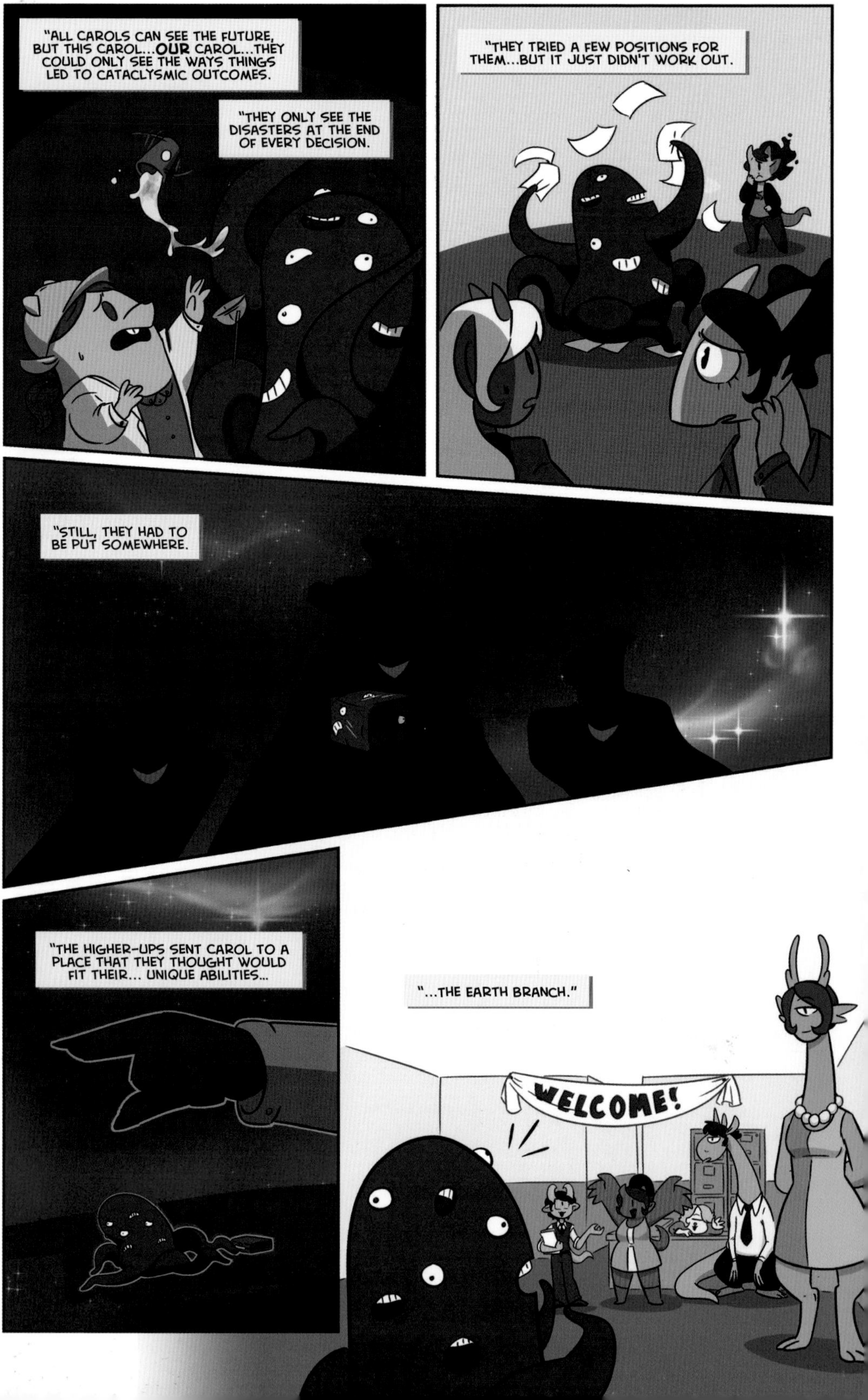
"ALL CAROLS CAN SEE THE FUTURE, BUT THIS CAROL...OUR CAROL...THEY COULD ONLY SEE THE WAYS THINGS LED TO CATACLYSMIC OUTCOMES.
"THEY ONLY SEE THE DISASTERS AT THE END OF EVERY DECISION.
"THEY TRIED A FEW POSITIONS FOR THEM...BUT IT JUST DIDN'T WORK OUT.
"STILL, THEY HAD TO BE PUT SOMEWHERE.
"THE HIGHER-UPS SENT CAROL TO A PLACE THAT THEY THOUGHT WOULD FIT THEIR... UNIQUE ABILITIES...
"...THE EARTH BRANCH."
WELCOME!

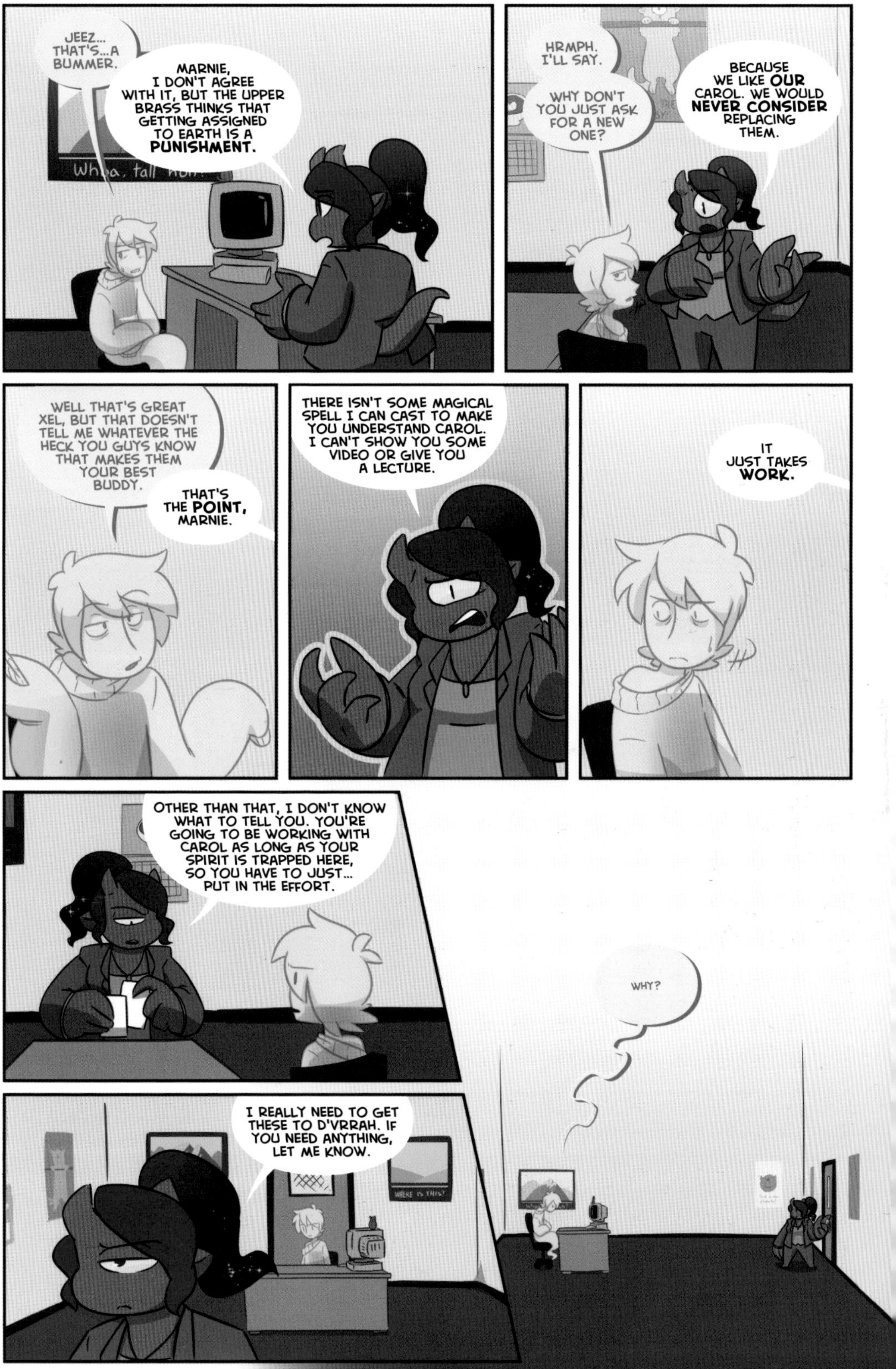

JEEZ... THAT'S...A BUMMER.
MARNIE, I DON'T AGREE WITH IT, BUT THE UPPER BRASS THINKS THAT GETTING ASSIGNED TO EARTH IS A **PUNISHMENT.**
HRMPH. I'LL SAY.
WHY DON'T YOU JUST ASK FOR A NEW ONE?
BECAUSE WE LIKE **OUR** CAROL. WE WOULD **NEVER CONSIDER** REPLACING THEM.
WELL THAT'S GREAT XEL, BUT THAT DOESN'T TELL ME WHATEVER THE HECK YOU GUYS KNOW THAT MAKES THEM YOUR BEST BUDDY.
THAT'S THE **POINT,** MARNIE.
THERE ISN'T SOME MAGICAL SPELL I CAN CAST TO MAKE YOU UNDERSTAND CAROL. I CAN'T SHOW YOU SOME VIDEO OR GIVE YOU A LECTURE.
IT JUST TAKES **WORK.**
OTHER THAN THAT, I DON'T KNOW WHAT TO TELL YOU. YOU'RE GOING TO BE WORKING WITH CAROL AS LONG AS YOUR SPIRIT IS TRAPPED HERE, SO YOU HAVE TO JUST... PUT IN THE EFFORT.
I REALLY NEED TO GET THESE TO D'VRRAH. IF YOU NEED ANYTHING, LET ME KNOW.
WHY?
WHERE IS THIS?

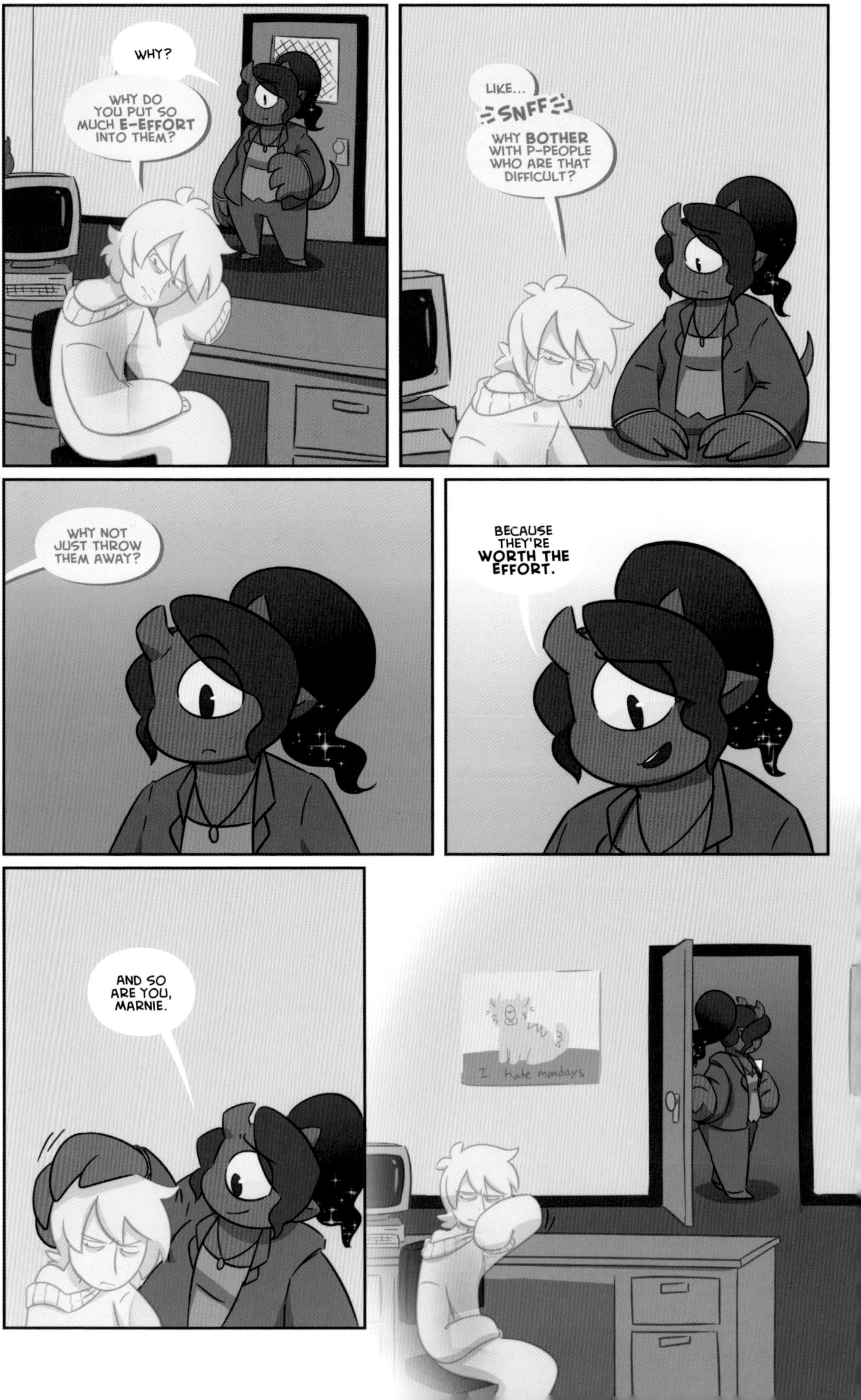
WHY?
WHY DO YOU PUT SO MUCH E-EFFORT INTO THEM?
LIKE...
SNFF
WHY BOTHER WITH P-PEOPLE WHO ARE THAT DIFFICULT?
WHY NOT JUST THROW THEM AWAY?
BECAUSE THEY'RE WORTH THE EFFORT.
AND SO ARE YOU, MARNIE.
I hate mondays

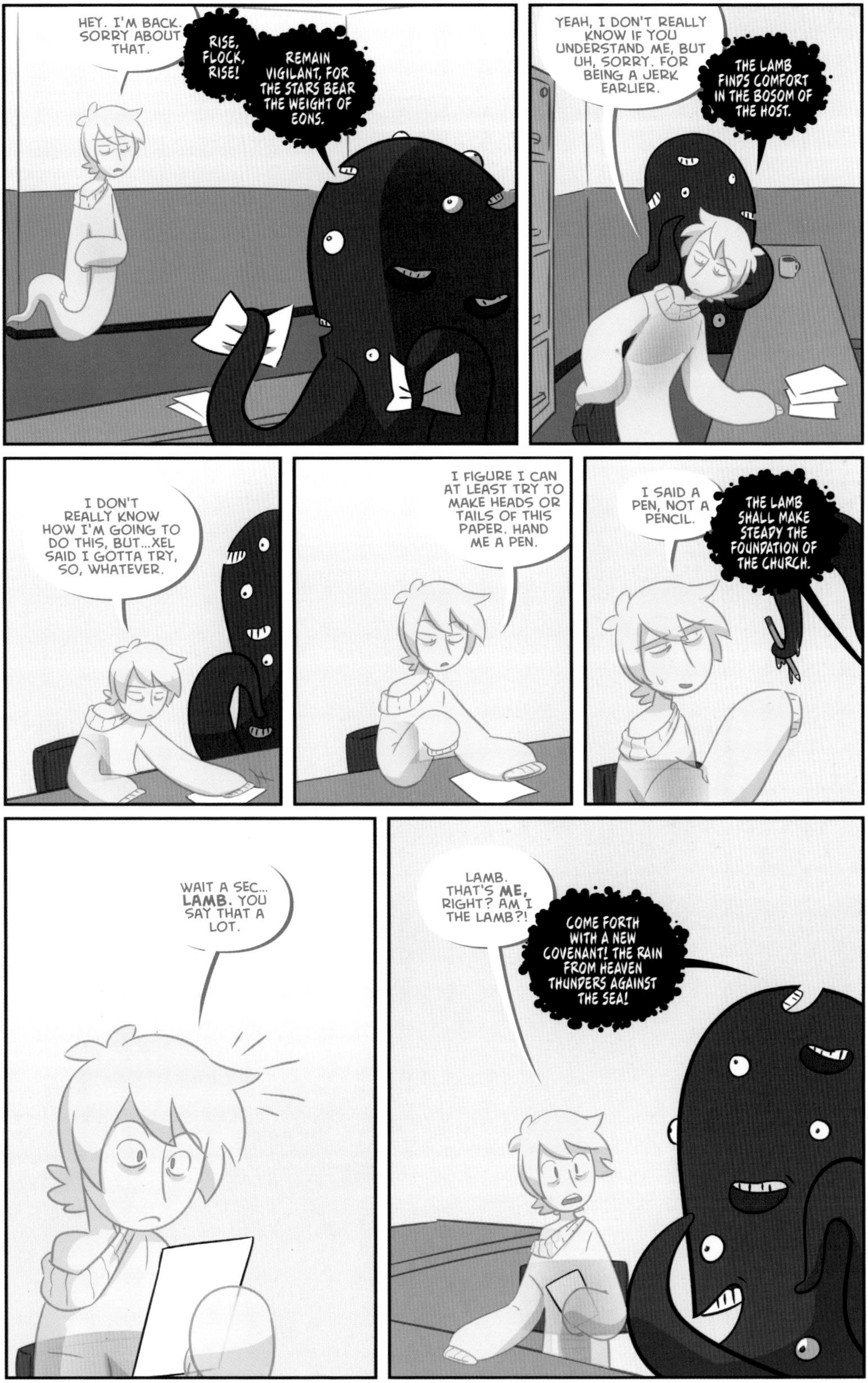
HEY. I'M BACK. SORRY ABOUT THAT.
RISE, FLOCK, RISE!
REMAIN VIGILANT, FOR THE STARS BEAR THE WEIGHT OF EONS.
YEAH, I DON'T REALLY KNOW IF YOU UNDERSTAND ME, BUT UH, SORRY. FOR BEING A JERK EARLIER.
THE LAMB FINDS COMFORT IN THE BOSOM OF THE HOST.
I DON'T REALLY KNOW HOW I'M GOING TO DO THIS, BUT...XEL SAID I GOTTA TRY, SO, WHATEVER.
I FIGURE I CAN AT LEAST TRY TO MAKE HEADS OR TAILS OF THIS PAPER. HAND ME A PEN.
I SAID A PEN, NOT A PENCIL.
THE LAMB SHALL MAKE STEADY THE FOUNDATION OF THE CHURCH.
WAIT A SEC... **LAMB.** YOU SAY THAT A LOT.
LAMB. THAT'S **ME,** RIGHT? AM I THE LAMB?!
COME FORTH WITH A NEW COVENANT! THE RAIN FROM HEAVEN THUNDERS AGAINST THE SEA!

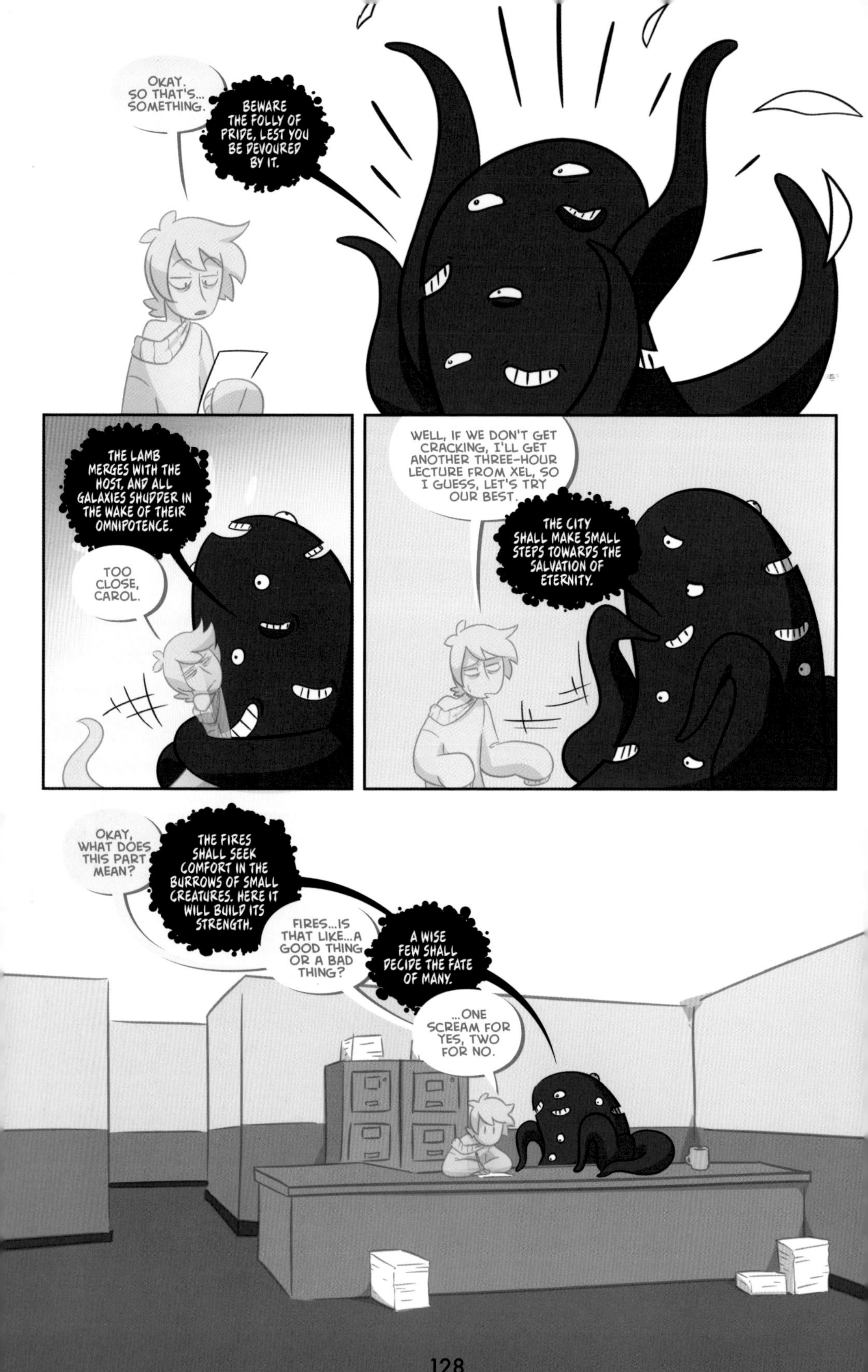
OKAY. SO THAT'S... SOMETHING.
BEWARE THE FOLLY OF PRIDE, LEST YOU BE DEVOURED BY IT.
THE LAMB MERGES WITH THE HOST, AND ALL GALAXIES SHUDDER IN THE WAKE OF THEIR OMNIPOTENCE.
TOO CLOSE, CAROL.
WELL, IF WE DON'T GET CRACKING, I'LL GET ANOTHER THREE-HOUR LECTURE FROM XEL, SO I GUESS, LET'S TRY OUR BEST.
THE CITY SHALL MAKE SMALL STEPS TOWARDS THE SALVATION OF ETERNITY.
OKAY, WHAT DOES THIS PART MEAN?
THE FIRES SHALL SEEK COMFORT IN THE BURROWS OF SMALL CREATURES. HERE IT WILL BUILD ITS STRENGTH.
FIRES...IS THAT LIKE...A GOOD THING OR A BAD THING?
A WISE FEW SHALL DECIDE THE FATE OF MANY.
...ONE SCREAM FOR YES, TWO FOR NO.

Department
of
Spectral Affairs

Chapter 5

V'attyr

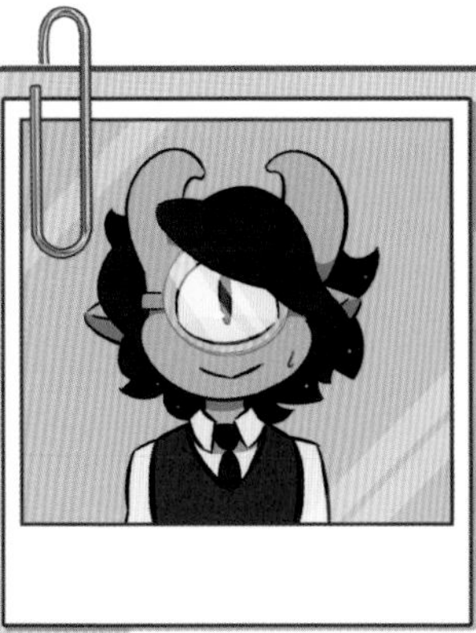

FOR OFFICIAL USE ONLY

Name: V'attyr

Pronunciation: Vik-Ter

Pronouns: he/him

Age: ∞

Position: case worker

Likes: Order, neatness, the smell of fresh laundry, worrying.

Dislikes: Messiness, that feeling where you feel like nothing is wrong which means something is definitely wrong and you're just forgetting about it!

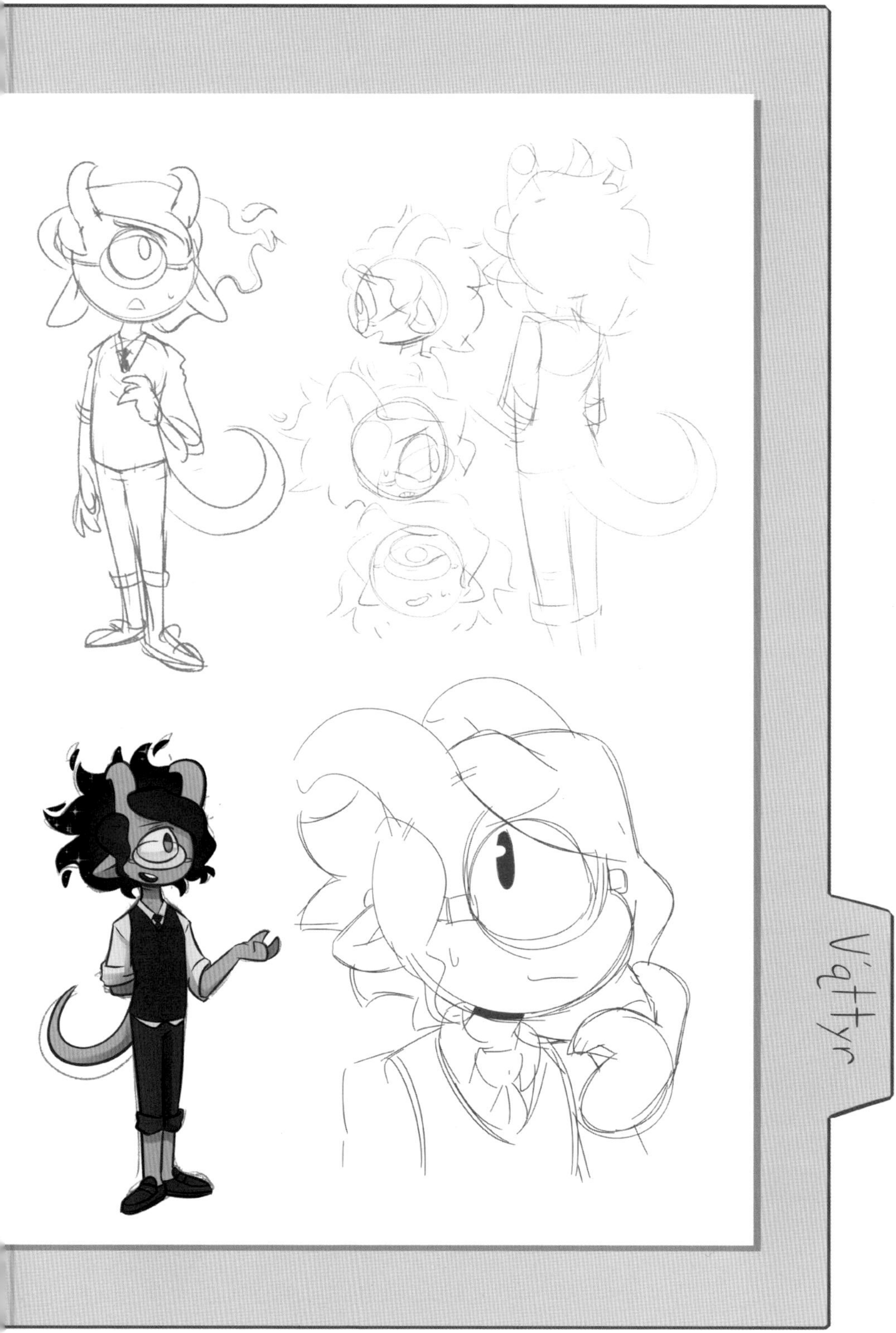
V'attyr

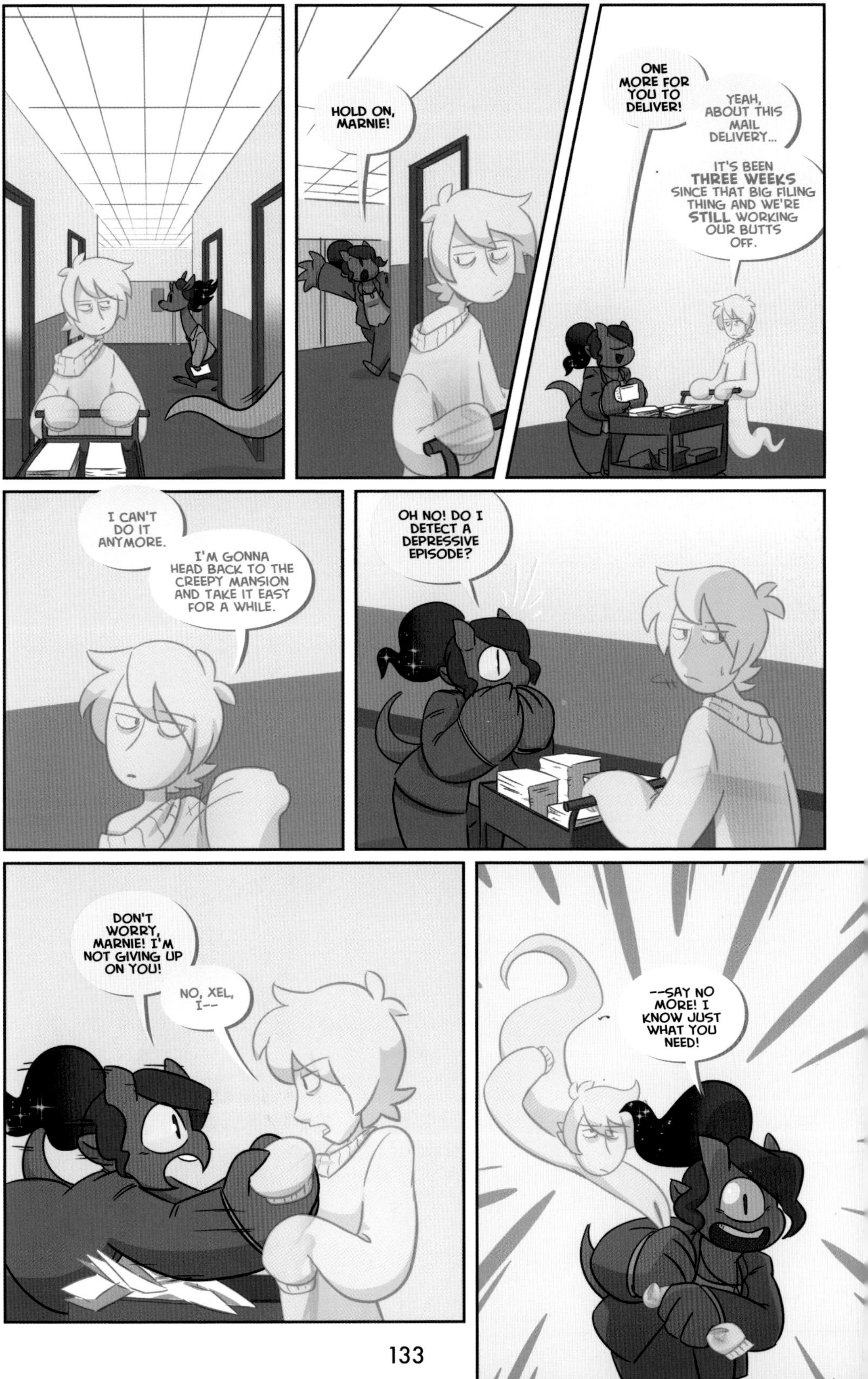
HOLD ON, MARNIE!
ONE MORE FOR YOU TO DELIVER!
YEAH, ABOUT THIS MAIL DELIVERY...
IT'S BEEN THREE WEEKS SINCE THAT BIG FILING THING AND WE'RE STILL WORKING OUR BUTTS OFF.
I CAN'T DO IT ANYMORE.
I'M GONNA HEAD BACK TO THE CREEPY MANSION AND TAKE IT EASY FOR A WHILE.
OH NO! DO I DETECT A DEPRESSIVE EPISODE?
DON'T WORRY, MARNIE! I'M NOT GIVING UP ON YOU!
NO, XEL, I--
--SAY NO MORE! I KNOW JUST WHAT YOU NEED!

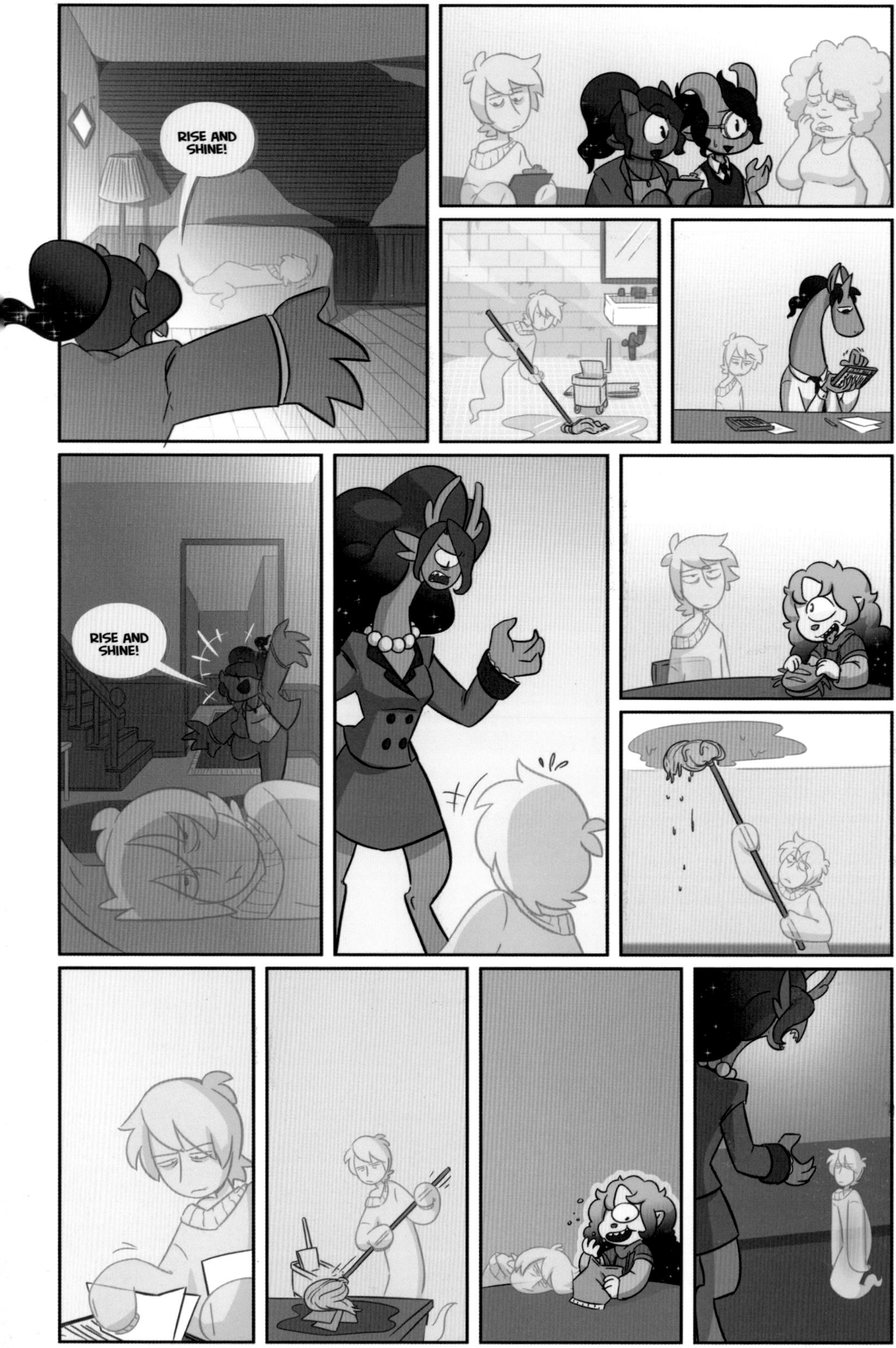
RISE AND SHINE!
RISE AND SHINE!

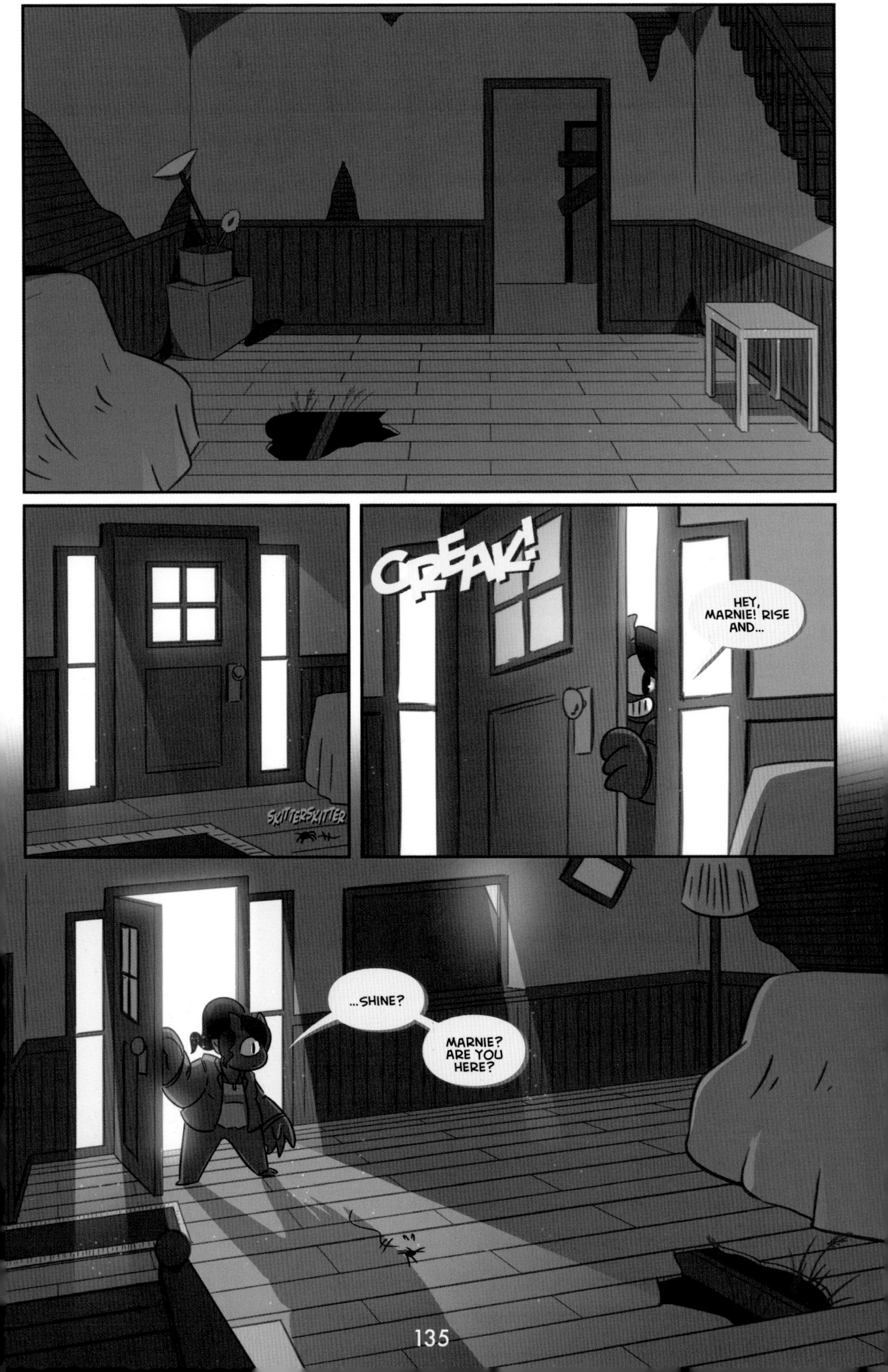
SKITTERSKITTER
CREAK!
HEY, MARNIE! RISE AND...
...SHINE?
MARNIE? ARE YOU HERE?

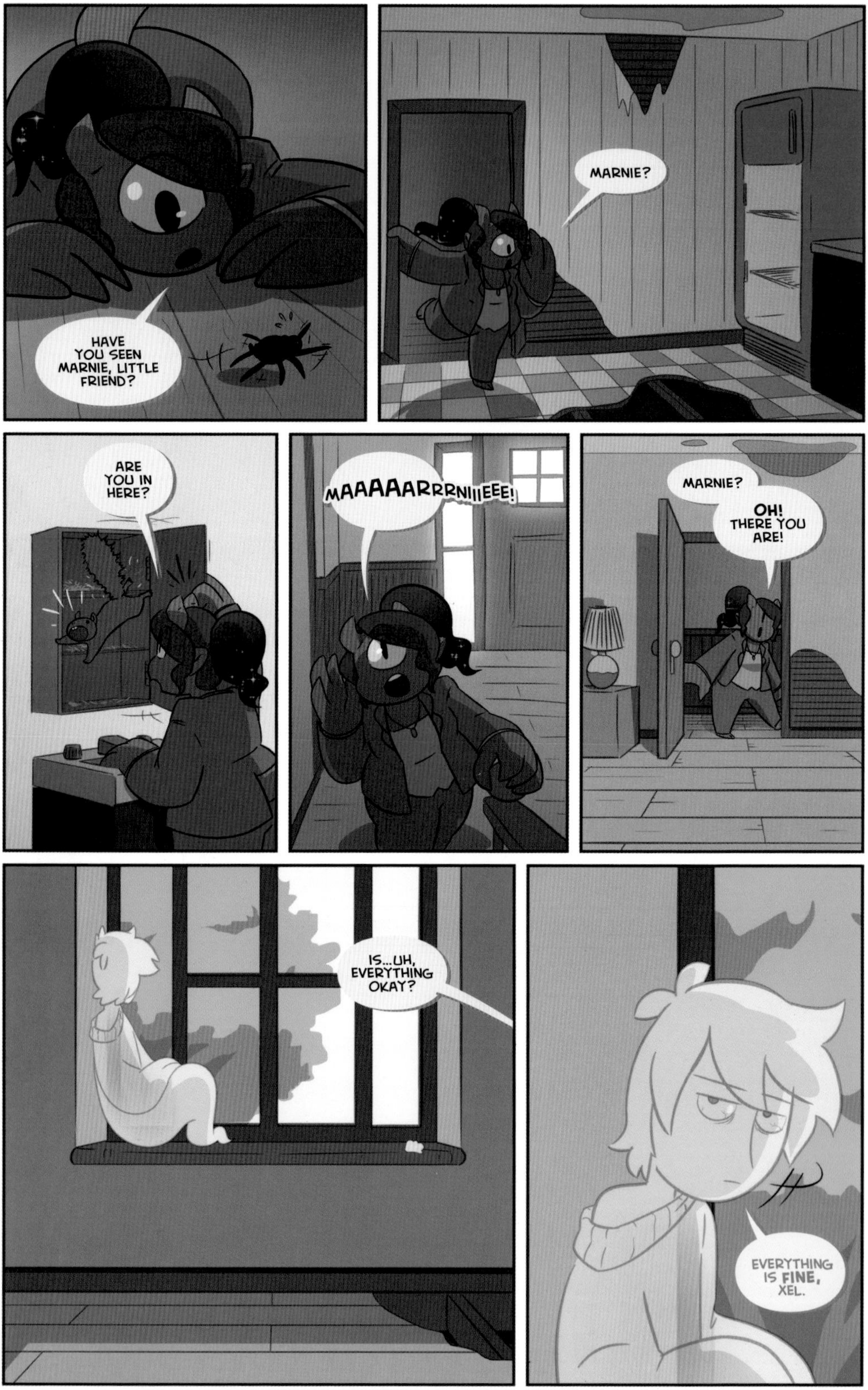
HAVE YOU SEEN MARNIE, LITTLE FRIEND?
MARNIE?
ARE YOU IN HERE?
MAAAAARRRRNIIIEEE!
MARNIE?
OH! THERE YOU ARE!
IS...UH, EVERYTHING OKAY?
EVERYTHING IS FINE, XEL.

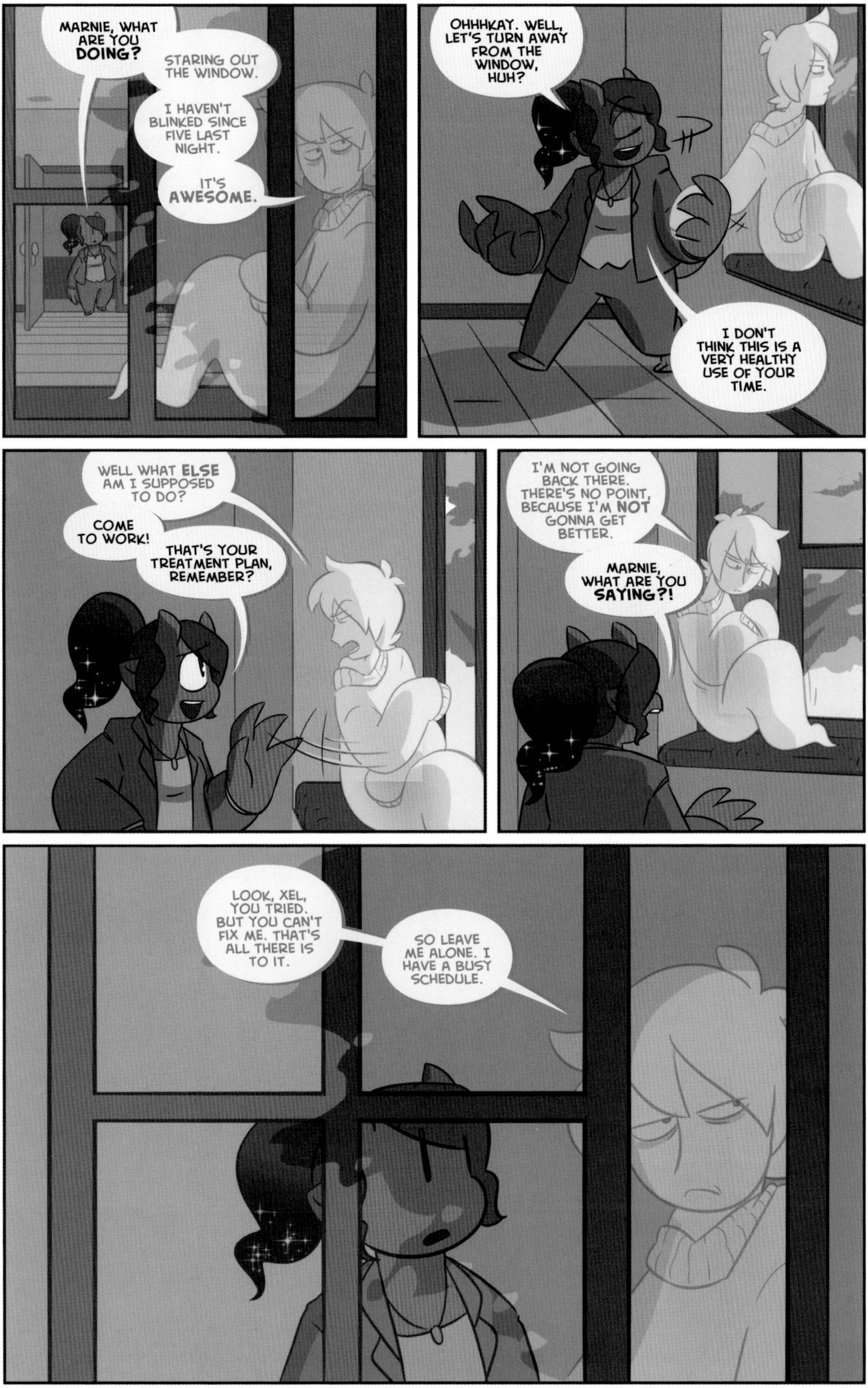
MARNIE, WHAT ARE YOU DOING?
STARING OUT THE WINDOW.
I HAVEN'T BLINKED SINCE FIVE LAST NIGHT.
IT'S AWESOME.
OHHHKAY. WELL, LET'S TURN AWAY FROM THE WINDOW, HUH?
I DON'T THINK THIS IS A VERY HEALTHY USE OF YOUR TIME.
WELL WHAT ELSE AM I SUPPOSED TO DO?
COME TO WORK!
THAT'S YOUR TREATMENT PLAN, REMEMBER?
I'M NOT GOING BACK THERE. THERE'S NO POINT, BECAUSE I'M NOT GONNA GET BETTER.
MARNIE, WHAT ARE YOU SAYING?!
LOOK, XEL, YOU TRIED. BUT YOU CAN'T FIX ME. THAT'S ALL THERE IS TO IT.
SO LEAVE ME ALONE. I HAVE A BUSY SCHEDULE.

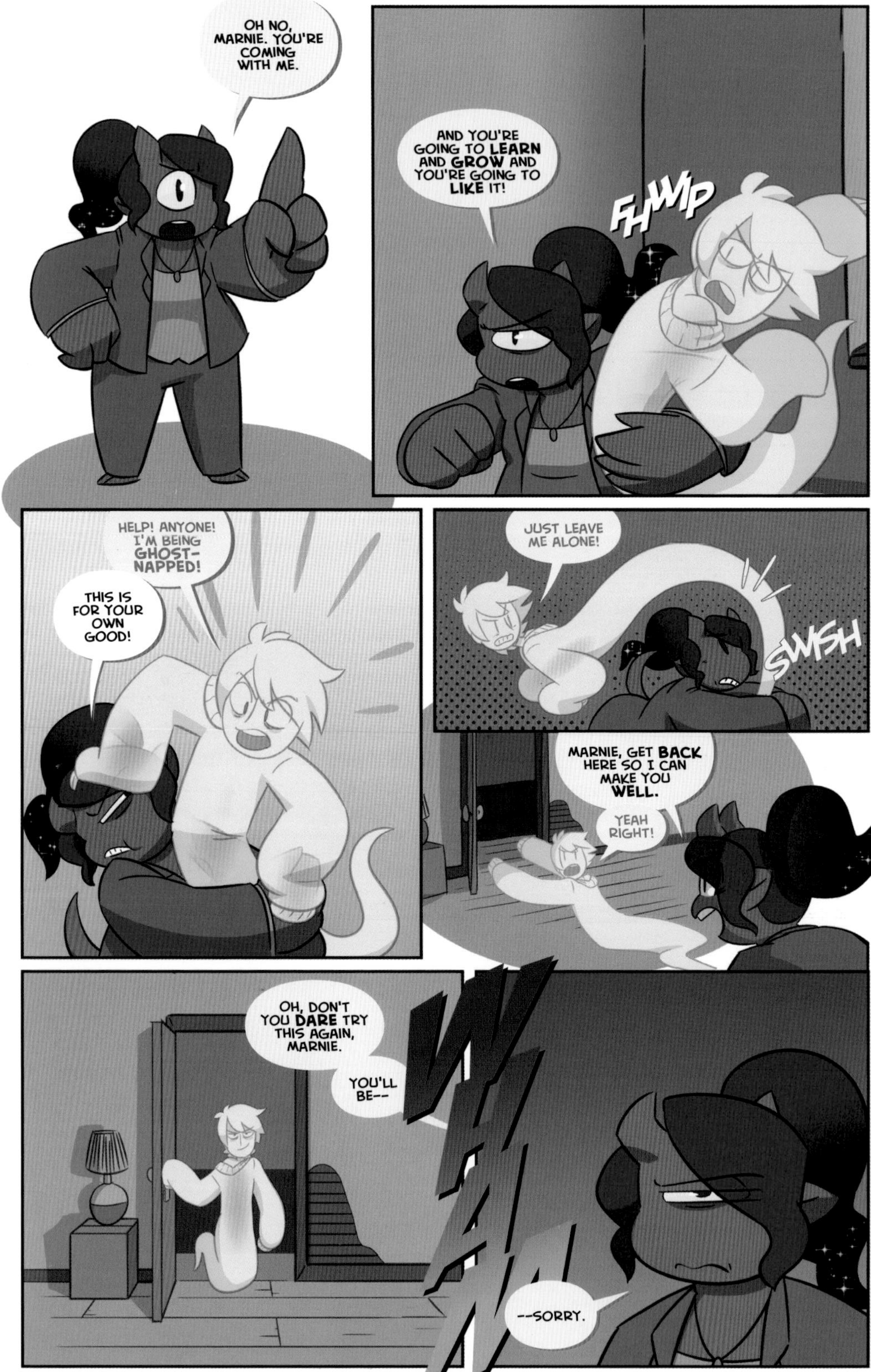
OH NO, MARNIE. YOU'RE COMING WITH ME.
AND YOU'RE GOING TO LEARN AND GROW AND YOU'RE GOING TO LIKE IT!
FHWIP
HELP! ANYONE! I'M BEING GHOST-NAPPED!
THIS IS FOR YOUR OWN GOOD!
JUST LEAVE ME ALONE!
SWISH
MARNIE, GET BACK HERE SO I CAN MAKE YOU WELL.
YEAH RIGHT!
OH, DON'T YOU DARE TRY THIS AGAIN, MARNIE.
YOU'LL BE--
--SORRY.

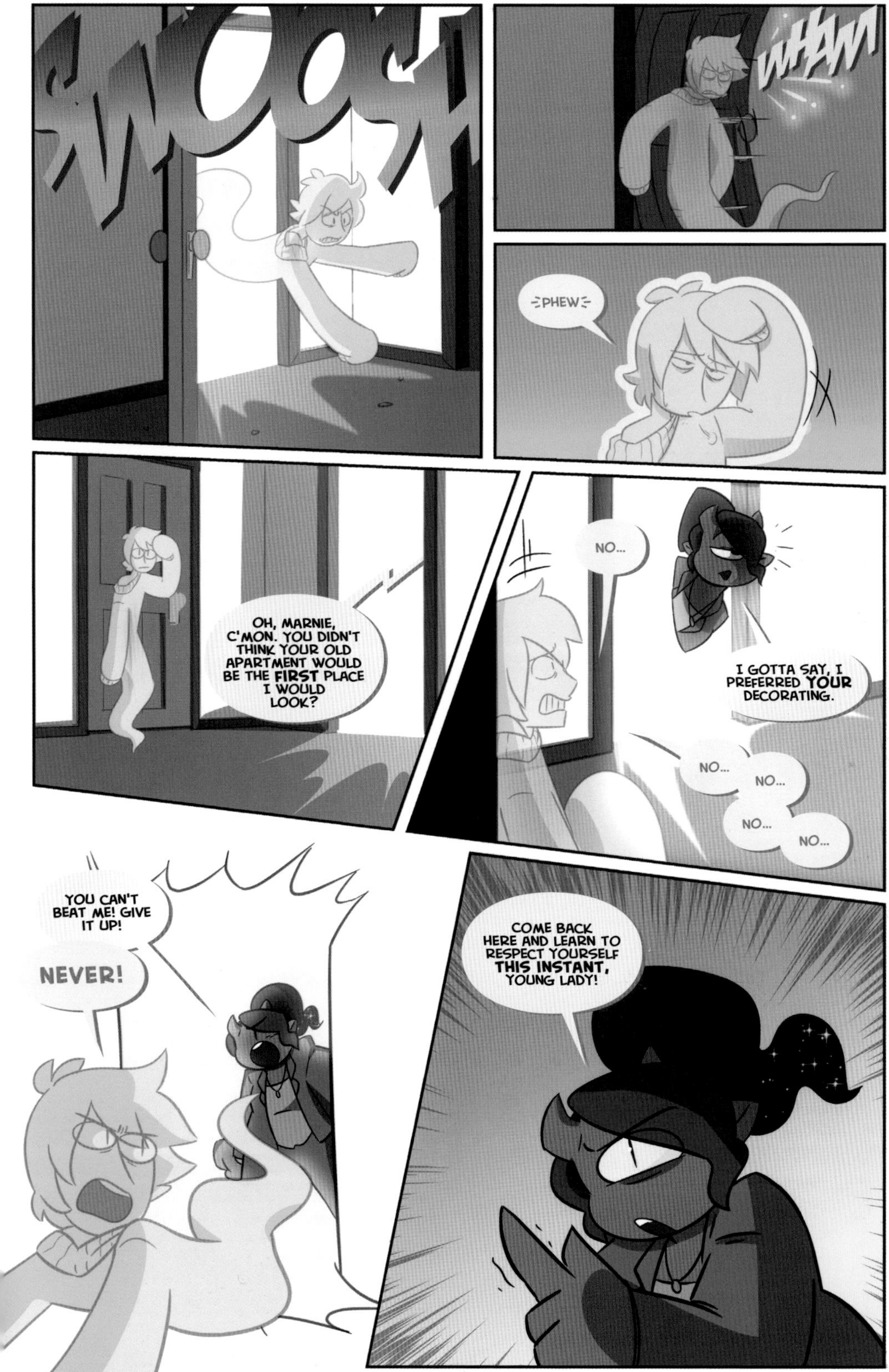
SWOOSH
WHAM
PHEW
OH, MARNIE, C'MON. YOU DIDN'T THINK YOUR OLD APARTMENT WOULD BE THE FIRST PLACE I WOULD LOOK?
NO...
I GOTTA SAY, I PREFERRED YOUR DECORATING.
NO...
NO...
NO...
NO...
YOU CAN'T BEAT ME! GIVE IT UP!
NEVER!
COME BACK HERE AND LEARN TO RESPECT YOURSELF THIS INSTANT, YOUNG LADY!

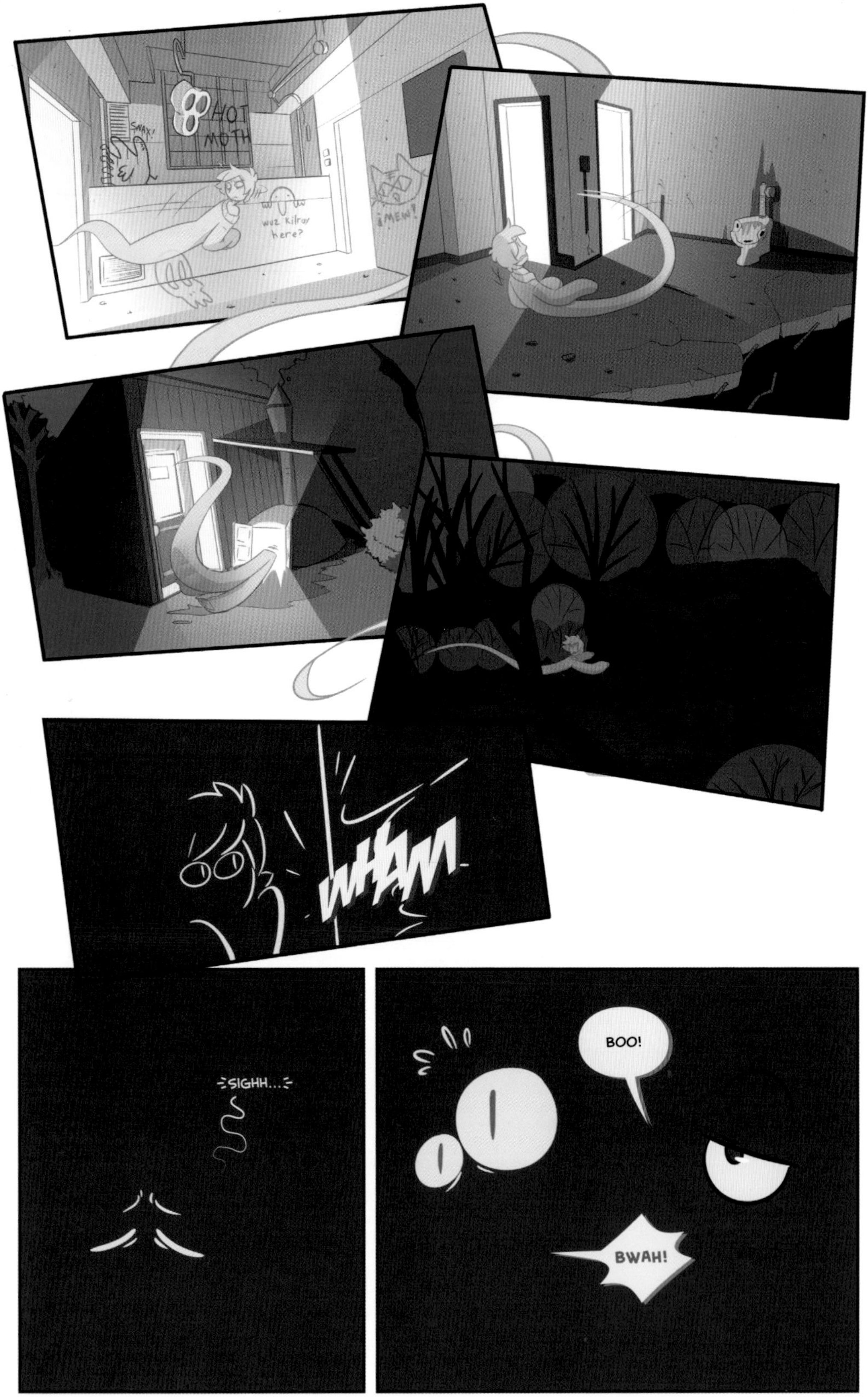
SNAX!
HOT MOTH
wuz Kilroy here?
¡MEW!
WHAM
SIGHH...
BOO!
BWAH!

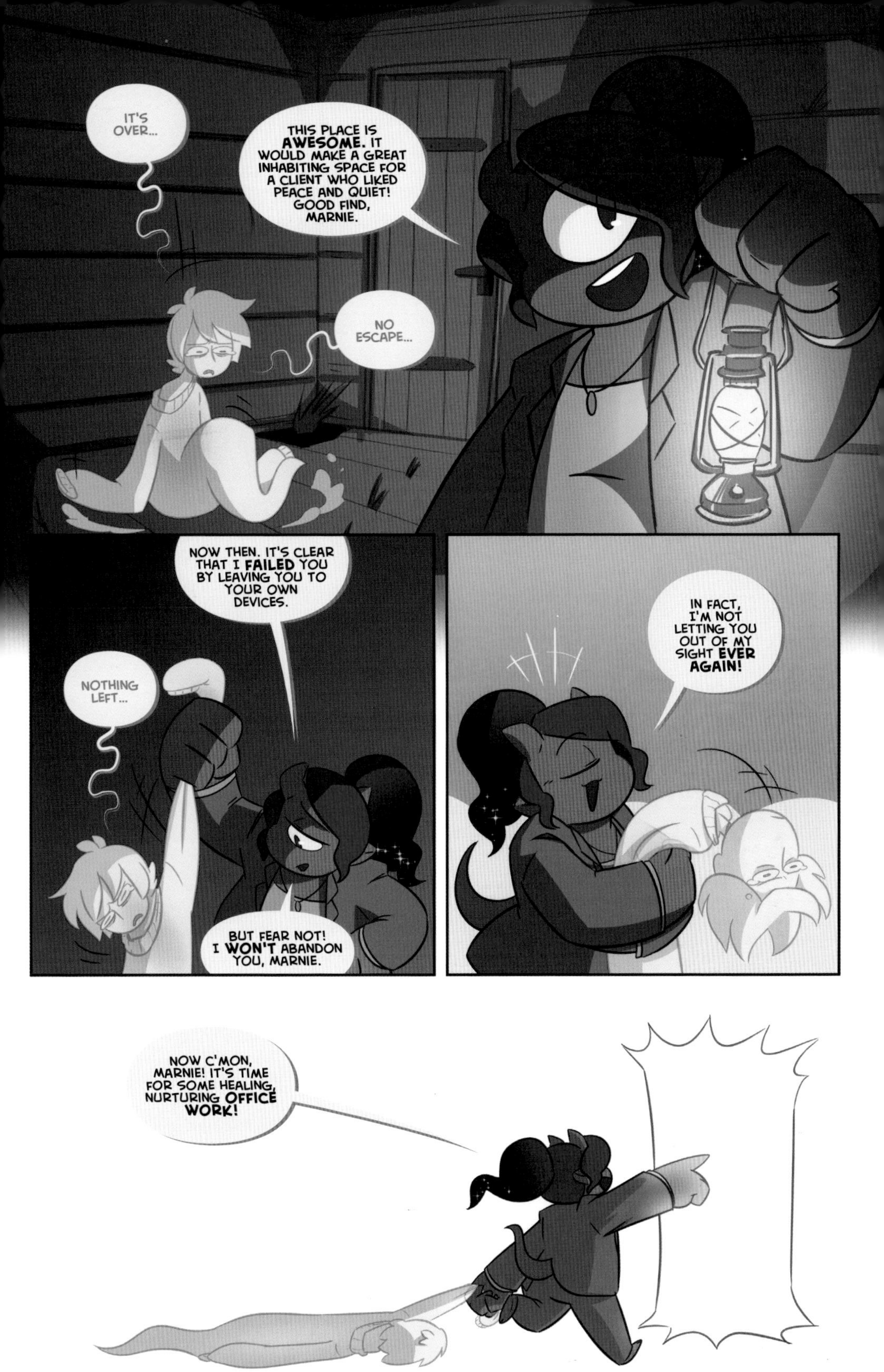
IT'S OVER...
THIS PLACE IS AWESOME. IT WOULD MAKE A GREAT INHABITING SPACE FOR A CLIENT WHO LIKED PEACE AND QUIET! GOOD FIND, MARNIE.
NO ESCAPE...
NOW THEN. IT'S CLEAR THAT I FAILED YOU BY LEAVING YOU TO YOUR OWN DEVICES.
NOTHING LEFT...
BUT FEAR NOT! I WON'T ABANDON YOU, MARNIE.
IN FACT, I'M NOT LETTING YOU OUT OF MY SIGHT EVER AGAIN!
NOW C'MON, MARNIE! IT'S TIME FOR SOME HEALING, NURTURING OFFICE WORK!

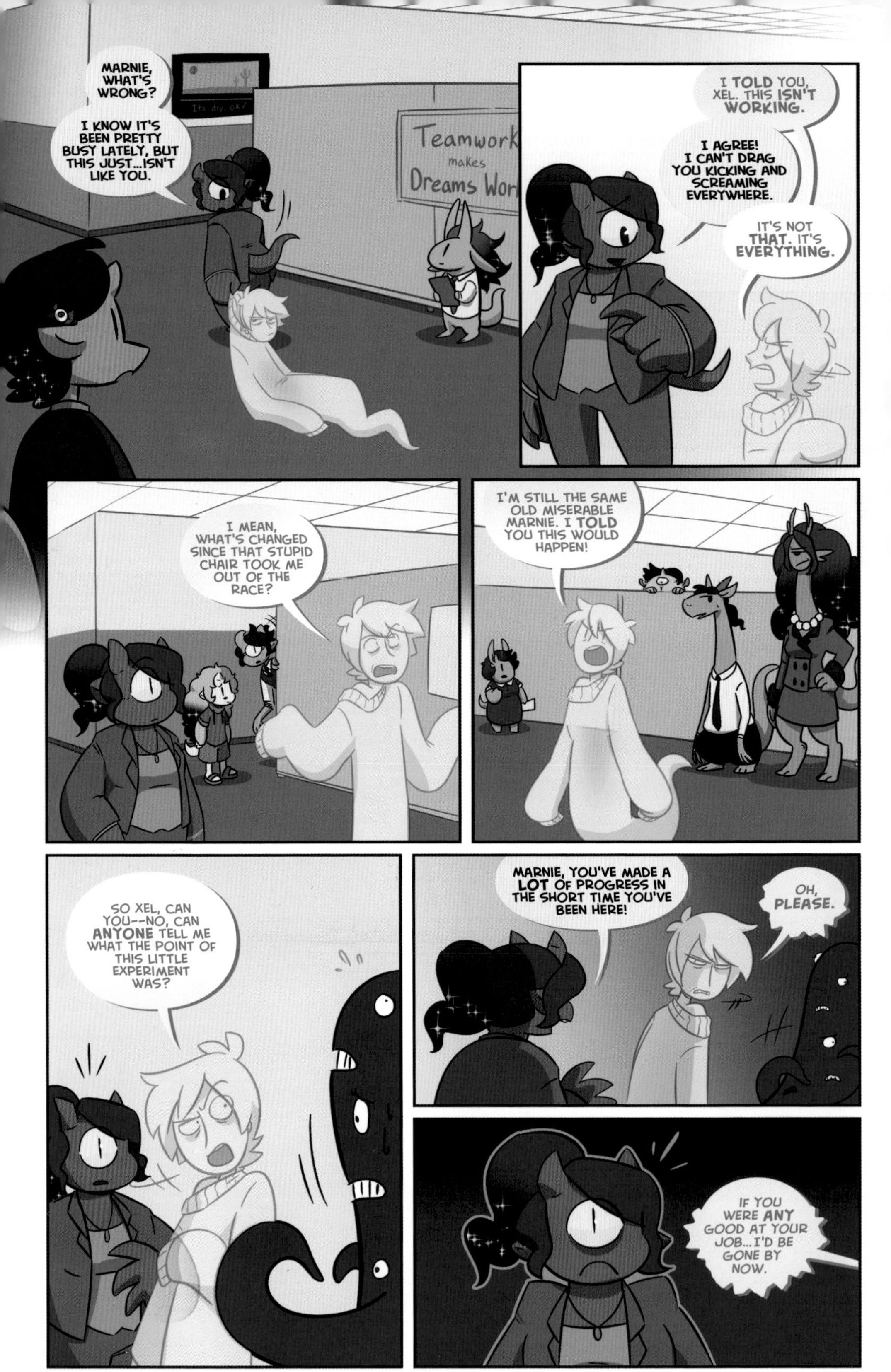
Its dry, ok?
Teamwork makes Dreams Work
MARNIE, WHAT'S WRONG?
I KNOW IT'S BEEN PRETTY BUSY LATELY, BUT THIS JUST...ISN'T LIKE YOU.
I TOLD YOU, XEL. THIS ISN'T WORKING.
I AGREE! I CAN'T DRAG YOU KICKING AND SCREAMING EVERYWHERE.
IT'S NOT THAT. IT'S EVERYTHING.
I MEAN, WHAT'S CHANGED SINCE THAT STUPID CHAIR TOOK ME OUT OF THE RACE?
I'M STILL THE SAME OLD MISERABLE MARNIE. I TOLD YOU THIS WOULD HAPPEN!
SO XEL, CAN YOU--NO, CAN ANYONE TELL ME WHAT THE POINT OF THIS LITTLE EXPERIMENT WAS?
MARNIE, YOU'VE MADE A LOT OF PROGRESS IN THE SHORT TIME YOU'VE BEEN HERE!
OH, PLEASE.
IF YOU WERE ANY GOOD AT YOUR JOB...I'D BE GONE BY NOW.

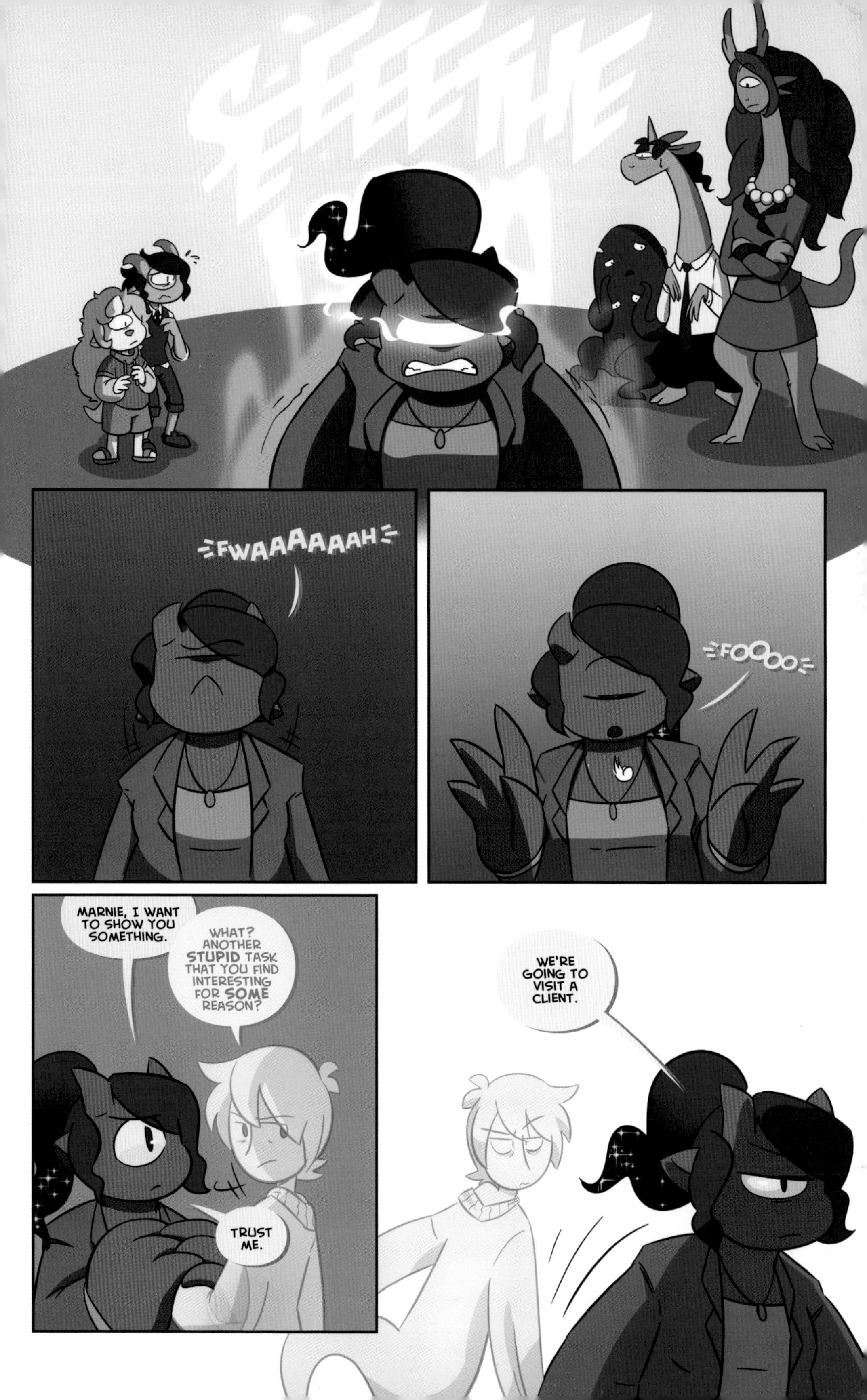
SEETHE
FWAAAAAAH
FOOOO
MARNIE, I WANT TO SHOW YOU SOMETHING.
WHAT? ANOTHER STUPID TASK THAT YOU FIND INTERESTING FOR SOME REASON?
TRUST ME.
WE'RE GOING TO VISIT A CLIENT.

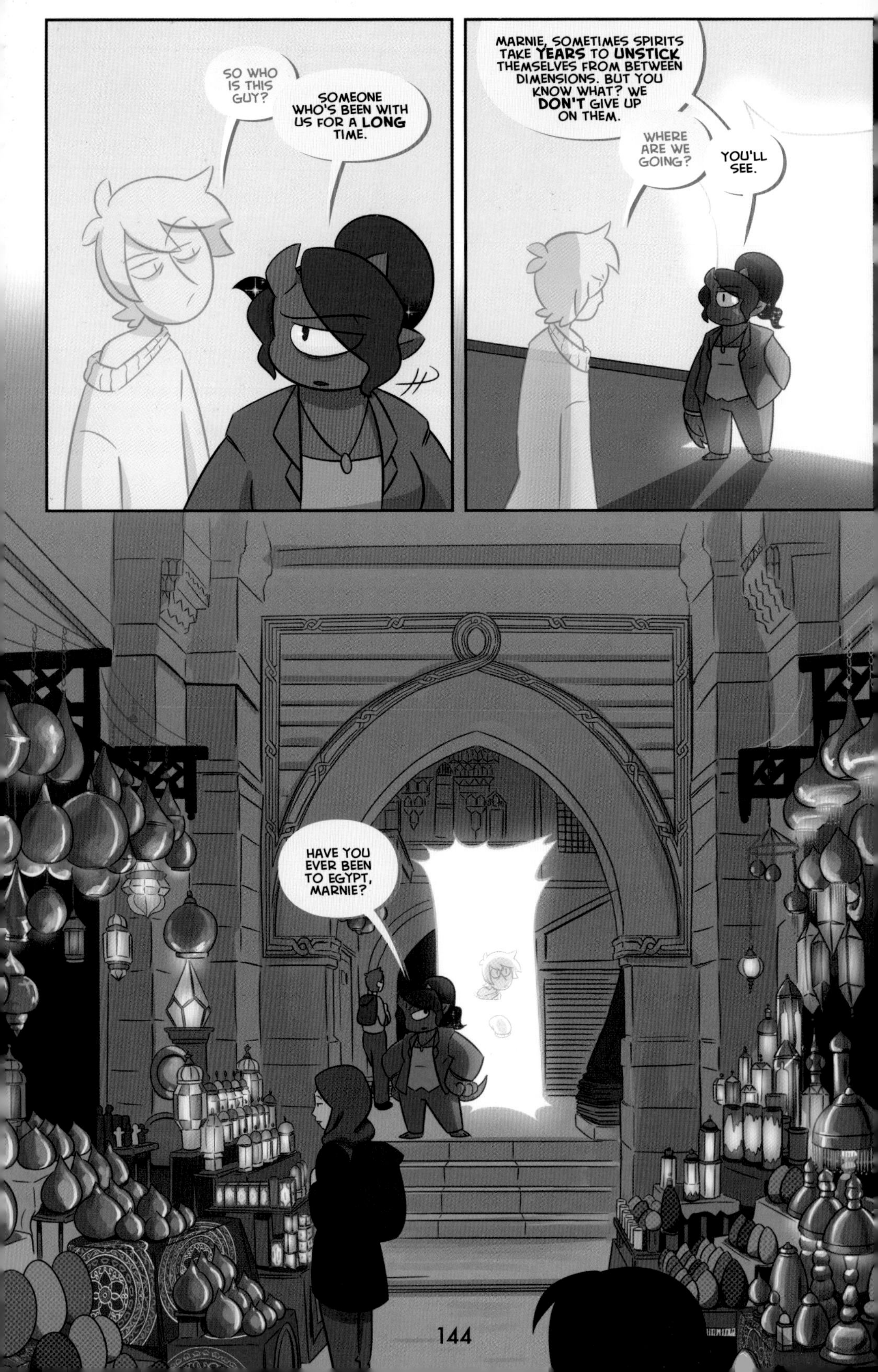
SO WHO IS THIS GUY?
SOMEONE WHO'S BEEN WITH US FOR A **LONG** TIME.
MARNIE, SOMETIMES SPIRITS TAKE **YEARS** TO **UNSTICK** THEMSELVES FROM BETWEEN DIMENSIONS. BUT YOU KNOW WHAT? WE **DON'T** GIVE UP ON THEM.
WHERE ARE WE GOING?
YOU'LL SEE.
HAVE YOU EVER BEEN TO EGYPT, MARNIE?

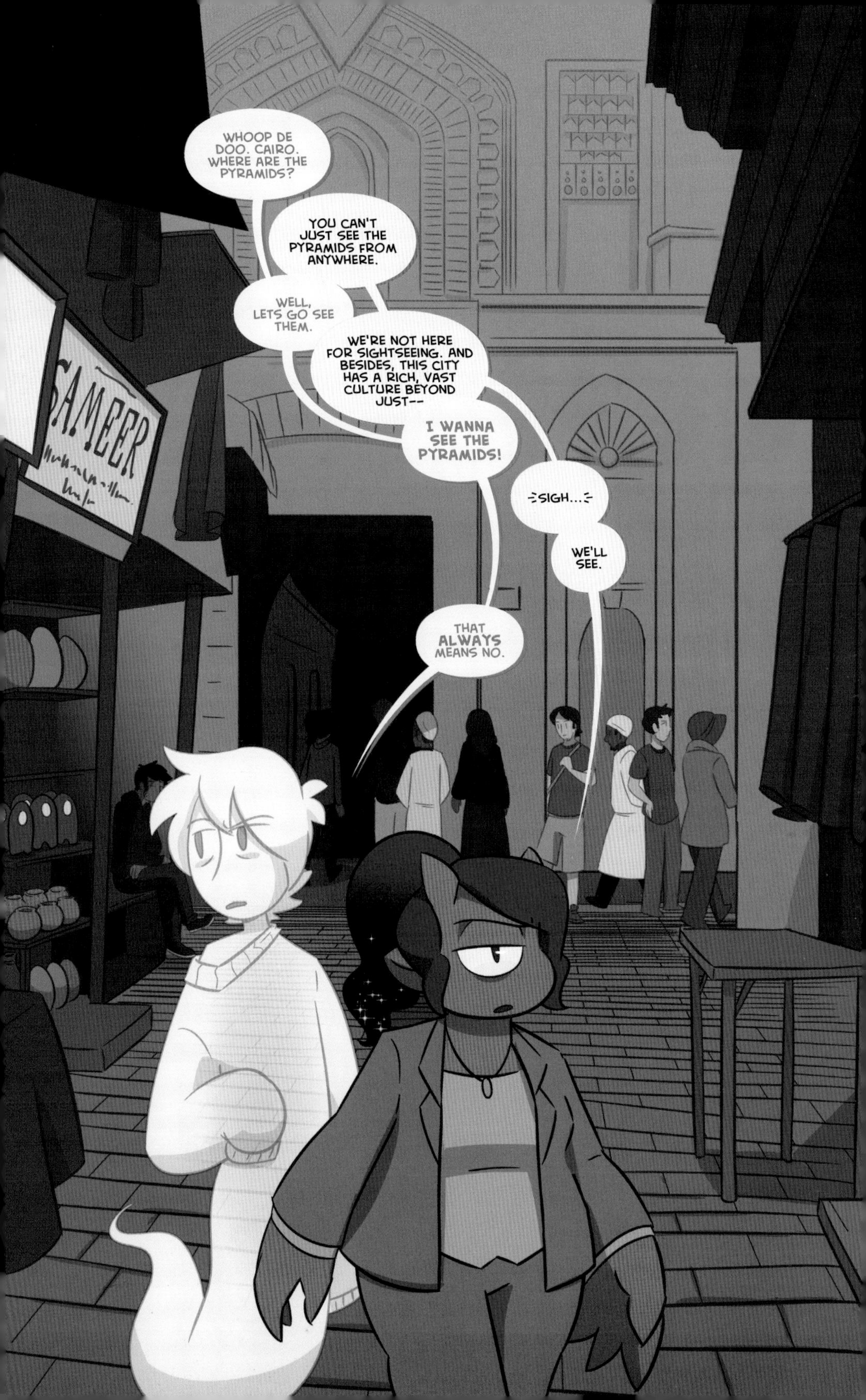
WHOOP DE DOO. CAIRO. WHERE ARE THE PYRAMIDS?
YOU CAN'T JUST SEE THE PYRAMIDS FROM ANYWHERE.
WELL, LETS GO SEE THEM.
WE'RE NOT HERE FOR SIGHTSEEING. AND BESIDES, THIS CITY HAS A RICH, VAST CULTURE BEYOND JUST--
I WANNA SEE THE PYRAMIDS!
SIGH...
WE'LL SEE.
THAT ALWAYS MEANS NO.
SAMEER

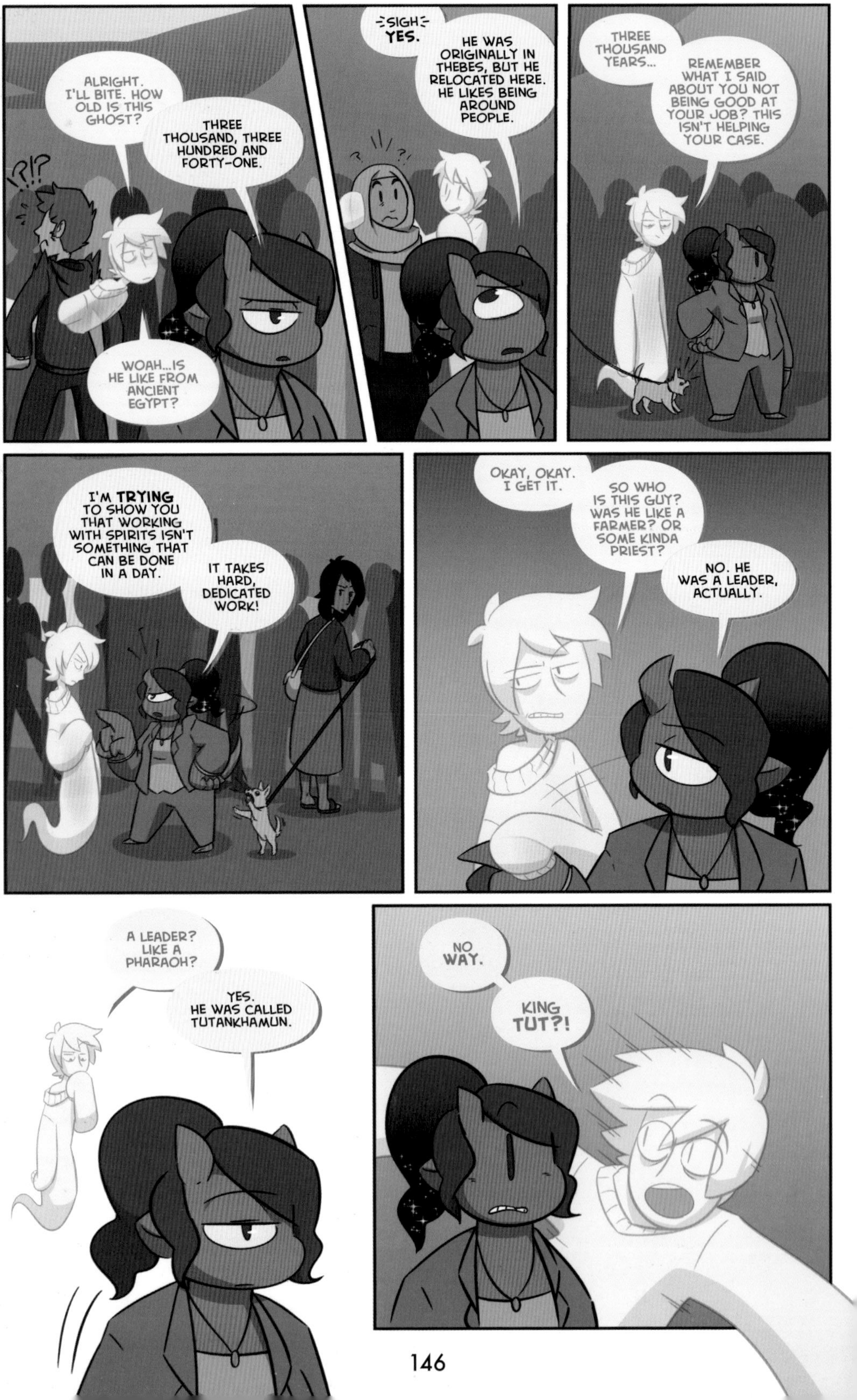
ALRIGHT. I'LL BITE. HOW OLD IS THIS GHOST?
THREE THOUSAND, THREE HUNDRED AND FORTY-ONE.
!?!?
WOAH...IS HE LIKE FROM ANCIENT EGYPT?
-SIGH- YES.
HE WAS ORIGINALLY IN THEBES, BUT HE RELOCATED HERE. HE LIKES BEING AROUND PEOPLE.
THREE THOUSAND YEARS...
REMEMBER WHAT I SAID ABOUT YOU NOT BEING GOOD AT YOUR JOB? THIS ISN'T HELPING YOUR CASE.
I'M **TRYING** TO SHOW YOU THAT WORKING WITH SPIRITS ISN'T SOMETHING THAT CAN BE DONE IN A DAY.
IT TAKES HARD, DEDICATED WORK!
OKAY, OKAY. I GET IT.
SO WHO IS THIS GUY? WAS HE LIKE A FARMER? OR SOME KINDA PRIEST?
NO. HE WAS A LEADER, ACTUALLY.
A LEADER? LIKE A PHARAOH?
YES. HE WAS CALLED TUTANKHAMUN.
NO **WAY.**
KING **TUT?!**

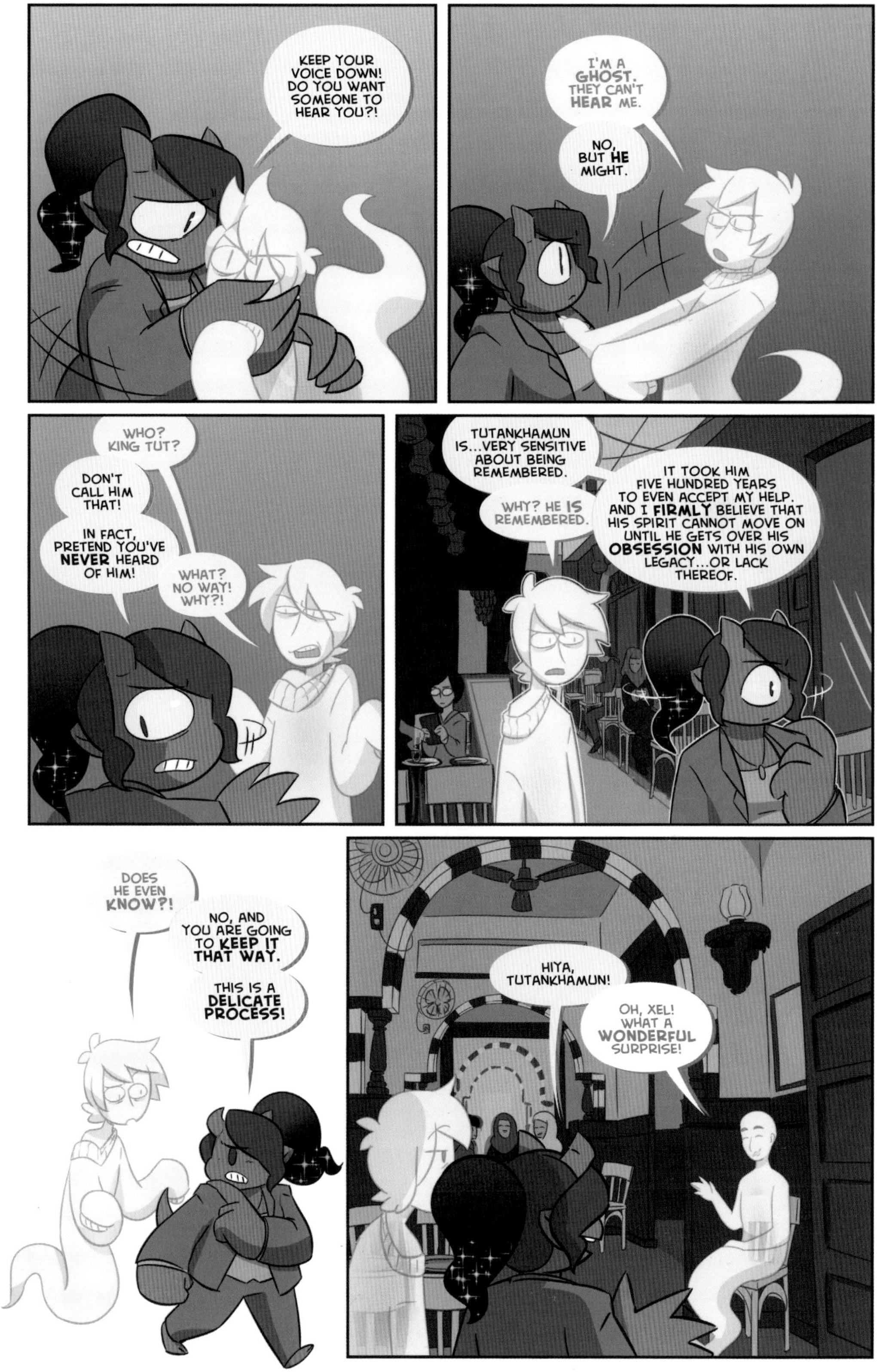
KEEP YOUR VOICE DOWN! DO YOU WANT SOMEONE TO HEAR YOU?!
I'M A GHOST. THEY CAN'T HEAR ME.
NO, BUT HE MIGHT.
WHO? KING TUT?
DON'T CALL HIM THAT!
IN FACT, PRETEND YOU'VE NEVER HEARD OF HIM!
WHAT? NO WAY! WHY?!
TUTANKHAMUN IS...VERY SENSITIVE ABOUT BEING REMEMBERED.
WHY? HE IS REMEMBERED.
IT TOOK HIM FIVE HUNDRED YEARS TO EVEN ACCEPT MY HELP. AND I FIRMLY BELIEVE THAT HIS SPIRIT CANNOT MOVE ON UNTIL HE GETS OVER HIS OBSESSION WITH HIS OWN LEGACY...OR LACK THEREOF.
DOES HE EVEN KNOW?!
NO, AND YOU ARE GOING TO KEEP IT THAT WAY.
THIS IS A DELICATE PROCESS!
HIYA, TUTANKHAMUN!
OH, XEL! WHAT A WONDERFUL SURPRISE!

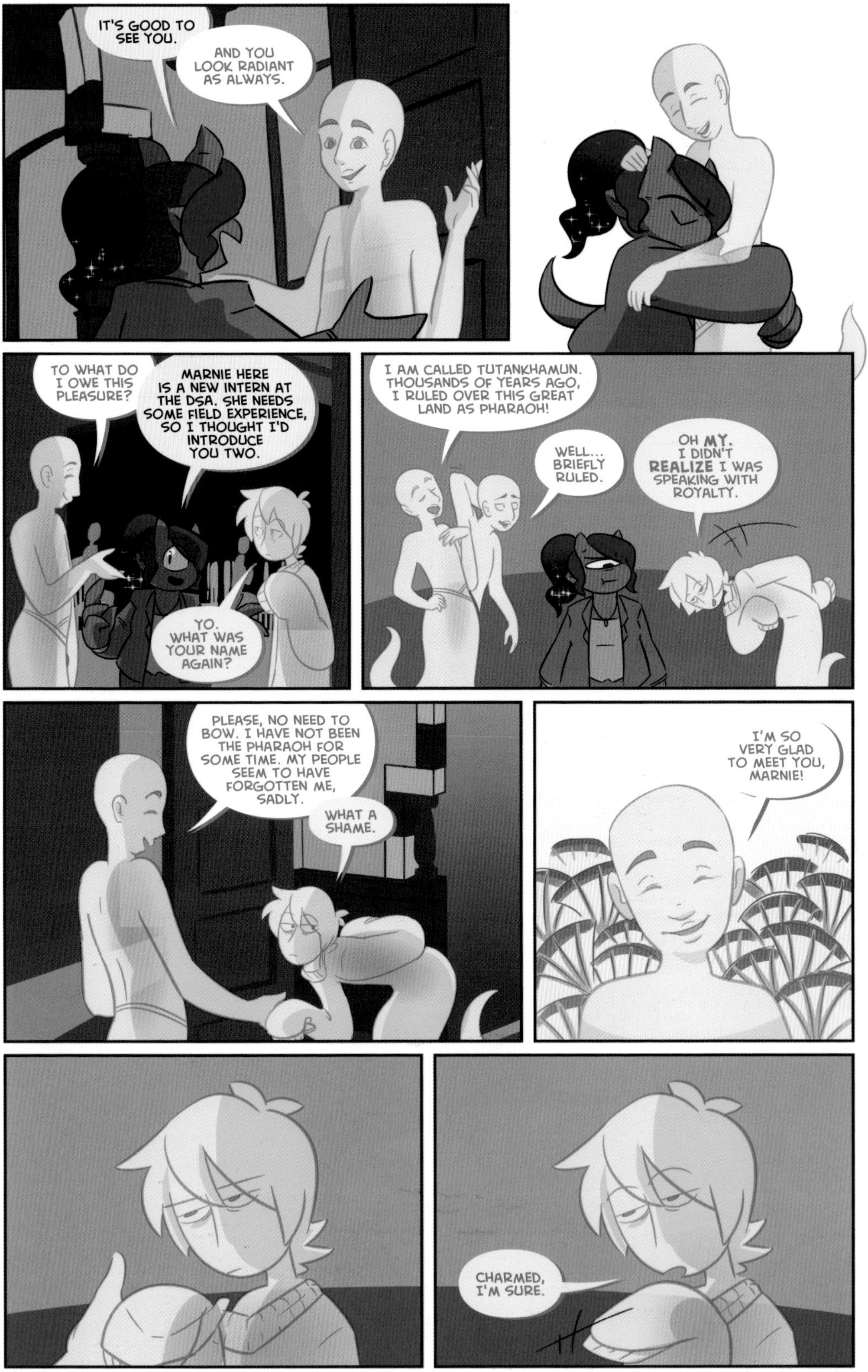
IT'S GOOD TO SEE YOU.
AND YOU LOOK RADIANT AS ALWAYS.
TO WHAT DO I OWE THIS PLEASURE?
MARNIE HERE IS A NEW INTERN AT THE DSA. SHE NEEDS SOME FIELD EXPERIENCE, SO I THOUGHT I'D INTRODUCE YOU TWO.
YO. WHAT WAS YOUR NAME AGAIN?
I AM CALLED TUTANKHAMUN. THOUSANDS OF YEARS AGO, I RULED OVER THIS GREAT LAND AS PHARAOH!
WELL... BRIEFLY RULED.
OH MY. I DIDN'T REALIZE I WAS SPEAKING WITH ROYALTY.
PLEASE, NO NEED TO BOW. I HAVE NOT BEEN THE PHARAOH FOR SOME TIME. MY PEOPLE SEEM TO HAVE FORGOTTEN ME, SADLY.
WHAT A SHAME.
I'M SO VERY GLAD TO MEET YOU, MARNIE!
CHARMED, I'M SURE.

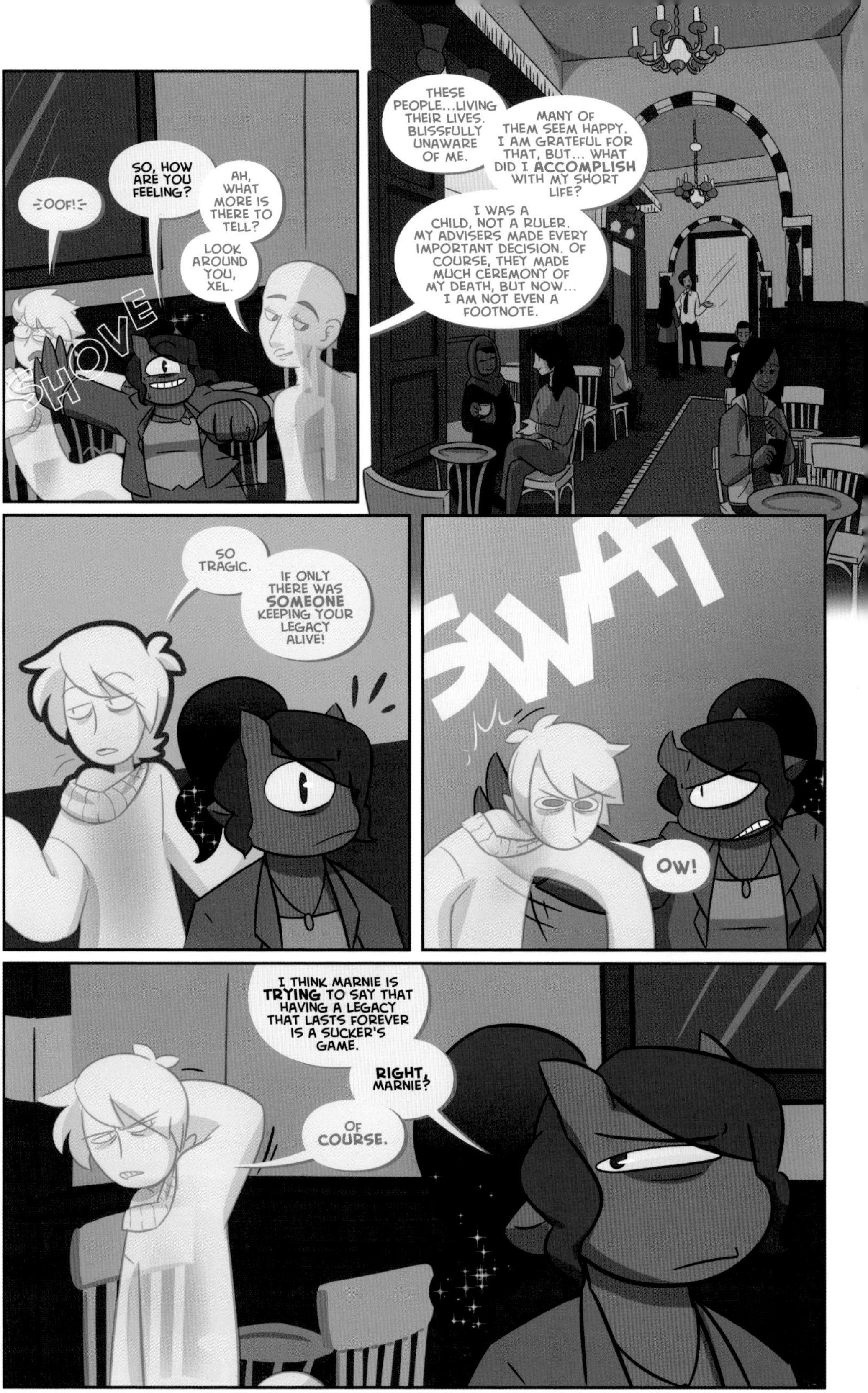
OOF!
SO, HOW ARE YOU FEELING?
AH, WHAT MORE IS THERE TO TELL?
LOOK AROUND YOU, XEL.
SHOVE
THESE PEOPLE...LIVING THEIR LIVES. BLISSFULLY UNAWARE OF ME.
MANY OF THEM SEEM HAPPY. I AM GRATEFUL FOR THAT, BUT... WHAT DID I ACCOMPLISH WITH MY SHORT LIFE?
I WAS A CHILD, NOT A RULER. MY ADVISERS MADE EVERY IMPORTANT DECISION. OF COURSE, THEY MADE MUCH CEREMONY OF MY DEATH, BUT NOW... I AM NOT EVEN A FOOTNOTE.
SO TRAGIC.
IF ONLY THERE WAS SOMEONE KEEPING YOUR LEGACY ALIVE!
SWAT
OW!
I THINK MARNIE IS TRYING TO SAY THAT HAVING A LEGACY THAT LASTS FOREVER IS A SUCKER'S GAME.
RIGHT, MARNIE?
OF COURSE.

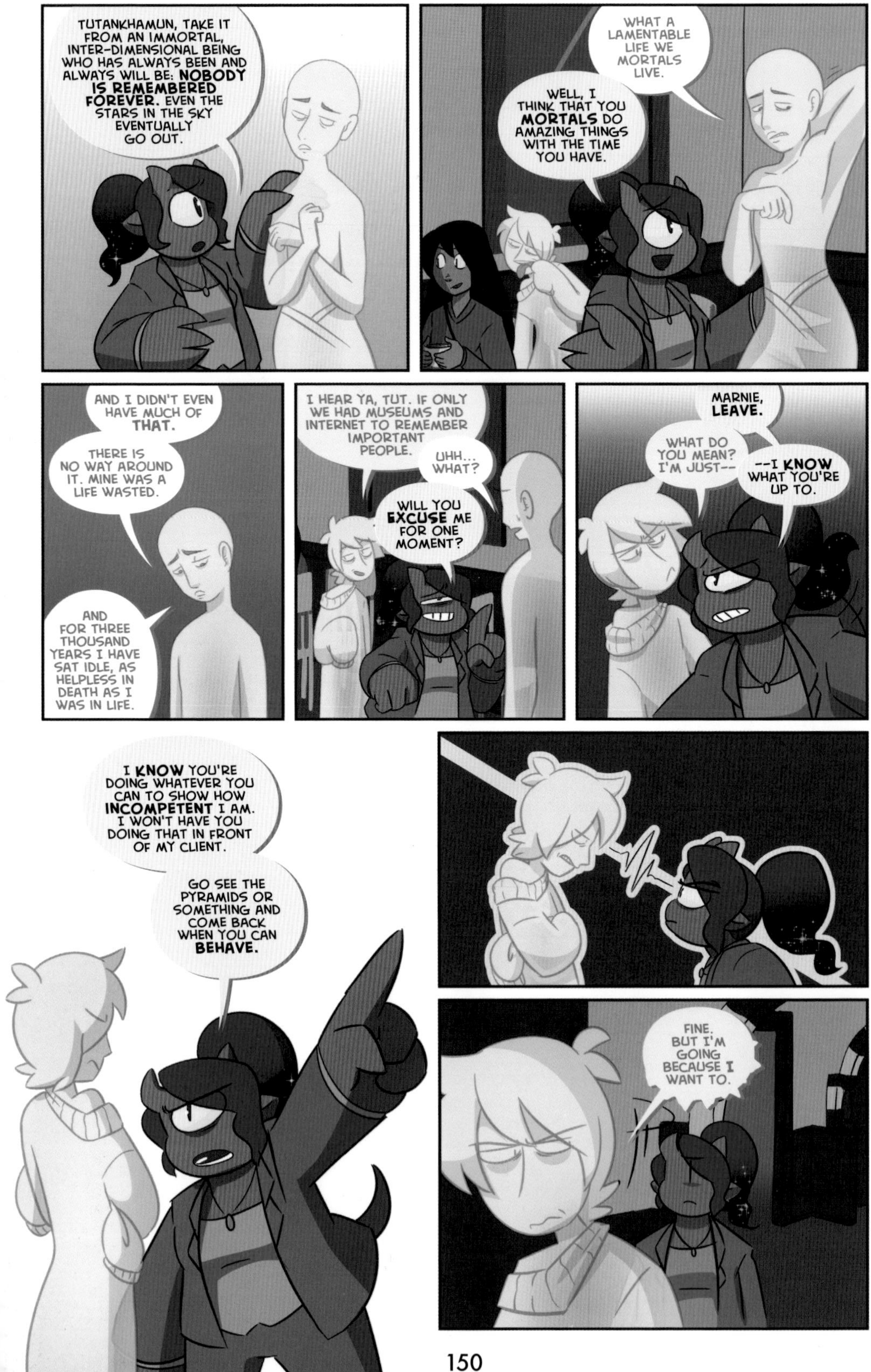
TUTANKHAMUN, TAKE IT FROM AN IMMORTAL, INTER-DIMENSIONAL BEING WHO HAS ALWAYS BEEN AND ALWAYS WILL BE: NOBODY IS REMEMBERED FOREVER. EVEN THE STARS IN THE SKY EVENTUALLY GO OUT.
WHAT A LAMENTABLE LIFE WE MORTALS LIVE.
WELL, I THINK THAT YOU MORTALS DO AMAZING THINGS WITH THE TIME YOU HAVE.
AND I DIDN'T EVEN HAVE MUCH OF THAT.
THERE IS NO WAY AROUND IT. MINE WAS A LIFE WASTED.
AND FOR THREE THOUSAND YEARS I HAVE SAT IDLE, AS HELPLESS IN DEATH AS I WAS IN LIFE.
I HEAR YA, TUT. IF ONLY WE HAD MUSEUMS AND INTERNET TO REMEMBER IMPORTANT PEOPLE.
UHH... WHAT?
WILL YOU EXCUSE ME FOR ONE MOMENT?
MARNIE, LEAVE.
WHAT DO YOU MEAN? I'M JUST--
--I KNOW WHAT YOU'RE UP TO.
I KNOW YOU'RE DOING WHATEVER YOU CAN TO SHOW HOW INCOMPETENT I AM. I WON'T HAVE YOU DOING THAT IN FRONT OF MY CLIENT.
GO SEE THE PYRAMIDS OR SOMETHING AND COME BACK WHEN YOU CAN BEHAVE.
FINE. BUT I'M GOING BECAUSE I WANT TO.

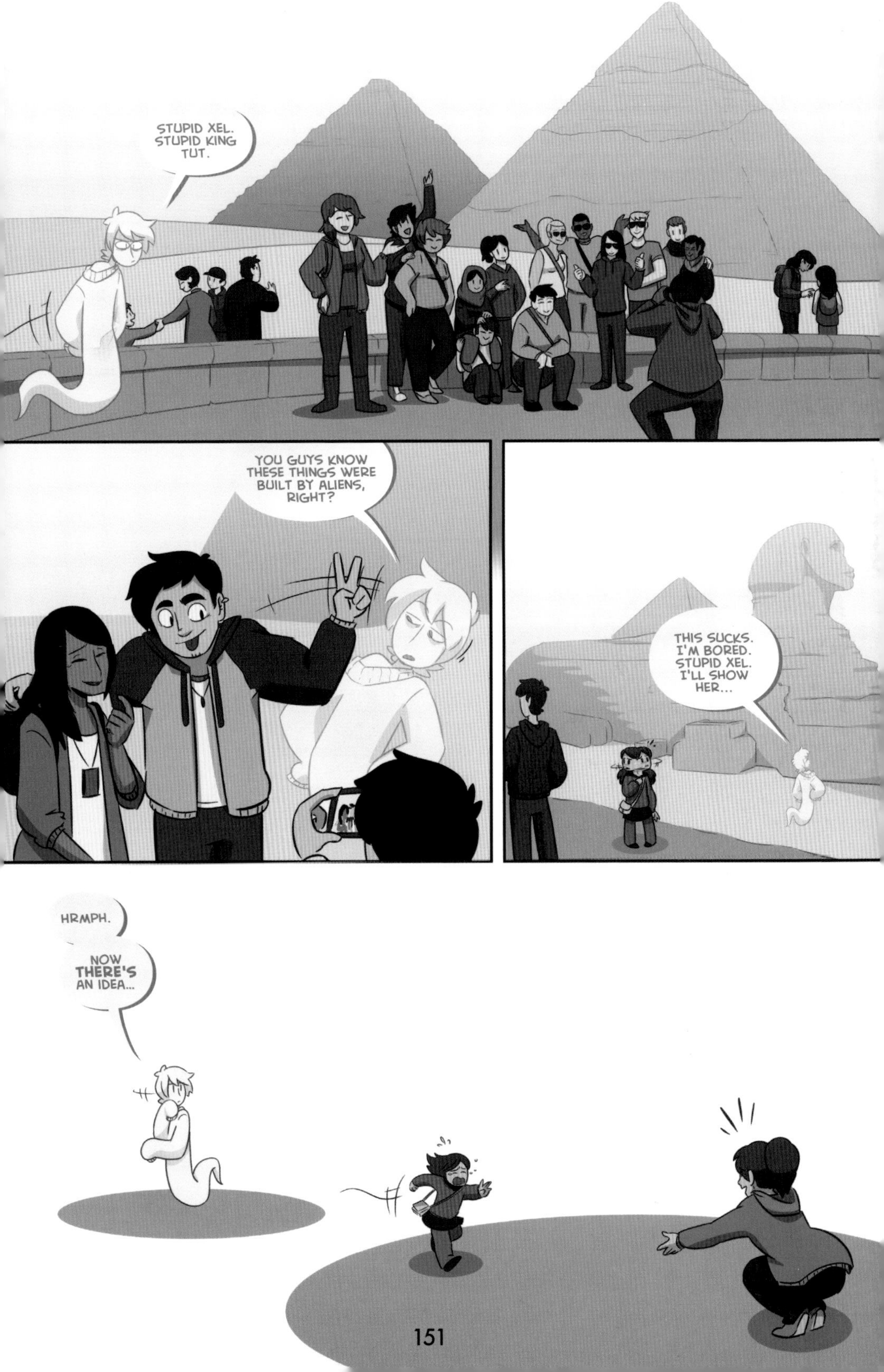
STUPID XEL. STUPID KING TUT.
YOU GUYS KNOW THESE THINGS WERE BUILT BY ALIENS, RIGHT?
THIS SUCKS. I'M BORED. STUPID XEL. I'LL SHOW HER...
HRMPH.
NOW THERE'S AN IDEA...

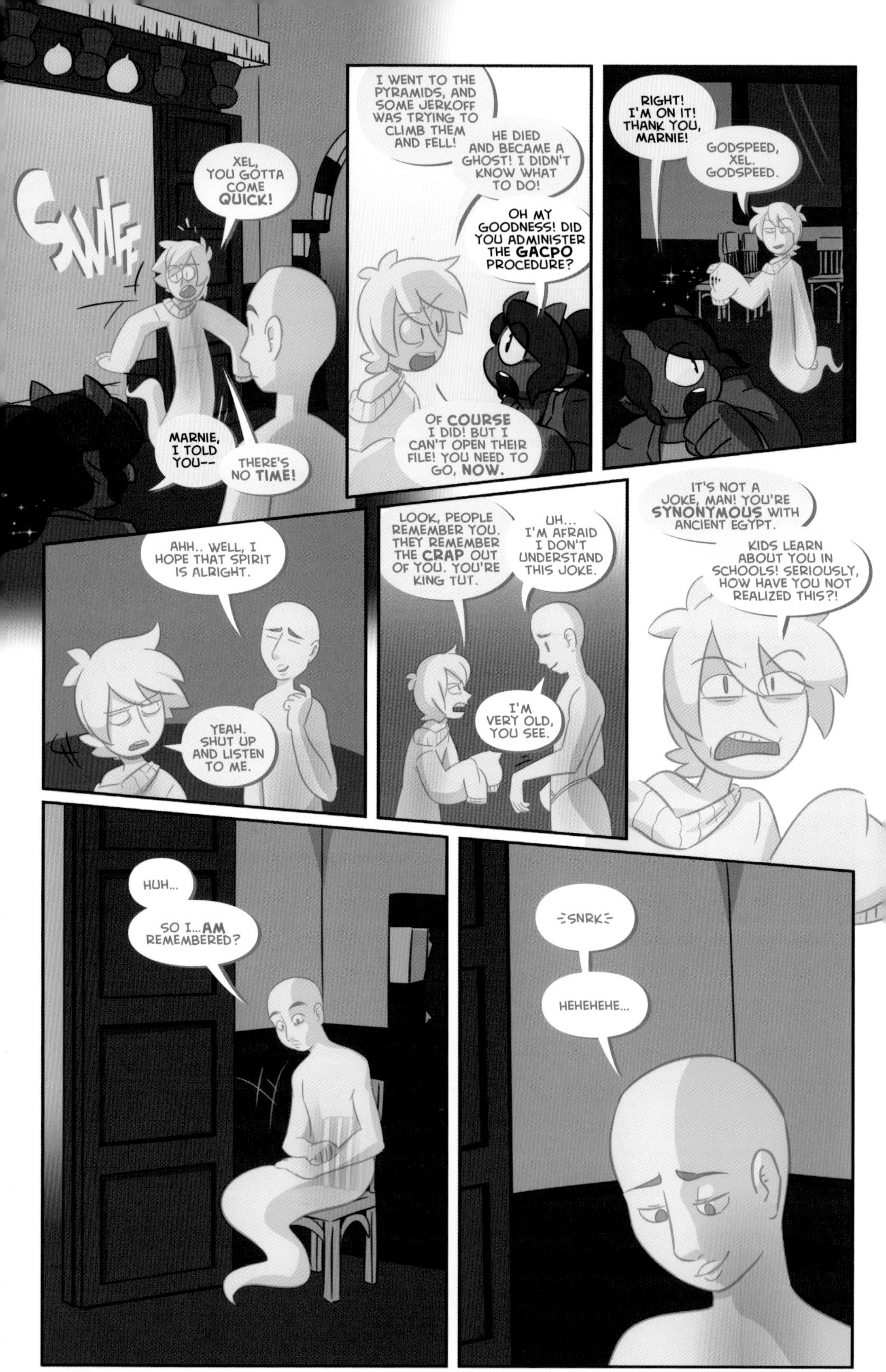
SWIFF
XEL, YOU GOTTA COME QUICK!
MARNIE, I TOLD YOU--
THERE'S NO TIME!
I WENT TO THE PYRAMIDS, AND SOME JERKOFF WAS TRYING TO CLIMB THEM AND FELL!
HE DIED AND BECAME A GHOST! I DIDN'T KNOW WHAT TO DO!
OH MY GOODNESS! DID YOU ADMINISTER THE GACPO PROCEDURE?
OF COURSE I DID! BUT I CAN'T OPEN THEIR FILE! YOU NEED TO GO, NOW.
RIGHT! I'M ON IT! THANK YOU, MARNIE!
GODSPEED, XEL. GODSPEED.
AHH.. WELL, I HOPE THAT SPIRIT IS ALRIGHT.
YEAH. SHUT UP AND LISTEN TO ME.
LOOK, PEOPLE REMEMBER YOU. THEY REMEMBER THE CRAP OUT OF YOU. YOU'RE KING TUT.
UH... I'M AFRAID I DON'T UNDERSTAND THIS JOKE.
I'M VERY OLD, YOU SEE.
IT'S NOT A JOKE, MAN! YOU'RE SYNONYMOUS WITH ANCIENT EGYPT.
KIDS LEARN ABOUT YOU IN SCHOOLS! SERIOUSLY, HOW HAVE YOU NOT REALIZED THIS?!
HUH...
SO I...AM REMEMBERED?
SNRK
HEHEHEHE...

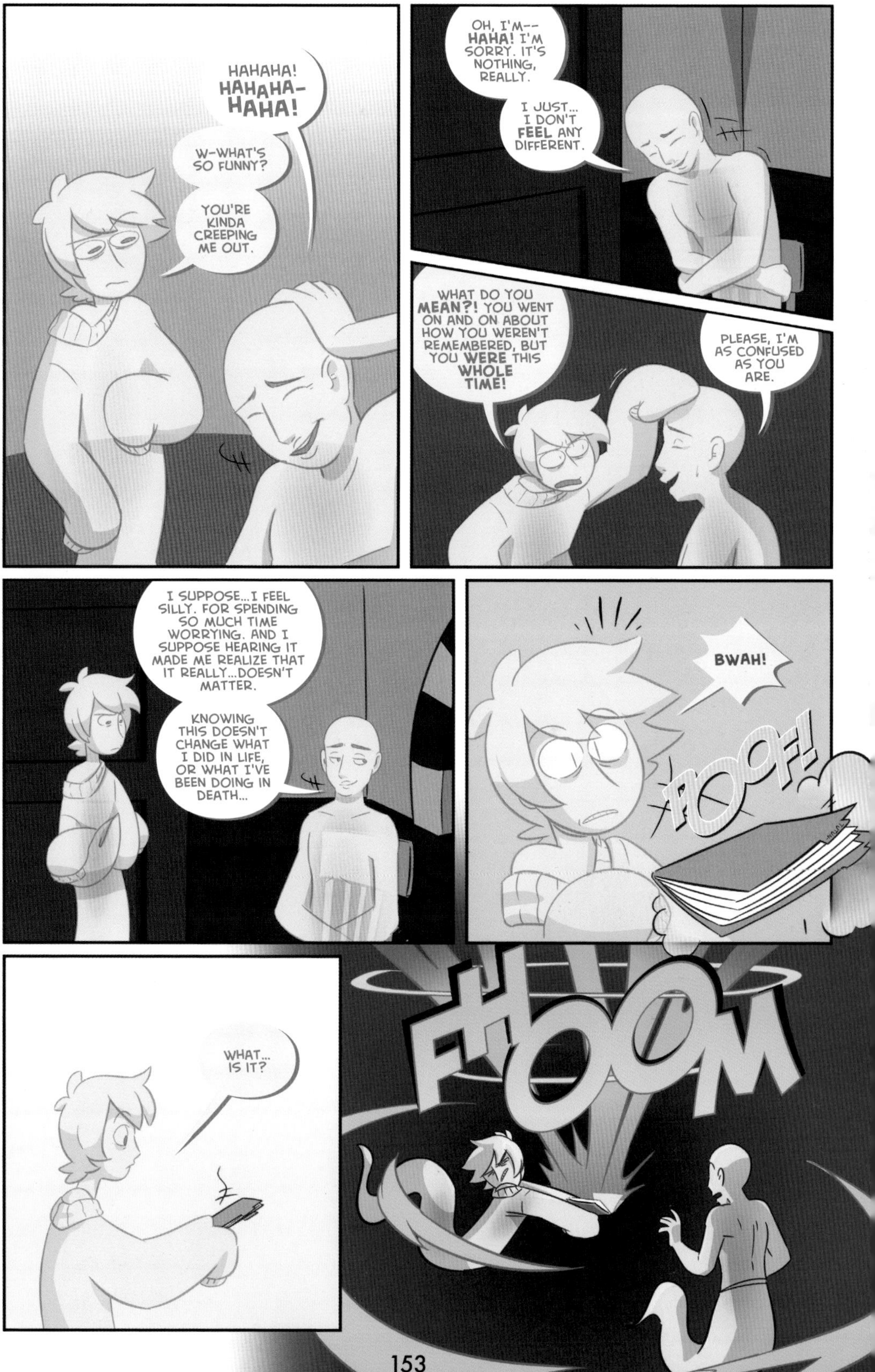
HAHAHA! HAHAHA-HAHA!
W-WHAT'S SO FUNNY?
YOU'RE KINDA CREEPING ME OUT.
OH, I'M-- HAHA! I'M SORRY. IT'S NOTHING, REALLY.
I JUST... I DON'T FEEL ANY DIFFERENT.
WHAT DO YOU MEAN?! YOU WENT ON AND ON ABOUT HOW YOU WEREN'T REMEMBERED, BUT YOU WERE THIS WHOLE TIME!
PLEASE, I'M AS CONFUSED AS YOU ARE.
I SUPPOSE...I FEEL SILLY. FOR SPENDING SO MUCH TIME WORRYING. AND I SUPPOSE HEARING IT MADE ME REALIZE THAT IT REALLY...DOESN'T MATTER.
KNOWING THIS DOESN'T CHANGE WHAT I DID IN LIFE, OR WHAT I'VE BEEN DOING IN DEATH...
BWAH!
POOF!
WHAT... IS IT?
F'BOOM

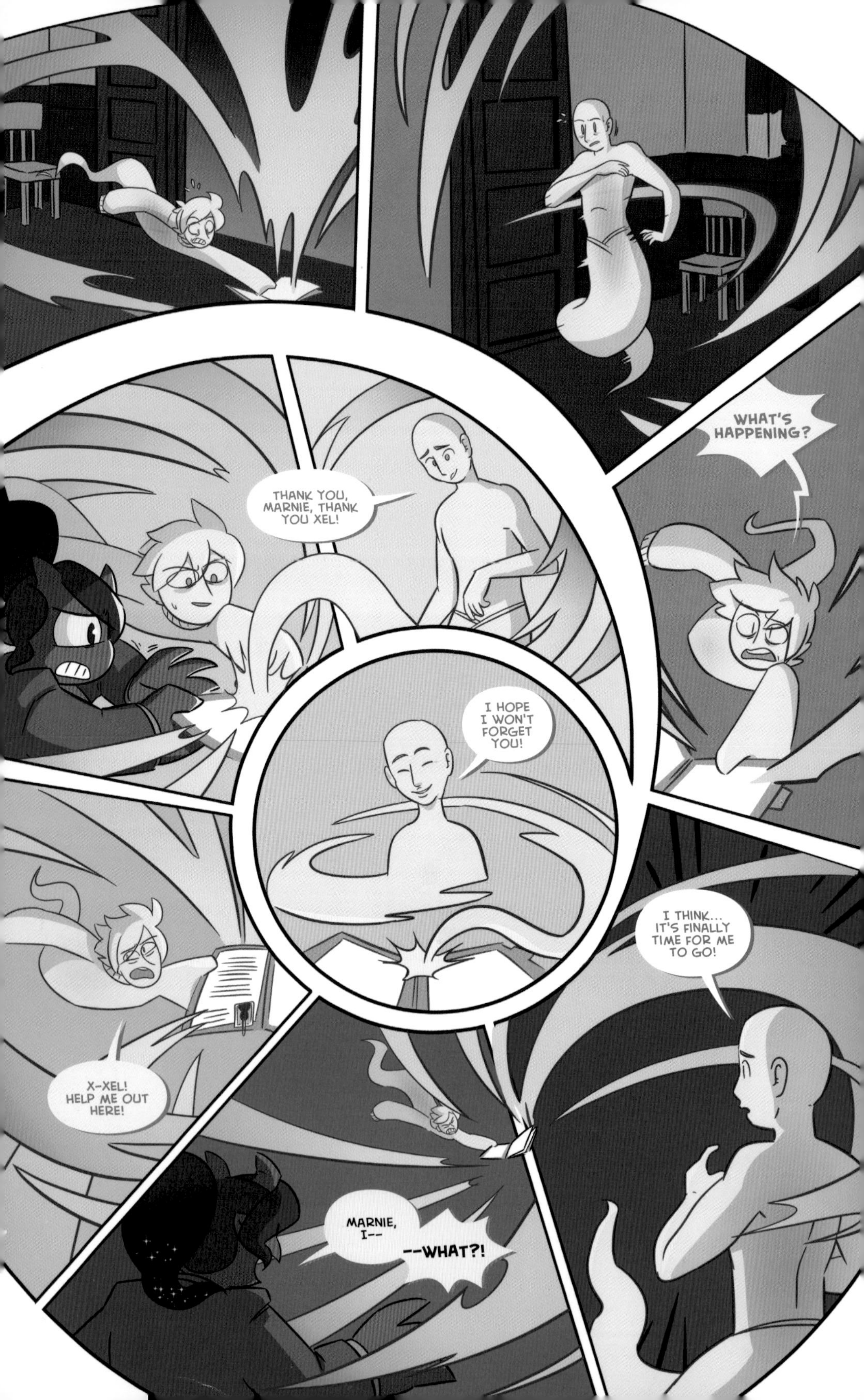
WHAT'S HAPPENING?
THANK YOU, MARNIE, THANK YOU XEL!
I HOPE I WON'T FORGET YOU!
X-XEL! HELP ME OUT HERE!
I THINK... IT'S FINALLY TIME FOR ME TO GO!
MARNIE, I--
--WHAT?!

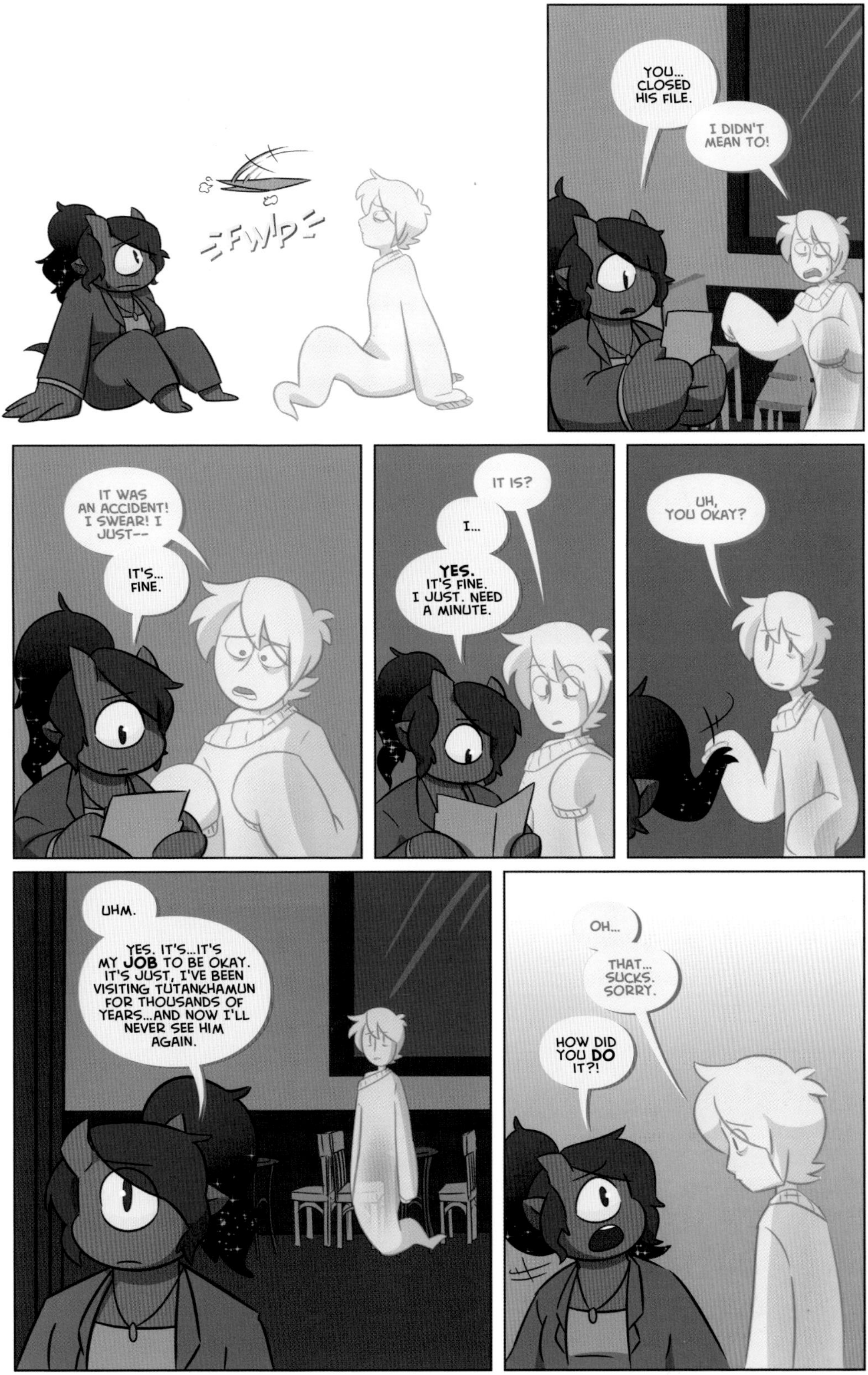
FWIP
YOU... CLOSED HIS FILE.
I DIDN'T MEAN TO!
IT WAS AN ACCIDENT! I SWEAR! I JUST--
IT'S... FINE.
IT IS?
I...
YES. IT'S FINE. I JUST. NEED A MINUTE.
UH, YOU OKAY?
UHM.
YES. IT'S...IT'S MY JOB TO BE OKAY. IT'S JUST, I'VE BEEN VISITING TUTANKHAMUN FOR THOUSANDS OF YEARS...AND NOW I'LL NEVER SEE HIM AGAIN.
OH...
THAT... SUCKS. SORRY.
HOW DID YOU DO IT?!

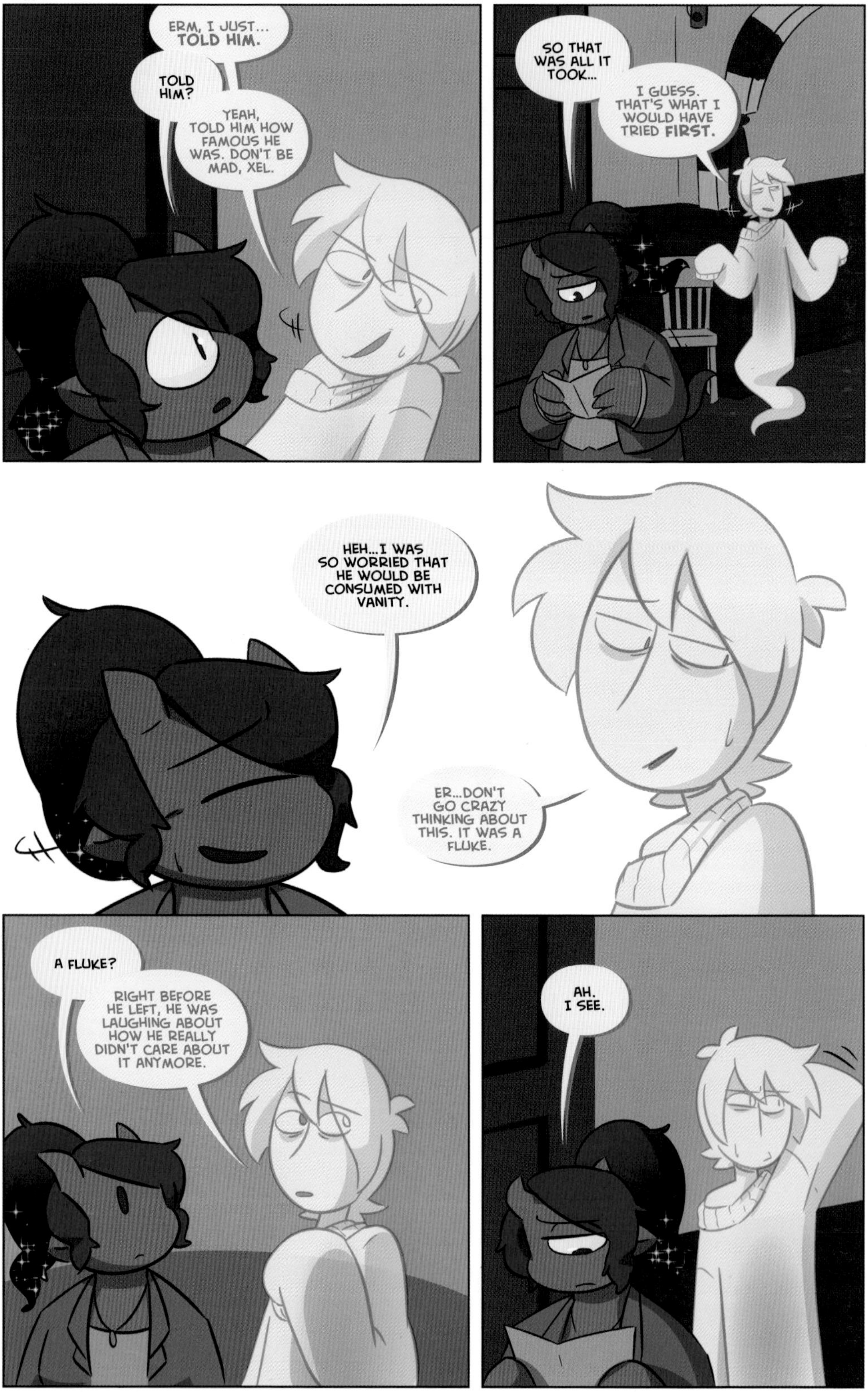
ERM, I JUST... TOLD HIM.
TOLD HIM?
YEAH, TOLD HIM HOW FAMOUS HE WAS. DON'T BE MAD, XEL.
SO THAT WAS ALL IT TOOK...
I GUESS. THAT'S WHAT I WOULD HAVE TRIED FIRST.
HEH...I WAS SO WORRIED THAT HE WOULD BE CONSUMED WITH VANITY.
ER...DON'T GO CRAZY THINKING ABOUT THIS. IT WAS A FLUKE.
A FLUKE?
RIGHT BEFORE HE LEFT, HE WAS LAUGHING ABOUT HOW HE REALLY DIDN'T CARE ABOUT IT ANYMORE.
AH. I SEE.

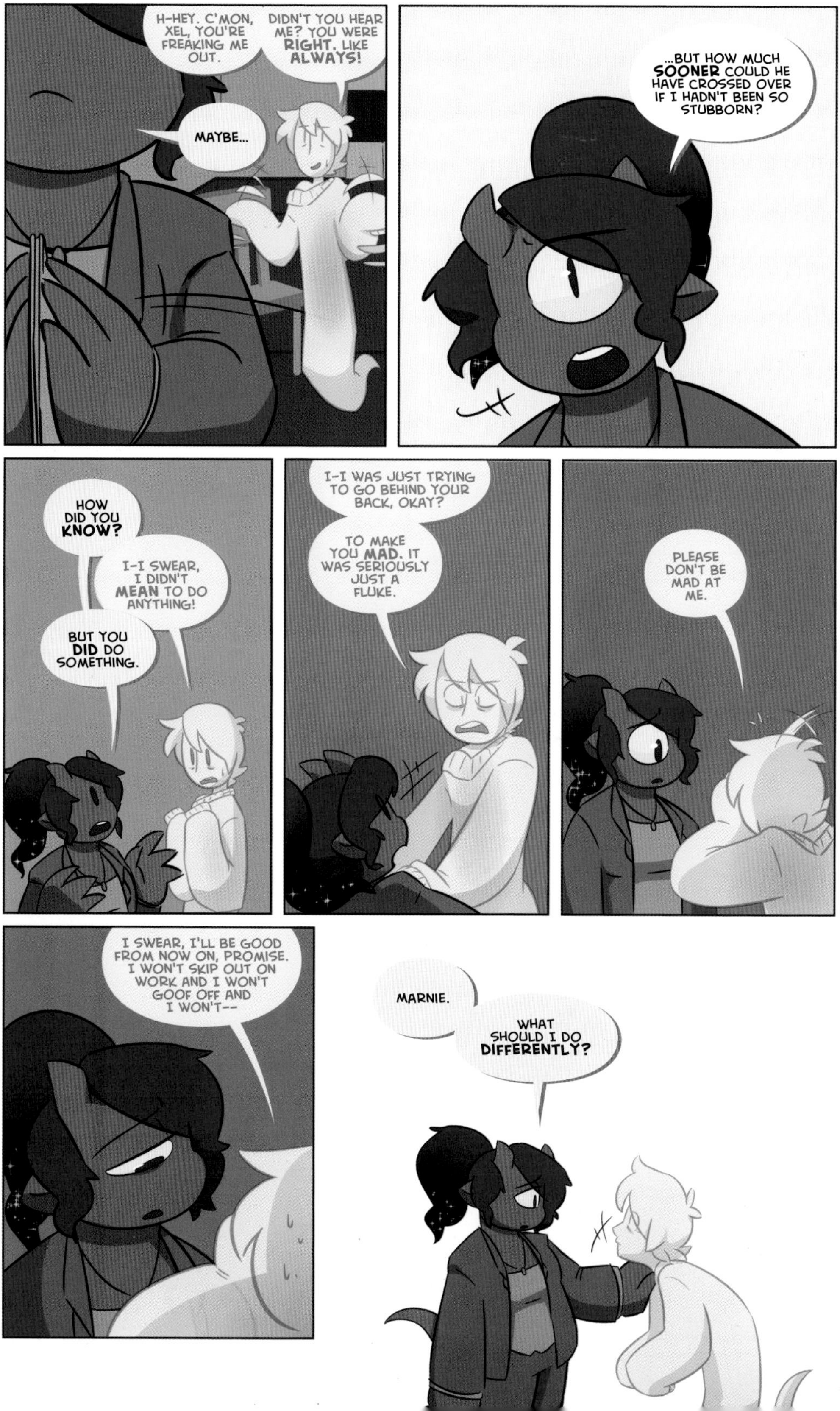
H-HEY. C'MON, XEL, YOU'RE FREAKING ME OUT.
DIDN'T YOU HEAR ME? YOU WERE RIGHT. LIKE ALWAYS!
MAYBE...
...BUT HOW MUCH SOONER COULD HE HAVE CROSSED OVER IF I HADN'T BEEN SO STUBBORN?
HOW DID YOU KNOW?
I-I SWEAR, I DIDN'T MEAN TO DO ANYTHING!
BUT YOU DID DO SOMETHING.
I-I WAS JUST TRYING TO GO BEHIND YOUR BACK, OKAY?
TO MAKE YOU MAD. IT WAS SERIOUSLY JUST A FLUKE.
PLEASE DON'T BE MAD AT ME.
I SWEAR, I'LL BE GOOD FROM NOW ON, PROMISE. I WON'T SKIP OUT ON WORK AND I WON'T GOOF OFF AND I WON'T--
MARNIE.
WHAT SHOULD I DO DIFFERENTLY?

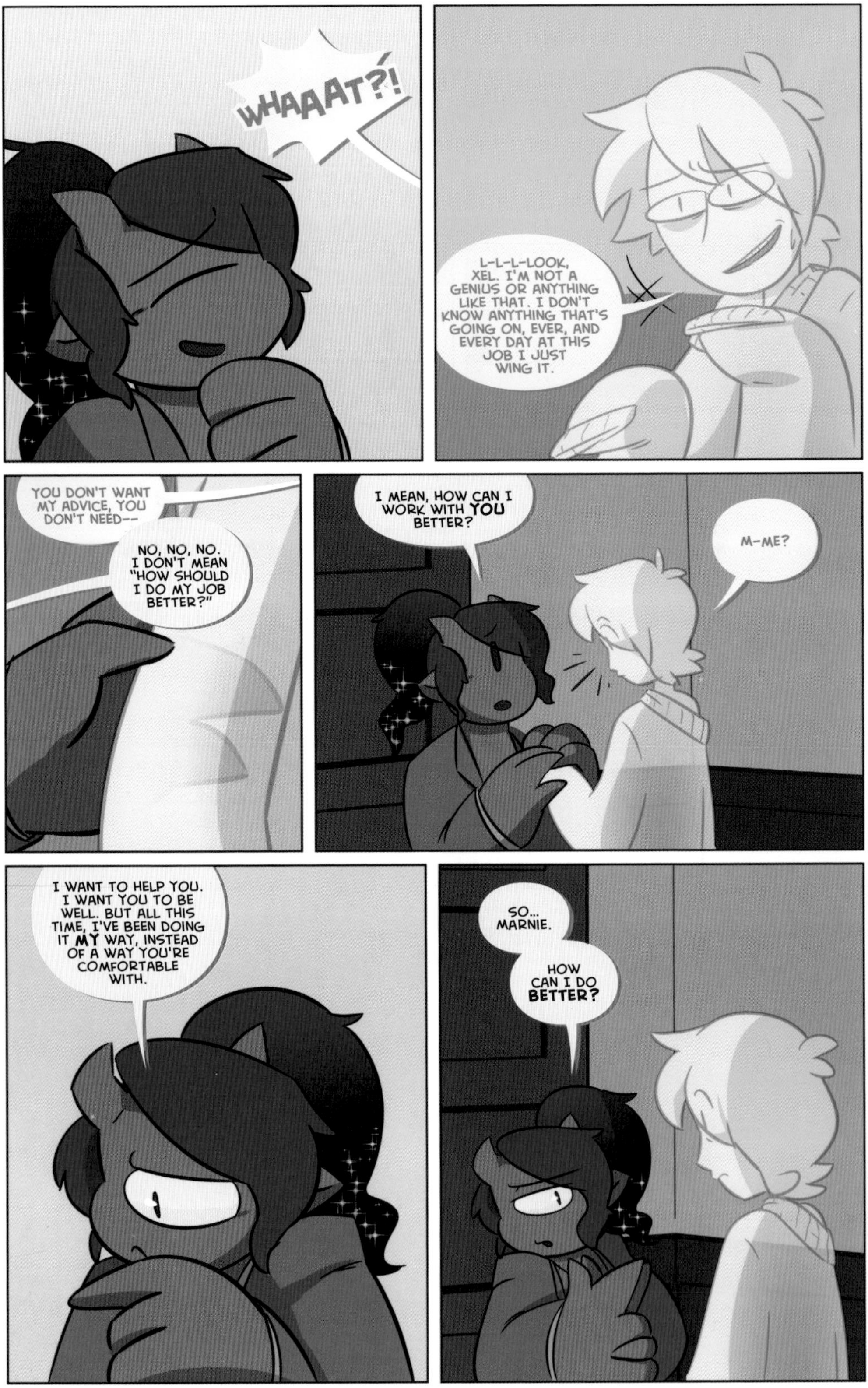
WHAAAT?!
L-L-L-LOOK, XEL. I'M NOT A GENIUS OR ANYTHING LIKE THAT. I DON'T KNOW ANYTHING THAT'S GOING ON, EVER, AND EVERY DAY AT THIS JOB I JUST WING IT.
YOU DON'T WANT MY ADVICE, YOU DON'T NEED--
NO, NO, NO. I DON'T MEAN "HOW SHOULD I DO MY JOB BETTER?"
I MEAN, HOW CAN I WORK WITH YOU BETTER?
M-ME?
I WANT TO HELP YOU. I WANT YOU TO BE WELL. BUT ALL THIS TIME, I'VE BEEN DOING IT MY WAY, INSTEAD OF A WAY YOU'RE COMFORTABLE WITH.
SO... MARNIE.
HOW CAN I DO BETTER?

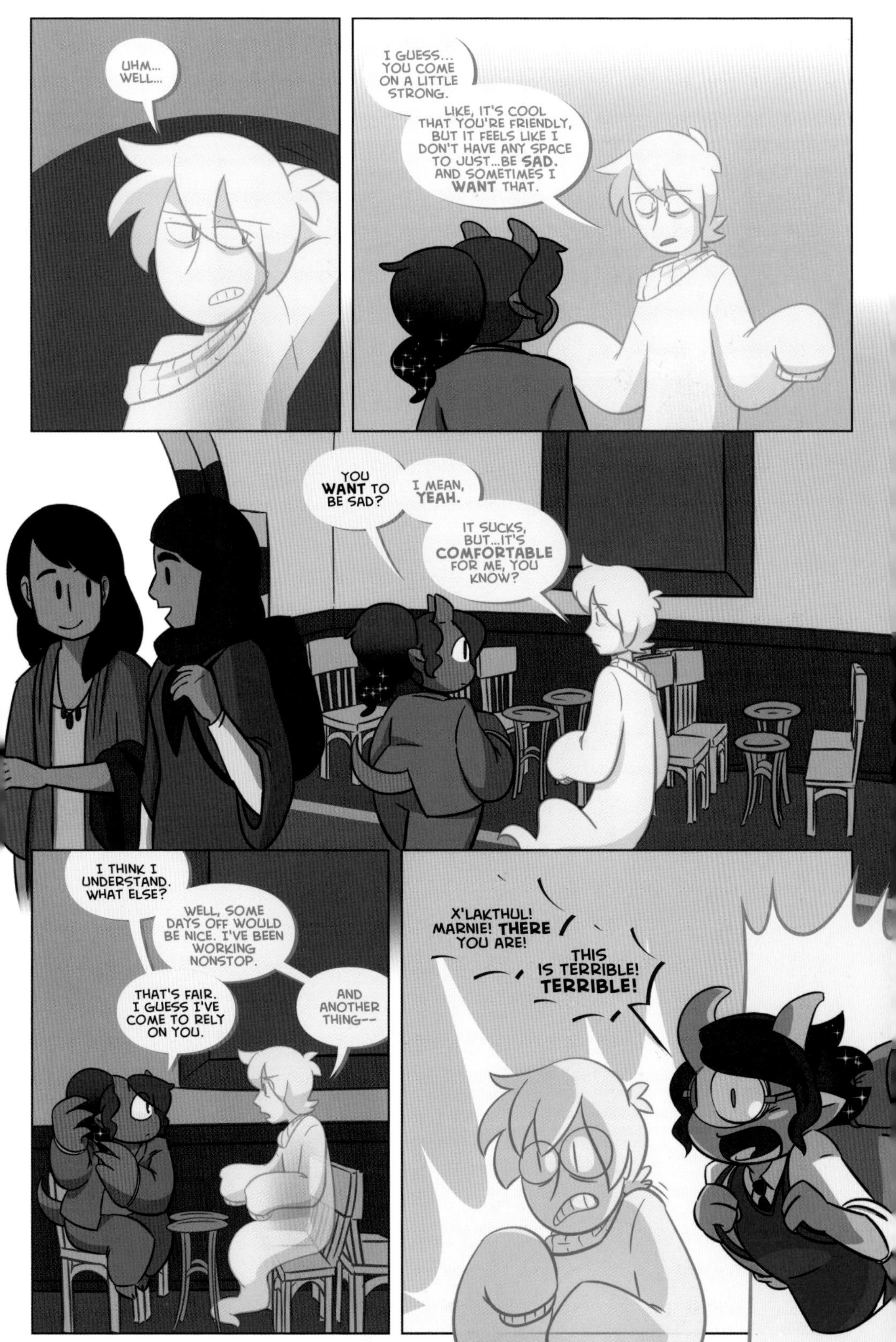
UHM... WELL...
I GUESS... YOU COME ON A LITTLE STRONG.
LIKE, IT'S COOL THAT YOU'RE FRIENDLY, BUT IT FEELS LIKE I DON'T HAVE ANY SPACE TO JUST...BE SAD. AND SOMETIMES I WANT THAT.
YOU WANT TO BE SAD?
I MEAN, YEAH.
IT SUCKS, BUT...IT'S COMFORTABLE FOR ME, YOU KNOW?
I THINK I UNDERSTAND. WHAT ELSE?
WELL, SOME DAYS OFF WOULD BE NICE. I'VE BEEN WORKING NONSTOP.
THAT'S FAIR. I GUESS I'VE COME TO RELY ON YOU.
AND ANOTHER THING--
X'LAKTHUL! MARNIE! THERE YOU ARE!
THIS IS TERRIBLE! TERRIBLE!

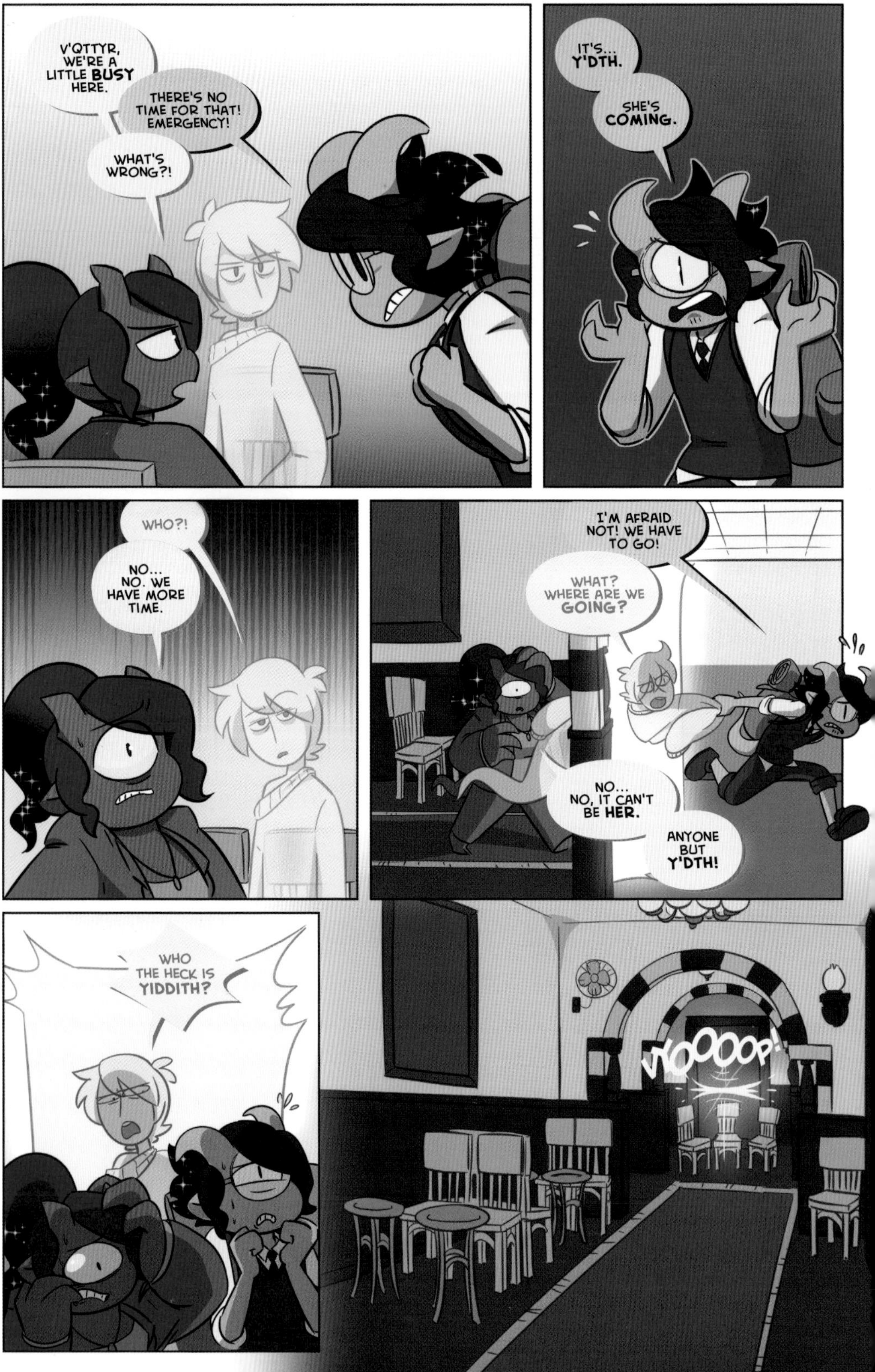
V'QTTYR, WE'RE A LITTLE BUSY HERE.
THERE'S NO TIME FOR THAT! EMERGENCY!
WHAT'S WRONG?!
IT'S... Y'DTH.
SHE'S COMING.
WHO?!
NO... NO. WE HAVE MORE TIME.
I'M AFRAID NOT! WE HAVE TO GO!
WHAT? WHERE ARE WE GOING?
NO... NO, IT CAN'T BE HER.
ANYONE BUT Y'DTH!
WHO THE HECK IS YIDDITH?
VYOOOOP!

Department of Spectral Affairs

Chapter 6

Winters, M.

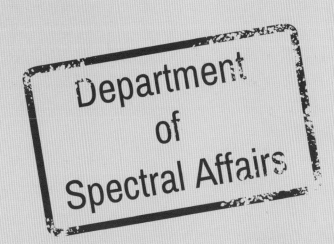

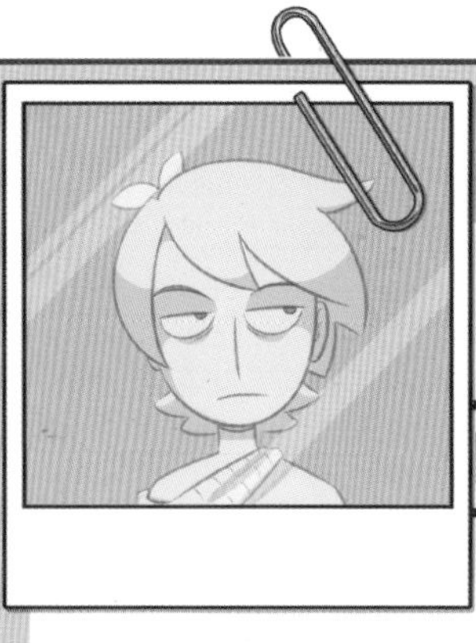

R OFFICIAL USE ONLY

Name: Marnie Winters

Pronunciation: Mar-Nee Win-Ters

Pronouns: she/her

Age: 19 (alive)

Position: Intern

Likes: Sarcasm, the spider that lives in my house.

Dislikes: Chairs, being told what to do.

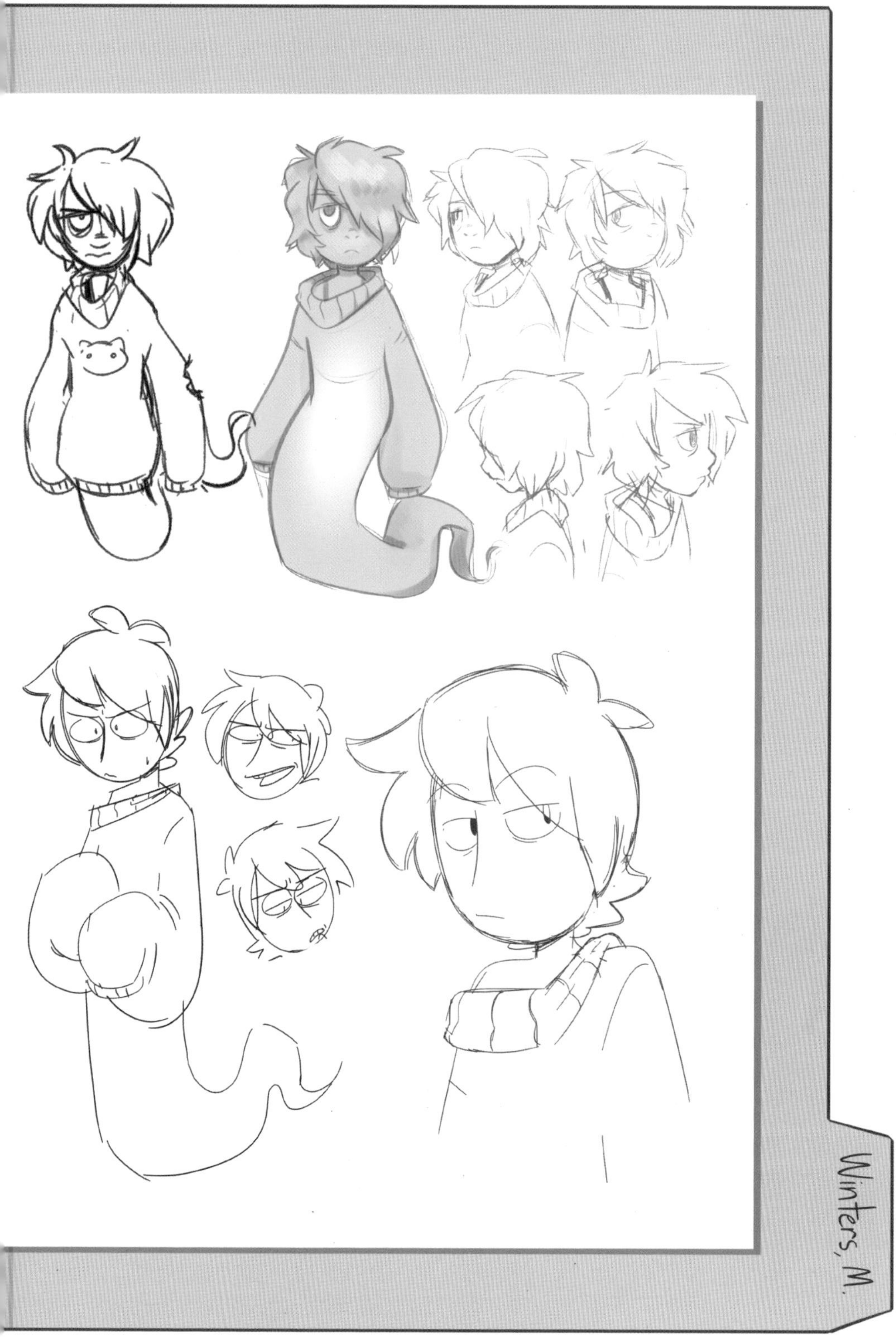
Winters, M.

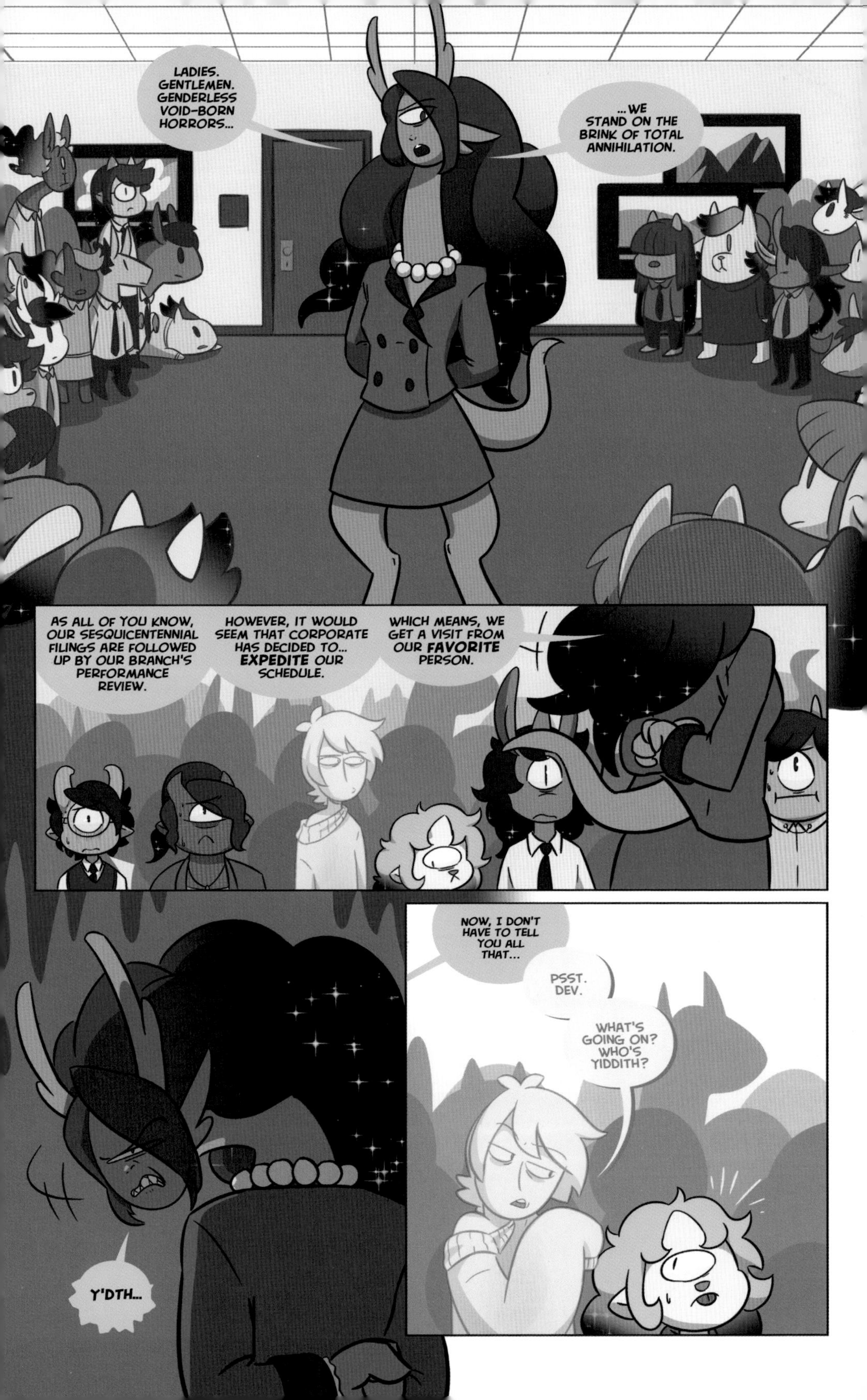
LADIES. GENTLEMEN. GENDERLESS VOID-BORN HORRORS...
...WE STAND ON THE BRINK OF TOTAL ANNIHILATION.
AS ALL OF YOU KNOW, OUR SESQUICENTENNIAL FILINGS ARE FOLLOWED UP BY OUR BRANCH'S PERFORMANCE REVIEW.
HOWEVER, IT WOULD SEEM THAT CORPORATE HAS DECIDED TO... EXPEDITE OUR SCHEDULE.
WHICH MEANS, WE GET A VISIT FROM OUR FAVORITE PERSON.
Y'DTH...
NOW, I DON'T HAVE TO TELL YOU ALL THAT...
PSST. DEV.
WHAT'S GOING ON? WHO'S YIDDITH?

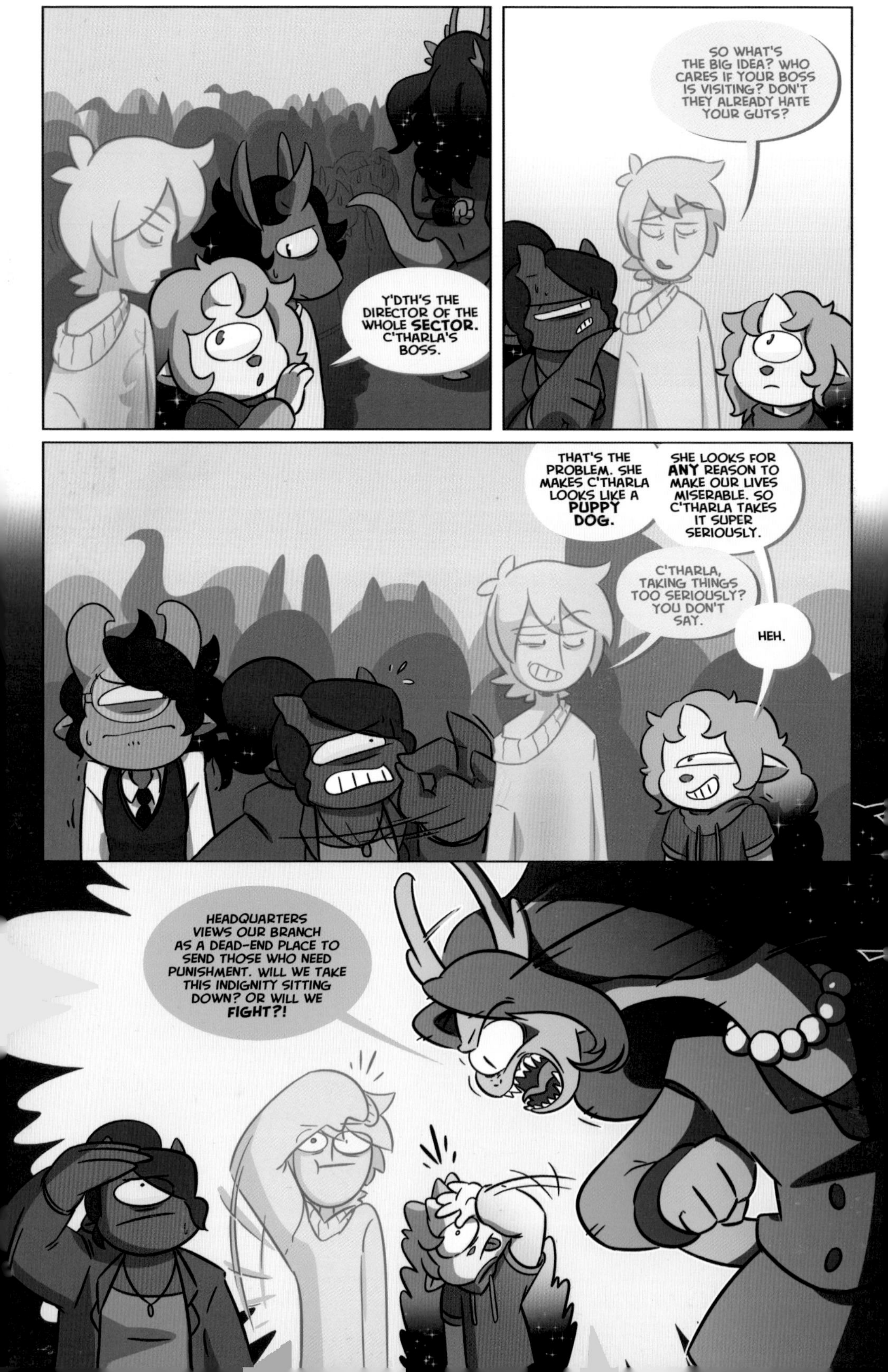
Y'DTH'S THE DIRECTOR OF THE WHOLE **SECTOR.** C'THARLA'S BOSS.
SO WHAT'S THE BIG IDEA? WHO CARES IF YOUR BOSS IS VISITING? DON'T THEY ALREADY HATE YOUR GUTS?
THAT'S THE PROBLEM. SHE MAKES C'THARLA LOOKS LIKE A **PUPPY DOG.**
SHE LOOKS FOR **ANY** REASON TO MAKE OUR LIVES MISERABLE. SO C'THARLA TAKES IT SUPER SERIOUSLY.
C'THARLA, TAKING THINGS TOO SERIOUSLY? YOU DON'T SAY.
HEH.
HEADQUARTERS VIEWS OUR BRANCH AS A DEAD-END PLACE TO SEND THOSE WHO NEED PUNISHMENT. WILL WE TAKE THIS INDIGNITY SITTING DOWN? OR WILL WE **FIGHT?!**

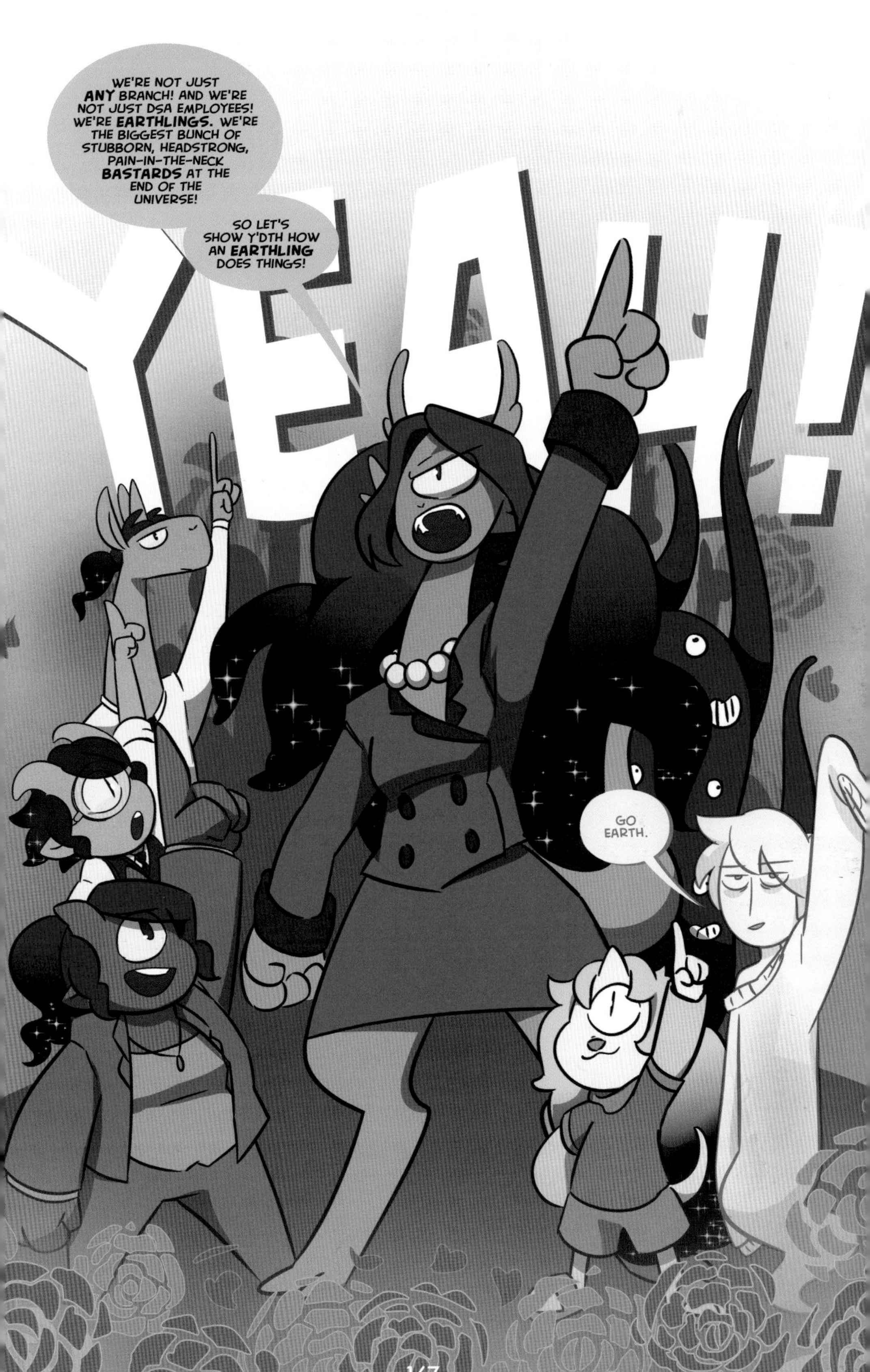
WE'RE NOT JUST ANY BRANCH! AND WE'RE NOT JUST DSA EMPLOYEES! WE'RE EARTHLINGS. WE'RE THE BIGGEST BUNCH OF STUBBORN, HEADSTRONG, PAIN-IN-THE-NECK BASTARDS AT THE END OF THE UNIVERSE!
SO LET'S SHOW Y'DTH HOW AN EARTHLING DOES THINGS!
YEAH!!
GO EARTH.

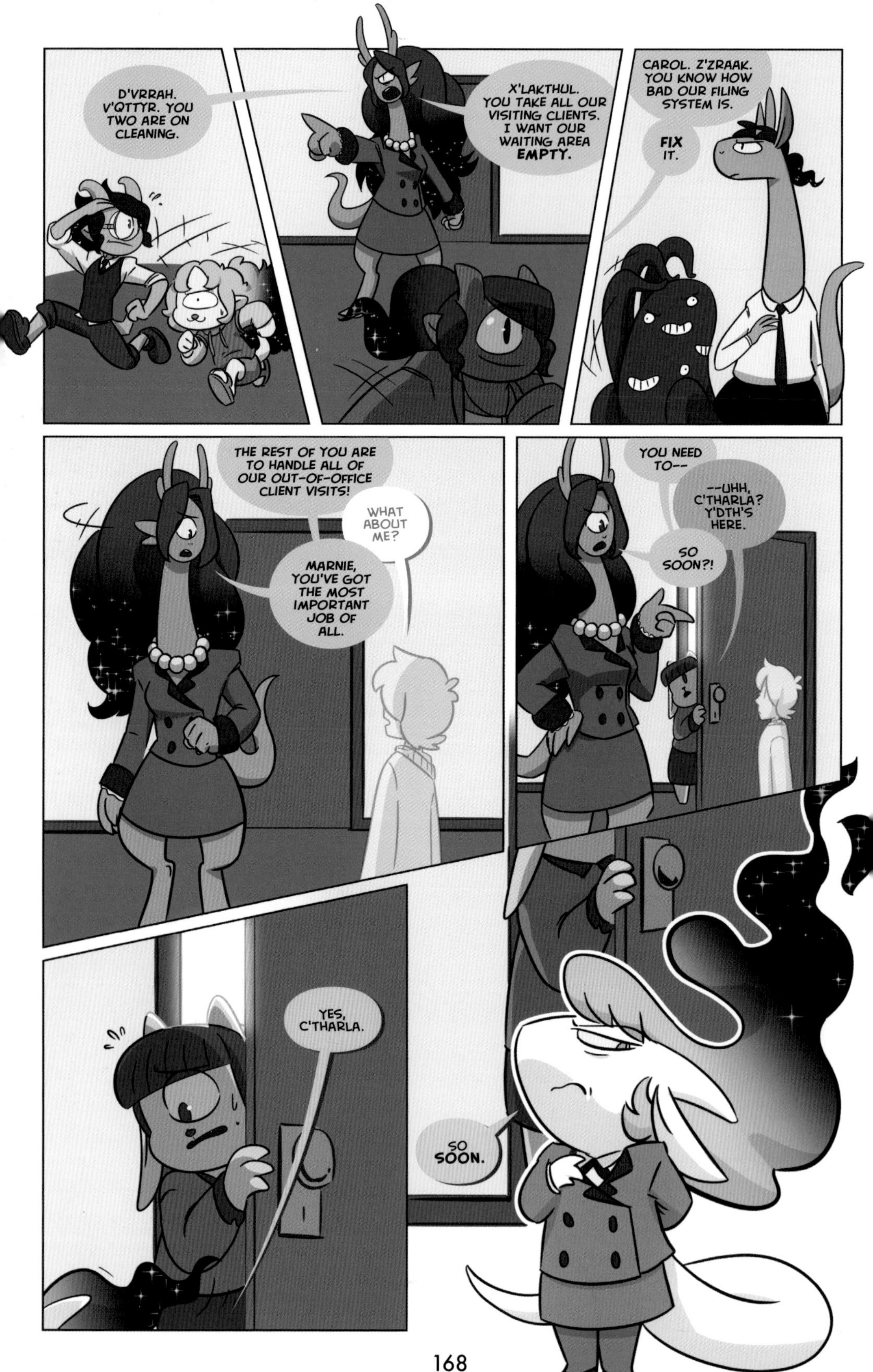
D'VRRAH. V'QTTYR. YOU TWO ARE ON CLEANING.
X'LAKTHUL. YOU TAKE ALL OUR VISITING CLIENTS. I WANT OUR WAITING AREA EMPTY.
CAROL. Z'ZRAAK. YOU KNOW HOW BAD OUR FILING SYSTEM IS.
FIX IT.
THE REST OF YOU ARE TO HANDLE ALL OF OUR OUT-OF-OFFICE CLIENT VISITS!
WHAT ABOUT ME?
MARNIE, YOU'VE GOT THE MOST IMPORTANT JOB OF ALL.
YOU NEED TO--
--UHH, C'THARLA? Y'DTH'S HERE.
SO SOON?!
YES, C'THARLA.
SO SOON.

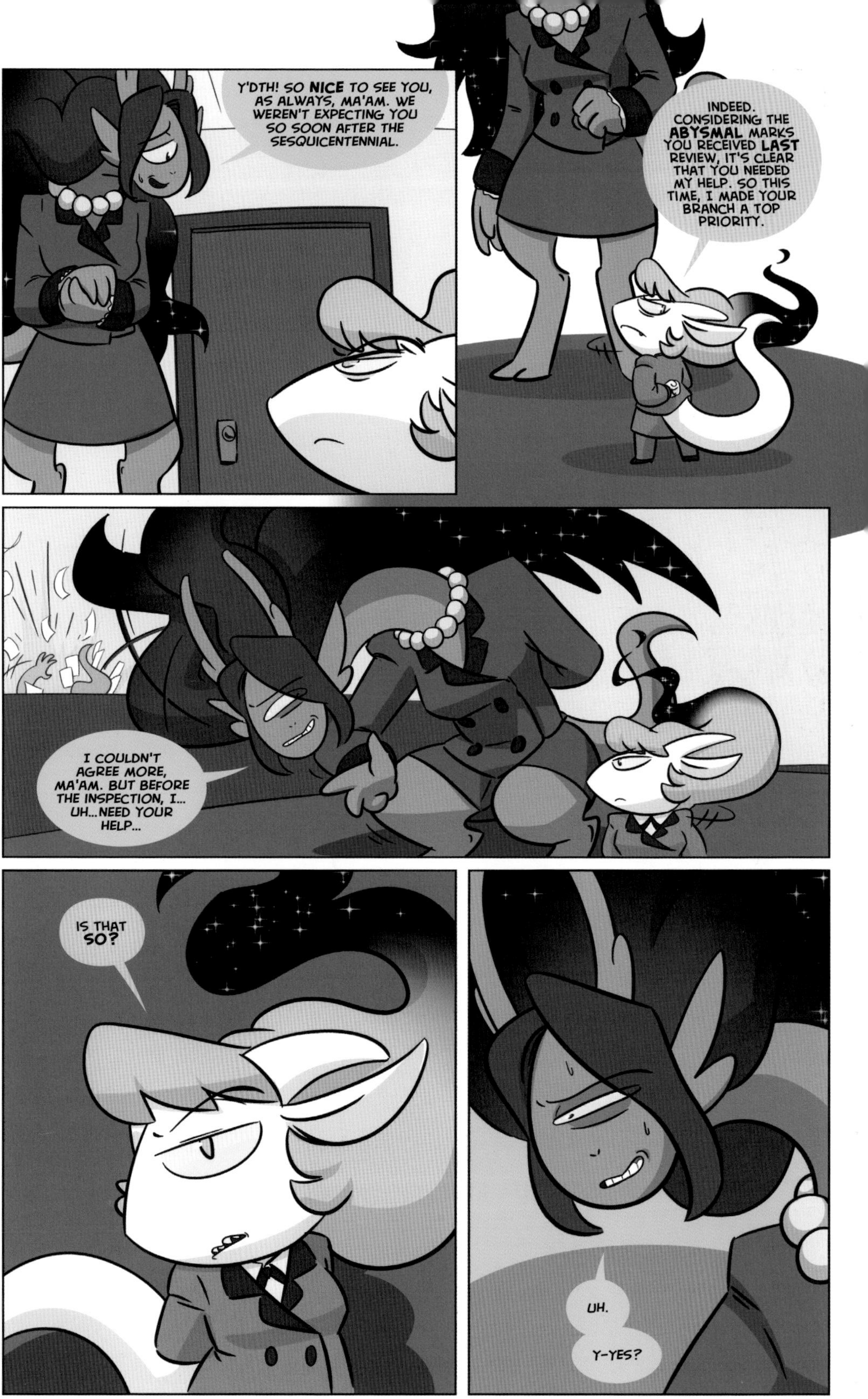
Y'DTH! SO **NICE** TO SEE YOU, AS ALWAYS, MA'AM. WE WEREN'T EXPECTING YOU SO SOON AFTER THE SESQUICENTENNIAL.
INDEED. CONSIDERING THE **ABYSMAL** MARKS YOU RECEIVED **LAST** REVIEW, IT'S CLEAR THAT YOU NEEDED MY HELP. SO THIS TIME, I MADE YOUR BRANCH A TOP PRIORITY.
I COULDN'T AGREE MORE, MA'AM. BUT BEFORE THE INSPECTION, I... UH...NEED YOUR HELP...
IS THAT **SO?**
UH.
Y-YES?

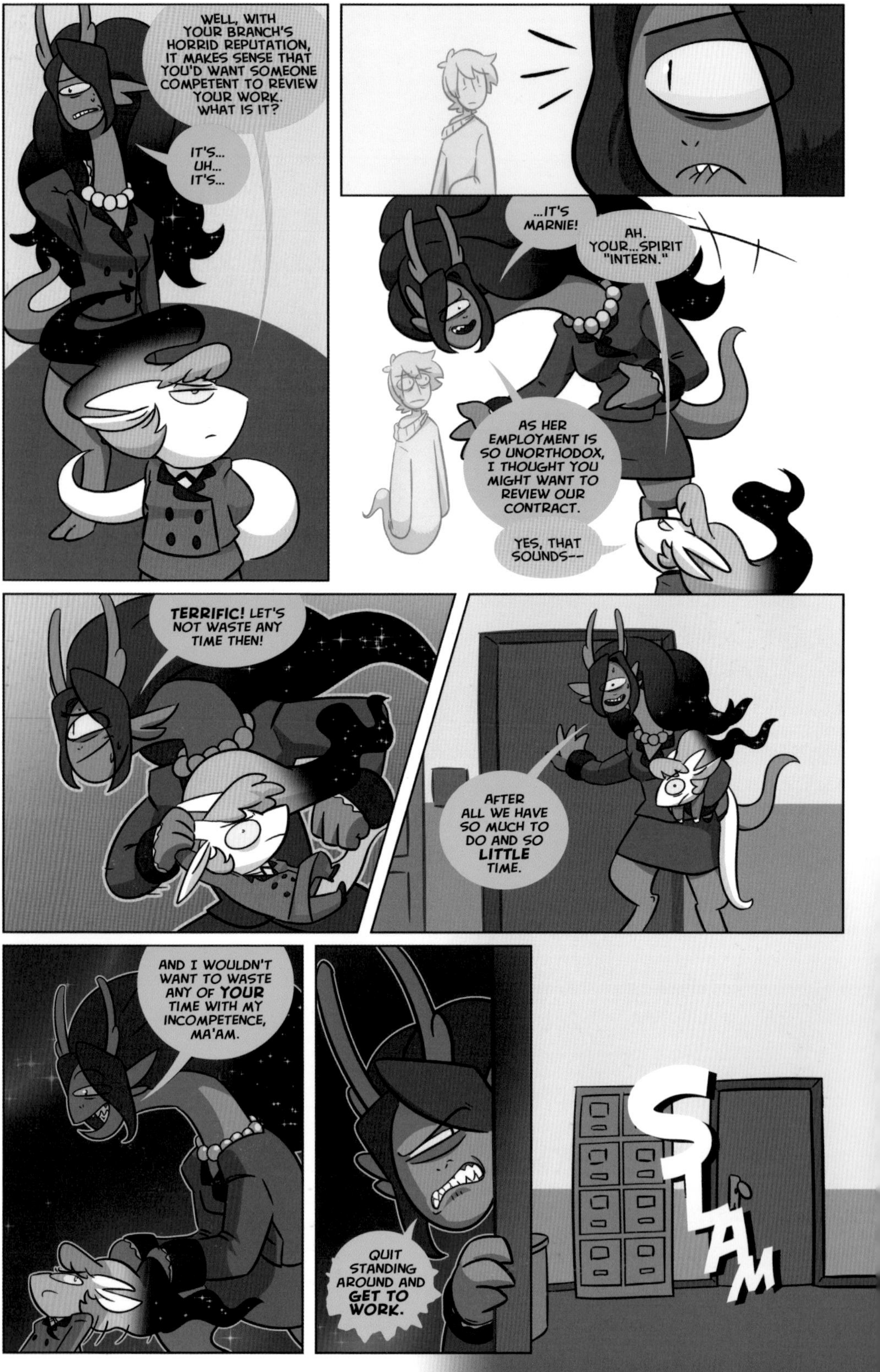
WELL, WITH YOUR BRANCH'S HORRID REPUTATION, IT MAKES SENSE THAT YOU'D WANT SOMEONE COMPETENT TO REVIEW YOUR WORK. WHAT IS IT?
IT'S... UH... IT'S...
...IT'S MARNIE!
AH. YOUR...SPIRIT "INTERN."
AS HER EMPLOYMENT IS SO UNORTHODOX, I THOUGHT YOU MIGHT WANT TO REVIEW OUR CONTRACT.
YES, THAT SOUNDS--
TERRIFIC! LET'S NOT WASTE ANY TIME THEN!
AFTER ALL WE HAVE SO MUCH TO DO AND SO LITTLE TIME.
AND I WOULDN'T WANT TO WASTE ANY OF YOUR TIME WITH MY INCOMPETENCE, MA'AM.
QUIT STANDING AROUND AND GET TO WORK.
SLAM

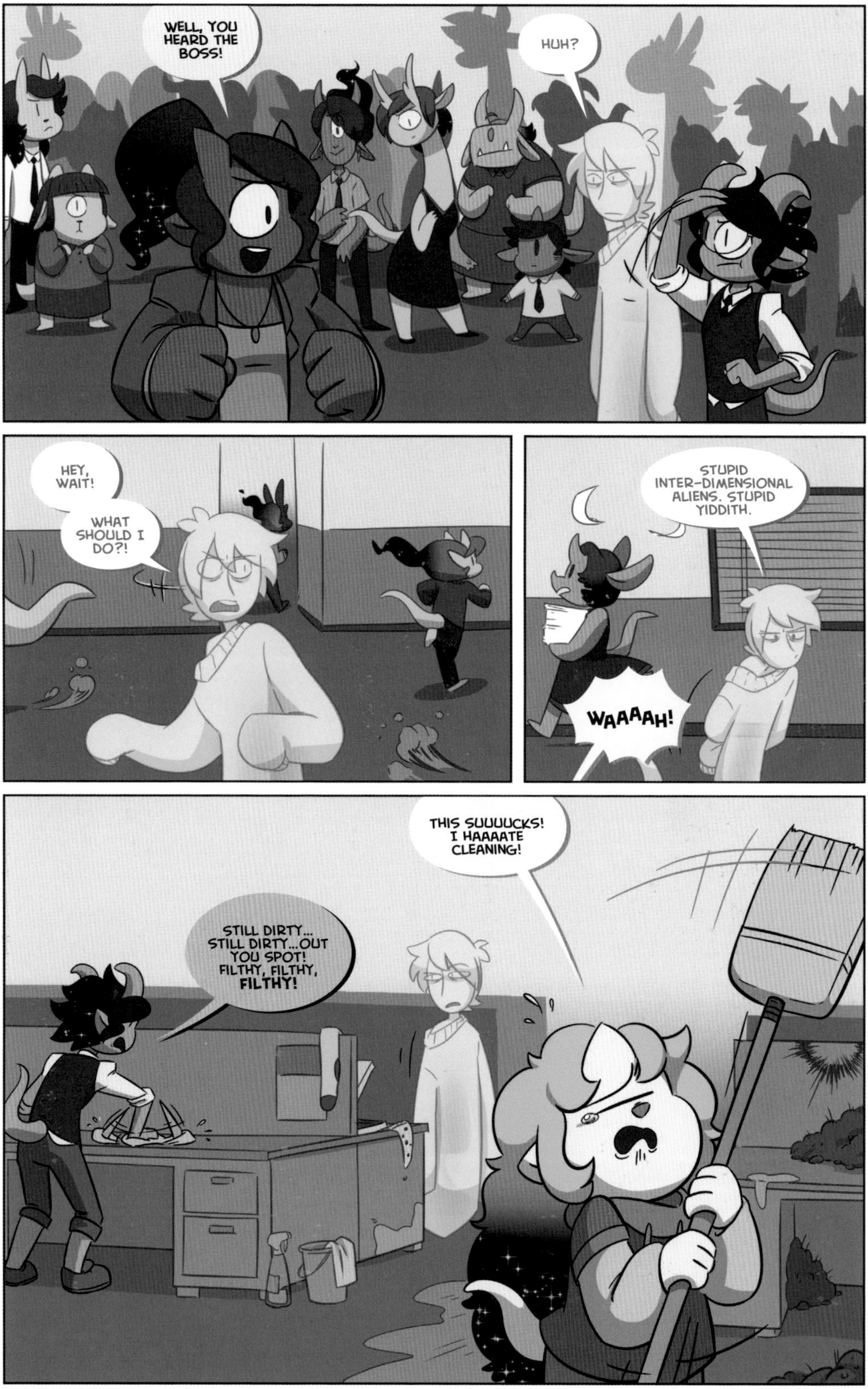
WELL, YOU HEARD THE BOSS!
HUH?
HEY, WAIT!
WHAT SHOULD I DO?!
STUPID INTER-DIMENSIONAL ALIENS. STUPID YIDDITH.
WAAAAH!
THIS SUUUUCKS! I HAAAATE CLEANING!
STILL DIRTY... STILL DIRTY...OUT YOU SPOT! FILTHY, FILTHY, **FILTHY!**

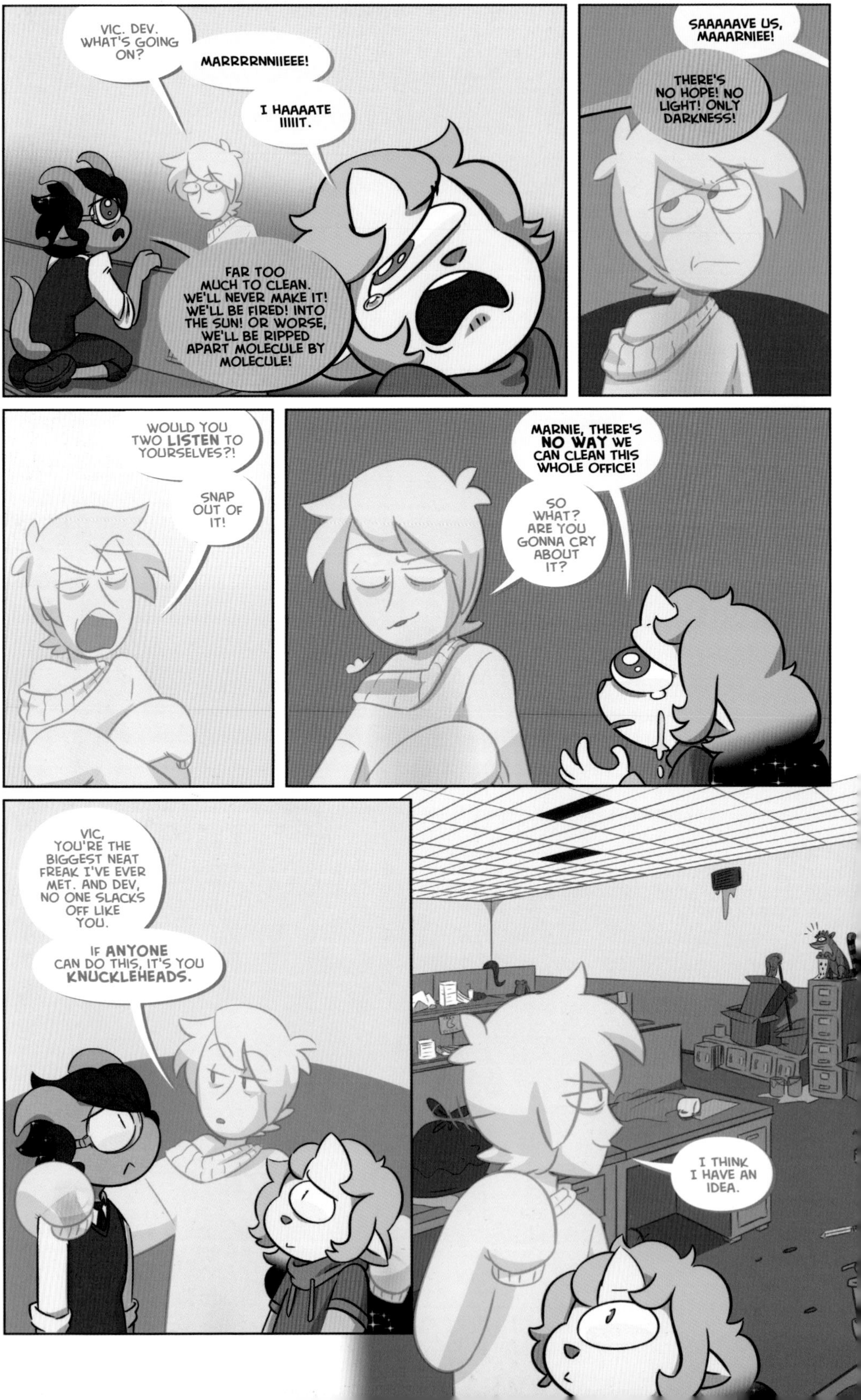

VIC. DEV. WHAT'S GOING ON?
MARRRRNNIIEEE!
I HAAAATE IIIIIT.
FAR TOO MUCH TO CLEAN. WE'LL NEVER MAKE IT! WE'LL BE FIRED! INTO THE SUN! OR WORSE, WE'LL BE RIPPED APART MOLECULE BY MOLECULE!
SAAAAAVE US, MAAARNIEE!
THERE'S NO HOPE! NO LIGHT! ONLY DARKNESS!
WOULD YOU TWO LISTEN TO YOURSELVES?!
SNAP OUT OF IT!
MARNIE, THERE'S NO WAY WE CAN CLEAN THIS WHOLE OFFICE!
SO WHAT? ARE YOU GONNA CRY ABOUT IT?
VIC, YOU'RE THE BIGGEST NEAT FREAK I'VE EVER MET. AND DEV, NO ONE SLACKS OFF LIKE YOU.
IF ANYONE CAN DO THIS, IT'S YOU KNUCKLEHEADS.
I THINK I HAVE AN IDEA.

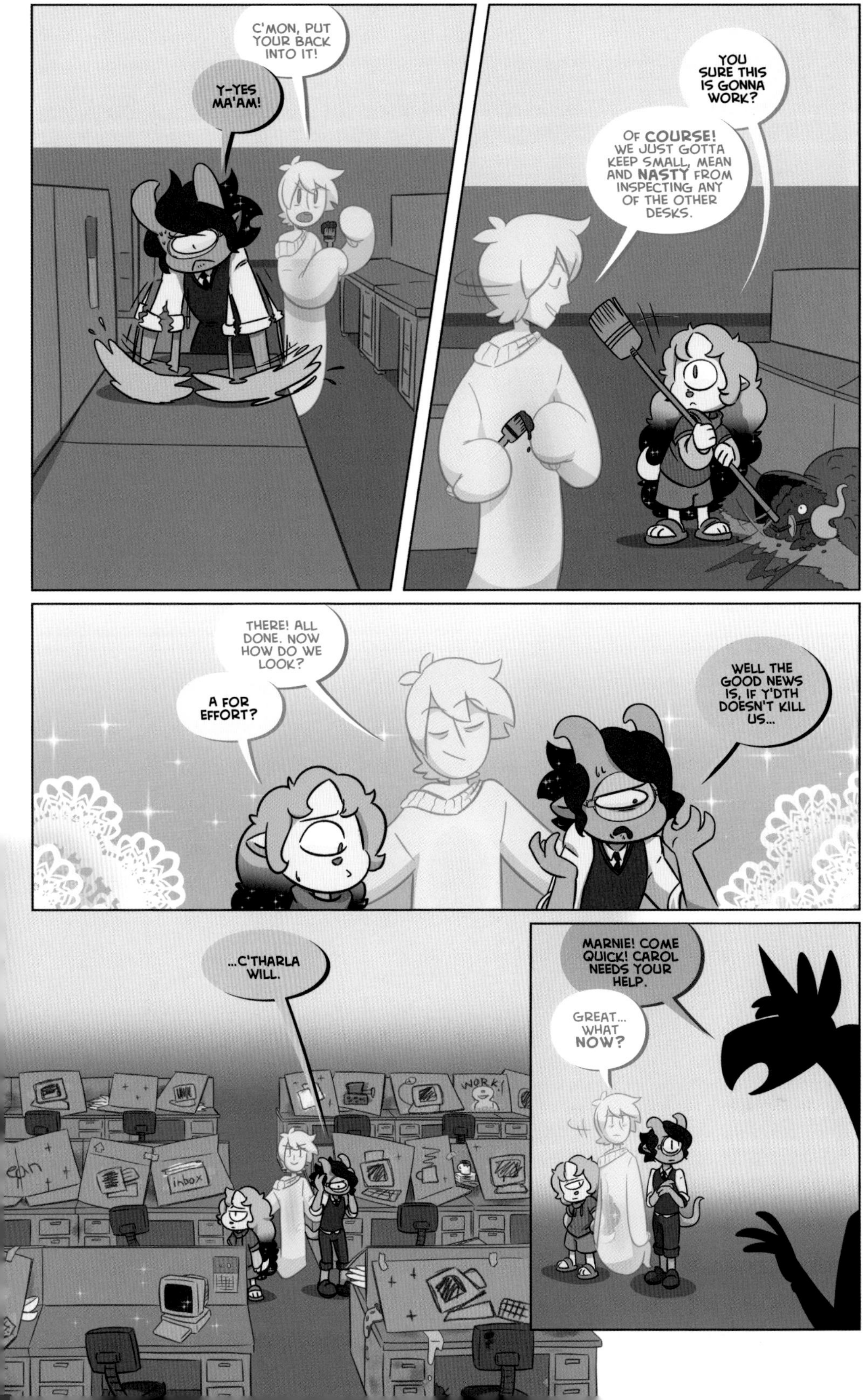
C'MON, PUT YOUR BACK INTO IT!
Y-YES MA'AM!
YOU SURE THIS IS GONNA WORK?
OF COURSE! WE JUST GOTTA KEEP SMALL, MEAN AND NASTY FROM INSPECTING ANY OF THE OTHER DESKS.
THERE! ALL DONE. NOW HOW DO WE LOOK?
A FOR EFFORT?
WELL THE GOOD NEWS IS, IF Y'DTH DOESN'T KILL US...
...C'THARLA WILL.
WORK!
inbox
MARNIE! COME QUICK! CAROL NEEDS YOUR HELP.
GREAT... WHAT NOW?

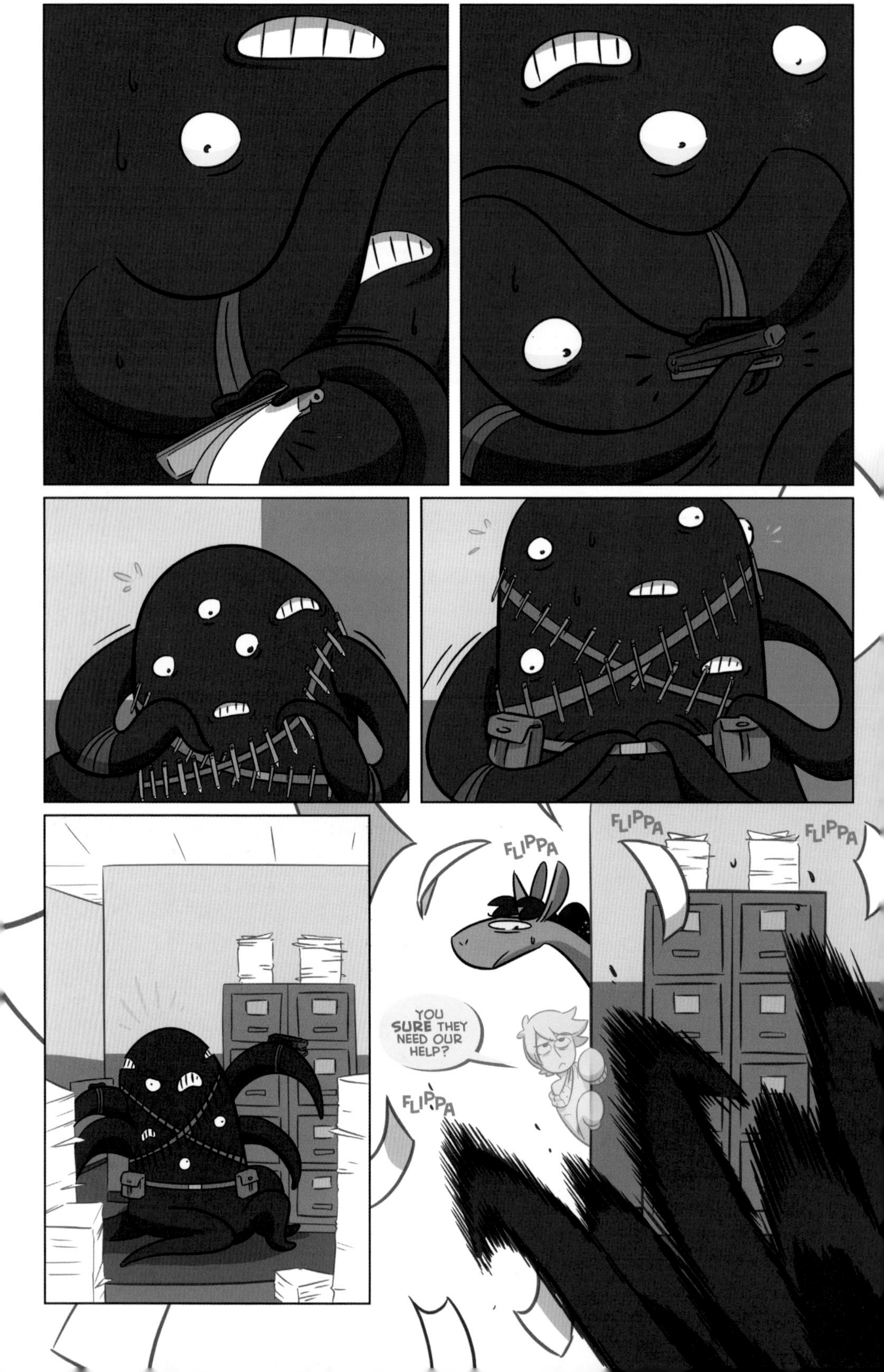
FLIPPA
FLIPPA
FLIPPA
YOU SURE THEY NEED OUR HELP?
FLIPPA

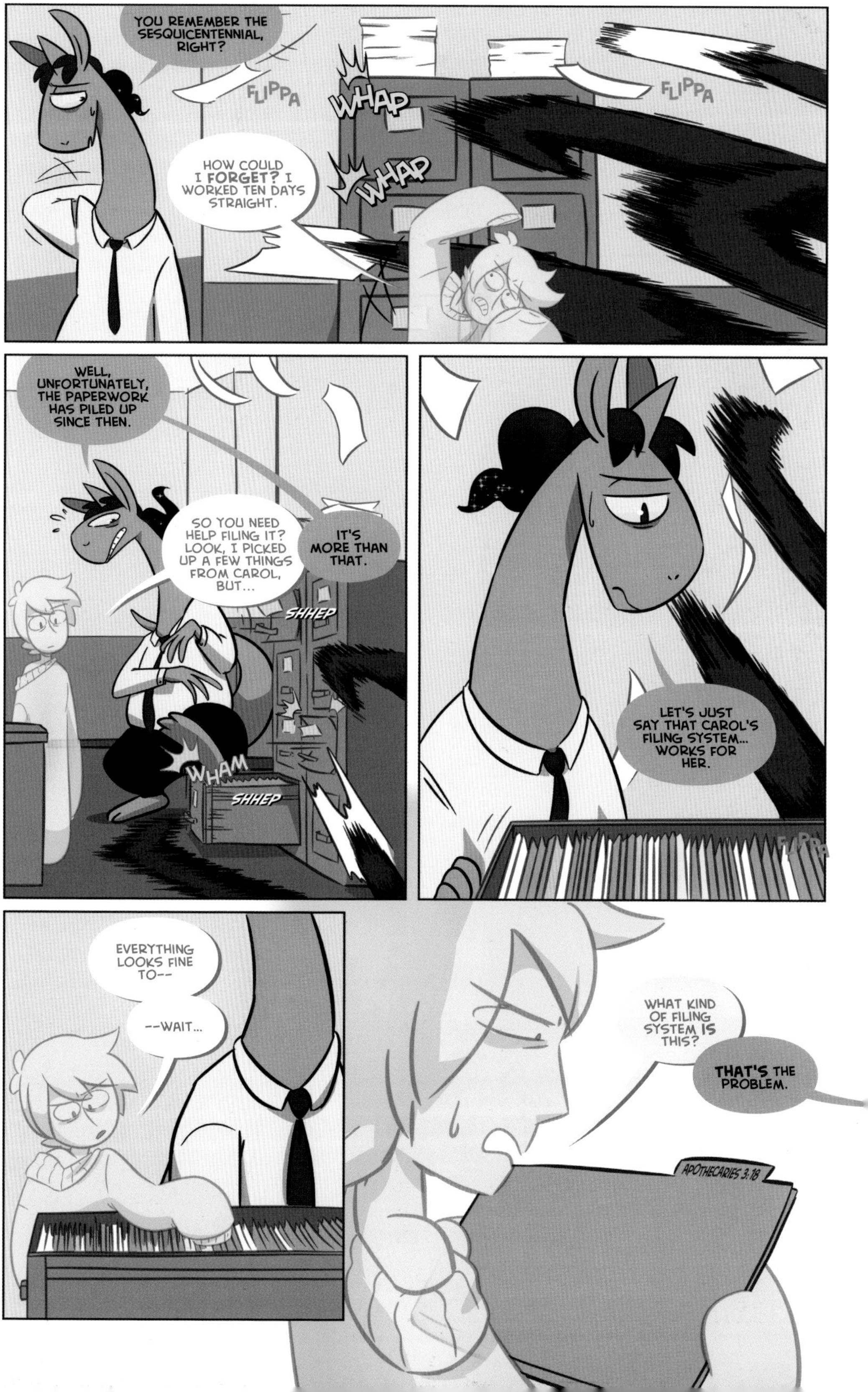
YOU REMEMBER THE SESQUICENTENNIAL, RIGHT?
FLIPPA
WHAP
FLIPPA
HOW COULD I **FORGET?** I WORKED TEN DAYS STRAIGHT.
WHAP
WELL, UNFORTUNATELY, THE PAPERWORK HAS PILED UP SINCE THEN.
SO YOU NEED HELP FILING IT? LOOK, I PICKED UP A FEW THINGS FROM CAROL, BUT...
IT'S MORE THAN THAT.
SHHEP
WHAM
SHHEP
LET'S JUST SAY THAT CAROL'S FILING SYSTEM... WORKS FOR HER.
EVERYTHING LOOKS FINE TO--
--WAIT...
WHAT KIND OF FILING SYSTEM **IS** THIS?
THAT'S THE PROBLEM.
APOTHECARIES 3:18

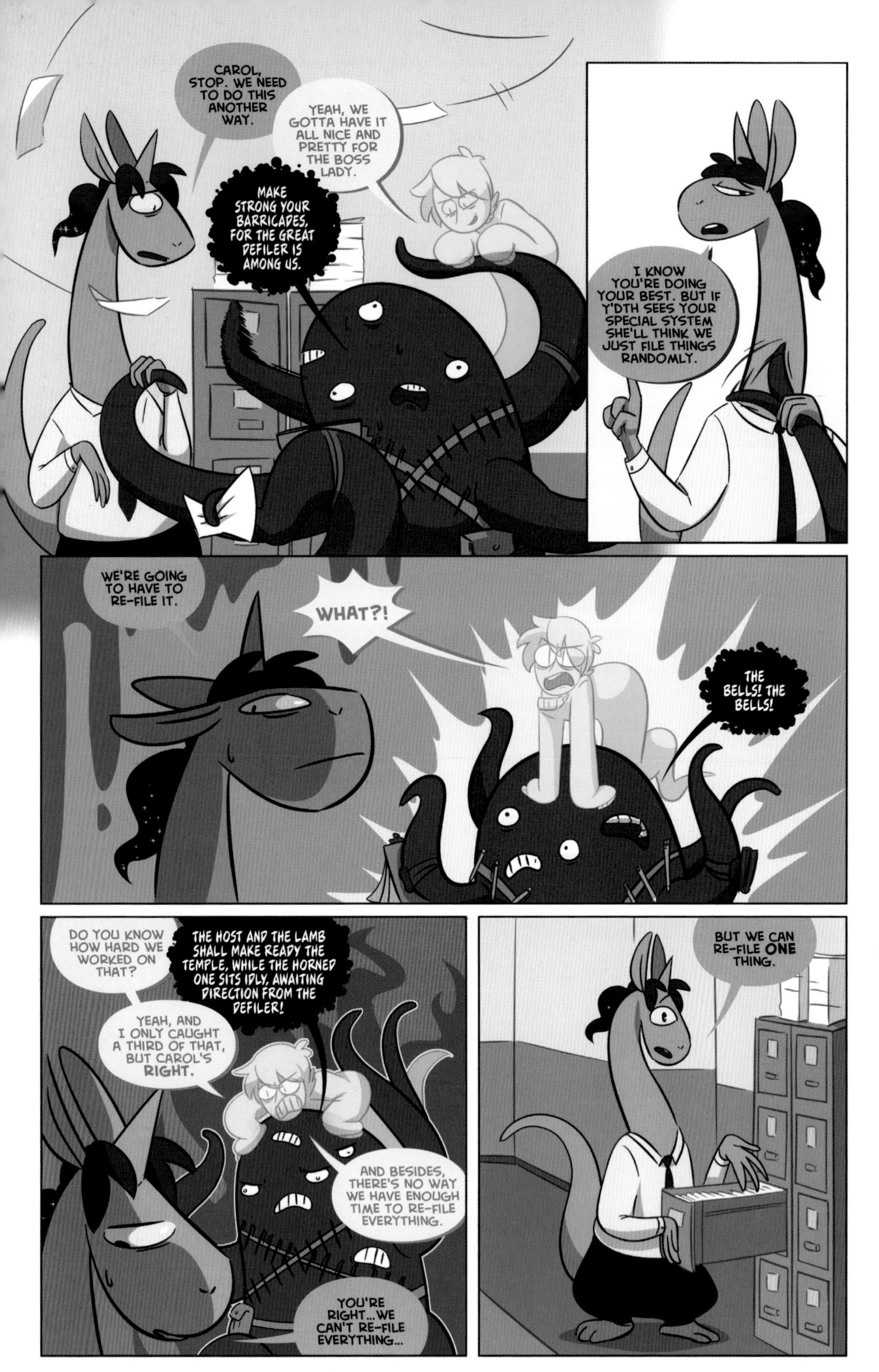
CAROL, STOP. WE NEED TO DO THIS ANOTHER WAY.
YEAH, WE GOTTA HAVE IT ALL NICE AND PRETTY FOR THE BOSS LADY.
MAKE STRONG YOUR BARRICADES, FOR THE GREAT DEFILER IS AMONG US.
I KNOW YOU'RE DOING YOUR BEST. BUT IF Y'DTH SEES YOUR SPECIAL SYSTEM SHE'LL THINK WE JUST FILE THINGS RANDOMLY.
WE'RE GOING TO HAVE TO RE-FILE IT.
WHAT?!
THE BELLS! THE BELLS!
DO YOU KNOW HOW HARD WE WORKED ON THAT?
THE HOST AND THE LAMB SHALL MAKE READY THE TEMPLE, WHILE THE HORNED ONE SITS IDLY, AWAITING DIRECTION FROM THE DEFILER!
YEAH, AND I ONLY CAUGHT A THIRD OF THAT, BUT CAROL'S RIGHT.
AND BESIDES, THERE'S NO WAY WE HAVE ENOUGH TIME TO RE-FILE EVERYTHING.
YOU'RE RIGHT...WE CAN'T RE-FILE EVERYTHING...
BUT WE CAN RE-FILE ONE THING.

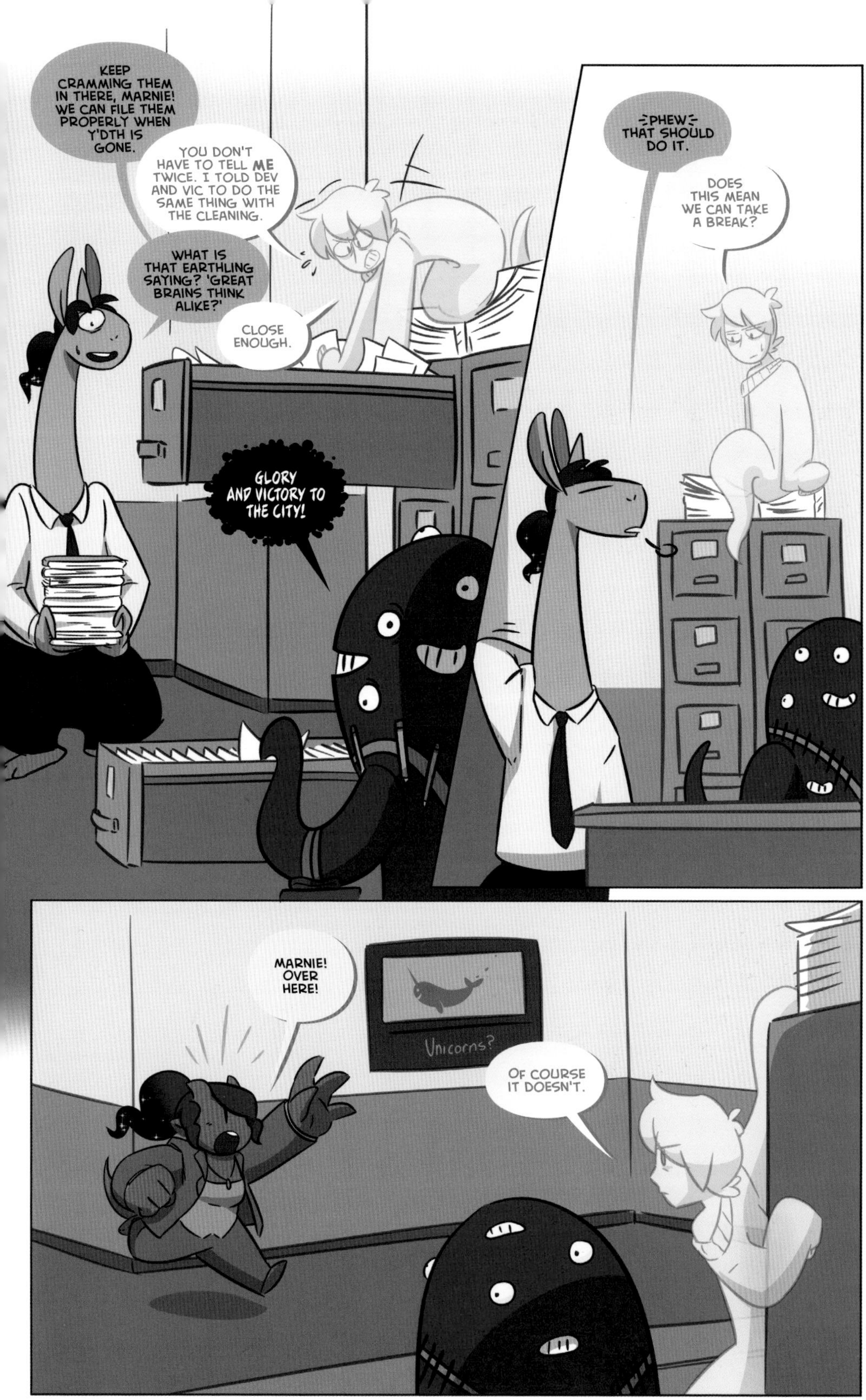
KEEP CRAMMING THEM IN THERE, MARNIE! WE CAN FILE THEM PROPERLY WHEN Y'DTH IS GONE.
YOU DON'T HAVE TO TELL ME TWICE. I TOLD DEV AND VIC TO DO THE SAME THING WITH THE CLEANING.
WHAT IS THAT EARTHLING SAYING? 'GREAT BRAINS THINK ALIKE?'
CLOSE ENOUGH.
GLORY AND VICTORY TO THE CITY!
PHEW THAT SHOULD DO IT.
DOES THIS MEAN WE CAN TAKE A BREAK?
MARNIE! OVER HERE!
Unicorns?
OF COURSE IT DOESN'T.

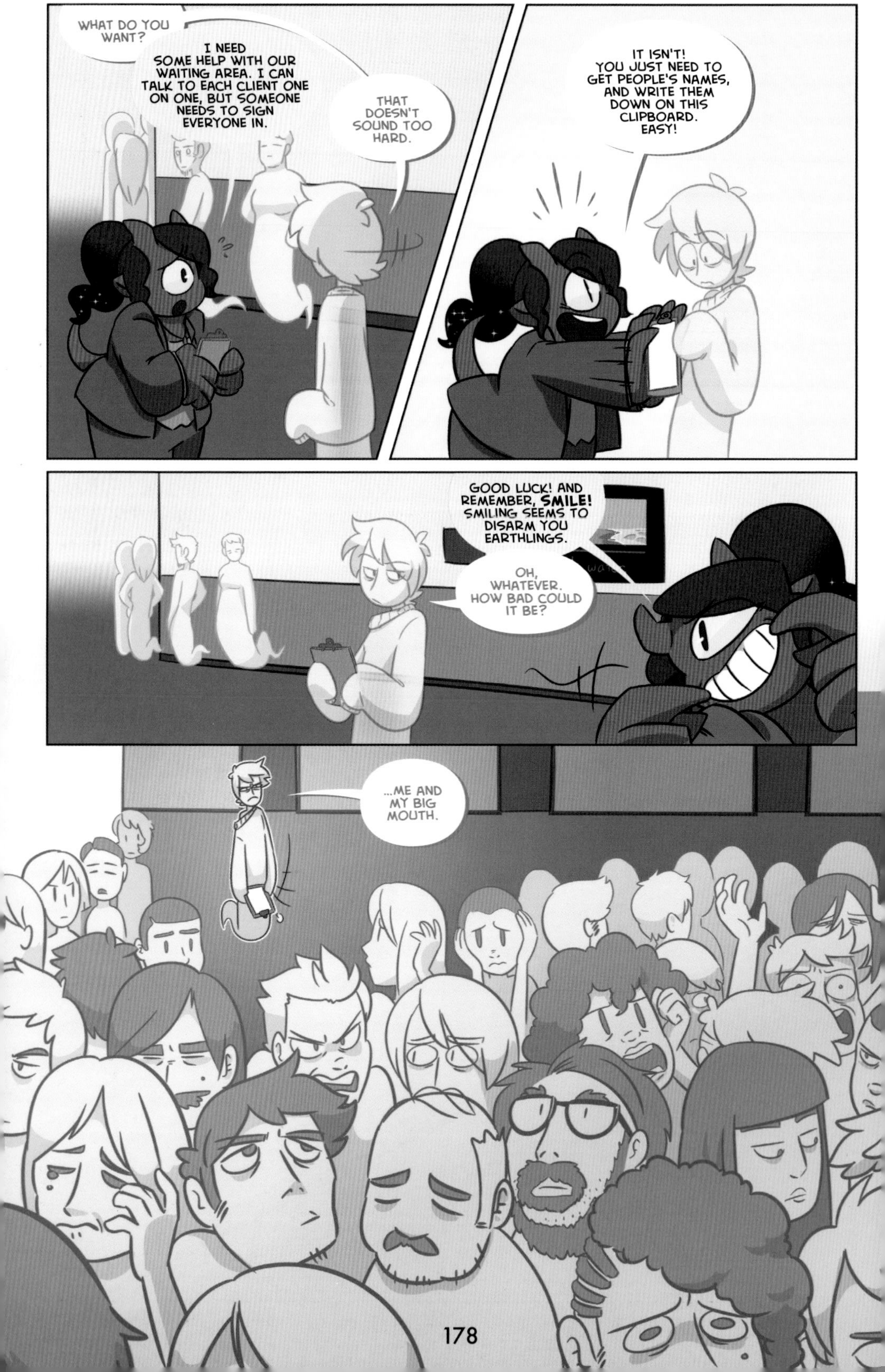
WHAT DO YOU WANT?
I NEED SOME HELP WITH OUR WAITING AREA. I CAN TALK TO EACH CLIENT ONE ON ONE, BUT SOMEONE NEEDS TO SIGN EVERYONE IN.
THAT DOESN'T SOUND TOO HARD.
IT ISN'T! YOU JUST NEED TO GET PEOPLE'S NAMES, AND WRITE THEM DOWN ON THIS CLIPBOARD. EASY!
GOOD LUCK! AND REMEMBER, **SMILE!** SMILING SEEMS TO DISARM YOU EARTHLINGS.
OH, WHATEVER. HOW BAD COULD IT BE?
...ME AND MY BIG MOUTH.

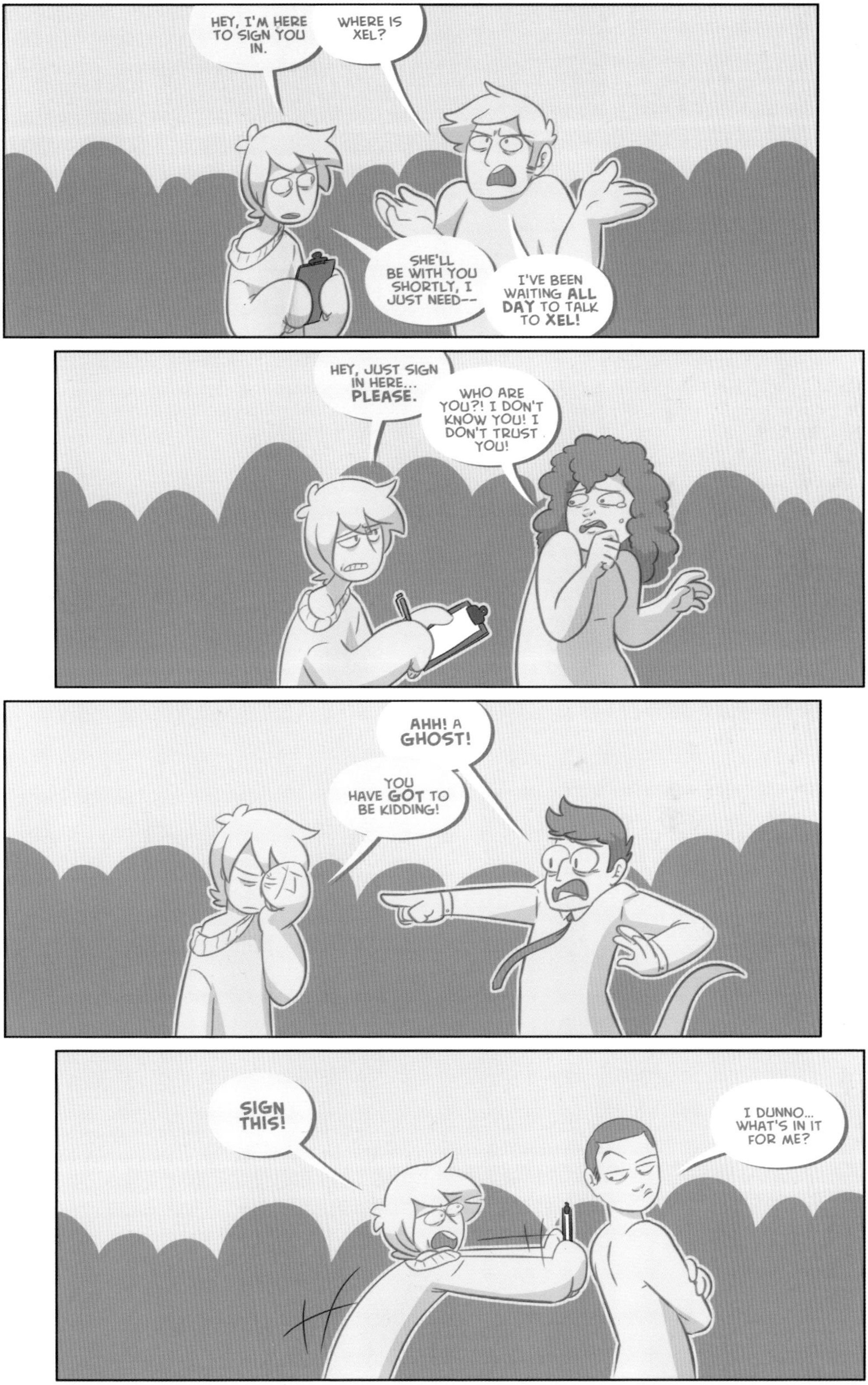
HEY, I'M HERE TO SIGN YOU IN.
WHERE IS XEL?
SHE'LL BE WITH YOU SHORTLY, I JUST NEED--
I'VE BEEN WAITING **ALL DAY** TO TALK TO **XEL!**
HEY, JUST SIGN IN HERE... **PLEASE.**
WHO ARE YOU?! I DON'T KNOW YOU! I DON'T TRUST YOU!
AHH! A **GHOST!**
YOU HAVE **GOT** TO BE KIDDING!
SIGN THIS!
I DUNNO... WHAT'S IN IT FOR ME?

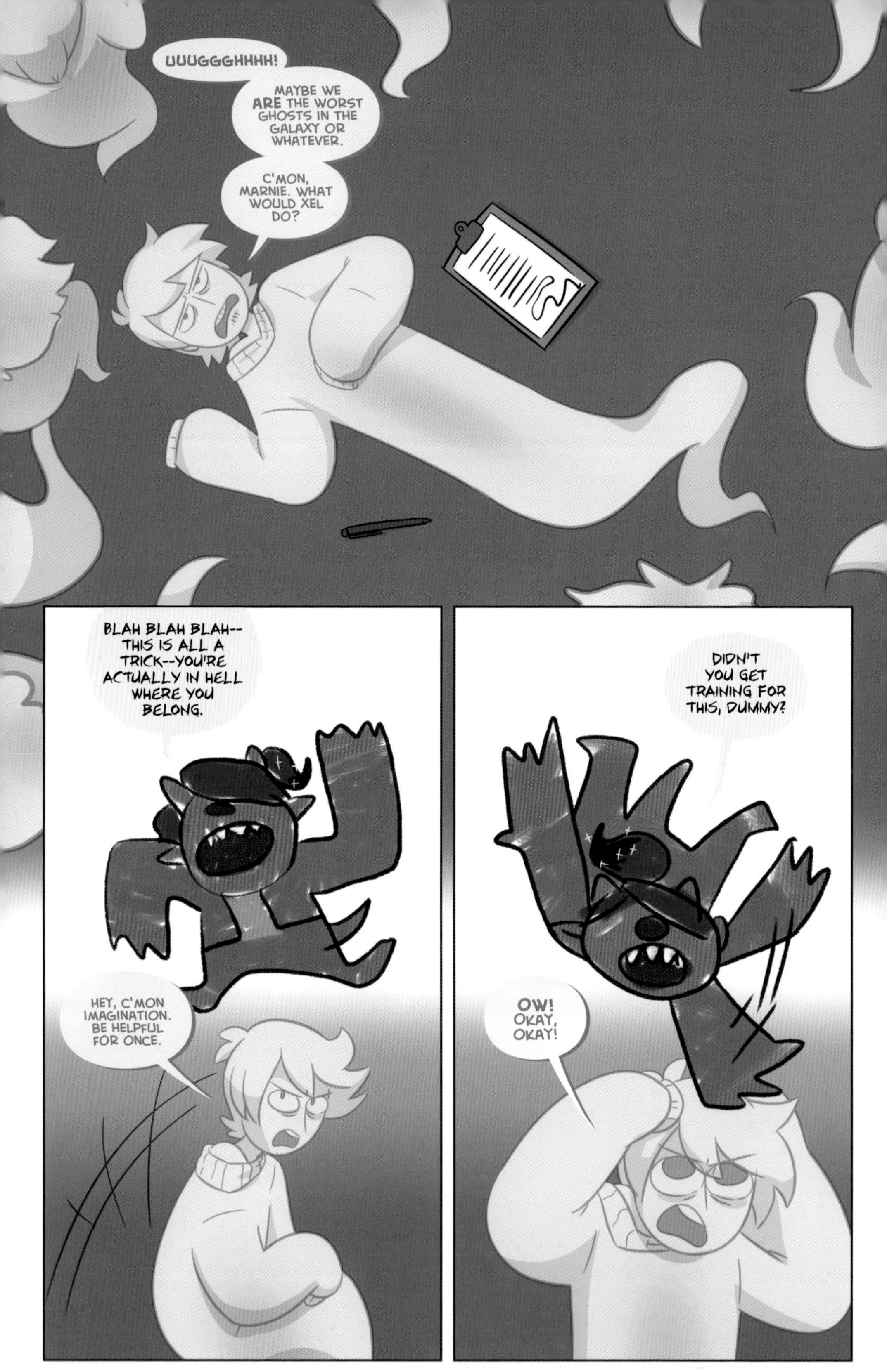
UUUGGGHHHH!
MAYBE WE **ARE** THE WORST GHOSTS IN THE GALAXY OR WHATEVER.
C'MON, MARNIE. WHAT WOULD XEL DO?
BLAH BLAH BLAH--THIS IS ALL A TRICK--YOU'RE ACTUALLY IN HELL WHERE YOU BELONG.
HEY, C'MON IMAGINATION. BE HELPFUL FOR ONCE.
DIDN'T YOU GET TRAINING FOR THIS, DUMMY?
OW! OKAY, OKAY!

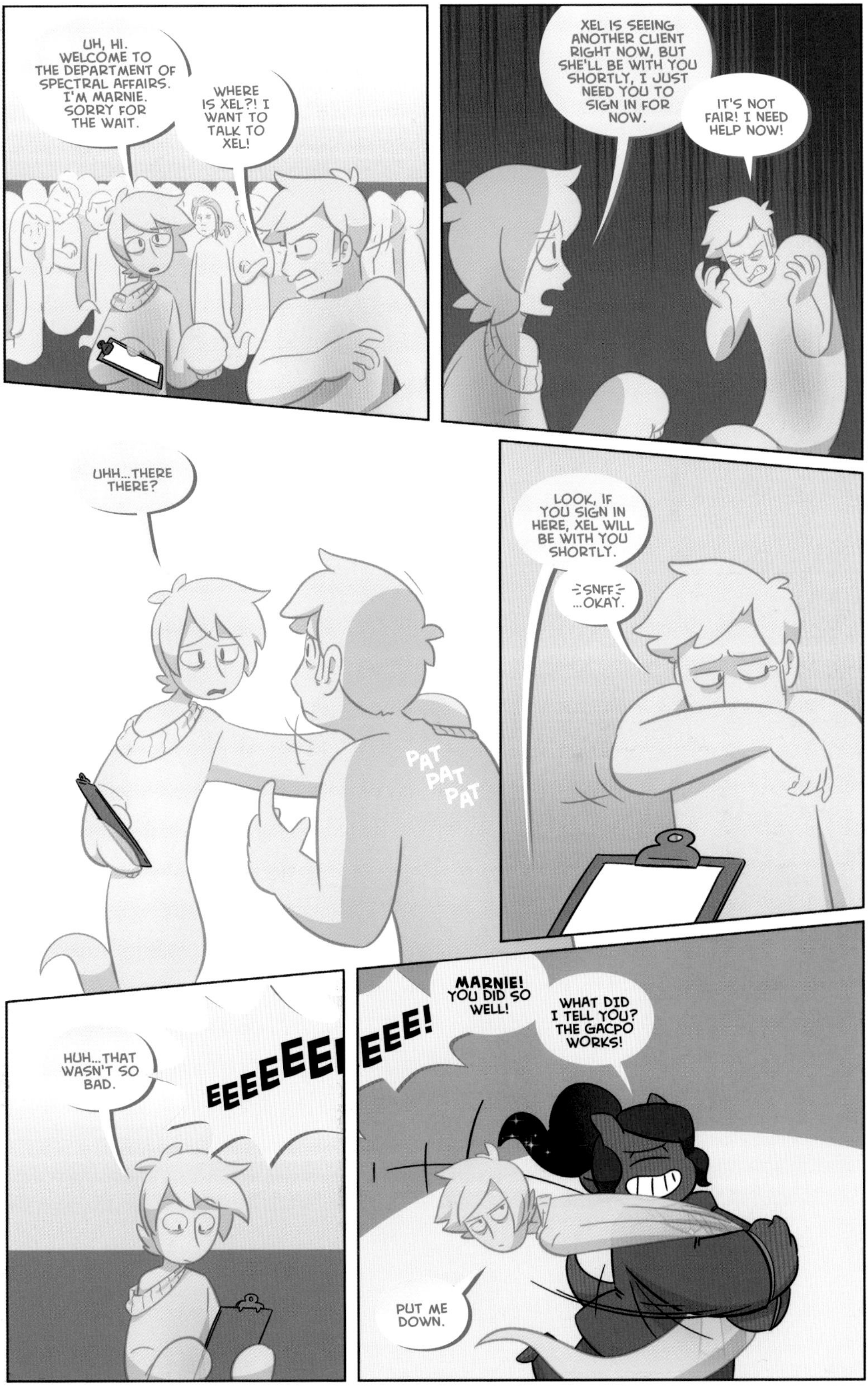
UH, HI. WELCOME TO THE DEPARTMENT OF SPECTRAL AFFAIRS. I'M MARNIE. SORRY FOR THE WAIT.
WHERE IS XEL?! I WANT TO TALK TO XEL!
XEL IS SEEING ANOTHER CLIENT RIGHT NOW, BUT SHE'LL BE WITH YOU SHORTLY, I JUST NEED YOU TO SIGN IN FOR NOW.
IT'S NOT FAIR! I NEED HELP NOW!
UHH...THERE THERE?
PAT PAT PAT
LOOK, IF YOU SIGN IN HERE, XEL WILL BE WITH YOU SHORTLY.
SNFF ...OKAY.
HUH...THAT WASN'T SO BAD.
EEEEEEEEE!
MARNIE! YOU DID SO WELL!
WHAT DID I TELL YOU? THE GACPO WORKS!
PUT ME DOWN.

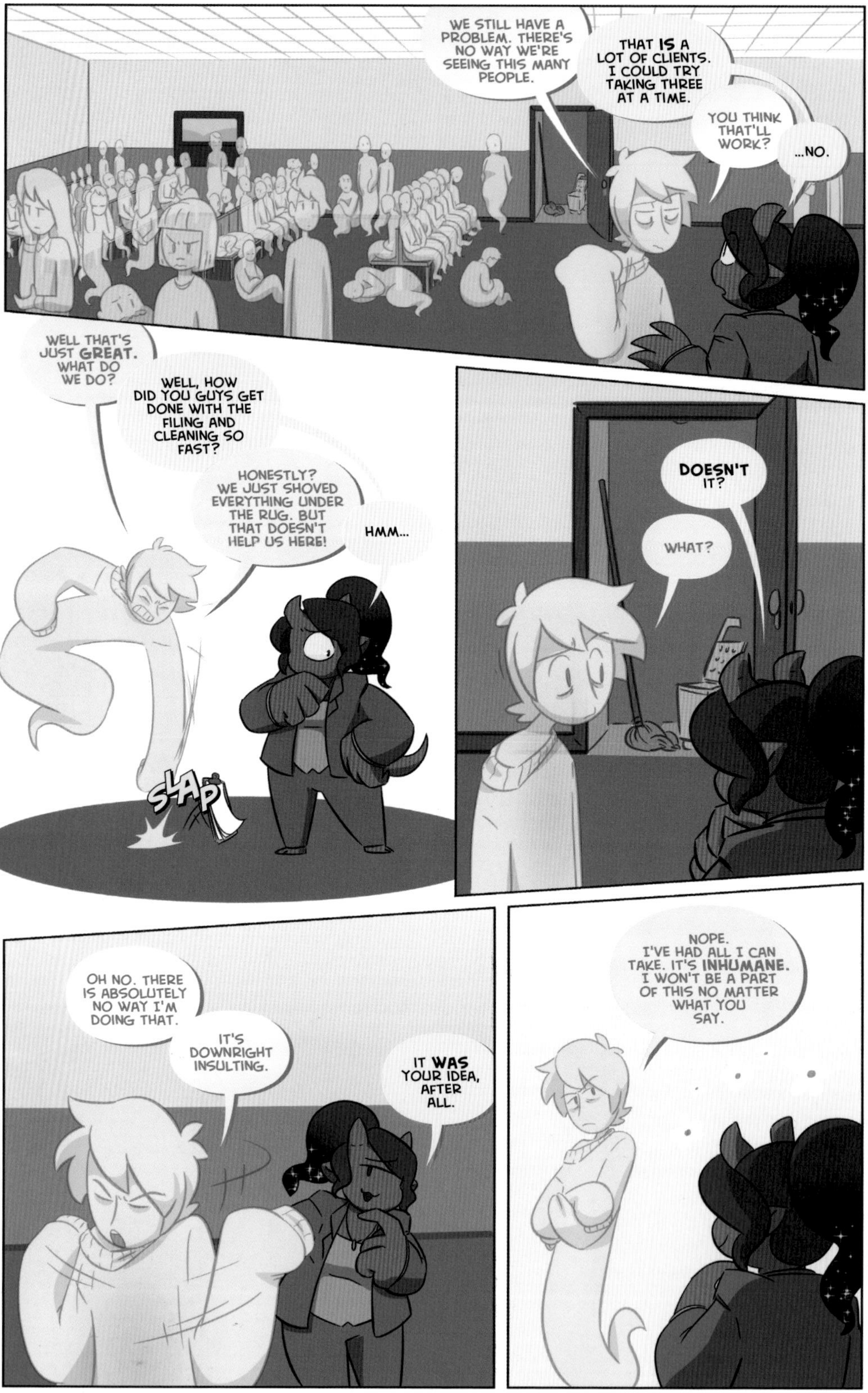
WE STILL HAVE A PROBLEM. THERE'S NO WAY WE'RE SEEING THIS MANY PEOPLE.
THAT IS A LOT OF CLIENTS. I COULD TRY TAKING THREE AT A TIME.
YOU THINK THAT'LL WORK?
...NO.
WELL THAT'S JUST GREAT. WHAT DO WE DO?
WELL, HOW DID YOU GUYS GET DONE WITH THE FILING AND CLEANING SO FAST?
HONESTLY? WE JUST SHOVED EVERYTHING UNDER THE RUG. BUT THAT DOESN'T HELP US HERE!
HMM...
SLAP
DOESN'T IT?
WHAT?
OH NO. THERE IS ABSOLUTELY NO WAY I'M DOING THAT.
IT'S DOWNRIGHT INSULTING.
IT WAS YOUR IDEA, AFTER ALL.
NOPE. I'VE HAD ALL I CAN TAKE. IT'S INHUMANE. I WON'T BE A PART OF THIS NO MATTER WHAT YOU SAY.

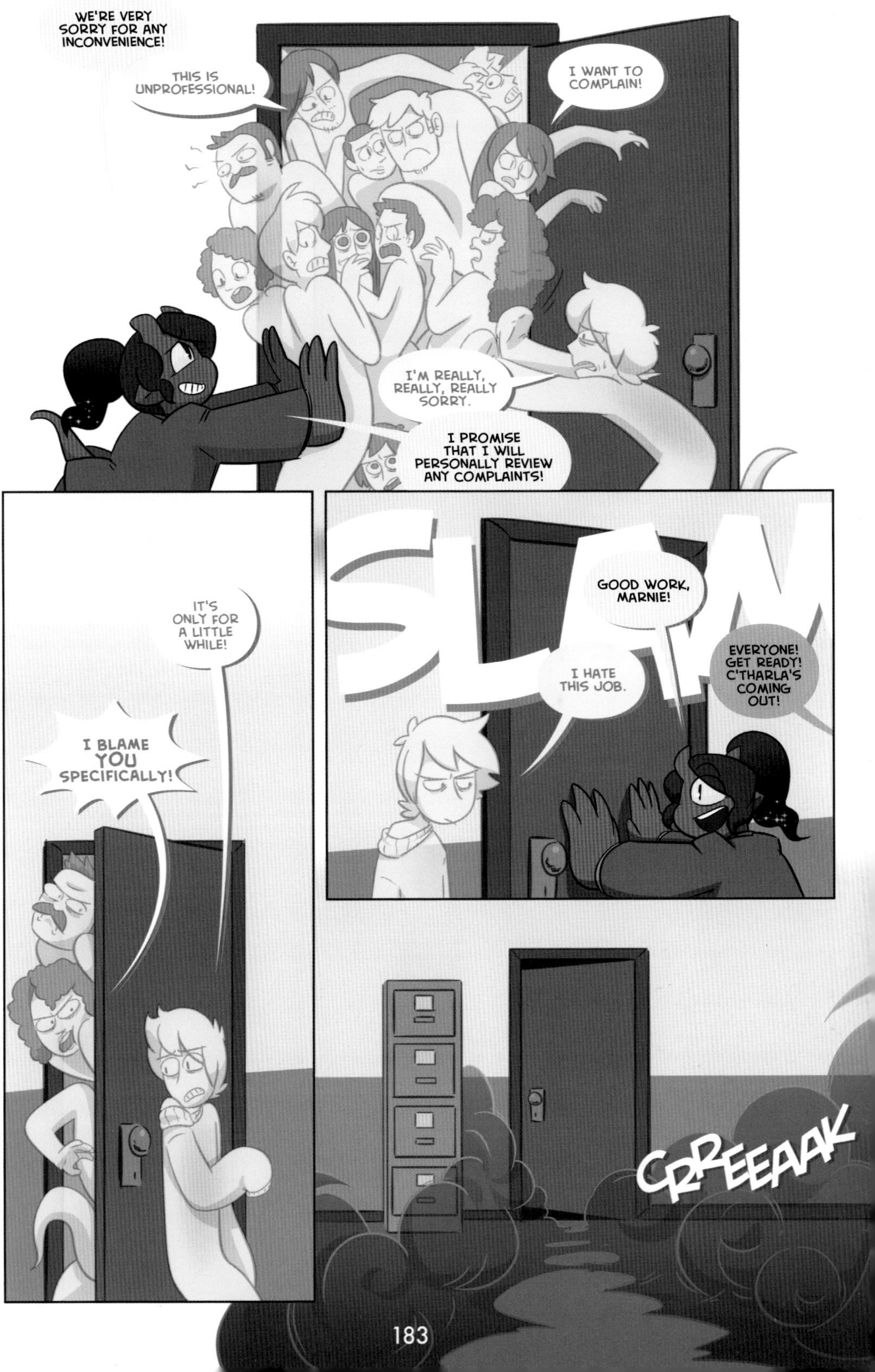
WE'RE VERY SORRY FOR ANY INCONVENIENCE!
THIS IS UNPROFESSIONAL!
I WANT TO COMPLAIN!
I'M REALLY, REALLY, REALLY SORRY.
I PROMISE THAT I WILL PERSONALLY REVIEW ANY COMPLAINTS!
IT'S ONLY FOR A LITTLE WHILE!
I BLAME YOU SPECIFICALLY!
SLAM
GOOD WORK, MARNIE!
I HATE THIS JOB.
EVERYONE! GET READY! C'THARLA'S COMING OUT!
CRREEAAK

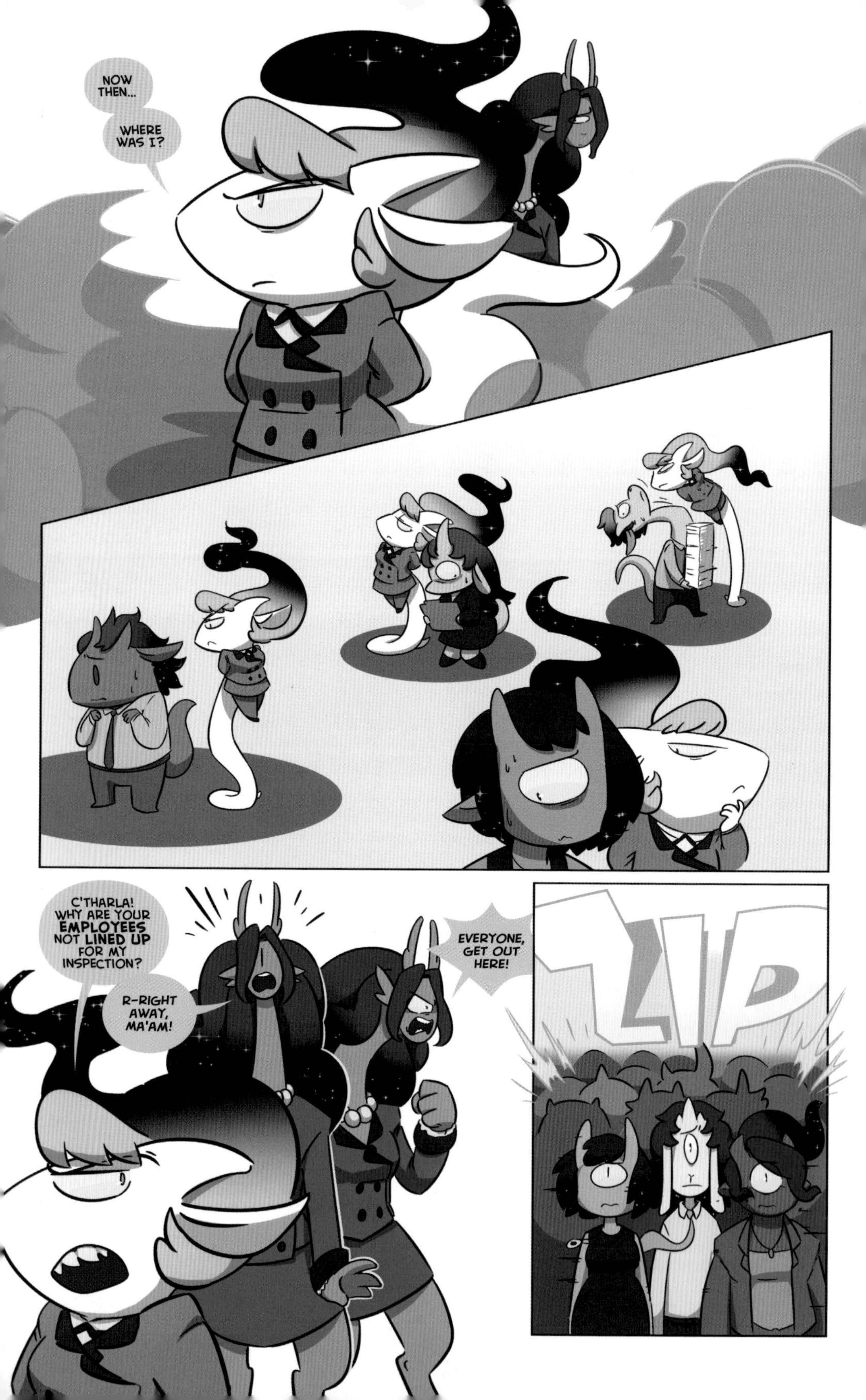
NOW THEN...
WHERE WAS I?
C'THARLA! WHY ARE YOUR EMPLOYEES NOT LINED UP FOR MY INSPECTION?
R-RIGHT AWAY, MA'AM!
EVERYONE, GET OUT HERE!
ZIP

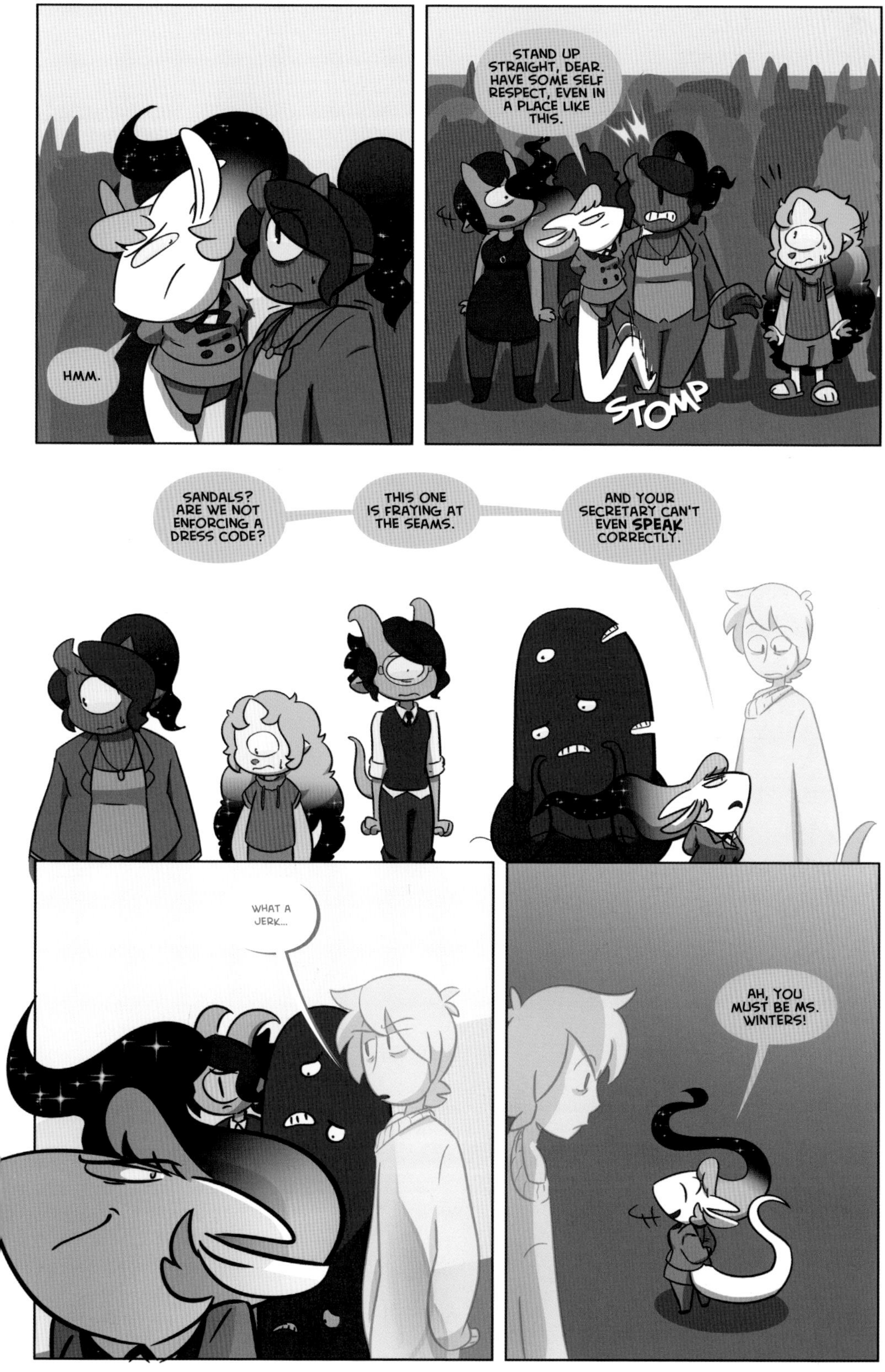
HMM.
STAND UP STRAIGHT, DEAR. HAVE SOME SELF RESPECT, EVEN IN A PLACE LIKE THIS.
STOMP
SANDALS? ARE WE NOT ENFORCING A DRESS CODE?
THIS ONE IS FRAYING AT THE SEAMS.
AND YOUR SECRETARY CAN'T EVEN SPEAK CORRECTLY.
WHAT A JERK...
AH, YOU MUST BE MS. WINTERS!

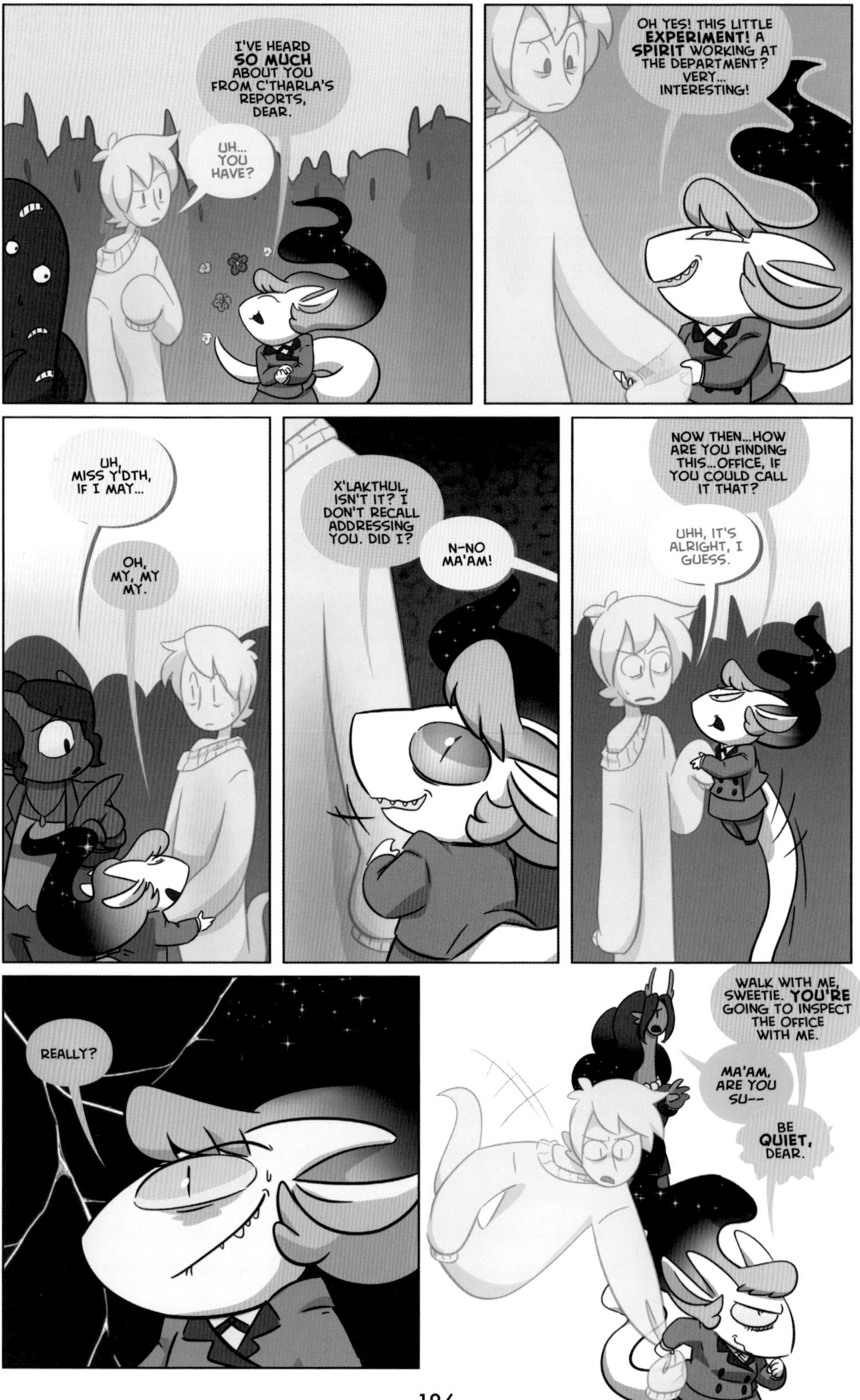
I'VE HEARD **SO MUCH** ABOUT YOU FROM C'THARLA'S REPORTS, DEAR.
UH... YOU HAVE?
OH YES! THIS LITTLE **EXPERIMENT!** A **SPIRIT** WORKING AT THE DEPARTMENT? VERY... INTERESTING!
UH, MISS Y'DTH, IF I MAY...
OH, MY, MY MY.
X'LAKTHUL, ISN'T IT? I DON'T RECALL ADDRESSING YOU. DID I?
N-NO MA'AM!
NOW THEN...HOW ARE YOU FINDING THIS...OFFICE, IF YOU COULD CALL IT THAT?
UHH, IT'S ALRIGHT, I GUESS.
REALLY?
WALK WITH ME, SWEETIE. **YOU'RE** GOING TO INSPECT THE OFFICE WITH ME.
MA'AM, ARE YOU SU--
BE **QUIET,** DEAR.

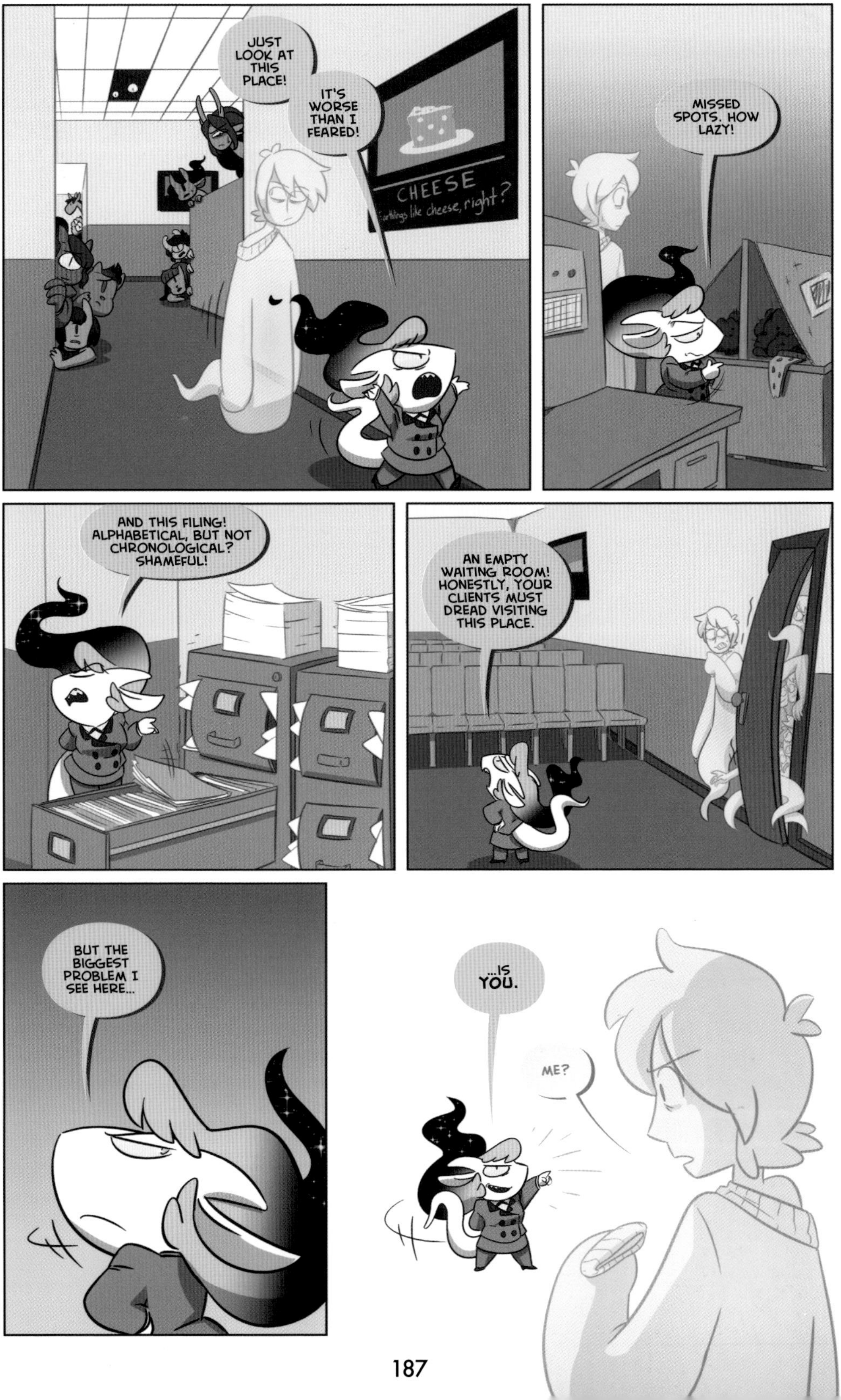
JUST LOOK AT THIS PLACE!
IT'S WORSE THAN I FEARED!
CHEESE
Earthlings like cheese, right?
MISSED SPOTS. HOW LAZY!
AND THIS FILING! ALPHABETICAL, BUT NOT CHRONOLOGICAL? SHAMEFUL!
AN EMPTY WAITING ROOM! HONESTLY, YOUR CLIENTS MUST DREAD VISITING THIS PLACE.
BUT THE BIGGEST PROBLEM I SEE HERE...
...IS YOU.
ME?

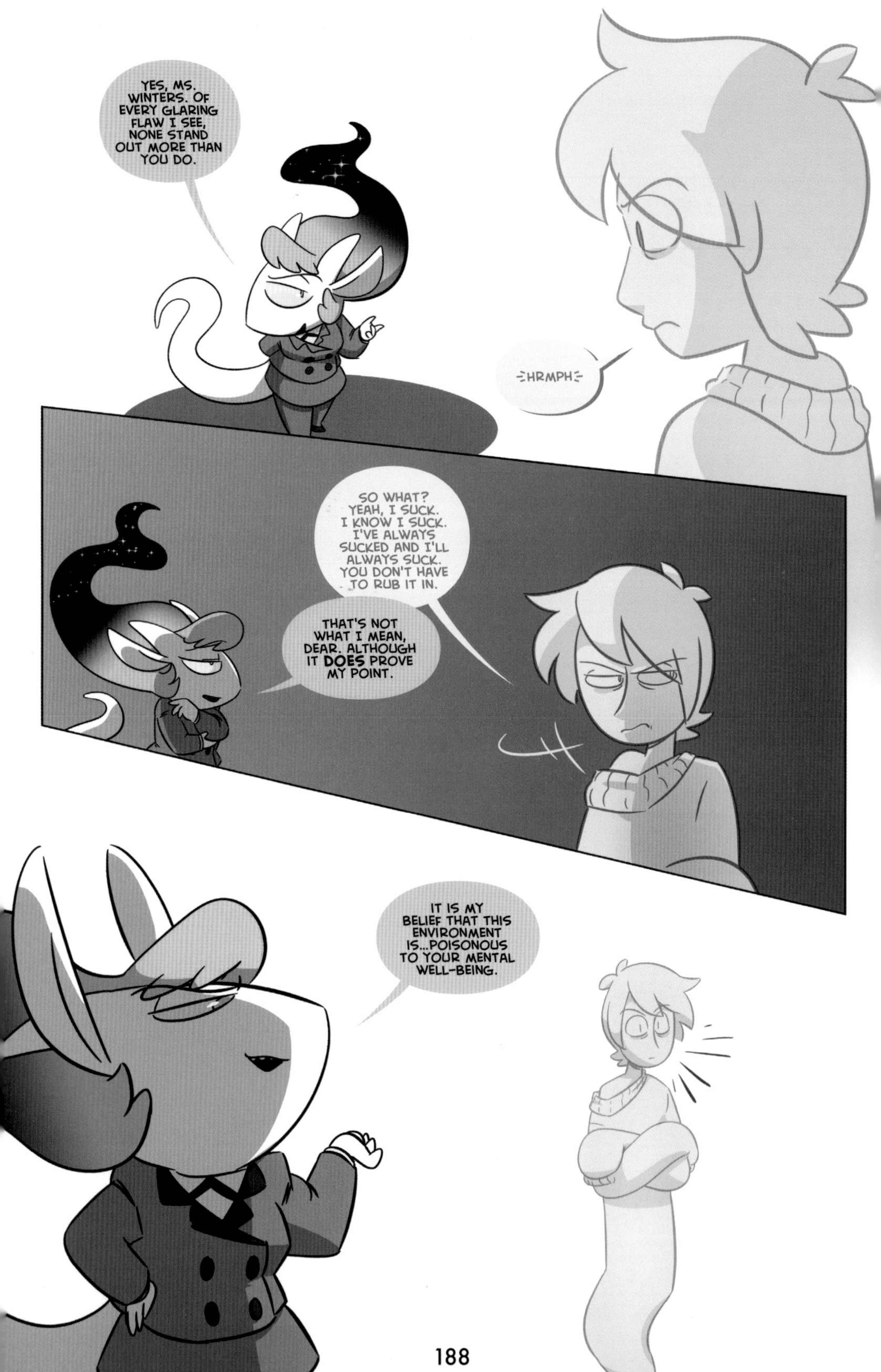
YES, MS. WINTERS. OF EVERY GLARING FLAW I SEE, NONE STAND OUT MORE THAN YOU DO.
HRMPH
SO WHAT? YEAH, I SUCK. I KNOW I SUCK. I'VE ALWAYS SUCKED AND I'LL ALWAYS SUCK. YOU DON'T HAVE TO RUB IT IN.
THAT'S NOT WHAT I MEAN, DEAR. ALTHOUGH IT DOES PROVE MY POINT.
IT IS MY BELIEF THAT THIS ENVIRONMENT IS...POISONOUS TO YOUR MENTAL WELL-BEING.

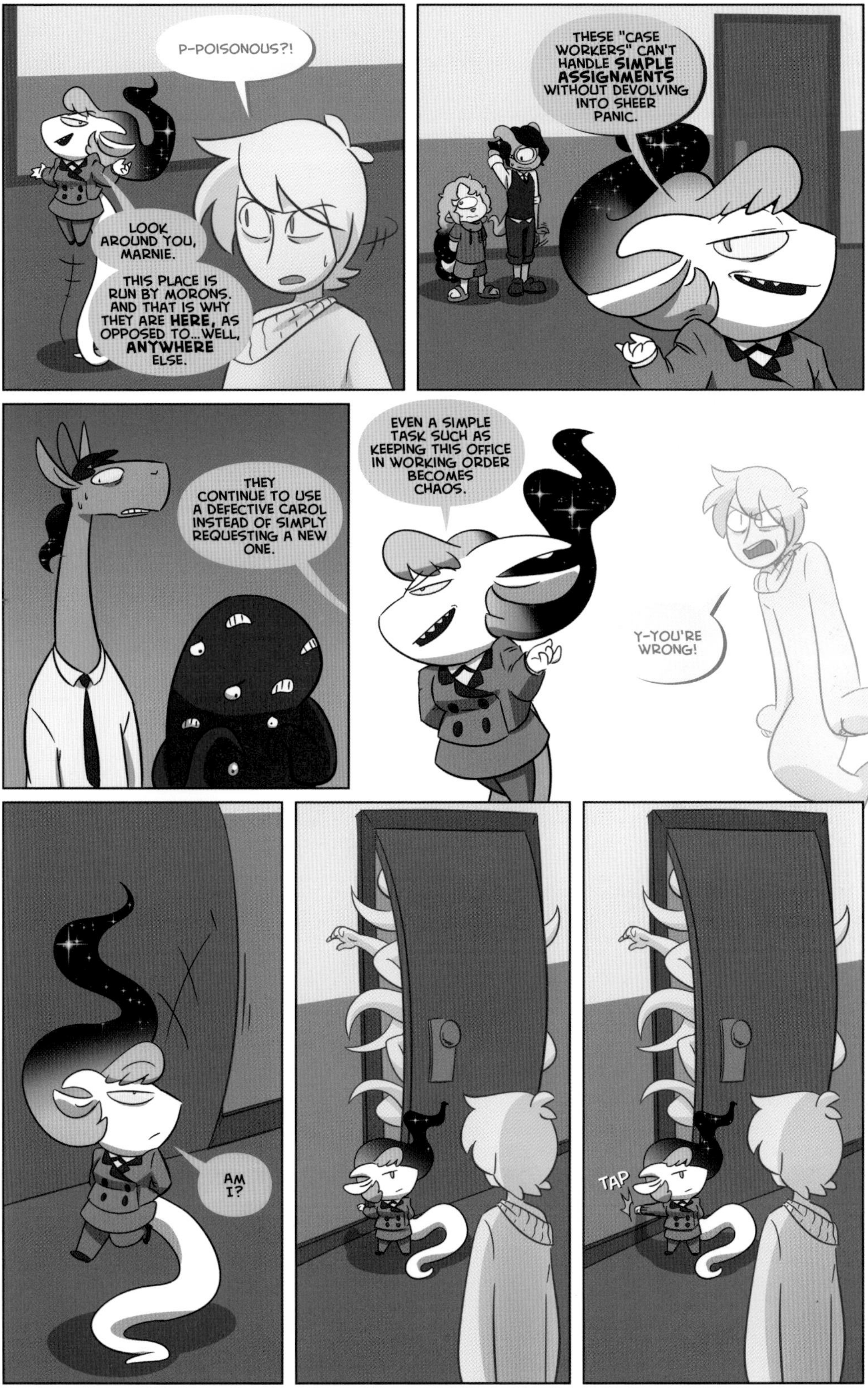
P-POISONOUS?!
LOOK AROUND YOU, MARNIE.
THIS PLACE IS RUN BY MORONS. AND THAT IS WHY THEY ARE **HERE,** AS OPPOSED TO...WELL, **ANYWHERE** ELSE.
THESE "CASE WORKERS" CAN'T HANDLE **SIMPLE ASSIGNMENTS** WITHOUT DEVOLVING INTO SHEER PANIC.
THEY CONTINUE TO USE A DEFECTIVE CAROL INSTEAD OF SIMPLY REQUESTING A NEW ONE.
EVEN A SIMPLE TASK SUCH AS KEEPING THIS OFFICE IN WORKING ORDER BECOMES CHAOS.
Y-YOU'RE WRONG!
AM I?
TAP

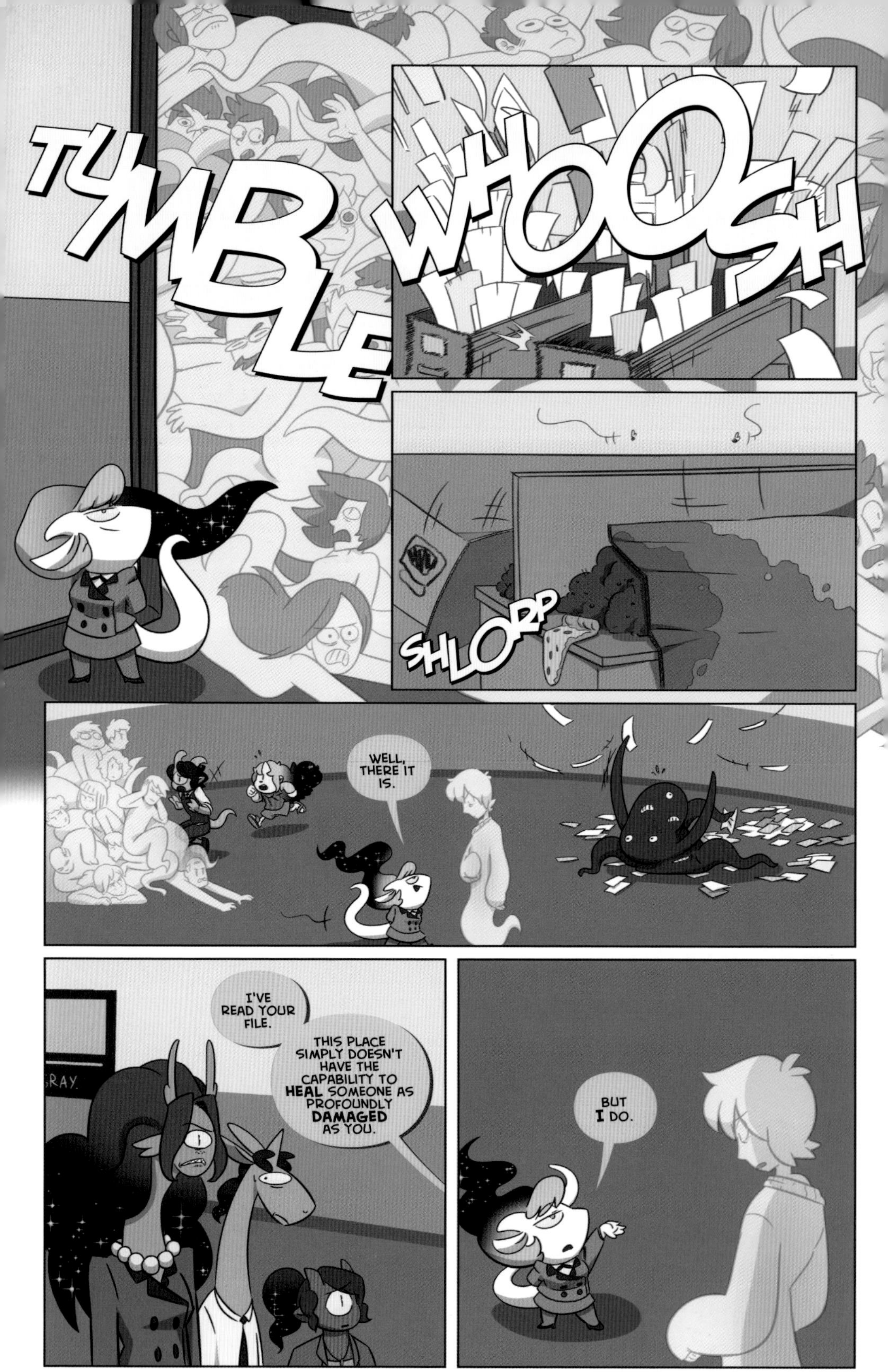
TUMBLE
WHOOSH
SHLORP
WELL, THERE IT IS.
I'VE READ YOUR FILE.
THIS PLACE SIMPLY DOESN'T HAVE THE CAPABILITY TO **HEAL** SOMEONE AS PROFOUNDLY **DAMAGED** AS YOU.
BUT **I** DO.

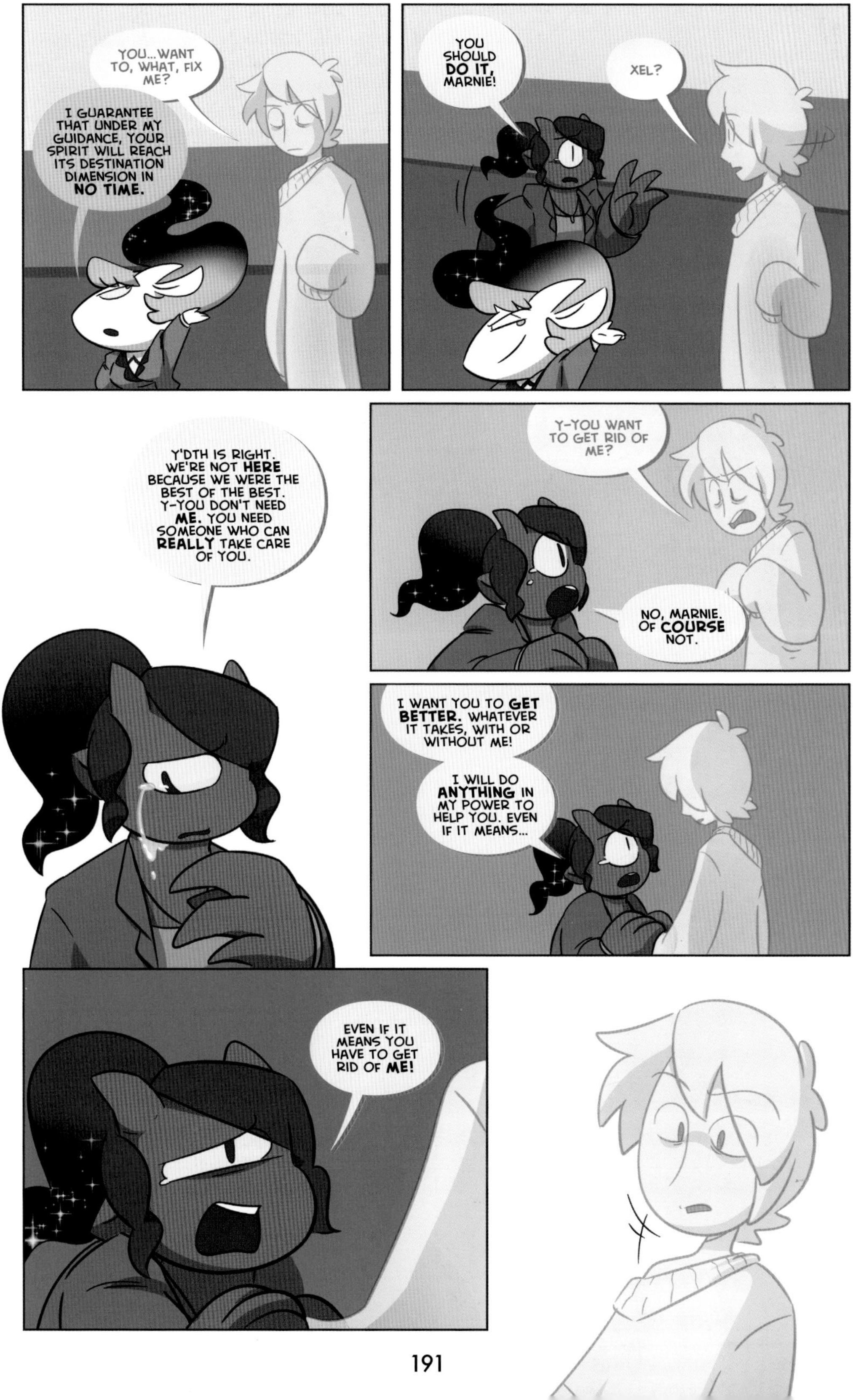

YOU... WANT TO, WHAT, FIX ME?
I GUARANTEE THAT UNDER MY GUIDANCE, YOUR SPIRIT WILL REACH ITS DESTINATION DIMENSION IN NO TIME.
YOU SHOULD DO IT, MARNIE!
XEL?
Y'DTH IS RIGHT. WE'RE NOT HERE BECAUSE WE WERE THE BEST OF THE BEST. Y-YOU DON'T NEED ME. YOU NEED SOMEONE WHO CAN REALLY TAKE CARE OF YOU.
Y-YOU WANT TO GET RID OF ME?
NO, MARNIE. OF COURSE NOT.
I WANT YOU TO GET BETTER. WHATEVER IT TAKES, WITH OR WITHOUT ME!
I WILL DO ANYTHING IN MY POWER TO HELP YOU. EVEN IF IT MEANS...
EVEN IF IT MEANS YOU HAVE TO GET RID OF ME!

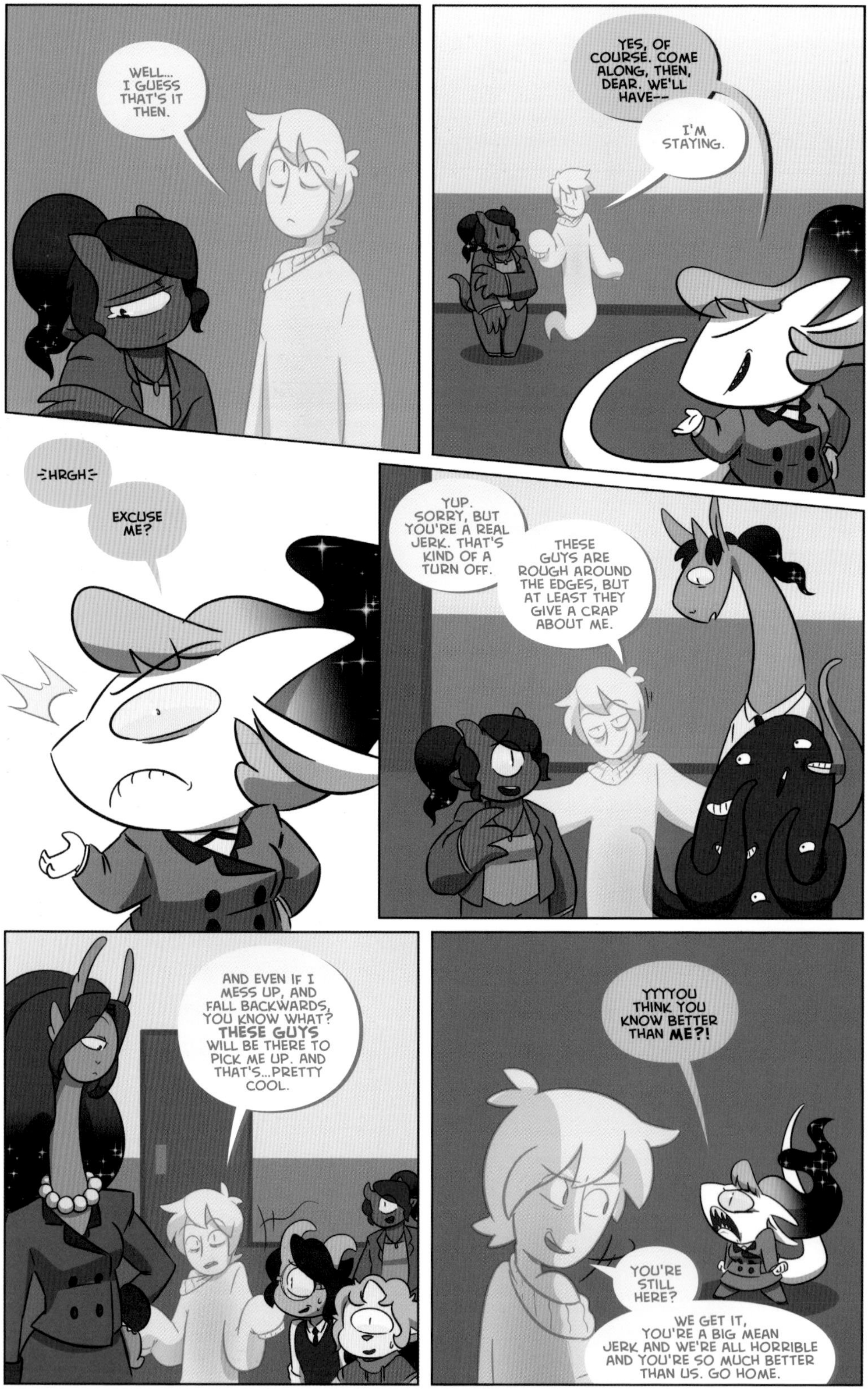
WELL... I GUESS THAT'S IT THEN.
YES, OF COURSE. COME ALONG, THEN, DEAR. WE'LL HAVE--
I'M STAYING.
HRGH
EXCUSE ME?
YUP. SORRY, BUT YOU'RE A REAL JERK. THAT'S KIND OF A TURN OFF.
THESE GUYS ARE ROUGH AROUND THE EDGES, BUT AT LEAST THEY GIVE A CRAP ABOUT ME.
AND EVEN IF I MESS UP, AND FALL BACKWARDS, YOU KNOW WHAT? THESE GUYS WILL BE THERE TO PICK ME UP. AND THAT'S...PRETTY COOL.
YYYYOU THINK YOU KNOW BETTER THAN ME?!
YOU'RE STILL HERE?
WE GET IT, YOU'RE A BIG MEAN JERK AND WE'RE ALL HORRIBLE AND YOU'RE SO MUCH BETTER THAN US. GO HOME.

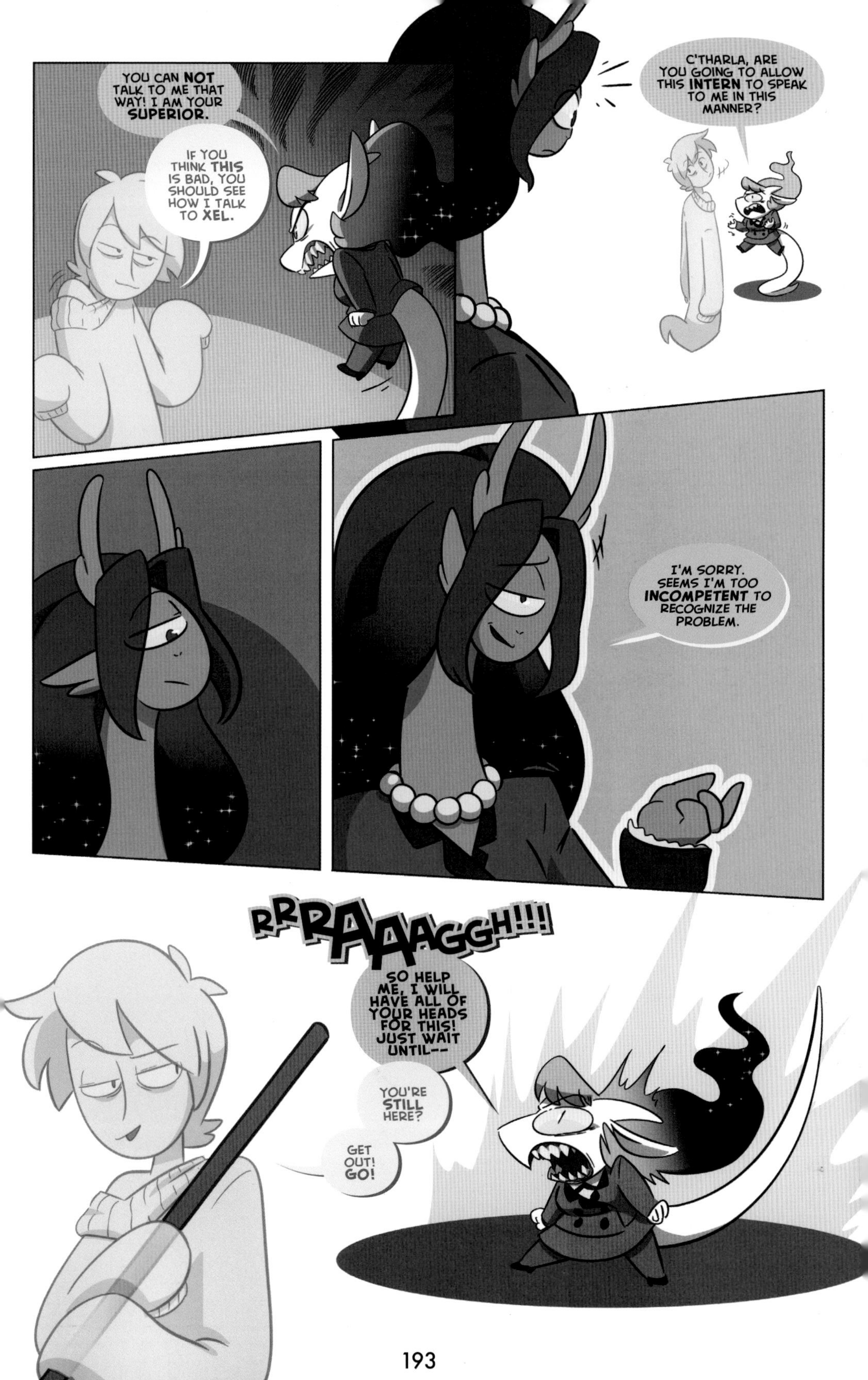

YOU CAN NOT TALK TO ME THAT WAY! I AM YOUR SUPERIOR.
IF YOU THINK THIS IS BAD, YOU SHOULD SEE HOW I TALK TO XEL.
C'THARLA, ARE YOU GOING TO ALLOW THIS INTERN TO SPEAK TO ME IN THIS MANNER?
I'M SORRY. SEEMS I'M TOO INCOMPETENT TO RECOGNIZE THE PROBLEM.
RRRAAAAGGH!!!
SO HELP ME, I WILL HAVE ALL OF YOUR HEADS FOR THIS! JUST WAIT UNTIL--
YOU'RE STILL HERE?
GET OUT! GO!

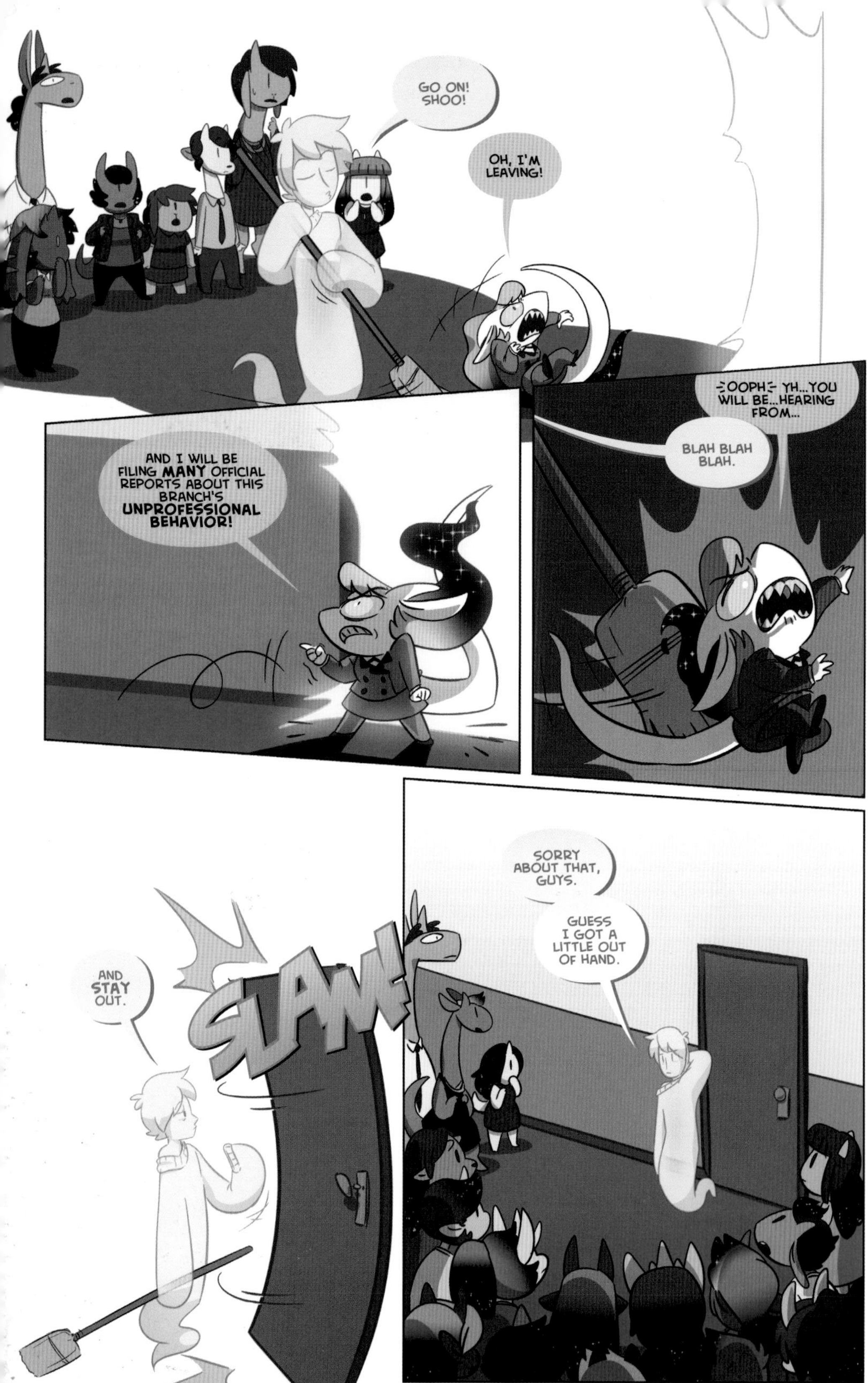
GO ON! SHOO!
OH, I'M LEAVING!
AND I WILL BE FILING MANY OFFICIAL REPORTS ABOUT THIS BRANCH'S UNPROFESSIONAL BEHAVIOR!
-OOPH- YH...YOU WILL BE...HEARING FROM...
BLAH BLAH BLAH.
AND STAY OUT.
SLAM!
SORRY ABOUT THAT, GUYS.
GUESS I GOT A LITTLE OUT OF HAND.

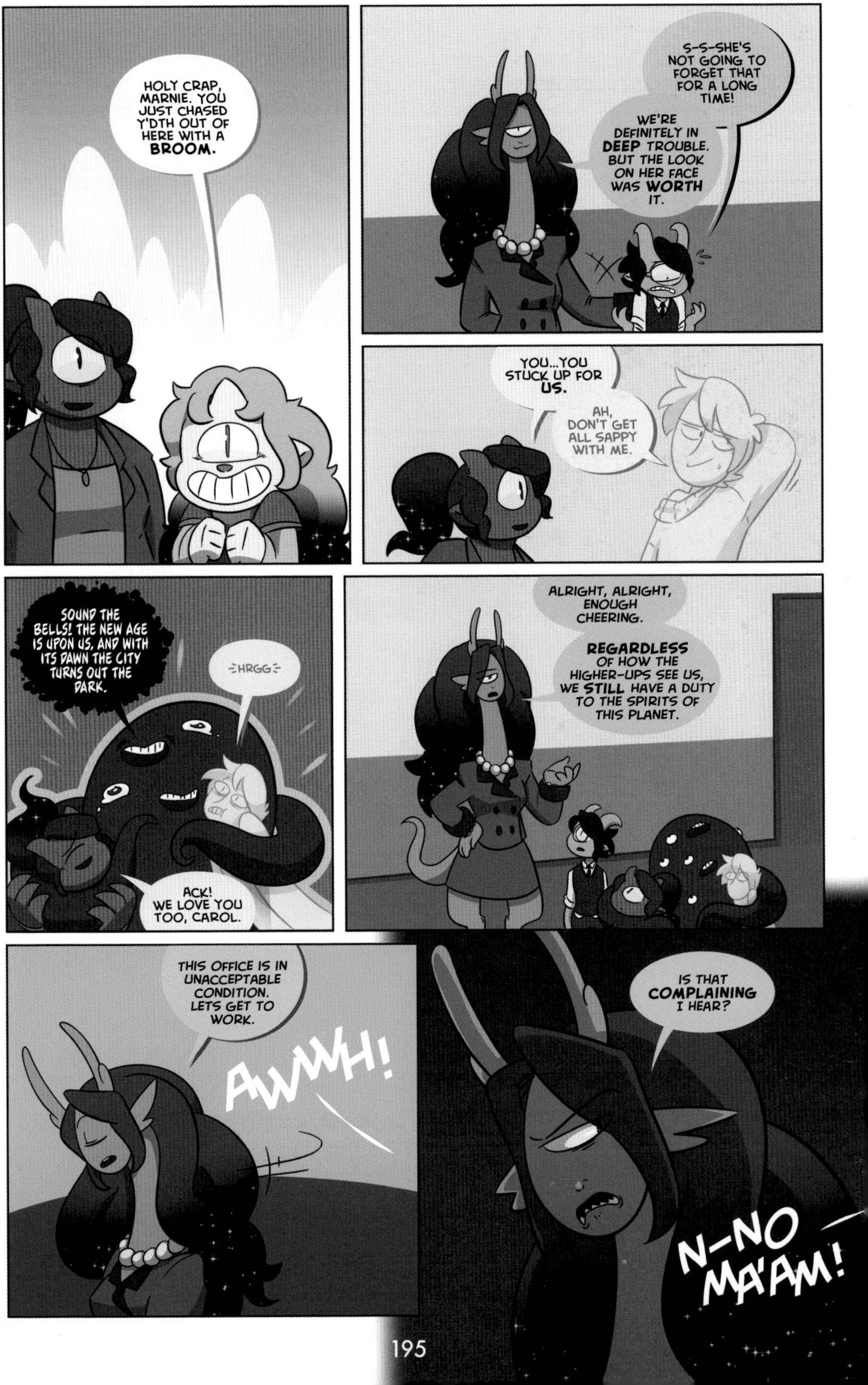
HOLY CRAP, MARNIE. YOU JUST CHASED Y'DTH OUT OF HERE WITH A BROOM.
S-S-SHE'S NOT GOING TO FORGET THAT FOR A LONG TIME!
WE'RE DEFINITELY IN DEEP TROUBLE. BUT THE LOOK ON HER FACE WAS WORTH IT.
YOU...YOU STUCK UP FOR US.
AH, DON'T GET ALL SAPPY WITH ME.
SOUND THE BELLS! THE NEW AGE IS UPON US, AND WITH ITS DAWN THE CITY TURNS OUT THE DARK.
HRGG
ACK! WE LOVE YOU TOO, CAROL.
ALRIGHT, ALRIGHT, ENOUGH CHEERING.
REGARDLESS OF HOW THE HIGHER-UPS SEE US, WE STILL HAVE A DUTY TO THE SPIRITS OF THIS PLANET.
THIS OFFICE IS IN UNACCEPTABLE CONDITION. LETS GET TO WORK.
AWWH!
IS THAT COMPLAINING I HEAR?
N-NO MA'AM!

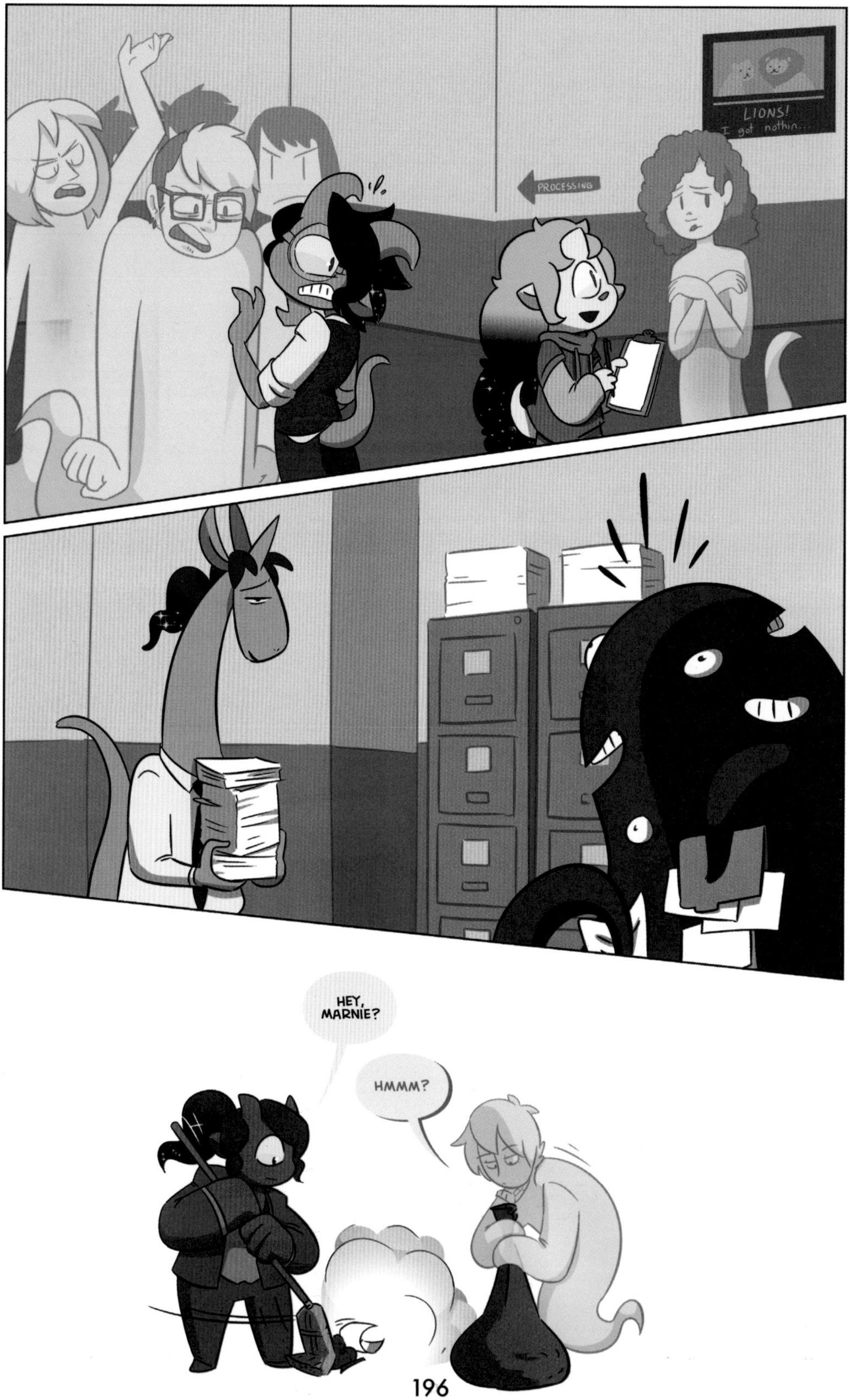
LIONS!
I got nothin...
PROCESSING
HEY, MARNIE?
HMMM?

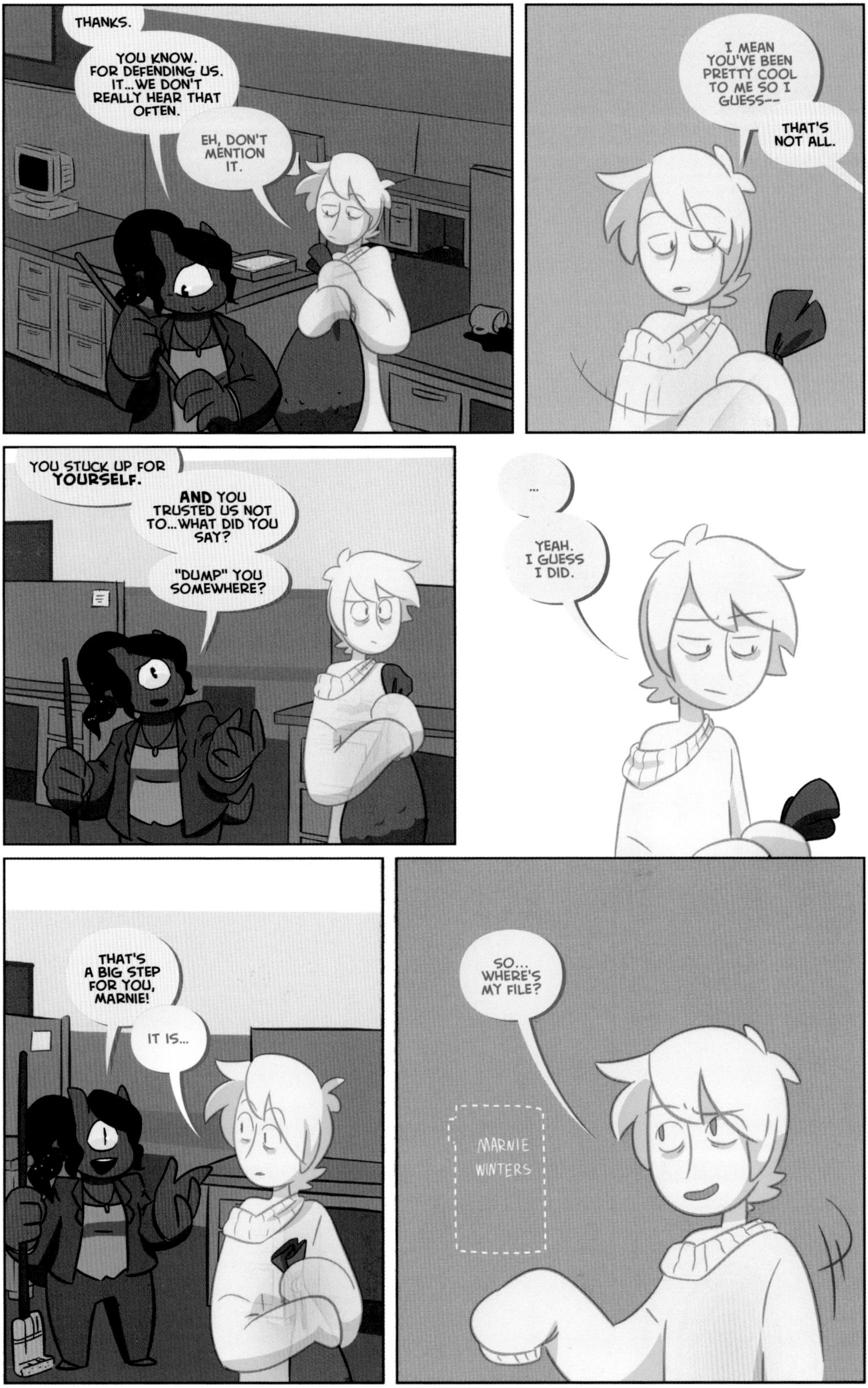
THANKS.
YOU KNOW. FOR DEFENDING US. IT...WE DON'T REALLY HEAR THAT OFTEN.
EH, DON'T MENTION IT.
I MEAN YOU'VE BEEN PRETTY COOL TO ME SO I GUESS--
THAT'S NOT ALL.
YOU STUCK UP FOR **YOURSELF.**
AND YOU TRUSTED US NOT TO...WHAT DID YOU SAY?
"DUMP" YOU SOMEWHERE?
...
YEAH. I GUESS I DID.
THAT'S A BIG STEP FOR YOU, MARNIE!
IT IS...
SO... WHERE'S MY FILE?
MARNIE WINTERS

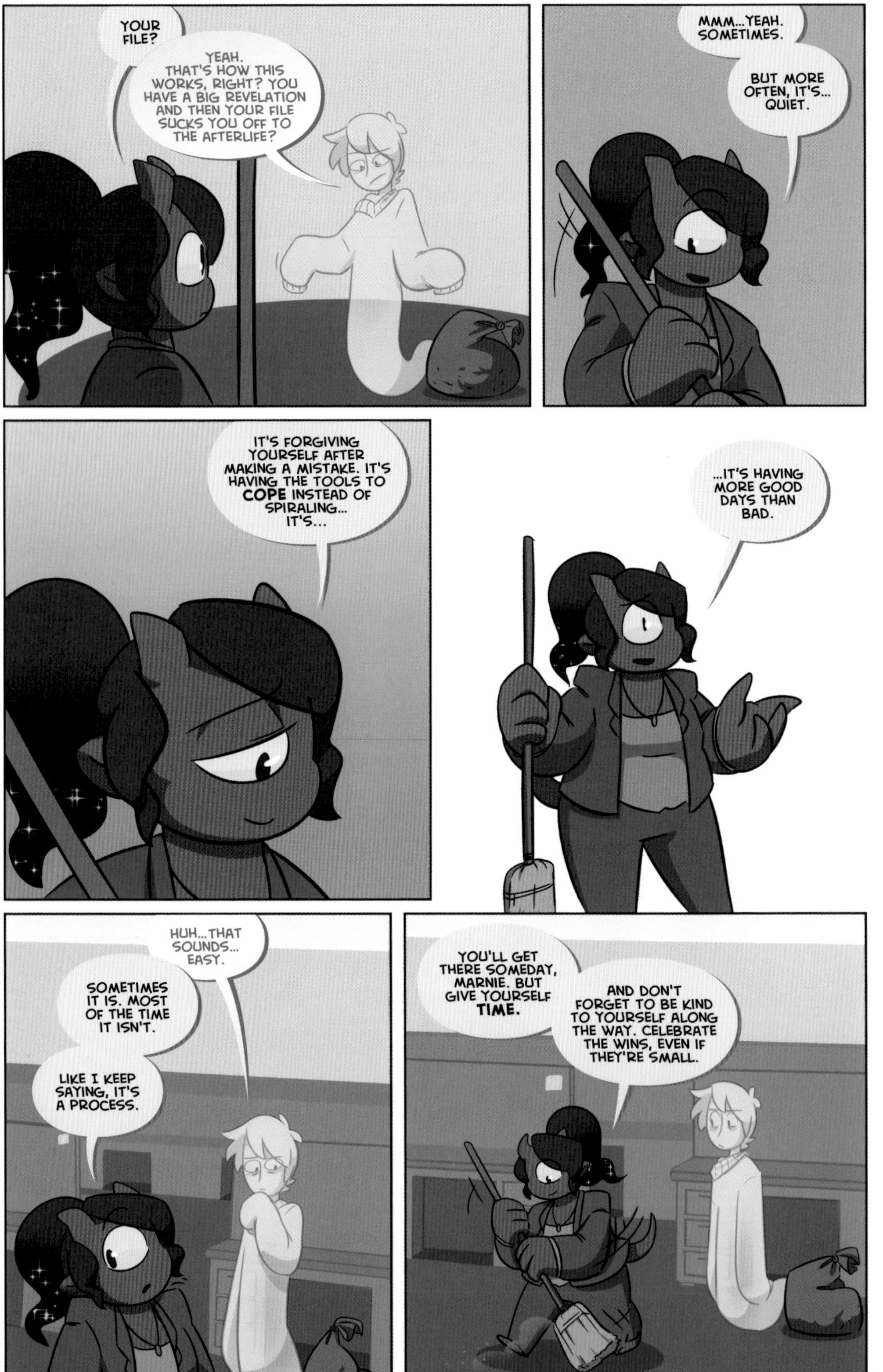
YOUR FILE?
YEAH. THAT'S HOW THIS WORKS, RIGHT? YOU HAVE A BIG REVELATION AND THEN YOUR FILE SUCKS YOU OFF TO THE AFTERLIFE?
MMM...YEAH. SOMETIMES.
BUT MORE OFTEN, IT'S... QUIET.
IT'S FORGIVING YOURSELF AFTER MAKING A MISTAKE. IT'S HAVING THE TOOLS TO COPE INSTEAD OF SPIRALING... IT'S...
...IT'S HAVING MORE GOOD DAYS THAN BAD.
HUH...THAT SOUNDS... EASY.
SOMETIMES IT IS. MOST OF THE TIME IT ISN'T.
LIKE I KEEP SAYING, IT'S A PROCESS.
YOU'LL GET THERE SOMEDAY, MARNIE. BUT GIVE YOURSELF TIME.
AND DON'T FORGET TO BE KIND TO YOURSELF ALONG THE WAY. CELEBRATE THE WINS, EVEN IF THEY'RE SMALL.

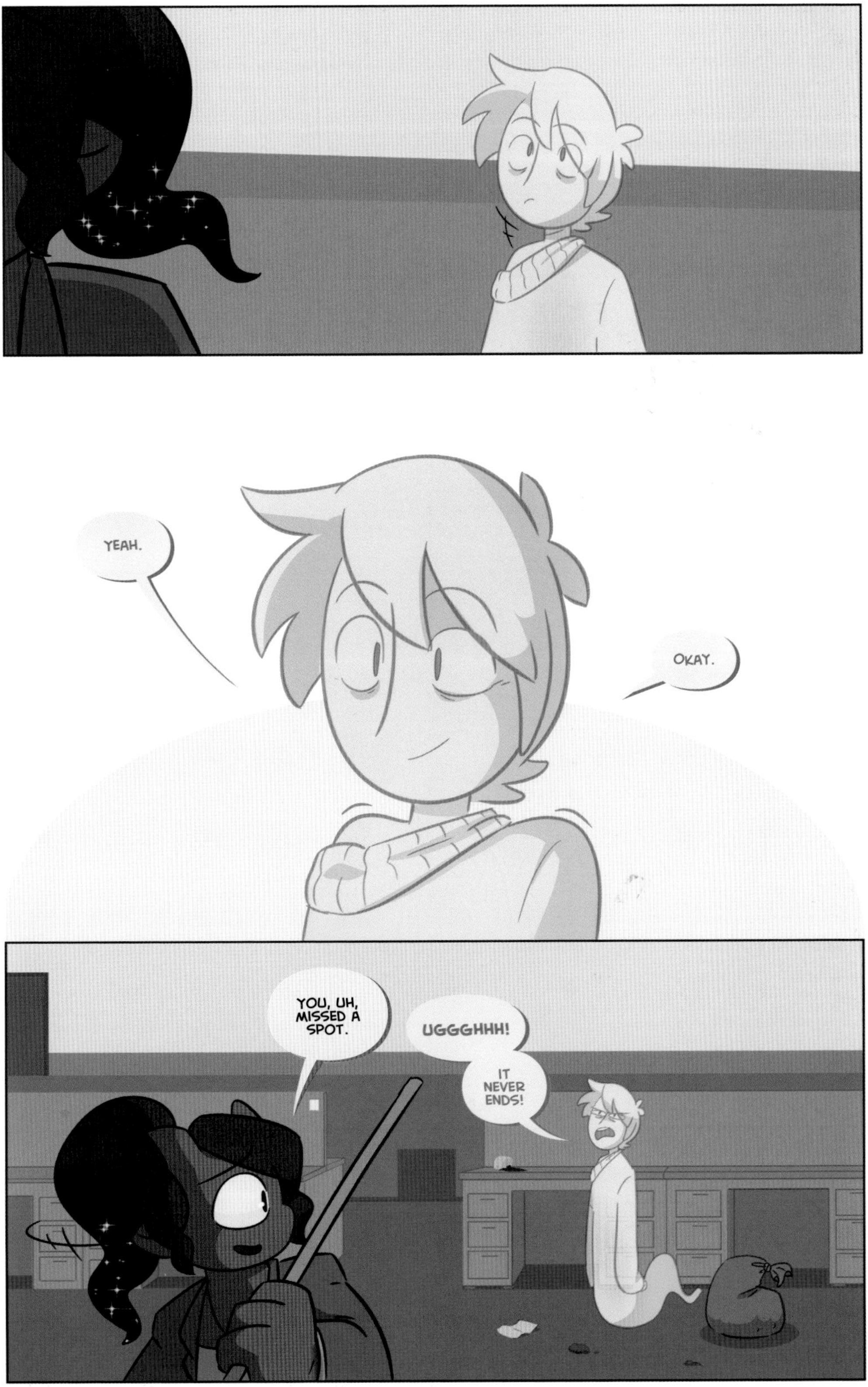
YEAH.
OKAY.
YOU, UH, MISSED A SPOT.
UGGGHHH!
IT NEVER ENDS!

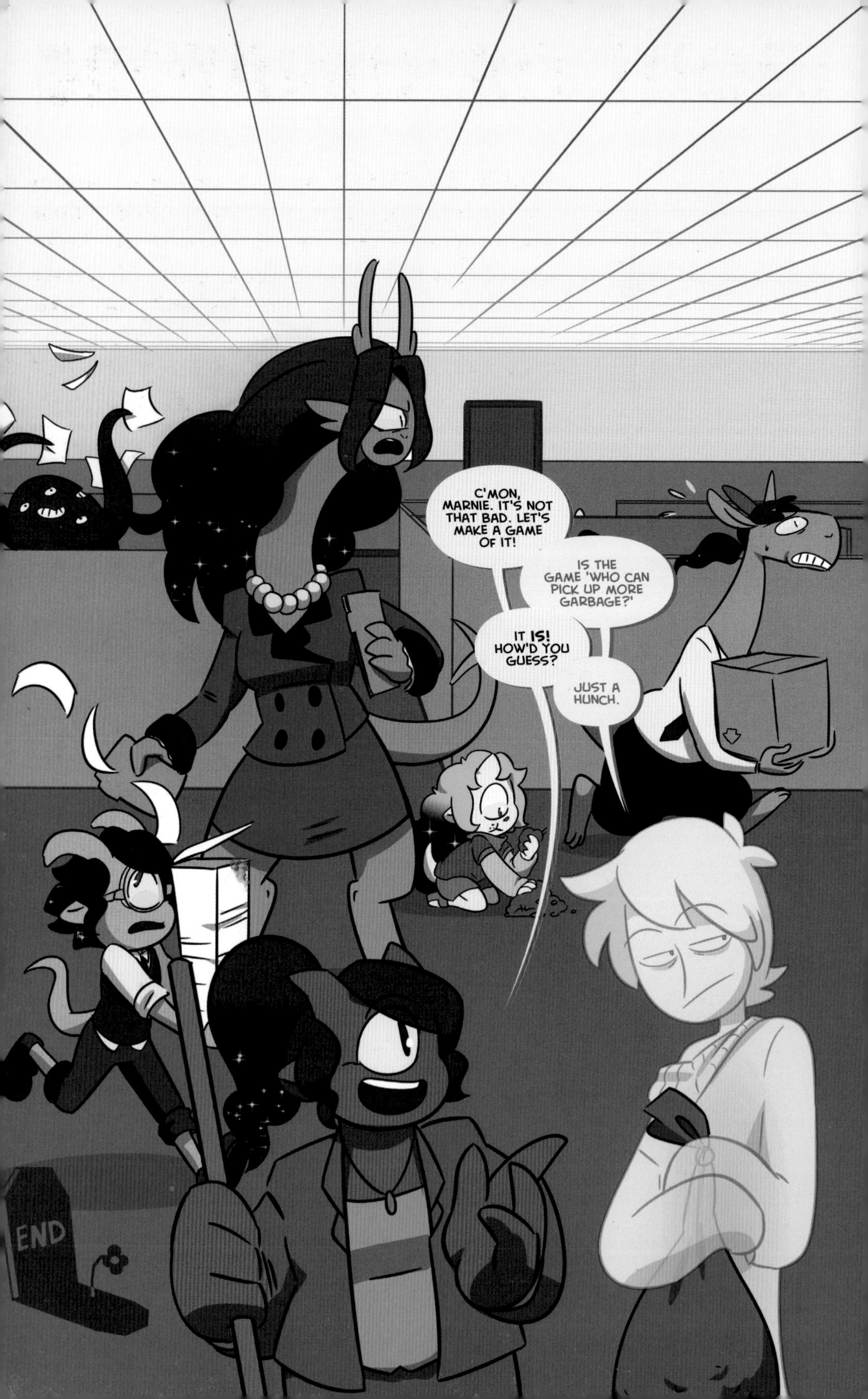
C'MON, MARNIE. IT'S NOT THAT BAD. LET'S MAKE A GAME OF IT!
IS THE GAME 'WHO CAN PICK UP MORE GARBAGE?'
IT IS! HOW'D YOU GUESS?
JUST A HUNCH.
END

ABOUT THE CREATORS

EMILY RIESBECK started writing comics at the ripe old age of ten, when they created their first original character, the superhero Aqua Guy. Since then, they've been publishing their superhero webcomic, *The Blue Valkyrie*. Their short comics have been featured in anthologies like *Chubby* and *Local Haunts*. You can find more of Emily's work at emilyriesbeck.com or follow them on Twitter at @emilyriesbeck, to hear them talk about werewolves and aliens and other monstrous things.

ELLEN KRAMER is a freelance artist and creator of the webcomic *Parisa*, self published for four years and most recently published by Hiveworks. She also contributed a short comic to BOOM! Studios' *Regular Show 2017 Special*. Ellen did not do well in school because she couldn't stop drawing all over her homework. Now she's a professional artist and all the people who doubted her have slugs coming from their mouth every time they try to speak. Probably.

MATT KROTZER gives voices to characters and adds sound to action. As a comic book letterer and graphic designer working for powerhouses like Image, Dark Horse, and many fine independent comics publishers around the world, he's collaborated with some of the brightest artists in comics. He is an optimist and frequent champion of lost causes, regularly found cheering for the mighty Bengals of Cincinnati. Matt lives in suburban Pennsylvania with his wife, daughter and faithful feline companion, Teddy.

SPECIAL THANKS

EMILY

A lot of thank you's, but this is my debut graphic novel and I only get one of those:

Thanks to Mom and Dad for their endless support throughout my life, Kevin for being the best twin brother I could ask for, Andromeda and Diane for continuing to share your love with me, Carl for the inspiration and for the name X'Lakthul which I stole without remorse, Jose for answering all my social work related questions, David for starting me on my comic-writing journey, and all my friends for putting up with me when this book was all I talked about.

ELLEN

Thanks to my best friends for their enthusiastic support. Thanks to Andres for always being there for me, to Orunmilla, Tony, and Sarah for never forgetting about me. I want to thank my sister Gretchen for allowing me to confide in her and a special thanks to Emily for doing all the legwork to get me my first big illustration gig.

MATT

Thank you to Kylene and Ellery for their never-ending love, patience, and support.

And finally, from all of us, thanks to you for reading our book.

BEHIND THE SCENES

Art process pages for page 135 from Ellen.

Thumbnails

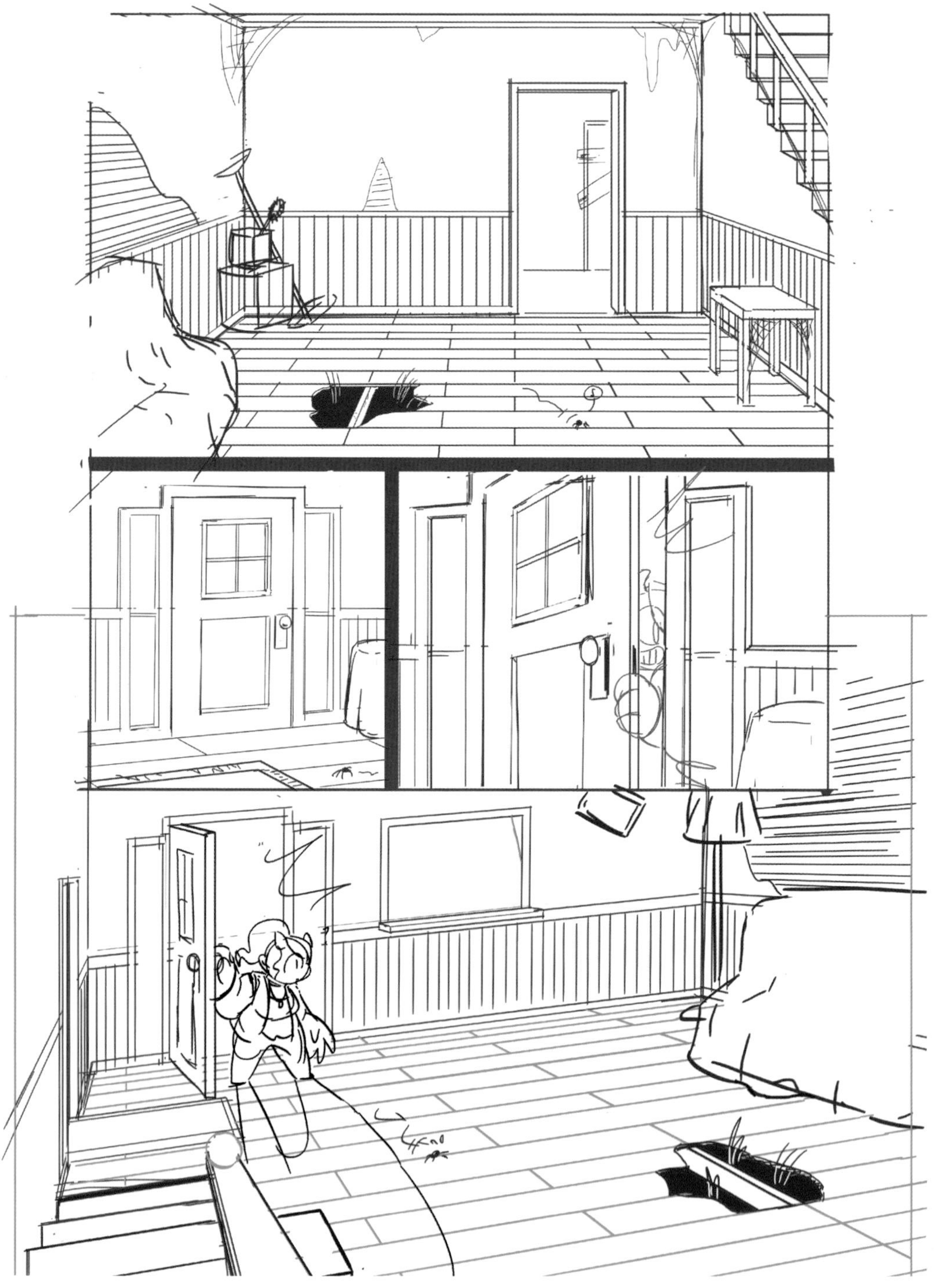

Layouts

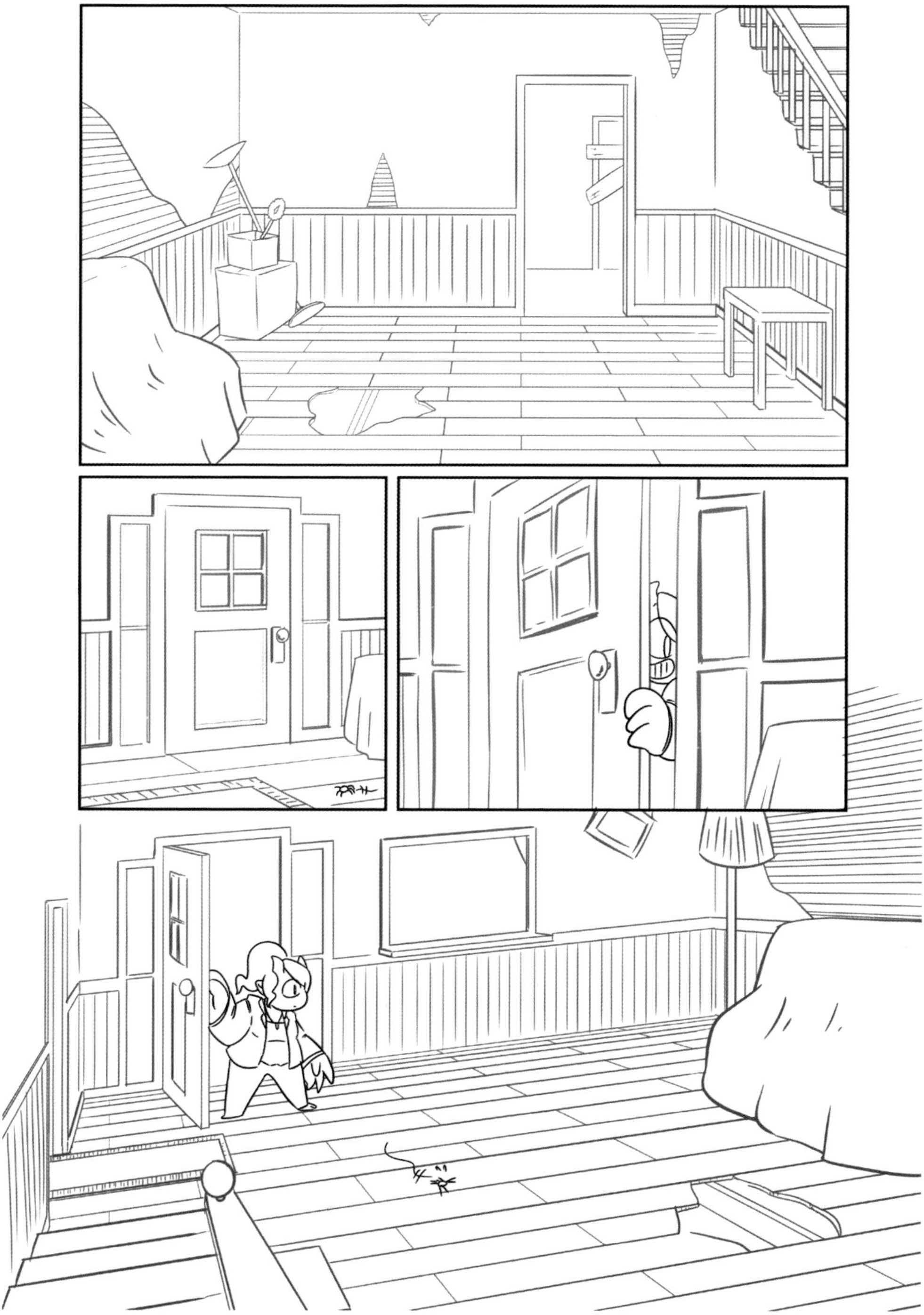

Inks

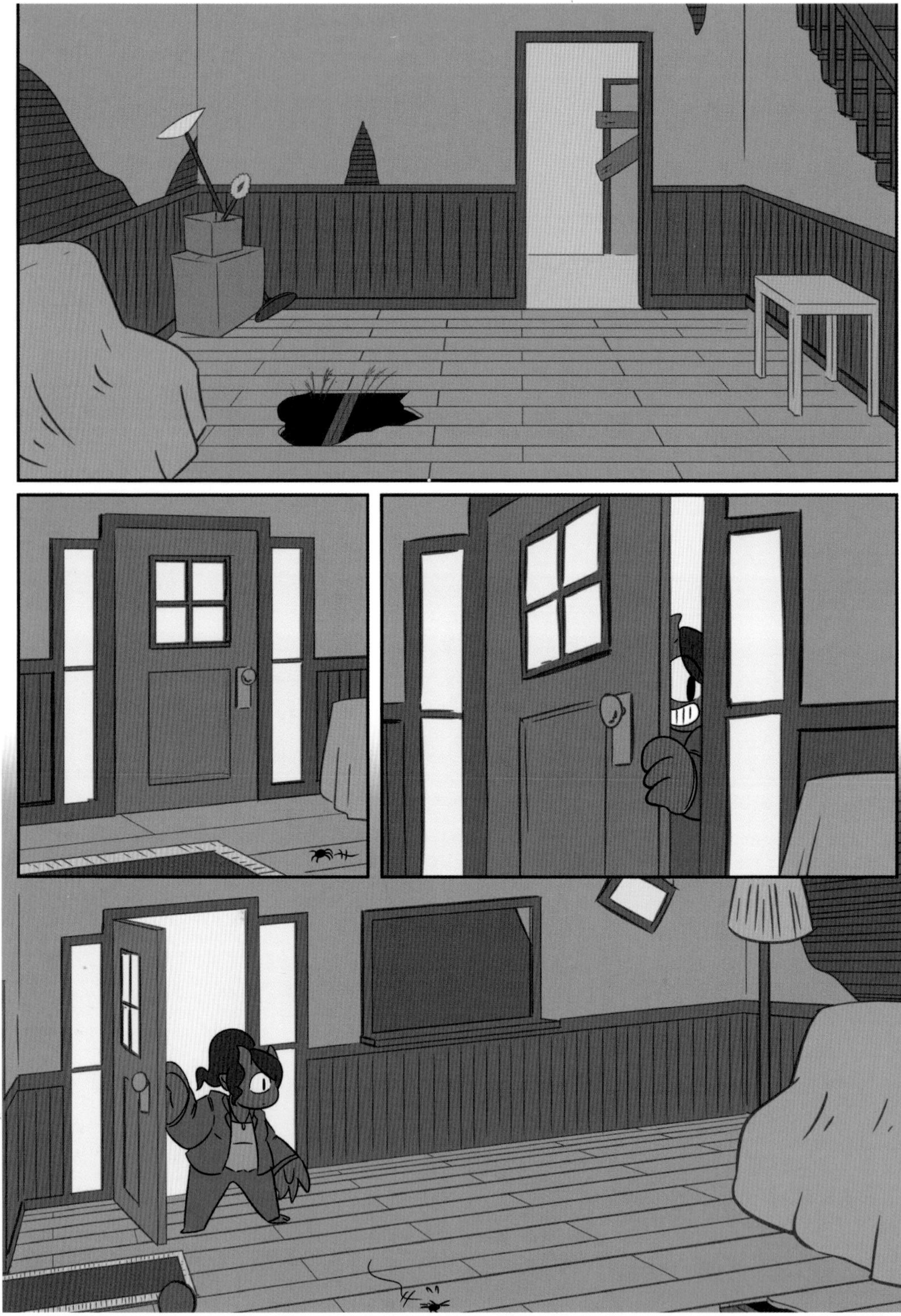

Flat Color

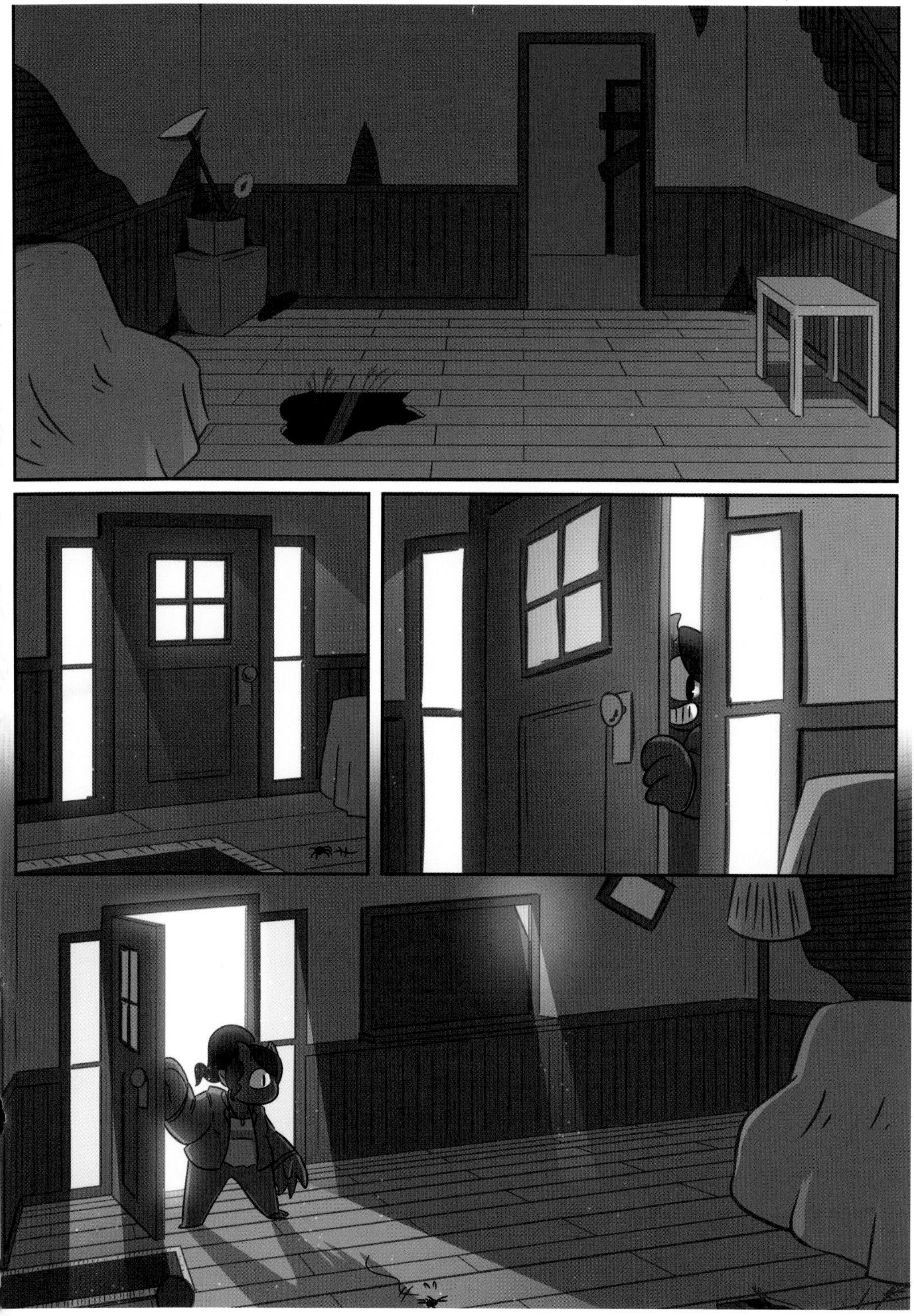

Final Color

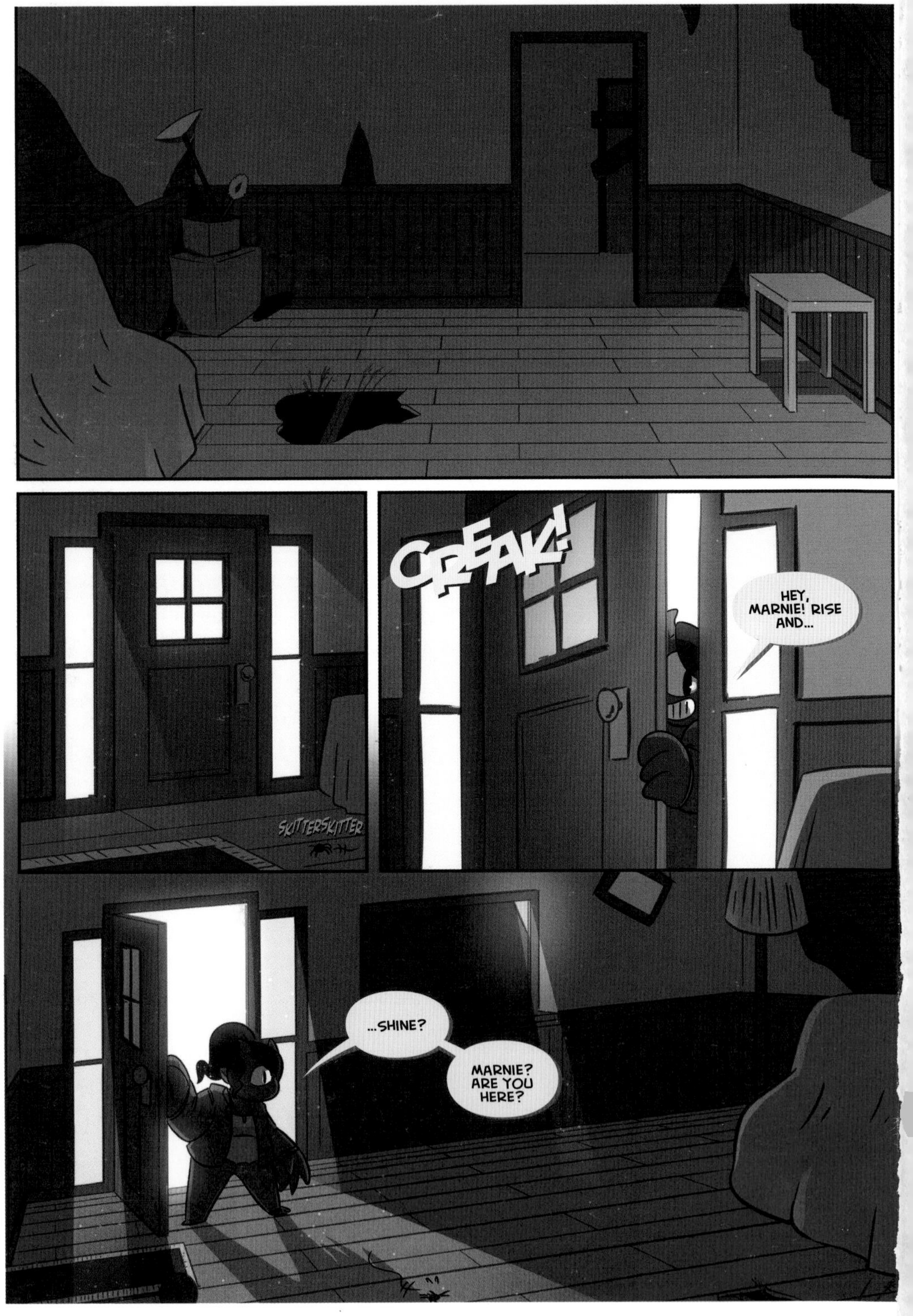
SKITTERSKITTER
CREAK!
HEY, MARNIE! RISE AND...
...SHINE?
MARNIE? ARE YOU HERE?

Final page with lettering by Matt